Kaden & Keegan

The Walkers of Coyote Ridge, 9

BY NICOLE EDWARDS

ALLURING INDULGENCE
Kaleb
Zane
Travis
Holidays with the Walker Brothers
Ethan
Braydon
Sawyer
Brendon

THE WALKERS OF COYOTE RIDGE
Curtis
Jared
Hard to Hold
Hard to Handle
Beau
Rex
A Coyote Ridge Christmas
Mack
Kaden & Keegan

BRANTLEY WALKER: OFF THE BOOKS
All In
Without a Trace
Hide & Seek

AUSTIN ARROWS
Rush
Kaufman

CLUB DESTINY
Conviction
Temptation
Addicted
Seduction
Infatuation
Captivated
Devotion
Perception
Entrusted
Adored
Distraction

DEAD HEAT RANCH
Boots Optional
Betting on Grace
Overnight Love

DEVIL'S BEND
Chasing Dreams
Vanishing Dreams

MISPLACED HALOS
Protected in Darkness
Salvation in Darkness
Bound in Darkness

OFFICE INTRIGUE
Office Intrigue
Intrigued Out of the Office
Their Rebellious Submissive
Their Famous Dominant
Their Ruthless Sadist
Their Naughty Student
Their Fairy Princess

PIER 70
Reckless
Fearless
Speechless
Harmless
Clueless

SNIPER 1 SECURITY
Wait for Morning
Never Say Never
Tomorrow's Too Late

SOUTHERN BOY MAFIA/DEVIL'S PLAYGROUND
Beautifully Brutal
Without Regret
Beautifully Loyal
Without Restraint

STANDALONE NOVELS
Unhinged Trilogy
A Million Tiny Pieces
Inked on Paper
Bad Reputation
Bad Business

NAUGHTY HOLIDAY EDITIONS
2015
2016

Kaden & Keegan

THE WALKERS OF COYOTE RIDGE, 9

NICOLE EDWARDS

Published by Nicole Edwards Limited
PO Box 1086, Pflugerville, Texas 78691

Kaden & Keegan
Walkers of Coyote Ridge, 9
Nicole Edwards

This is a work of fiction. Names, characters, businesses, places, events and incidents either are the products of the author's imagination or used in a fictitious manner. Any resemblance to actual persons, living or dead, business establishments, events, or locals is entirely coincidental.

COVER DETAILS:

Image: © Wander Aguiar Photography
Model: Michael, Natasha & Luke
Design: © Nicole Edwards Limited

INTERIOR DETAILS:

Formatting: Nicole Edwards Limited
Editing: Blue Otter Editing | BlueOtterEditing.com | Fairest Reviews Editing |Fairestofallbookreviews.blog

ISBN:
Ebook 9781644180358 | Paperback 9781644180365 | Audio 9781644180372

SUBJECTS:
BISAC: FICTION / Romance / General
BISAC: FICTION / Romance / Western

Dear reader,

This is a standalone book, HOWEVER…

Before you start reading, I want to let you know that you'll see quite a bit of Travis Walker in this book. His storyline is continuing from the **Brantley Walker: Off the Books** series. While you don't have to read that series to get the gist, you should check out **ALL IN** if you haven't done so to learn what happens to Travis and his family.

Thanks for reading!

Nicole Edwards

Dedication

To all those little surprises in life.

Prologue

Twenty-one years ago
Friday, September 17, 1999

"A RANCH, KADEN. WE WILL OWN ONE day. If we have nothin' else, we'll have a ranch." Keegan Walker stretched out his arms and did a three sixty as he continued to walk. "None of this suburban, cookie-cutter crap. A house we can make our own, a barn worthy of some horses."

Beside him, his twin brother Kaden's boots scraped as they walked along the fancy sidewalks leading home. He missed the dirt road to the old place, the dust they kicked up as they clomped along the tree-lined path that had been formed by hard work and heavy vehicles.

"One day," Kaden agreed.

His brother wasn't much for talking. Of the two of them, Keegan was the one who'd gotten the boisterous personality. Or so his parents had been saying since the day they were born.

"And while we're dreamin' big, we'll have ourselves one woman," Keegan announced, grinning wide.

"We're sixteen," Kaden noted. "Don't think that's somethin' we need to worry about for some time."

Definitely not, but it was something they would plan for. Until that time came, they would find joy in moving from one hot girl to the next. That was one of the good things—perhaps the only good thing—about living in suburban hell. Just in the short time they'd been there, it was clear these chicks were hot for a couple of twins who sported cowboy hats and boots, and they didn't bat an eyelash at making out with both of them at the same time.

The big two-story red brick house their parents bought came into view and grew larger with every step. He missed the old house, the giant pecan tree in the front yard, seeing their devoted retriever, Roscoe, run out the door to greet them when they walked up the path. He would never understand how his father could give all that up to live in a neighborhood with nosy neighbors who brought over pies they'd purchased in the freezer section of the grocery store and pretended they wanted to get to know them when what they really wanted was to see how the rednecks lived. Yep, he'd heard a couple of the jock assholes call them that.

But Keegan would make the most of it because they only had two more years here, then they could go off and do whatever the hell they wanted. Which would be, "A ranch, one woman, and … we're gonna live in Coyote Ridge."

Kaden's head snapped his way. "Seriously?"

Keegan shrugged. "In the country with our cousins on every street corner. Not this"—he waved his hand in the direction of the house—"uppity-housewife-screwin', picket-fence-havin', briefcase -carryin' bullshit."

Kaden snickered. "Sometimes, Keeg, you say the nicest things."

"Don't I?" He grinned.

While Keegan loved his parents beyond measure, couldn't imagine living anywhere they weren't, he despised this residential mecca Gerald and Sue Ellen Walker had moved into last year. It drove him absolutely batshit crazy that they had neighbors right next door. Why Mom and Dad had up and sold the ranch and moved here, he would never know. Nor had they shared the reason the few hundred times he'd asked.

"It's not so bad," Kaden said, as though reading his thoughts. "We've got a pool."

"Only good thing about it," Keegan grumbled.

"We don't have to share a bedroom with Quinn anymore," Kaden added.

"Okay, only *other* good thing," he agreed.

When his mother and father had presented them with the idea of moving—something they quickly learned they had no say in—their parents had used the number of bedrooms as a way of getting them on board with the idea. Six kids, seven bedrooms. Enough for them to have their own.

Keegan had immediately disputed the idea. So had Kaden. They shared a bedroom and that was that. Why he felt compelled to be where his twin was, he didn't know, but it had been that way since birth, and he didn't feel the need to justify his reasons. Separate beds were a must, but the room had to be the same. Their argument had taken some of the pizazz out of their parents' presentation—at least for them—but it hadn't changed the outcome. And here they were, living in this monstrosity of a house, going to a big-city school with their big-city rules, and trying to fit in. Not that the latter was difficult for them. Gauging by the number of girls who bombarded the house phone with calls, they were doing a damn fine job.

"So a ranch, not a farm?" Kaden asked as they tromped across the perfectly manicured lawn toward the front door.

"Yep. Livestock'll be our focus." Keegan smirked. "But you can have a garden if you want it."

Kaden rolled his eyes. "How big then?"

"Size don't matter. Just as long as we've got some cows and pigs. Maybe some chickens."

"Chickens?"

Keegan peered over at his twin. He could see Kaden's brain working, doing the calculations, likely figuring out what they would need to make their dream into a reality. Once he did that, he would move on to the ROI, determining how many of each they would have to send to slaughter to make ends meet. Never mind the fact they were teenagers and God only knew when they'd have the money necessary to buy a ranch. If he knew Kaden—and he most certainly did—his brother would have it all figured out before Momma and Daddy's front door hit 'em in the ass on their way out into the world in a couple of years.

Speaking of Momma and Daddy's front door, Keegan reached it first, turned the knob, and pushed it open. He stepped back, bowed slightly, and said, "Ladies first."

"Screw you, Keeg."

The fact that his brother laughed made it okay.

No sooner had he shut the door behind him than their little sister shouted Keegan's name. A second later, Roscoe came charging toward them, his feather-duster tail wagging with excitement.

"What?" Keegan shouted to Eve while he squatted down to rub Roscoe's head.

"Phone!"

He glanced at Kaden again, shrugged in answer to the silent question.

"Who is it?" he asked Eve when she shoved the cordless handset toward him.

"How should I know? Probably another girl who wants to play kissy-face with you."

One could only hope.

Keegan grinned, took the phone. "Hey."

"Keegan?"

"Yep. Who's this?"

"Anna," she replied as though he should've known.

While he mentally flipped through images in an attempt to remember which one she was, he said, "Oh, hey, Anna. Whatcha up to?"

"I wanted to see if you wanted to hang out."

Then he remembered which one she was. Redheaded cheerleader with the giant tits and the sweet little ass. She'd been cozying up to him in Texas History, batting those eyelashes and putting an extra pout in her lips.

"Me and Kaden, right?"

"Umm ... yeah. Of course."

Keegan heard the uncertainty in her tone, knew this was going to go nowhere fast. As hot as she was, he knew better than to mix it up with the girls who didn't want the two of them together. No way was he brushing off his brother for some chick. No way, no how.

"Where do you live, girl?" he asked, sauntering through the living room toward the kitchen.

She went on to give directions. Turned out, she lived in the same neighborhood, only a couple of streets over.

"Your momma and daddy gonna be all right if we both come over?" he asked directly.

Keegan knew what the girls at school were saying about them. They'd already pegged Keegan as the bad boy, the one without a care in the world. And they were calling Kaden studious and sweet.

"They're not home right now," Anna said.

Keegan mouthed her response to Kaden and waited for him to answer.

He got one. A quick jerk of his head and Kaden had relayed his lack of desire to hang out with the firecracker known as Anna Benson.

"You know what, Anna? I think we've got homework. Maybe another time?"

"Maybe Kaden could do your homework for you," she said, a teasing tone in her voice. "And you could come by. Doesn't have to be both of you."

"Sorry. He's not good at math."

Kaden glared his way.

"Talk to you later," he said into the phone, then hung it up and set the cordless receiver near the charging base.

"I'm not good at math?" Kaden grumbled.

"Hey, I coulda told her we'd come over and you coulda watched her paw at me like a cat toy. Which way'd you rather have it?"

"Whatever." Kaden marched to the fridge, yanked open the door, stared inside.

Before they could rummage through the kitchen for some after-school snacks, the doorbell rang. Footsteps sounded overhead, then trampled down the stairs.

"I got it!" Eve shouted.

What was it with twelve-year-old girls having to be the first one to answer the phone and the door? Eve had certainly mastered the art of getting there first.

From where he leaned against the kitchen counter, Keegan heard a soft female voice. "Are your brothers home?"

Keegan glanced at Kaden, cocked an eyebrow in question, and got a shrug for an answer.

"I've got five," Eve said snidely. "Which one?"

"The twins."

Okay, that piqued his curiosity, had Keegan marching through the house toward the front door, Kaden right on his heels.

"Who're you?" Eve asked the woman.

"Shauna Whitley. Your next-door neighbor."

"Really?" Eve didn't sound impressed.

"Eve, don't be rude," Kaden said, stepping in front of Keegan as they reached the door. "I'm Kaden. This is my brother Keegan. It's nice to meet you, Mrs. Whitley."

Shauna Whitley smiled, and Keegan was almost positive she radiated.

That was the day they'd been introduced to the woman who would forever change their lives. It would be months of manual labor—mowing her yard, cleaning her pool, tending to her flowers—before Mrs. Whitley finally got around to her real reason for introducing herself that day.

By the time they were seventeen, they would and did consider themselves men in every sense of the word, thanks to the sassy, sexy, suburban housewife whose husband spent a majority of the year away on business. Or with his mistress, if Mrs. Whitley was to be believed.

They had whiled away many afternoons over at Mrs. Whitley's, and as the months passed, after she'd taught them things that would last a lifetime, they continued to show her all they'd learned. After all, practice made perfect, did it not?

Turned out, Mrs. Whitley was the woman who had sealed their fates, made them realize their idea of sharing one woman between them was exactly what they wanted in life.

And one day, like the ranch, Keegan was damn sure they would finally find exactly what they were looking for.

Twenty Years Later…
Wednesday, December 25, 2019

KEEGAN WALKER GRINNED OVER AT HIS BROTHER as he lifted his hand. "Last chance to back out."

He waited for Kaden to change his mind, something his twin was prone to do.

"She told us she'd meet us," Keegan reminded him. "True gentlemen will check on a lady, right?"

Before Kaden could say a word, Keegan dropped his knuckles to the door. Three quick raps and he was stepping back.

Kaden sighed. "She's probably as—"

The door opened and Bristol appeared, fresh-faced, her silky brown hair pulled back into her normal ponytail. Her eyebrows lowered, confusion written all over her beautiful face.

"Hey," she greeted even as she stuck her head out the door and peered down the hall. "What are you doing here?"

Keegan smirked. "The real question is why aren't you downstairs?"

Her eyes widened as though she just remembered she'd promised to meet them in the bar.

"I am so sorry. I must've forgotten."

Yep. Or she chickened out, which was likely her real reason for avoiding them.

"No worries. Mind if we come in?" Keegan asked, knowing his brother would be too tongue-tied to get the sentence out.

"In?"

Keegan held up the bottle of Goose, grinned. "Figured we'd bring the party to you. Hang out for a bit. Chat."

Bristol's eyes remained on his. "Chat?"

"Yeah. You know, that thing friends do?"

"Friends?"

Figuring they could spend half an hour doing this, Keegan took a step forward. "Perhaps we could have this discussion inside. Before we wake up any of those kiddos."

That seemed to get through to her, because Bristol took a step back, but she never took her eyes off them.

"I was getting ready for bed."

"Well, I was hopin' we could hang out," Keegan said, realizing Kaden really had lost the ability to speak.

Figured.

"And do what?" The edge of caution in Bristol's voice made him smile.

"Watch a movie? Play cards? Gossip? Doesn't matter," he told her, then held up the bottle. "As long as we come up with a way to finish off this bottle."

Bristol laughed and she seemed to settle somewhat. "Finish that off? It's not even open."

Keegan took care of that right quick. "Is now."

While Bristol and Kaden acted like teenagers who were forced to play seven minutes in heaven, Keegan made his way into the bathroom, retrieved the two glasses the hotel kept stashed there. Why did they put them in the bathroom? he wondered. Seemed an awkward place for glasses.

Not that it mattered.

"All right," he said when he returned. "You sit there." He motioned for Bristol to move to the bed. "You"—he pointed to Kaden—"can sit in that chair. And I'll take the floor."

"You're serious," Bristol said, but at least she was following directions, making her way over to the bed.

"Very. So what'll it be? Movie? Strip poker?" And because he'd thought of it and it sounded appealing, he added, "Seven minutes in heaven? We could play spin the bottle"—Keegan held up the bottle—"but we should probably wait till it's empty."

"I am not playing spin the bottle," Bristol said with a laugh.

"Seven minutes in heaven it is."

She laughed again and Keegan found he very much liked the sound. While he hadn't found himself quite as infatuated with the cute little daycare owner—not the way Kaden was, anyway—he certainly understood the appeal. When she wasn't on edge, she was fun and sweet and damn easy on the eyes.

Since neither of them had any suggestions, Keegan poured two fingers in each of the glasses, passed one to Bristol, the other to Kaden. Since he didn't have another, he figured he'd drink straight from the bottle.

No one spoke and Keegan realized it was going to get awkward really fast if he didn't do something.

"All right. Never have I ever, it is."

Bristol's cheeks turned a pretty shade of pink. "Seriously?"

"Yep. I assume you know how to play?"

She nodded. "Someone tells something they've never done before and anyone who has done it has to drink."

Keegan mock toasted her with the bottle. "You can go first."

"Me?"

Yep, he could totally understand why Kaden was head over heels for this chick. Seriously.

* * *

BRISTOL KNEW SHE SHOULDN'T HAVE ANSWERED THE door. She'd even considered it. It would've been easy to play it off tomorrow, to tell them she'd fallen asleep early, but her hand had turned that knob before her brain could get out the instruction.

And here she was, sitting in a semi-dark room with two of the sexiest men on the planet. She knew she would regret standing them up tonight, but she'd never anticipated they'd make a house call. Or hotel room, as was the case now.

Not that she had any intention of letting them know she wasn't entirely disappointed that they'd tracked her down. In fact, she planned to continue with the ruse, making them believe she had absolutely no interest. Which, of course, was a painful lie. But sometimes self-preservation was the most important thing.

"Should we put a time limit on this?" Keegan asked, a teasing note in his voice.

"I'm thinkin'," she argued, though she hadn't given a second's thought about something she'd never done.

Taking a deep breath, she willed her mind to quiet, to ignore the fact that Kaden and Keegan Walker had interrupted what would've been a perfectly boring night.

"Ten, nine..."

Bristol laughed. "Hush it. I'm thinkin'. Okay, fine. Never have I ever ... stolen a car."

Keegan's sexy mouth curved into a wide grin while his twin's twitched. Kaden lifted his glass, drained it, while Keegan took a swig on the bottle.

Bristol's eyes widened. "You've stolen a car?"

"Technically," Kaden said, "we misappropriated it. Temporarily."

Bristol raised her eyebrows, urging him to continue.

"It was our old man's car," Keegan explained. "Needless to say, we spent a good portion of our freshman year grounded."

Bristol realized she shouldn't have been surprised. Kaden and Keegan were the very definition of a bad boy. In duplicate.

"My turn," Keegan said. "Never have I ever snuck a boy in my bedroom window."

Realizing the twist he'd put on that, Bristol chuckled, only it came out as a snort. A very unladylike one, at that.

"Well?" Kaden prompted, his blue-gray eyes locked on her as though he couldn't wait to find out the answer.

Bristol took a big swallow of her drink.

"I knew it!" Keegan laughed. "Explain yourself, young lady."

"I was a junior, I think. His name was David. He was a senior and I thought he hung the moon."

"Did you get caught?" Kaden inquired.

"Nope. But I never did it again after that. I was so freaked out that my dad would catch me, I couldn't even look at him. He stayed for about twenty minutes, then hightailed it. Never talked to me again after that."

"Probably for the best," Keegan noted, then glanced at Kaden. "Your turn."

Kaden seemed to consider it, then said, "Never have I ever cried while watching a movie."

"Good one," Keegan said.

Bristol was the only one to drink.

"Last movie you cried at," Kaden prompted.

"Oh, geez." Bristol tried to think but wasn't even sure. "I have no idea, but I can admit, I tend to get weepy. I have no shame."

The game took off from there.

Bristol: "Never have I ever lied to get a job."

Kaden and Keegan both drank.

"Mechanic shop," Keegan supplied. "We were seventeen. Lied and said we were eighteen."

"Did you get hired?"

"Yep."

Keegan: "Never have I ever been on a fad diet."

Bristol drank, Kaden didn't.

"More than one," she admitted.

Kaden: "Never have I ever cut my own hair."

Keegan drank, Bristol did, too.

"I wanted bangs," Bristol said when Kaden stared at her. "For the record, it did not turn out well."

"Well, I shaved my head," Keegan admitted, getting to his knees to add more vodka to her glass.

"Did you do it, too?" she asked Kaden.

"Hell no. He looked like a douche."

That made her laugh so hard tears came to her eyes. It took a minute or two, but she finally calmed herself.

Bristol: "Never have I ever played strip poker."

"Totally missin' out, darlin'," Keegan said as he took a pull on the bottle.

Kaden downed his drink, held his glass out for more.

At this point, Bristol was feeling no pain, so she offered up her glass, too.

Keegan: "Never have I ever eaten food that fell on the floor."

Kaden drank, Bristol didn't.

"Five-second rule," Kaden said defensively, and followed it with a sinful smirk.

More vodka was added.

Kaden: "Never have I ever gotten a tattoo I regretted."

Keegan drank, Bristol didn't.

"I was drunk and stupid."

"What's the tattoo of?"

"An anchor." He tapped over his left shoulder to show where it was. "Luckily, I never have to look at it."

Bristol: "Never have I ever slept in the nude."

Both men drank. Kaden had to get more.

"Every night, darlin'," Kaden supplied.

Keegan: "Never have I ever regifted something someone gave me."

Bristol downed what was in her glass, laughing. She knew she should chill on the shots, but she couldn't seem to help herself. For the first time in a long time, she was totally chill.

"It gets worse," she explained, giggling. "It was a gift from Bianca. I gifted it back to her two years later. She totally busted me."

Both men laughed and she realized how much she loved the rough grind of their voices.

Keegan supplied more alcohol.

Kaden: "Never have I ever talked my way out of a ticket."

Bristol drank, Keegan didn't.

"I was sixteen," she told them. "And in my defense, I've never been pulled over since."

Another refill.

Bristol: "Never have I ever hated a gift but said I loved it."

Both men looked at one another, then drank.

"Our mother buys us socks for Christmas every year," Kaden noted.

Keegan: "Never have I ever tried to make someone jealous."

Bristol grinned, drank, and so did Kaden.

"That same guy in high school," she told them. "David."

"Did it work?"

She grinned at the memory. "Nope. But I figure that was my good fortune. He's been married three times now."

Kaden: "Never have I—"

"Okay," Bristol interrupted. "One more, then I have to stop or I'll be sick."

"Party pooper," Keegan teased as he poured a small amount in her glass.

Kaden: "Never have I ever wanted to date two men at one time."

Bristol's head was spinning from the alcohol. She blamed that for why she downed her drink. Luckily, their wide eyes stopped her from blurting exactly who she'd wanted to date at the same time.

Of course, Keegan didn't let it go.

"Spill it," he insisted.

She shook her head.

He was smiling as he got to his feet, moved over to the bed.

Bristol's lungs stopped working as she stared up at the handsome man. He was tall and lean and so freaking beautiful.

"Okay, give me a hint," he urged.

No way could she tell them. No freaking way.

"How old were you when you wanted to date two men at one time?" Kaden asked, joining his brother, both of them looming over her.

Bristol shook her head again. If she told them…

"Do I need to tickle it out of you?" Keegan's barely disguised threat made her laugh.

"Not ticklish," she told him. Luckily, it was true.

Evidently, he didn't believe her, because Keegan took her empty glass, set it on the nightstand, then put one knee on the bed as he reached for her.

When his hand gripped her side, she couldn't have laughed if she'd wanted to. The air in the room became scarce, and a fierce heat took up residence inside her, flooding her veins. That was when she realized neither of them was laughing. Something had shifted in the air, taking their carefree game and turning it into something far more dangerous.

"Tell me somethin'," Keegan whispered, his eyes imploring her.

"Hmm?"

"Have you ever kissed twins?"

"No."

"Do you want to?"

His warm hand was still on her side, even though he kept a decent distance between them.

Bristol looked over at Kaden, held his gaze for a second, then revealed the one secret she'd sworn she would take to her grave.

KADEN HAD KNOWN THE SECOND KEEGAN SUGGESTED they pay Bristol a visit that there was a good chance things were going to get out of control. He'd been doubly certain of that when Keegan procured the vodka.

Then again, out of control was the name of the game when Keegan was in charge, and no doubt about it, his twin had taken the reins from the moment he knocked on her door.

His lungs were constricted as he waited with bated breath for her to answer Keegan's question of whether or not she wanted to slide down the slippery slope and kiss the two of them, to try some twin action on for size.

"Yes," Bristol whispered. "I do."

He was pretty damn sure his heart skipped a few beats as soon as those words tumbled out of her sweet, pouty lips.

Blame it on the alcohol or the game or, hell, on the setting, didn't matter. While Kaden was usually the level-headed one, he found himself doing something he never would've done had they not been in this particular room, with this particular woman.

Kaden put one knee on the bed, then leaned over Bristol, shouldering Keegan out of the way in the process. His brother was not about to sample the goods before him, because Christ Almighty, Kaden had been waiting too long for this.

He held Bristol's gaze as he got closer, waited for her to throw up the big red stop sign. That was the only reason he nearly fell over when Bristol reached for him, her soft, smooth fingers curling around his neck as she pulled him down until their mouths touched. His lips brushed hers ever so lightly, then more insistently. His tongue got with the program, sliding over her bottom lip. They shared air for a moment, and when she sighed, Kaden sealed his mouth to hers, kissing her the way he'd fantasized for months. Her soft moan reverberated against his lips, and it took tremendous effort not to press her into the mattress.

When he pulled back, he watched as her eyes slowly opened, glittering with a heat he'd only caught glimpses of before.

"My turn."

His brother's raspy words pulled him back from the edge. Rather than get up, though, Kaden drew his other leg up on the bed and shifted to the side, watching as Bristol locked lips with his twin.

Most people wouldn't understand their desire to share a woman between them, but that was the only thing they'd ever wanted. Hell, sometimes Kaden couldn't wrap his head around how it had come to be, but he'd long ago stopped trying to figure it out because this … here … with Bristol…

This was fucking perfect.

More so than any other moment in Kaden's entire existence.

Keegan growled low in his throat as he leaned over her. Bristol's hand remained curled around Keegan's neck, and she was pulling him down as she leaned back on the pillow. Kaden knew he should put a stop to this. Come tomorrow, when the three of them were battling hangovers, he damn sure didn't want regret to intrude, and there was no doubt in his mind that would happen. For Bristol, of course. Kaden wasn't going to regret a thing, unless, of course, he managed to push her away with this little stunt. While he'd suspected she was interested in them, Kaden had noticed she did her best to pretend otherwise.

He was just about to call a halt when Keegan's hand locked onto Kaden's wrist. His twin relocated his hand, setting it on Bristol's thigh before Keegan refocused on the kiss.

Bristol didn't push his hand away, even as he slid his palm down her shin until he reached her ankle. He caressed her smooth skin, working his way up her calf, pushing the thin pajama pants upward. He wasn't working to get them off her, merely wanted to touch, to explore. She was definitely as soft as he'd imagined, maybe softer.

God, he'd wanted this for so damn long. Wanted her.

Bristol moaned again, drawing Kaden's attention to the way her lips were still fused to Keegan's. Kaden didn't move, didn't interrupt, though he wanted to feel her mouth on his more than he wanted oxygen. He mimicked a statue, right up until she reached for him, her fingers gliding over his wrist. When she tugged, evidently wanting him closer, Kaden shifted, his thigh brushing hers. It was then she pulled back from Keegan.

Again, he waited for her to stop, but she surprised him, reaching for him.

Kaden had always prided himself on his self-control, but when it came to Bristol, it seemed to fail him. Epically. As his lips covered hers once more, he knew he needed to back off. The vodka had lowered her inhibitions, and if they moved forward, she would hate them both come morning.

And Kaden wasn't willing to risk that.

"God, you're sweet," he whispered, pulling his mouth back and pressing his forehead to hers. "So fucking sweet, Bristol."

She was breathing hard, as was he, more so when her hand slid beneath his shirt, her cool fingers brushing against his abs. Fucking hell.

This had to stop.

Kaden took a deep breath, reached for her wrist, and removed her hand, though it pained him to do so.

"You're gonna leave, aren't you?" she asked, her voice so soft he barely heard her.

"We are, yes. But when you're ready ... *really* ready, Bristol ... just know we're waitin' for you." Kaden lifted his head, met and held her gaze. "Only you."

He could see the hint of uncertainty in her eyes, but Kaden knew this was the only option. Falling into bed with her would be amazing. They could rock her world all fucking night long, but Kaden wanted a hell of a lot more than one night with her.

Forcing himself to his feet, Kaden met Keegan's eyes. His twin nodded once. They were on the same page, thank God.

"Dream about us," Keegan said softly, smiling down at her.

When Kaden stepped out into the hallway, his body ached with the need for her, but he was getting used to it. As it was, he'd wanted Bristol for so long, he wasn't sure he remembered a time when he wasn't aching for her.

"She's gonna push us away," Keegan said, lifting the vodka bottle to his lips as they headed toward the elevator to their floor.

"She is," he agreed, but good things came to those who waited.

And Kaden was willing to wait as long as it took, because in the end, it would be so fucking worth it.

Chapter One

Present Day
Monday, October 19, 2020

KEEGAN WALKER STARED AT HIS TWIN, DOING his damnedest to get the man to come over to his way of thinking. Being as he'd been working on Kaden for the better part of ten minutes, it wasn't looking good for him.

"All right. What about a bakery?"

"Coyote Ridge already has a bakery," Kaden countered.

"Pet store?"

"No."

"Gym?"

"No."

"Vape shop?"

Kaden shot him a *get real* look. "No."

"Thrift shop?" Of course, that had Keegan doing his rendition of Macklemore's "Thrift Shop." "I'm gonna *pop* some *tags* … only got twenty *dollas* in my pocket."

A little too much twang, he thought, but not terrible.

"Stick to your day job, Keeg."

Yeah, yeah, yeah. Whatever. "Fine. No thrift shop. What about an arcade?"

Kaden narrowed his eyes in that manner that spoke of disbelief combined with a modicum of concern. "Seriously?"

"Yeah. Seriously." Keegan *was* serious, and he wasn't sure how much clearer he could be. Yet Kaden didn't seem to be on board, hence the reason he was feigning ignorance.

"Is this some sorta midlife crisis?" Kaden questioned, his dark eyebrow lowered at a sharp slant, his incredulity evident.

"First off, we're a long damn way from *midlife*. And two, it's a damn fine idea and you know it."

"Oh, yeah? And who in their right mind is gonna hang out in an arcade? In Coyote Ridge?"

"Just because *you're* old doesn't mean we all are," Keegan argued, staring at the man who was more or less his mirror image. "Have you seen the town lately? They're finally gettin' with the program."

"Yada, yada, I got it," Kaden sniped. "Ever since Rex opened the B and B, blah, blah. I know the spiel, Keeg."

But what a spiel it was. The Double R Bed and Breakfast had been open for a year, and it had proven to be a fruitful venture in just a short time. The big, renovated farmhouse right in the heart of town had been at capacity every weekend since the opening, and it didn't appear they'd be letting up anytime soon. What more could a small-town hotel ask for? Or those who had invested in the project from the jump?

Keegan grinned wide. "Damn good idea, wasn't it? I knew that place would be a helluva investment."

"Frog giggin', cow tippin', and a B and B. What more could Coyote Ridge *possibly* offer?" Kaden grumbled.

"An arcade," Keegan answered, deadpan.

Kaden rolled his eyes again.

Keegan had known his brother would react this way. They might share the same DNA code, but there was no denying their personalities were polar opposite. Kaden had always been the level-headed one, the one who came up with a plan even when a plan wasn't necessary. Keegan was more of the fly-by-the-seat-of-your-pants kinda guy. He tried not to take things too seriously, while Kaden spent more time thinking than actually doing. And sure, Keegan could admit his brother was usually right when it came down to their arguments.

Didn't mean Keegan agreed with his twin. In fact, most of the time they didn't see eye to eye at all.

But...

Yes, but. Backing Rex Sharpe in the bed-and-breakfast had been a stellar idea if he did say so himself. And now, who was to say an arcade couldn't bring some life to this sleepy little town? Of course, Keegan was only considering it because his true dream couldn't be realized yet. It had always been his goal to own a ranch, but without one available to acquire, that was unfortunately on the back burner.

"Well"—Keegan lifted his coffee mug, offered his brother a casual one-shoulder shrug—"I think it's a smart idea. Think about all the things Coyote Ridge has goin' for it. Just in the time we've been here, they've opened a toy store and a bookstore, right on Main Street. I heard they're plannin' to expand the bookstore to include a coffee shop. An arcade might kick it up a notch."

"I get my coffee at the bakery," Kaden retorted.

"*Options*, Kaden. We're always open for *options*."

"No. No way," Kaden retorted. "I'll admit, I doubted the B and B in the beginning, and it turned out all right, but I'm not at all on board with an arcade."

"Okay, fine," Keegan conceded. "What then? It's not set in stone and the place is still for sale. We can snatch it up, put in somethin' of our own." He leaned in, lowered his voice. "For fuck's sake, everyone else is doin' it. Why can't we?"

"If everyone else was jumpin' off a cliff, would you wanna do that, too, Keeg?"

He grinned. "Damn straight I would."

Those familiar steel-blue eyes glinted with incredulity. "You're serious? You want... *Us*? You and me...?" Kaden exhaled with a sigh and shook his head. "Ain't gonna happen, Keeg."

Keegan chuckled. He happened to enjoy getting his brother riled. Especially first thing in the morning.

"I'll come up with somethin'," he told his twin. "You just wait." Although he certainly wasn't giving up on the arcade.

Kaden challenged him back with a simple tilt of his eyebrows upward.

Keegan knew that look. Kaden thought he was off his rocker. And perhaps he was, but hey, everyone else seemed to be making their mark on this town. Why couldn't they?

Kaden leaned back, allowed the waitress to set his plate down in front of him. "Thanks." He turned his full attention to Keegan. "Might I remind you, we've got enough on our plates."

Keegan smiled at the waitress. "Thanks, doll." He peered over at his brother. "What? With Walker Demo? That's gonna be our claim to fame?" It was his turn to shake his head. "In case you didn't notice, it just kicked over leadership again."

Granted, that was because Reese Tavoularis had moved on to the governor's task force, another brainchild of their cousin Travis Walker. In Reese's place, Autumn Jameson—one of Travis's many cousins on his mother's side—had come on board to run things. She'd been in her new role for nearly a month, and to his surprise, she was doing pretty darn well. He was tempted to say she could pinpoint an issue with an engine faster than he could. But that didn't change the fact that even the family business didn't seem all that stable.

"What about the time we're puttin' in on the ranch?" Kaden asked.

"Key word there bein' *the*. *The* ranch infers that it doesn't belong to us."

As much as he enjoyed working on the Walker ranch, which belonged to Uncle Curtis and Aunt Lorrie, it had always been a dream of his to have one of his own. And yes, Keegan was keeping his eyes open for that opportunity. If it were to arise tomorrow, he'd drop every damn thing else and follow his dream. Until then...

Silence settled between them as Kaden covered his scrambled eggs in tabasco sauce. Rather than stir him up more, Keegan took a sip of his orange juice, stared at his pancakes. He always had pancakes. Every damn day. Why? At what point in his thirty-seven years had he gotten so damn … boring?

"Are you really serious about this? Openin' a place of our own?" Kaden finally asked, his voice lowered.

"Hell, I don't know. I'm just…" He met his twin's eyes. "I'm tired of watchin' everyone else doin' their thing while we settle for bein' along for the ride."

Kaden sighed.

Keegan sat up straight, picked up his fork. "Tell you what. I'm gonna stuff my face with these pancakes and we can pretend this conversation never happened. Deal?"

Kaden's blue-gray eyes locked on his face, but Keegan didn't flinch. He knew how he sounded. Petulant, whiny, sullen. Take your pick.

In his defense, Keegan had always allowed Kaden to make the final decisions. Sure, he threw in his two cents, like where they were gonna put down roots. His choice had always been Coyote Ridge, and since they were metaphorically attached at the hip, where one of them went, the other followed. When they arrived here, they'd thought it would be a fruitful venture. Years later, although they'd technically settled in, they weren't completely settled.

"Fine," Kaden huffed, grabbing his coffee mug. "Let's talk to Travis. Get his thoughts."

Great. Go to the man with the plan and tell him what? That they didn't have a plan? Yeah, no thank you. Their cousin Travis was not just *paving* the way here in Coyote Ridge, he *was* the way. Hell, after Travis's daughter was kidnapped a few weeks back, a task force governing the state of Texas had been formed to search for other missing people. Thank the good Lord, Kate had been located and returned seemingly unharmed two painfully long days after she went missing, but still. Guy had some serious pull. Not to mention, half the town went to Travis for advice. Keegan didn't want to be another in that long line.

Keegan sipped his juice, glared at his pancakes.

They finished their breakfast in silence, although it was obvious Kaden's mind was running a million miles a minute. That was the way his twin's brain worked. Whenever Keegan planted an idea, his brother would veto it immediately, then spend considerable time mulling it over until he came to a final decision. Generally, Keegan would go along with whatever his brother wanted, because truth was, Keegan was the laid-back one. Most things he could simply take or leave. Didn't matter. But something hadn't been sitting well with him lately.

While living and working in this small town had always been a dream of his, there was only one teeny tiny problem... They hadn't really put down roots. When Keegan took stock of what they had to call their own ... besides their trucks, there wasn't much of anything.

Take the house they occupied, for instance. Someone else's. Technically, it was now just one of seven separate structures Curtis had built for his boys when they were old enough to venture out on their own. Originally, it had been Kaleb's place. Then it was Jared's for a bit. Now it was theirs until they figured out what they wanted to do.

To buy or not to buy? Coyote Ridge or bust? For the moment, their options were open although real estate in Coyote Ridge was scarce and what did come available was usually snatched up within hours of being listed. If it ever made it to listing at all. Just like the building on Main Street. If they didn't make their play, it would be gone before they knew it. There wasn't even an apartment to be had. Not that Keegan had any desire to live in an apartment. He preferred wide-open spaces.

Sure, he loved Coyote Ridge. Had since he was a kid, when their parents would bring them and their brothers and sister down to visit their aunts and uncles. He remembered one summer—they were probably twelve, maybe thirteen—his brothers and sister all ganged up on their parents, tried to convince them to move to the small town their father had grown up in. Their parents won in the end, determined to hold down the fort in El Paso, but they'd all talked about moving here eventually.

Their oldest brother was the first to take the leap, relocating to Coyote Ridge permanently. Jared had fled a bad situation only to have it all turn around for the best once he settled down here. Of course, Quinn and Eve had rolled in only a month ago, with Wesley promising to pull up the rear sometime in the next year. At the very least, Wesley had promised to make it down here at some point during the holidays. Keegan was looking forward to seeing their overachieving doctor brother as well as their parents.

Even having his family close wasn't doing what it used to though. Keegan wanted something more.

Then again, perhaps that didn't have anything to do with the house they lived in or the jobs they held or the hobbies they'd picked up along the way. In most ways, they had the life they'd hoped for. Perhaps his settling-down issue had more to do with a some*one*, not necessarily a some*thing*.

That, of course, was Kaden's fault. His twin was still adamant they would eventually have the big wedding and greet some sweet young thing at the end of the aisle where they would vow to love endlessly, blah, blah, fucking blah. Keegan was no longer disillusioned in that area. Been there, done that. Twice. Another ride on the merry-go-round that was shitty relationships? No fucking thank you.

Unfortunately, he was starting to suspect Kaden had a specific woman in mind.

Did he still want to share women with his twin? Damn straight. He didn't know any other way. Their desire to share women between them was something that had come naturally since they were old enough to don a condom. Then it had been sealed thanks to Mrs. Whitley, the sexy housewife who'd turned two horny teenagers into men. Some found their untraditional need an abomination, but that had always been the way it was for them, and Keegan wasn't the sort to make excuses for it.

It was the marriage part he wasn't on board with. Nothing permanent, either. Fucking for the sake of fucking, that was his motto. Why, you ask? Well, that was because their attempts at happily ever after had blown up in their faces not once but twice in their history. Thank the good Lord, they'd never made it to the altar either time, but that had been the plan.

He was still on board with shagging the same chick, but he was no longer interested in seeing if it would lead to something more. It wouldn't. Might as well steer clear of the heartache.

Which was another reason Keegan was content to live in Coyote Ridge. He saw the way people treated Travis, Kylie, and Gage. They certainly weren't abominations and they were making the ménage à trois work. Of course, that was a different version of what Keegan and Kaden engaged in. Travis was in love with both Kylie and Gage, he was intimate with both of them, while Keegan and Kaden merely wanted to bang a willing, sexy woman from both ends. At the same time.

Crude, yeah, he could see that.

And yes, he was jaded.

So fucking what.

Kaden's cell phone rang, drawing Keegan from his rambling thoughts.

His brother snatched the phone off the table. "What's up, Trav?"

Keegan watched Kaden's face, waited to see what emergency they were being dragged into now. For whatever reason, they were the go-tos when it came to helping out Curtis's branch of the Walker family tree.

"Absolutely. We can run by there now, take them to the daycare. No problem."

Keegan grinned. Looked as though they were on chauffeur duty again.

When Kaden hung up, he grabbed his napkin, wiped his mouth, and signaled the waitress over.

"What was that about?"

Kaden reviewed the check, pulled out some cash. "Travis needs us to run by his house and pick up Kade, Avery, and Maddox. Asked us to drop them off at the daycare."

"Somethin' wrong?"

Kaden got to his feet. "Said Haden isn't feelin' well. Runnin' a fever. Kylie's hesitant to get him outta the house."

"Can't blame her there. What about Kate? She back at school yet?" Keegan asked, hopeful the little darling was finding some normalcy again after her horrific ordeal with the crazy psycho bitch who'd snatched her.

"Not yet. Travis said she's with him at the resort. Gonna take her to Lorrie this afternoon."

Keegan got to his feet, grabbed a five out of his wallet, and tossed it onto the table along with the money his brother left.

"I covered the tip already," Kaden mumbled as they were walking toward the door.

"And I bumped it a little. Now she'll be happy to see us next time we come in."

Kaden smirked. "She's happy to see us already."

Yeah, but Keegan was still on the fence as to whether he was going to attempt to get her phone number or not. Never hurt to be extra nice.

You know, just in case.

HALF AN HOUR LATER, KADEN WAS HOPPING out of the truck while his brother carried on a conversation with the three kids strapped into their car seats in the back seat. Kaden couldn't help it, he was laughing at some ridiculous joke Keegan told. Didn't matter that it was juvenile and rather simple, he still laughed.

Kaden had to admit, he was a tad jealous of how easily Keegan got along with the little ones. His twin was the guy all the kids wanted to be around, the one they chased over and under the jungle gym, shot with water guns on Sunday afternoons, hunted Easter eggs with, opened presents with. In recent months, Keegan had even claimed Beau's title belt as the favorite uncle, although technically they were cousins, not uncles.

Granted, that transition only happened because Beau was ear-deep in dirty diapers of his own with the rowdy triplets. Beau had promised Keegan he would be back to challenge him for the title, but he needed some time to settle in. Kaden had to wonder how true that was because the triple terrors were now one, and Beau was still on hiatus, his return to glory still iffy.

Didn't seem to bother Keegan in the least. In fact, Kaden was pretty sure Keegan was mighty proud of the title.

Funny thing was, Keegan didn't have to try too hard to be the favorite. He was merely good with kids. Kaden, on the other hand, loved the little munchkins, but he didn't have the smooth way that Keegan did. His brother would talk them into damn near anything, including brushing their teeth and eating their vegetables. The guy was a miracle worker.

At one point, Kaden had figured they'd have a houseful of their own rugrats by now, a ranch to raise them on. Some sweet woman sleeping between them, waking them up with a smile, a woman they could love beyond reason, spoil because she deserved it. So far, it hadn't happened, but he hadn't lost faith.

Kaden even had one particular woman in mind, but he found himself trying to navigate a couple of obstacles.

One: Bristol Newton, the sassy daycare owner he'd set his eye on, was proving to be resistant to their charms. A problem Kaden figured could be remedied if he just put his heart into it.

Two: Keegan. His twin was adamantly opposed to happily ever after. According to him, it wasn't possible, so why bother. He did, however, say *just sex* was always on the table.

Kaden didn't really see Bristol as the *just-sex* kinda girl, which brought him around to those obstacles he was still attempting to hurdle.

"Man, y'all are lucky," Keegan was saying when Kaden opened the truck door to help Avery out of her car seat.

"Why? Why are we lucky, Uncle Keeg?" four-year-old Kade asked, smiling widely as Keegan leaned in on the other side of the truck to assist him out.

"Because y'all get to come here," Keegan explained, motioning toward the daycare.

And see Bristol. Kaden kept that thought to himself as he set Avery on her feet because, at three, the little girl was already too independent to be carried.

Kaden took her hand before shutting the rear door. When he reached the front of the truck, Keegan was joining him, one hand firmly held in Kade's, the other arm filled with eighteen-month-old Maddox.

"There's all kinds of cool stuff to play with here," Keegan continued.

Kaden grinned. It was pretty much the same conversation they had anytime they brought one of the kids here. There were currently twenty-three little ones between Curtis and Lorrie's seven sons, the last of the herd—Zane and V's Dustin—born last December. For the first time in years, none of the women were pregnant. And due to being far outnumbered by the short-legged Walkers, Kaden and Keegan were often called in to help out in one capacity or another.

As for the daycare, they'd brought almost all of them here at some point. Keegan had mastered the art of hyping them up to want to go in. On occasion, one would make a mad dash for the door in an attempt to escape, but by the time Kaden was leaving, the kids were always excited. That was Keegan for you.

"There is," Kade assured Keegan with a huge grin. "All *kinds* of stuff."

"That's just not fair," Keegan said as he opened the outer door, allowing Kade and Avery to step in before him, then Kaden. "I wanna play with the cool stuff."

Once inside, they remained in the small vestibule, waiting for the interior doors to be unlocked. No one was allowed in who wasn't on the approved list of visitors, had their fingerprints on file, and knew their specialized code. No exceptions.

Kaden stepped up to the keypad, typed in the six-digit code, pressed his finger to the scanner, and waited.

"Maybe Miss Bristol'll let you play, too," Kade told Keegan, his brow furrowed as he peered up, the spitting image of Travis only in miniature form. "I can ask her."

Keegan's response was a conspiratorial grin and a quick nod.

Kaden chuckled. God, he loved these kids. They were so damn innocent, reminding him of a simpler time. And he felt blessed to have a chance to hang out with his cousins and their little ones on a daily basis. Plus, from time to time, he got to hang with his brother Jared, spend some quality time with his own nephew and niece.

"You do that," Keegan told Kade. "If Miss Bristol says it's cool, maybe we can play for a few minutes."

On more than one occasion, Kaden had had to sit back and watch Keegan build block castles with the little kids. Sometimes he wondered if his twin wouldn't mind spending his day here just so he could do that.

The lock disengaged, allowing them to open the interior door. The instant Kade stepped inside, he released Keegan's hand and began jumping up and down. "Miss Bristol! Miss Bristol!" he squealed.

Bristol Newton peered up from her spot at the desk, her light blue eyes glittering, a smile tilting the corners of her full lips. Clearly Kade knew to wait until he was acknowledged.

She turned in her chair, giving Kade her full attention as she rested her elbows on her knees, leaning toward him. "Good mornin', Kade."

God, he loved that soft twang, the raspy sound of her voice.

Hi, Miss Bristol." Based on the puff of his cheeks, Kade was trying to stifle his energy, but his hands couldn't seem to remain still.

Bristol peered up at them, then back to Kade. She stood and stepped around the desk. "What has you so excited this mornin'?"

"Uncle Keegan wants to play with the cool stuff. Can he? Just for a little while? Purty please?"

While Bristol chatted it up with the kids, Kaden took a minute to admire her. From her shoulder-length brown hair pulled back in a sleek ponytail, to the pink Converse on her feet. She looked all of sixteen, although Kaden knew she'd hit the big three-one earlier in the year. He'd even been invited to the shindig. Of course, he'd come up with an excuse as to why he couldn't go. In his defense, Bristol had been dating some jackass at the time—a temporary thing that had lasted all of two weeks—and he hadn't been keen on subjecting himself to seeing her with another man.

In fact, ever since their incident at Alluring Indulgence last December, it seemed Bristol was attempting to keep them at a distance by flaunting other men. Didn't matter that they never lasted much past a first date and she never shared any stories of hope for something more with the many women in her orbit. If she had, perhaps he would've had to intervene. Since she seemed to be doing what she could to push him and his brother away, he'd been biding his time.

But she was single now.

Very single.

When those glittering eyes lifted to meet his, a wide grin on her face, he was hard-pressed to keep from winking at her, a bad habit he'd acquired when picking up women. Fortunately, he knew better. Bristol was not the sort of woman who would be impressed by a wink and a smile. She was far too smart for that. In fact, she'd rebuked every attempt he'd made to flirt with her in the past. Except for that one alcohol-fueled night. Still, that hadn't deterred him in the least. Of course, he'd thought for sure they'd made inroads with her last Christmas, but he should've known better.

"Well, all right," she told Kade with a chuckle before peering up at Keegan. "I think it'll be fine if Uncle Keegan hangs out for a bit."

"Yay!" Kade squealed, jumping up and down as he grabbed Keegan's hand and jerked him toward the door leading to the inner sanctum.

"Hold up, speedy. Your sister's gonna wanna join us."

Kaden remained in the front office as Keegan keyed his passcode in a secondary keypad and then motioned Avery in front of him, making the little girl giggle as Kade grabbed Avery's hand and took off at a trot toward the back the instant the door opened.

"Sometimes I think you should charge him for bein' here," Kaden told Bristol as he stepped over to the wide window that overlooked the room where the kids congregated, watching his brother pass Maddox off to a waiting teacher.

"I think it's sweet," she said, bending over to jot something down in her notebook before standing tall once more.

The outfit she wore was more for comfort than fashion, he figured, but the woman would've looked damn fine wearing a potato sack. The light blue skinny jeans couldn't have been more formfitting if they'd been painted on. The plus was how they showcased toned legs and a sinful ass while the oversized cream-colored sweatshirt hid the nice curves he knew she rocked on that petite frame.

Truth was, Kaden was usually drawn to leggy women, the ones who were closer to his six foot two inches. Bristol couldn't have been but a few inches over five feet. Still there was something about her that did it for him.

"I'll be sure to tell him you said that." Kaden grinned. "He likes when women call him sweet."

Speaking of sweet, Bristol was sweet enough to cause a toothache and sassy enough to square a man's shoulders. Not to mention, she was as stubborn as she was beautiful. Oddly enough, he didn't even have to wink to make Bristol blush. Despite the fact they'd spent countless hours in her presence, usually at one Walker function or another, he always detected a hint of nerves when she was around them.

"So, will you be attendin' the fall festival?" she asked while they stood watching as a group of kids built a block fort around Keegan.

Fall festival? They'd just had the back to school festival, hadn't they? He did a mental calculation, realized the fall festival was only a few days away. Next weekend, in fact.

"Is it just me or does Coyote Ridge have a festival for everything?"

Bristol smiled up at him, a flash of those pretty white teeth. "I think the mayor's responsible for that."

"It hasn't always been that way?"

"Oh, no." She shook her head. "Not like this, anyway. We've had one or two a year, but only for the past couple of years has it ramped up. It's kinda nice."

Nice wasn't the word he would've used. Saying there was a festival for everything wasn't an exaggeration. Just in the past year, he'd been suckered into attending a Valentine's festival, Founder's Day festival, Easter, Memorial Day, the Kick Off to Summer festival, July Fourth, Back to School, some kind of Ode to Pets festival, and now the town's long-running annual fall festival.

How exactly did anyone get anything done around this place when they spent so much damn time decorating and organizing events?

"I think it's her way of revitalizin' the town," Bristol continued. "Mayor Stewart is all about bringin' the residents together."

Kaden found himself mesmerized by Bristol's glossy pink lips and the twinkle in her eyes. He wanted to kiss those lips again, to slide his tongue along the seam and dip inside, hear her reaction. It had been too damn long since he'd gotten a taste of her.

"Does that mean you'll be attendin'?" he asked, breaking the hold she had over him and forcing his eyes to meet hers.

Bristol grinned. "Of course. Mayor Stewart roped me into it."

"I find it amusin' you refer to her as Mayor Stewart considerin' Bianca's your best friend."

Bristol laughed. "One of them, yes. But I do it because it irritates her."

That made him smile. He liked her sassiness. Kaden only wished she'd turn all that attitude on him sometime.

"Well?" she asked, still staring at him.

Kaden frowned. "Well, what?"

"Can I add you to the list of people attendin'?"

"Depends."

"On?"

Kaden held her stare and offered his best smile. "What's in it for me?"

Chapter Two

WHAT'S IN IT FOR ME?

That was a loaded question if Bristol had ever heard one.

More so because there were so many answers she wanted to give. Not a one of them appropriate. Not only because she was currently at work and there were a few dozen kids in the building. No. Her reasoning had everything to do with the fact that she had sworn off Kaden and Keegan Walker. No matter how much she wanted to play with fire, Bristol knew there was no way she walked away without a burn or two if she entertained the idea of mixing it up with them.

Even knowing that—plus running the mantra over in her head a couple dozen times a day—she couldn't seem to help herself. The ridiculously attractive twins appealed to her on a base level, even if they scared the daylights out of her.

Not that she would admit that to anyone. Well, no one except for Bianca, the one person in the world who probably knew everything there was to know about her. She could blame margarita night as the reason she'd blurted out her deepest, darkest fantasy. Lord knows she hadn't intended to do it, but now that it was out there, she couldn't take it back.

However, she *could* keep Kaden and Keegan from finding out.

"I'm sure there'll be some cute women there vyin' for your attention," she said, keeping her tone teasing.

"And you know this how?"

Bristol rolled her eyes. "Well, it's a given."

Kaden turned to face her, leaning his shoulder against the wall. "You think?"

Oh, he could act all sweet and innocent, but she knew better. "I know."

"So, you'll be there, huh?"

"Well, of course." It only took the words coming out of her mouth before she realized how he'd twisted them into something else entirely. "But not vyin' for your attention."

"Well, that's disappointin'." His gaze shot to Keegan in the other room, but his smile didn't falter.

The man had a very, very nice smile. It caused the dimple in his scruffy cheek to wink at her.

Bristol shook off the thought, forced her attention to the kids in the central playroom. There were currently two teachers in there, both paying close attention to all the little ones while Keegan sat in the center of a block fort being erected around him.

"I hear there's gonna be an auction that coincides with it," Bristol admitted, aiming for casual as she dropped the real reason for her inquiry.

"An auction?" Kaden's smoky blue eyes glittered with mischief when he shot her a sideways glance.

"Yes. Highest bidder gets a date with a hunk. I think that's how she's marketing it. Bianca's lookin' for eligible bachelors to sign up."

For a second, she was almost certain she saw disappointment in his eyes.

"Is that right?"

Bristol nodded. "I suggested she approach you and Keegan, see if you'd be willing to join in the festivities."

Kaden laughed and the sound was so sexy Bristol had to look away. She turned her attention to Keegan, who was helping the kids rebuild the block fort that continued to fall down around him. Bristol wasn't sure she'd ever met a man who could interact so easily with kids. Well, other than Beau. Like Beau, Keegan had a natural talent for keeping the kids engaged.

"What makes you think we're eligible?" he asked, a taunting tone to his deep voice.

She giggled. "You're single, aren't ya?"

His gaze heated for a moment, his smirk sexy. "Like I said earlier, what's in it for me?"

"Don't tell me you're worried someone won't bid on you," she teased, not wanting to answer the question with what was really on her mind.

"Does that mean you'll be biddin' on us?" Kaden asked.

Bristol's attention snapped to Kaden as his words sank in.

"Oh, no. I'm not..." She shook her head. "I'm not in the market for a date. But I'll be there to watch the action. I mean, it's for a good cause. Bianca's raisin' money for the church's annual Thanksgiving Dinner. To ensure every resident has a hearty meal."

"Does sound like a good cause."

"It is." Bristol held his gaze. "So, can I tell Bianca she has two more entries?"

Kaden's gaze shot over to his brother momentarily. "No."

Bristol couldn't deny she was a little hurt that he'd turned her down so easily. She thought for sure she'd be able to convince them. If she'd been smart, she would've approached Keegan about it first. He seemed to be the more amenable of the two of them.

"Well, I'm sorry to hear that." Bristol injected as much cheer into her tone as she could. No way would she let him hear her disappointment or misconstrue it in any way.

Kaden's eyes locked on hers. "If I do agree, you'd get one entry."

Bristol nodded, smiled as curiosity won out. "You're signin' Keegan up, I presume?"

He shook his head, his voice gruff and low when he said, "We're a package deal, sweetheart. I think you've figured that out by now."

Heat coiled in her belly, tightening something deep in her core. Her thoughts instantly drifted back to the night at Alluring Indulgence, the three of them in her hotel room. Games and alcohol had led to some rather intense moments, and yes, she'd gotten her first taste of the twins.

At the time, she'd been somewhat surprised despite the fact she'd heard about their unconventional methods to dating. Not that they hid their intentions. Every so often, Bristol would catch a glimpse of the two of them with one woman, usually at the bar. In their defense, they never did anything in public. Not so much as kissing, but she'd seen them at Moonshiners, the way the two of them managed to convince some lucky woman to go home with them.

And yes, perhaps she'd fantasized about being the filling in that sexy twin sandwich a time or two. She was human.

Bristol swallowed hard, forced herself not to look at Kaden. She had to get this conversation back on track.

Taking a deep breath, she cleared her throat. "If you do agree … well, like I said, it's for a really good cause." Smiling, she turned toward her desk, keeping her eyes down as she reached for a Post-it note. "And I'm sure there's one lucky lady out there who'll be thrilled to go on a date with the two of you."

She jotted down a message to call Bianca.

When she straightened, her eyes shot to Kaden's face. That was when she noticed he'd moved toward her. He took another step closer and Bristol fought the urge to step back. He smiled and she forced herself to look him in the eye rather than let her gaze drift down to his sensuous mouth.

"Sweetheart, there's only one lady we'd be interested in."

"Who's that?" She couldn't help it if her voice came out in a strangled whisper.

Kaden didn't respond, but his wicked smirk told her everything she needed to know.

Before she had to come up with an excuse as to why that would never happen, he broke eye contact and whistled for his brother. Bristol remembered where she was, shaking off the lust that had infused her blood. She managed a smile as Kaden made his way to the front doors.

"So is that a yes?" she blurted.

"I'll think about it," he said softly. "Get back to you."

She was so busy watching Kaden that she didn't prepare for the big, hard body that slipped past her, purposely brushing up against her. She told herself Keegan did it because she was standing in the path to the door, but the look he shot back at her said she was so very wrong.

Keegan tipped his hat and winked. "Thanks for lettin' me hang, darlin'."

"Anytime." The word came out breathless, that very brief moment when the heat of his body had pressed against her back having made her head spin.

Heat flashed inside her as the two men headed for the door.

And when Kaden grinned back at her over his shoulder, she rolled her eyes, remembering her pledge to herself.

No way was she going to get caught up in that mess. No way, no how.

"Miss Bristol! Jessica threw a block at me!"

She jerked her attention back to the task at hand and turned toward the kids just as one of her teachers was making her way over to address the situation.

Bristol took a deep breath, added a smile, then forced her feet to move.

By the time nap time rolled around, Bristol was exhausted.

Jennifer, one of her afternoon teachers, had called in sick, so they'd all been juggling to distribute the kids without overburdening anyone in the process. When they were at full capacity, it was a tight squeeze, but she always managed to make do. Of course, it required her to get into the thick of things and help out, putting aside her daily duties.

Bristol knew she should probably hire one more teacher since this seemed to be a recurring problem, but she'd been putting it off. She employed four full-time teachers and two part-timers in order to maintain a low student-teacher ratio. Plus Renee, their full-time cook/nurse/bus driver.

During the school year, it wasn't too bad since a good portion of her students were in elementary school. Summers usually required her to flip the two part-time teachers to full so they could manage. But it was never enough when she had one or more teachers calling in.

Truth was, she'd been hoping for the reprieve the holidays would bring. A lot of her full-time kids were known to take two weeks off around Christmas, the parents keeping them home for whatever reason. She'd been hoping to keep her overhead low until the new year. If she had any hopes of fixing up her house, she had to save some money, and that started with managing her business wisely.

As she sat at her desk in the front office, writing up an incident report for the bruise caused by Jessica's flying block, her cell phone rang. She glanced at the screen, grinned, then answered the call. "Hey, girlie. I was meanin' to call you."

"I just bet you were," Bianca Stewart, the town's beloved mayor and Bristol's best girlfriend, said with a chuckle. "Everyone's first order of business is to call the mayor. Did you have a complaint, too?"

Bristol grinned. "No, ma'am."

"Well, you're the first for the day."

"I doubt that's true."

"Oh, it's definitely true. I knew this position wouldn't be a walk in the park, but seriously. People bitch about the most mundane shit." Bianca sighed. "But I didn't call you to complain."

"No?"

"I'll save that for our next margarita night. Now I've got to tell you about a very interesting phone call I received."

"From?"

"Kaden Walker."

Bristol's insides clenched painfully tight, a weird shock of jealousy jolting her.

"Kaden?" She leaned back in her chair, tried to sound casual. "What—" She had to clear her throat. "What did he want?"

"He's volunteered himself for the auction."

She swallowed hard. "He did?"

"Yep. Him *and* his brother. One entry. I hear I've got *you* to thank for that."

"I … uh … yeah. I talked to Kaden this mornin', asked him about the auction."

"Do you have any idea how hot a commodity those two'll be?"

Oh, she had some idea.

"The two of them alone'll probably bring in enough to cover the cost of all the meals. Which means we'd have money left over for more meals, more hungry mouths fed. Oh, sweet Jesus, Bristol. This is amazing."

Yes. Amazing.

"And you couldn't ask for a better opening than this," Bianca said.

"Opening?" She was totally lost.

"You and two smokin'-hot cowboys?"

Bristol choked on a laugh. "What are you talkin' about?"

"You can't fool me, honey. I know the thought of them up on the auction block is more than you can stand."

"Not true," she lied easily. "I think it's great. For the town."

"And for you."

"No. Not for me." Bristol lowered her voice, glanced around to make sure there were no teachers nearby. "We talked about this. You're supposed to take that secret to your grave."

"And I will. You, on the other hand, have a very rare opportunity to get what you want without anyone bein' the wiser."

Bristol felt her face flame and she was grateful her friend wasn't there to see it. Yes, she had fantasized about being with Kaden and Keegan, but it wasn't something she dwelled on because *seriously*. She wasn't dumb enough to ever act on those desires. She'd learned her lesson the night she'd kissed them in her hotel room. It had gotten her exactly nowhere.

"So, how many entrants does that give you?" Bristol asked, needing to change the subject.

"Adding Kaden and Keegan, that gives me…" There was a lengthy pause. "Nine total. I'm hopin' for ten. I think ten's a good number but I'm running out of time. Can you think of anyone else?"

"Who do you have so far?"

"Hold on. Let me find my list of names." There was a rustle of paper. "Ah, yes. Here it is. Aside from Kaden and Keegan, we've got Jaxson Briggs. Plus, his younger brother. Carson agreed last night. Then there's Chase Jameson a.k.a. CJ. We've got Luca Switzer, Ryan Brehm, plus Leif and Lance Walker."

"Leif and Lance? They're twins. Are they doing the solo entry?"

Bianca laughed. "No. They don't share like Kaden and Keegan."

Bristol fought the blush. "Oh."

"I need one more. Can you think of anyone else?"

Glancing at the list of names she had jotted down, Bristol frowned. "That's nine names, but only eight entries. You need *two* more. Kaden and Keegan only count as one."

"Oh, crap." Bianca grunted. "You're right. I need two more. Dang it. Give me some options."

Bristol ran through faces in her head, tried to think of who else Bianca could add, but couldn't come up with anyone. Most of the men she knew were married with children because that was her business and all.

"Do you think Callen Mosier would be interested?" Bianca asked.

"Callen?" Bristol didn't know Callen well, but he was good friends with Rex, her oldest and dearest friend. Callen's family owned the hardware store in town, and she'd talked to him on occasion, but never at length.

"Last I heard, he was datin' some city girl," Bianca explained, "but they broke up. He'd be perfect."

"If you say so." Bristol figured anyone was perfect at this point. At least as far as Bianca was concerned.

"What about Reese Tavoularis?" Bianca suggested.

"He is officially off the market."

"Seriously? When did that happen?"

Bristol wasn't entirely sure as to the timeline, but she'd seen Reese and Brantley Walker out and about a few times lately and there was some definite chemistry there. Although it seemed they were pretending otherwise.

Clearly not needing a response, Bianca continued, "Fine. What about Cassius King?"

"Really? You want that hot-headed cowboy in your auction?"

"Personally, I think he gets a bad rap. If not him, what about Rafe Sharpe?"

"No," she said quickly. "Not Rafe."

"Ohh-kay."

Bristol would not go into the reasons for leaving Rafe alone, so she focused on Cassius. "I think Cassius'll do. I'm sure he can mind his manners for a little while. He'll be the youngest in the group," she told Bianca. "But why not?"

"Fine. You twisted my arm. I'll drop in at the hardware store and talk to Callen, then I'll see if I can track down Cassius."

"He works for Jeremiah Tucker. On his ranch."

"Perfect. If he's not there, I'm sure he'll be at Moonshiners on Friday night when I go in for a celebratory drink."

"What are you celebrating?"

"The fact that I've got the auction filled up, of course."

"Will you be ready by Saturday?"

"Yep. Easy peasy."

"You still plannin' to have the stage set up outside?"

"Yes. Not too far from the haunted house. Cross your fingers the weatherman holds true to his word. It's supposed to be nice. Might as well take advantage of it."

"I'll help you any way I can," Bristol told her friend.

"You can start by celebratin' with me at Moonshiners on Friday," Bianca said, sounding somewhat distracted now.

"I'd love to. I'll call the girls. See if they wanna come." It was the first Friday night in a long time that she didn't have babysitting plans. In fact, because of the fall festival, she'd kept the entire weekend open.

"Perfect. Friday at eight?"

Bristol noted it on her calendar so she wouldn't forget. "I'll be there with bells on. But we're also meetin' for breakfast one day this week. You promised."

Bianca grumbled. "I know. Up with the chickens. Yes, we'll meet for breakfast. Just tell me which day when you figure it out."

"I will." After disconnecting the call, Bristol leaned back in her chair and briefly wondered if Kaden and Keegan would be at Moonshiners on Friday. Then she snapped out of it and remembered she didn't want them to be.

Or so she tried to tell herself.

KEEGAN SPENT THE MORNING WORKING ON ONE of the Walker Demo trucks, giving it a much needed oil change, then shifting hats and helping Ethan out with some of the paperwork. Although he wasn't as quick with the numbers as Kaden, he could hold his own. Not exactly his favorite thing to do, but he knew it had to be done.

After spending three hours holed up in the office, he ventured out to grab lunch for him and Kaden, brought it back. They ate in their makeshift break room—toolbox for table, stools to sit on— then they both went back to work.

It was the same thing they did every single day. A routine they'd somehow fallen into. When they'd first offered to help out with Walker Demo, it had been before Ethan and Beau had the triplets. A temporary gig until something else came along. That was a year and a half ago. Then they'd agreed to stay on when Ethan told them he was hoping Beau could stay home with the babies. On most days, Keegan didn't mind it. Work was work, and since he was good with an engine, it wasn't too bad.

Didn't mean he wasn't dreaming of the day they were working for themselves. It wasn't that he was all that hyped on the idea of a business on Main Street, arcade or otherwise. No, Keegan still held out hope of owning a small cattle ranch, running it with his brother. Some days he felt the itch so bad, he wanted to toss the wrenches and go in search of something bigger. Unfortunately, he knew Kaden would spend hours talking his ear off, convincing him this was where they belonged for now, so Keegan knew better than to get all twisted up inside.

He was just about to bring up the subject again when a voice sounded from just outside the bay door.

"I hope to God y'all are decent in there."

Keegan glanced over at Kaden. "You think she'll say that *every* time she stops by?"

"If she's smart she will."

"Ain't no one naked off in here," Keegan announced, heading up to greet their boss.

Autumn Jameson stepped into the building, a Walker Demo cap on her head. She pulled it off, used her fingers to tousle her short, multi-hued, curly hair, and offered a winning grin. "Figure it pays to be cautious."

"Oh, trust me, it does."

Keegan had walked in on Ethan and Beau a couple of times during the time he'd been working here. It wasn't that he cared what they did when they were alone, but he'd learned the hard way that Ethan expected to be left alone if he was caught—quite literally—with his pants down. None of that *oops, you caught us, better get dressed* stuff for Ethan. No, sir. Which led to the awkward part, having to leave and come back, timing it perfectly. And then pretending you didn't get an eyeful.

"What brings you by?" Kaden asked, getting to his feet as he crumpled his paper sack and tossed it into the garbage.

"Just checking in. Thought I'd see if you needed me to get anything." Her brown eyes scanned the interior of the building. "Or maybe y'all needed some help."

Keegan chuckled. He had learned early that Autumn did not have a problem getting her hands dirty. In fact, he was pretty sure she enjoyed it more than running the business.

So when she offered, he did his best to take her up on it.

"Got one machine that's givin' us trouble," he said, shooting a quick look to Kaden, warning his brother to shut it.

"Yeah?" She sounded relieved and more than a little hopeful. "What's the problem with it?"

He motioned to the backhoe that continued to give them shit.

"Is that the same one we worked on before?"

"Yep. Seems to want to hang out here forever."

Autumn tossed her cap onto the toolbox, grabbed a wrench, and strolled away.

Knowing that was his cue, Keegan followed. "Changed out all the plugs and wires again."

"But we tuned it up the last time it was here."

"We did. And here it is again."

"Mind if I give it a look?"

"Be my guest. You got a lot of experience with heavy equipment?"

Autumn glanced over, her brown eyes smiling. "I know a thing or two, yeah. Helped my daddy out growin' up. He sells farm equipment."

Well, that was damn good to know. One day he might need the contact.

"That why you decided to venture into this business?"

She shook her head, her short hair swinging as she tinkered with something. "I got tired of the corporate world. My old life, really. Figured this was right up my alley. Fresh start, I guess."

"You sure an office job's what you want?" he asked when she continued to focus on the engine.

Her head turned and a smile formed. "Why do you think I'm in here, cowboy? Figure if I keep showing up, y'all will put me to work."

"If it'll get me in good with the boss," he said with an answering smile, "you're more than welcome to take over."

A couple of hours later, they called it a day. Before they headed back to the house, Keegan called Kylie, asked if she needed them to pick up the kids from the daycare. She thanked him for the offer, but evidently Gage was handling it.

Without anyone else to lend their assistance to, they fell into their regular routine of heading home. Keegan was the first to hit the shower, then went to the kitchen to rummage for dinner. While he poked around, never quite making a decision, his brother showered, then joined him. It took Kaden all of a minute to pull out what he wanted because, evidently, he'd planned on steaks and potatoes early that morning.

As soon as he saw the slabs of red meat, Keegan dragged out the small indoor grill his brother had purchased a couple of months ago.

"I think Autumn's gonna eventually work her way into the shop," he said absently as he got it set up, snagging the seasoning rub when he was done.

"Nah. I think she likes it as a hobby, but she's enjoyin' the rest of it," Kaden said.

"You know this how?"

"Because I talk to her." The tone implied the *duh*.

"Yeah? That all you been doin' with the boss lady? Talkin'?" Keegan teased.

"You know she's not interested in men, right?"

Keegan's gaze darted to Kaden. "Seriously?"

His brother laughed. "Sometimes you're clueless, you know that?"

A lesbian?

Hmm. Sounded kinda hot.

Shaking off the lewd and completely inappropriate thoughts of his boss, Keegan shifted topics. "What were you talkin' to Bristol about this mornin'?"

He remembered the way the pair had looked standing in that office. Almost cozy.

Kaden's eyes cut his way briefly, then turned back to the potatoes he was poking with a fork. "She asked if we were goin' to the fall festival."

Seemed an odd topic, but whatever. "When have we missed one? What did you tell her?"

"She asked if we'd participate in the auction."

"Auction? As in what? We sellin' Kaleb's coffee table?"

"Not that sort of auction."

"Good. I kinda like that coffee table." He grabbed a beer from the fridge, passed one to his brother. "So what's she wantin' to auction?"

"Us. To the highest bidder."

It took a minute for the words to process. When they did, Keegan barked a laugh, unable to control himself.

"Did you shudder and shriek? Wouldn't that kinda thing offend your delicate sensibilities?"

"Fuck off."

"I assume you told her no."

"Actually, I called Mayor Stewart and told her to count us in."

Turning his full attention to Kaden, he waited for him to deliver the punch line, because surely this was a joke. Keegan was the type to jump at the opportunity to have women throwing money his way. Kaden was the one who insisted on flowers and wine and shit.

"It's on Saturday, by the way."

"You're serious?"

On a normal day, his tight-ass brother would've been quick with the hell no. Then again, Kaden had a thing for Bristol, and somewhere in that warped and twisted brain, he probably figured this was their way in with her. After all, the effort Kaden had made over the last ten months had gone so well.

"What's the catch?" There had to be one.

"No catch. It's for a good cause, and Bristol asked nicely. Who was I to disappoint?"

"You're hopin' she'll bid on us," he accused.

"I'm hopin' we won't stand up there lookin' like a coupla idiots."

Keegan took a long pull on his beer, let the information his brother just sprang on him set in. "So the girl you've got the hots for wants to auction you for a date. You're quick to say yes and there's nothin' you're hopin' to gain from this?"

Sounded like heartache waiting to happen.

Bristol Newton had been playing games with them for the past year, stringing Kaden along. Enough to keep his interest, but never enough to allude to the possibility of more. Typical woman shit. And while he wouldn't turn Bristol down if she asked, Keegan damn sure wasn't the sort who was interested in playing games.

"I'm goin' with the flow," Kaden stated. "Just like you told me to do."

"Since when do you listen to me?"

"It's rare, but it happens."

He grinned, watching Kaden put the potatoes in the microwave. "You got a date in mind?"

"What?"

Keegan chuckled. "A date. You know, the good time we're supposed to be offerin'. What do you think those eager ladies will be biddin' on?"

"Us."

"Wow." Keegan's cheeks hurt from his smile. "How exactly do you carry the weight of that ego around all day?"

Kaden's responding "fuck you" lacked any heat.

"So why're you backin' off from Bristol now? 'Cause we both know you're not givin' up completely."

"What would you have done?"

"Hell, I would've signed us up a long time ago. But I'm not the one with the hard-on for the daycare owner."

Not that he would cop to anyway.

Chapter Three

THURSDAY MORNING ROLLED AROUND AND KADEN FOUND himself picking up breakfast at the bakery rather than sitting down to a hot meal at the diner. Keegan's fault, of course. His brother had stayed up too late playing GTA on his Xbox and had refused to get out of bed in time, something that usually happened once, maybe twice a week.

So Kaden had left his brother at the house and ventured into town, figuring he could spring for some donuts before making his way to the Walker Demo office to check on Autumn. He'd learned yesterday that she was having trouble with one of the general contractors. From what he could tell, she had it handled, but he figured he could be the nice guy, check in with the new boss, see if she needed him to have a chat with the guy. Of course, he had to broach the subject without sounding condescending because that certainly wasn't how he intended it, so the donuts were more of a way to pave the way.

When he stepped into the small bakery, he was assaulted with the scents of sweet pastries, the aroma of strong coffee, and the dull din of conversations taking place. The few scattered tables were full, the regulars out early to grab a quick breakfast before heading off to do their thing.

Like most up that early, Kaden went through the motions, moving by muscle memory behind the other customers, patiently waiting his turn.

"Good mornin', Mr. Walker."

The sassy tone, one he recognized belonging to Coyote Ridge's mayor, had his head turning, curious as to which of his uncles were there because, when he thought of Mr. Walker, they were the first to come to mind.

His gaze slid right over Bianca Stewart and landed on the woman sitting next to her at one of the few small tables scattered about. Bristol was seemingly very interested in the blueberry muffin sitting in front of her.

"Mornin'," he returned Bianca's greeting, smiling and letting his gaze linger on Bristol a little longer as he moved closer so he didn't have to shout.

"I didn't figure you for the donut type," Bianca said conversationally. "Don't you usually frequent the diner in the morning?"

Kaden found it amusing that she had yet to use his first name. Now that he thought about it, Bianca rarely did. He had to wonder if she knew who he was or if she considered them interchangeable.

He smiled, peering down at Bristol while answering Bianca. "Tryin' to mix it up a bit." When Bristol finally looked up, he tacked on, "Mornin'."

Her smile was forced. "Good mornin'."

She looked good. Then again, she looked good every time he saw her, didn't matter the time of day or what she was wearing. Today's attire consisted of her usual: skinny jeans, a long-sleeve T-shirt that was a size too big—pumpkin orange with some sort of sequined design on the front—and low-top Converse in black. Her hair was pulled back in a ponytail, minimal makeup on her beautiful face.

Kaden continued to stare at her, knowing this was the perfect opportunity for him to say something. Ask her out, invite himself to sit down. Anything that would move this conversation in the direction it should've been going for the past year.

"Oh, dear. Look at the time," Bianca blurted. "I'm so sorry. I totally forgot. I've got to … a thing. Yes. I've got a thing at a place, and I…" Bianca shot to her feet. "If you'll excuse me… I'll catch you later," she said to Bristol before sauntering out in her usual streamlined manner.

"Wow." Bristol laughed. "If *that* wasn't obvious."

"Obvious?" he asked, turning his attention back to Bristol.

She glanced over at the chair Bianca had just vacated, then up to him. "Would you … care to sit?"

It was his turn to assess the chair before nodding and sitting.

"Where's Keegan?"

"Still in bed. Stayed up too late."

Bristol smiled, peered down at her muffin. "A woman keepin' him busy?"

"Video game."

Her blue eyes were apologetic. "Oh. Sorry. I just…"

Rather than let her flounder for a reason, he said, "He's cranky without breakfast. Figured I'd entice him with chocolate donuts. He's got a thing for the cake ones."

"Mmm." Bristol's eyes lifted. "My favorite, too."

Kaden nodded at her muffin. "Yet you're havin' blueberry this mornin'."

"I don't indulge very often." Her hand went to her midsection, her chin jerking toward the muffin. "And this one's low calorie." A small smile turned the corners of her lips up. "Watchin' my weight and all. I'd do good to lose five pounds or so."

He openly eyed her, recognizing her too-large shirt did as it was intended, hiding the curvy figure beneath. When he met her gaze again, he shook his head. "That's the last thing you need to do."

Her cheeks turned a pretty, soft pink with her blush. God, she really was beautiful. She had that whole girl-next-door thing down pat.

"Yes, well. That's very kind of you to say, but—"

"No buts," he countered. "Give me a minute. I'll be right back." Kaden stood, turned toward the counter before glancing back. "Don't move, Bristol."

Her eyes flared and he knew she heard the slight command in his tone. It appeared to confuse her, but he had expected no less. Bristol had never seen that side of him because he tended to be more reserved, relying on Keegan's laid-back charm and devil-may-care attitude that generally got them the ladies. Didn't mean Kaden didn't have a side that knew damn well how to take the reins.

Kaden left her at the table, went to the counter. He greeted Bailey Weber, who wasn't only a waitress at Moonshiners, she was also the daughter of the bakery's owner. She helped out her mother several days a week, mostly during the week since late nights kept her busy on the weekends.

"What can I get ya?" Her smile was brilliant.

Kaden ordered a dozen chocolate cake donuts for Autumn, Keegan, and Ethan, and two additional—one for him, one for Bristol—as well as a cup of coffee. After Bailey boxed up his order, poured his coffee, and took his money, Kaden was heading back to Bristol. He noticed she hadn't touched the muffin, and rather than drink her coffee, her hands were wrapped firmly around the paper cup, as though it was anchoring her to the table.

"Here you go," he said, setting down the paper plate holding the two donuts.

"Kaden…"

"Enjoy it, Bristol. You deserve it."

"But—"

He shook his head, lifted his coffee cup. "No buts."

Bristol's sigh was sweet, and he was happy to see she wasn't going to refute him for long. Her eyes drifted to the donut repeatedly, as though it was calling her. When she finally gave in, it was with a wide grin that had his insides spinning.

Kaden wasn't sure what it was about this woman. Perhaps it was her beauty or her brains, maybe a combination of both. Could be her sassy attitude and the softer, sweeter side he sensed. Whatever it was, he'd been drawn to her from the beginning. For as long as he could remember, he'd been attempting to get her attention. Subtly, of course. But he was starting to believe subtle wasn't the way to go about it.

And truth be told, Kaden was damn tired of watching her mixing it up with other men. Initially, he'd thought she was doing it to piss him off, but he wasn't sure she had a devious bone in her body. Bristol was simply being Bristol. She was living her life the only way she knew how.

However, she was doing a damn fine job keeping them on the periphery and avoiding them at every turn.

"So are you ready for the auction?" she asked casually, breaking off a piece of her donut.

"What's to get ready for?" He took a bite of his donut, chewed. "Someone bids or they don't."

He hoped like hell that someone was her.

"I seriously doubt you'll have a problem in that department. It might come down to a fight, knowing some of the women in this town."

"You'll be there to protect us though, right?"

Another blush infused her cheeks.

"Actually…" Kaden met her gaze and it was then he knew that subtle was *definitely* no longer an option with Bristol. If he had any chance of taking this friendship to the next level, it was time to act on it.

Her dark eyebrows rose in question.

"I did have a few questions about how it all works. Thought maybe you'd talk me through it over dinner."

Bristol's gaze immediately lowered, her cheeks turning a pretty shade of pink. "What about Keegan?"

"What about him? He'll be there, too. Questions of his own."

When she looked back up, he saw the recognition in her gaze. Bristol was all too aware of what it meant to be with them.

"Tonight," he added. "At our place."

She swallowed, reached for her coffee. "I don't know if that's a good idea."

Kaden leaned forward, held her gaze. "Consider it a favor."

Sensing she was going to argue some more, Kaden got to his feet, smiled down at her. "It's a damn good idea, darlin'. You and I both know it. See you tonight."

With that, he took his coffee and the box of donuts and strolled out.

He could feel those pretty blue eyes lingering on him as he made his exit.

IT'S A DAMN GOOD IDEA, DARLIN'. YOU and I both know it.

Kaden's comment stuck with Bristol for most of the day, rattling around in her head, making it nearly impossible to concentrate. How she managed to make it through her tasks, she wasn't sure, but she had.

Now, as she sat in her car in the parking lot of the daycare, she debated on going home, pretending Kaden hadn't invited her to their house, hadn't checked in via text message twice to make sure she was coming.

As her heart began a steady gallop in her chest, Bristol realized avoiding them would be the wise thing to do. Perhaps she could come up with an excuse.

Oops. Slipped my mind because I had a rough afternoon…

Darn. I forgot I had to go to the grocery store…

Sorry, Kaden, I forgot. Now I'm home, in my pj's…

She glanced up in the rearview mirror, peering at her face. "You're not a chicken."

The eyes looking back at her seemed skeptical.

Bristol took a deep breath, squared her shoulders. Adding some Shakespearean flair, she said, "To do or not to do. That is the question."

With a heavy sigh, she flopped back against the seat, stared out into the darkness. It was only six thirty, but thanks to the short days, it was dark, the same as it had been when she had strolled into the daycare after her impromptu breakfast with Kaden.

A smile formed because that was what happened when she thought about the twins. She wasn't sure what that said about her sanity, but it wasn't something she'd been able to change no matter how hard she tried. And she had certainly tried. Numerous times.

"It's just dinner," she stated firmly. "Nothing's gonna happen. Dinner, conversation. I can answer their questions. That's all."

Yep, that was her trying to talk herself into it, just as she'd done for the majority of the day. Dinner and conversation sounded simple. She knew it would be anything but where Kaden and Keegan were concerned. Kaden had invited her under the guise of the auction, but she knew better. Of course, she'd agreed under that same pretense, knowing deep down there was the potential for something that didn't involve questions and answers.

In some ridiculous attempt to get a rational perspective on the situation, she'd told Bianca about Kaden's request for dinner. She should've known Bianca would not be the voice of reason. Her friend was over the moon for her, encouraging her to go, to let loose a little.

Did she want to? Yes. Yes, she did. She'd been fighting this absurd attraction to Kaden and Keegan for so long.

Problem was, Bristol feared that was exactly what she would do. Let loose. And doing so would likely lead to losing her clothes and theirs, then…

Turning the key in the ignition, she sat up straight, lifted her chin. She could do this. One dinner. A little conversation. Nothing more. By the time they were finished, she would have quashed that strange jealousy about them being auctioned off to the highest bidder and all would be right in her world.

Another sigh escaped as she pulled out of the parking lot and headed toward the Walker ranch.

Although she'd never been inside, she knew Kaden and Keegan lived in Kaleb's old house. It seemed to be the designated guesthouse on the property ever since Kaleb had moved in with Zoey years ago. As she made her way down the dirt drive, past Curtis and Lorrie's big, white two-story farmhouse, she wondered whether the twins had decorated the place or if it was still the same as Kaleb had left it. Probably not, she decided. Why would they? From the bits and pieces she'd collected over the past year or two, she'd learned Kaden and Keegan weren't entirely sure they were staying in Coyote Ridge indefinitely. It had been one of the reasons she'd kept her distance. She had no intentions of leaving the small town she'd grown up in. It had always been her plan to settle down here, get married, have some babies.

Of course, the marriage had come and gone, blowing up in her face before the latter could ever happen. A good thing, no doubt. Her ex wasn't exactly father material even though she had done her best to pretend otherwise.

Before she knew it, she was pulling up to the small, rustic cabin, parking her car beside one of the two big Chevy trucks. There was no driveway, or grass for that matter. Only a patch of dirt they evidently used as a parking lot.

Taking a deep breath, she grabbed her phone, left her purse on the passenger seat, and forced herself to get out of the car. Last thing she wanted was for one of them to see her sitting out here trying to talk herself into going inside. She had more backbone than that. There was no reason for her to fear Kaden or Keegan. Sure, they had the ability to break her heart if she gave them the chance, but she had no intention of doing so.

"Dinner. Conversation," she whispered, a reminder to herself she would get through this in one piece.

Ignoring the nerves jangling in her belly, Bristol managed to knock on the door. She took a step back, waited. When the door finally opened, she smiled up at Kaden.

Despite the fact they were identical, something that apparently ran in the Walker family, and still resembled one another almost perfectly, Bristol could tell them apart rather easily. There were some distinct differences she'd caught on to. Like, they had unique ways of walking. Kaden's gait was rigid, while Keegan ambled. As though he didn't have anywhere to go and all the time in the world to get there. Also, the hair. They both maintained a short shave on the sides and back of their head, but Kaden's dark hair was a little longer on top than Keegan's. But the biggest difference was in their eyes. Not the size or shape or the color. No, it was what she saw in them. Kaden's blue-gray eyes had fewer laugh lines than Keegan's, but Keegan's were the ones that held the storm clouds.

"Come in," Kaden urged, stepping back out of the way as the door opened wide.

Keeping her smile plastered on her face and gripping her cell phone to keep her hands from trembling, Bristol stepped into the house. She could smell food cooking, but she couldn't make out what it was, but it was enough to have her stomach rumbling in invitation.

"I was startin' to think you'd stand us up," Kaden said softly, stepping in close as he shut the door.

"Why would I?" she asked, injecting cheer into her tone. No way would she let him think she was intimidated by him.

Or attracted.

Yeah. That was the most important part to remember. Bristol could not let him or his twin know she was attracted to them. They were like piranhas in the water, waiting for the first sign of life so they could … bite.

"Smells good," she said in order to make conversation.

"My brother's a half-decent cook."

"Yeah?"

Kaden was nodding his head at the same time he said, "No. It's all me."

She laughed, couldn't help it. "I believe that."

"I'm the one responsible for dessert," another deep voice said.

Bristol turned in time to see Keegan stepping out of the small kitchen, his blue-gray eyes twinkling with mischief. He was wearing a pair of dark jeans, a stone-gray T-shirt, his feet bare. Odd how the man seemed to get hotter every time she saw him. There was a darker aspect to Keegan, one she'd never really understood. As though beneath that good ol' boy charm, there was an animal gearing up to pounce.

"And what's for dessert?" she asked before she could think better of it.

"Let's see how the night goes," he answered with a wink. "I'll let you know as soon as I know."

Oh, boy.

She was in so much trouble here.

WHEN KADEN HAD INFORMED HIM THEY WERE having company for dinner, Keegan figured it was his punishment for staying up too late, playing video games well into the early hours.

When Kaden had refused to tell him who was coming to dinner, he figured it was Kaden's way of pissing him off.

The frustration he'd suffered throughout the day had been worth it.

Maybe.

As usual, his first response to seeing a beautiful woman was to lay on the charm. He offered the innuendo, the wink, the crooked smile, long before he thought about his reasons for keeping his distance from this particular woman.

And he had damn good reasons. Really.

For months now, Bristol had said very little to them, interacting only when it was unavoidable, steering clear whenever possible. In doing so, she had succeeded in pissing Keegan off and as time went on, he'd begun to harbor a grudge against her for leading them on, making him hope for something that she had no intention of giving.

And no, he wasn't referring to sex. Not *only* sex, anyway.

Now she was here, and he'd made the mistake of flirting with her, pretending everything was hunky-dory when he honestly wished she'd take her pretty little ass on back to her house so he could go on being oblivious to her sweetness. He had no desire to be hooked by her the way Kaden had been.

However, she was here and his parents had raised him to be respectful to everyone. The least he could do was be polite.

Considering she was looking at them like she was Goldilocks and they were the bears gearing up to take a bite out of her, he wondered exactly what she thought they would do to her. She of all people should know they were the epitome of self-restraint. After all, they'd walked away that night at the resort despite the fact it could've very well ended with the three of them naked.

Even thinking about that night and the months that followed put a bad taste in his mouth.

Why she'd come, he didn't know, but clearly, she had an ulterior motive. The auction, maybe? Curiosity?

It wasn't that he didn't think Kaden capable of persuading a woman. He certainly was. But he seriously doubted Bristol had sexy, naked fun on her agenda. As far as Keegan was concerned, that was all they had to offer her. He knew his twin was hoping for something more, but Keegan had no intention of entertaining that notion. Not with her or any other woman. Never again.

He watched the way Bristol looked at Kaden and he didn't like the feeling he got.

She liked him, there was no way she could disguise it. Her emotions were worn on her sleeve, and though she was nervous to be here, Keegan got the sense it wasn't entirely off-putting for her. And she was staring at Kaden like the man was a knight in shining armor, gearing up to save her from the tower.

Yeah, okay, maybe he should lay off reading fairy tales to the munchkins for a while.

Where would it leave him if Bristol and Kaden went off and did something royally stupid? Like fall in love. Deep down he knew there was a connection there, one she clearly wanted to explore but was refusing to give in to. Interesting thing was, at one time he'd thought they had shared a similar connection except she'd been purposely avoiding them since that one intoxicating night.

Why was she here? What did she want? What was her end game?

He figured there was only one way to find out.

"Come in," he urged. "Don't be shy. We don't bite." He forced a smile. "Much."

She laughed and it sounded strained. He understood. This wasn't exactly comfortable.

Kaden helped her along, placing his hand on her back and nudging her toward the kitchen.

Keegan made a show of stepping back out of the way. "You two wanna be alone?"

Kaden frowned.

Bristol's gaze held firm to his before she glanced back at Kaden. "I thought you said it would be the three of us."

"It is," Kaden said with a sigh.

Two could play this game.

"Mmm." Keegan moved around the island, stopping when he was standing behind Bristol. Leaning down, he whispered in her ear. "And what might the three of us be doin', darlin'?"

"Ignore him. He's bein' an ass."

Keegan stood tall, stared at his brother. An ass. Right.

"Why do I get the feelin' he didn't know I was comin' to dinner?" Bristol prompted as she took a few steps away, looking between them.

"My brother thought it'd be fun to fuck with me all day," he admitted, still glaring at Kaden.

What the hell was his brother up to?

"Have to take the opportunity when it arises," Kaden said.

"Ain't no opportunity here," he muttered under his breath as he moved away.

"Keegan, be nice," Kaden commanded, that all too familiar warning in his tone.

It struck him wrong. So much so, he turned around and stared at the two of them. "What the fuck is goin' on here?"

Kaden was the one to respond. "We're just havin' dinner. And maybe some polite conversation."

"Dinner?"

"Yes."

Keegan looked at Bristol. "*Only* dinner?"

Her dark eyebrows dipped low. "Yes. Why else would I be here?"

It was an opening he couldn't pass up. "Oh, I don't know, Bristol. Maybe to pick up where we left off last year? Remember that night? You. Us. The hotel room?"

"Keegan…" The warning in Kaden's tone was lethal.

He held up a hand to his brother, kept his eyes pinned on Bristol. "Forgive me if I don't welcome you with open arms, darlin'. I seem to recall doin' that once." He tilted his head to the side. "Look where it got me."

When she didn't speak, he studied her gaze, wondering what her motivation was here. He knew Bristol wouldn't have come simply because she wanted to spend time with them. It wasn't her style. No, Bristol was the sort of woman who ran from her desires, ignored them, pretended they didn't exist. Hell, he'd witnessed it firsthand.

"Set the table, Keegan." There was frustration in Kaden's tone this time.

"I can help," Bristol offered, sounding only a tad flustered.

Keegan stared at her.

Seriously?

"I've got it," he insisted, making his way around the island to the cabinet that housed the plates.

While he went through the motions of laying out the plates, the silverware, the napkins, his thoughts drifted back to another time.

He recalled doing this very thing on more than one occasion for a woman they thought they'd spend the rest of their lives with. Two women, in fact. Separate incidents, of course. Kim and Meredith, two names that still made him cringe when he thought about them. The last one being the most memorable. Meredith Marsh. A sweet woman with a smile that had been almost as sweet as Bristol's.

It had started off much like this. The chasing game, the giving in, a constant push and pull. Time had passed while Meredith had made them believe the possibility of happily ever after was within their grasp. The nights had felt endless, the three of them together. Passion, indulgence in abundance.

Little had they known but Meredith had been making her own plans. It had been her intention to land Kaden, to slowly but surely push Keegan out of the picture. Why? Well, that was easy. Kaden was the mature one. Level-headed, financially stable. The perfect husband according to Meredith.

And Keegan's role in all of it? Meredith had informed him he was good for two things: a good laugh and an even better orgasm.

Yep. That was him.

Meredith's efforts to break Kaden and Keegan apart had never worked, but he'd spent far too much time pretending not to notice while she'd been making future plans for her and his brother.

To his shock, Kaden had been the one to put an end to that ridiculous ruse but not before Meredith had proposed marriage. To Kaden.

That had been when the veil on the illusion had slipped away. Since then, Keegan made a point to keep women at arm's length. One night was all he had to offer, because the last fucking thing he intended to be was on the back burner. Never again. Meredith was the reason Keegan refused to think Bristol could be a real possibility, despite his brother's obvious interest.

And this … this *dinner*… This was the first step in repeating history, making the same fucking mistake all over again.

He knew what Kaden was up to. His brother'd had his eye on Bristol Newton since the first time they'd laid eyes on her at the hospital back when Ethan and Beau's babies were born. Since then, they'd attempted to pursue her a little. Back at Christmas, they'd even managed to get close enough to tease her while they'd been cozied up in her hotel room. Damn, but that woman had been so fucking hot. And then her flame had extinguished. Just poof. Disappeared.

And now Kaden was attempting to go at her a different way.

Keegan couldn't deny he liked Bristol even if he harbored some anger toward her. She was pretty, smart, funny. All the qualities he admired in a woman. But if he was being honest, she didn't quite tick off all the boxes for him. Mostly because Bristol wasn't the one-and-done type and that had been their only prerequisite for the past decade or so. Women who wanted to know what it was like to be shared by two men, pleasured in ways they'd never experienced.

Of course, he might've entertained thoughts of the cute little daycare owner before Christmas. On a different level. If he factored in his age and his recent thoughts about settling down ... yeah, Keegan had given the whole forever thing a thought a time or two. Same thoughts he'd had for much of his life, even after Kim, the first one to dump him in hopes of having Kaden all to herself. But Meredith had ruined him completely, confirming that women didn't really want to be with two men for a lifetime, they merely wanted to be fucked by two at the same time.

Burned not once but twice. Keegan wasn't interested in reliving it for a third time.

Not that Bristol would give them the time of day. While she was sweet as cherry pie, not to mention hot as all get out, Keegan wasn't an idiot. They didn't have what it took to catch her eye. No, Bristol Newton was interested in someone with more ... life goals. Yeah. That was a good way to look at it. He knew from overhearing her conversations that Bristol wasn't interested in a couple of redneck boys who lived life to its fullest without all the worries of which university had the best programs, which companies offered the best benefits. None of that had ever mattered to them and Bristol knew it, too. She had her sights set much higher than the two of them. Hence the parade of men she'd had since Christmas.

Not that his brother would ever accept that. Kaden was still disillusioned when it came to love.

Did Keegan want to fuck her?

Oh, yeah. Nine ways to Sunday, in fact. He'd even dreamed about it a couple of times.

Would he act on it?

As he listened to her soft laughter, he had to wonder whether he would or not. It was tempting. But despite the real heat he felt between them, Keegan had no desire to go through it all again.

Twice was more than enough, thank you very fucking much.

Chapter Four

KADEN COULD FEEL THE TENSION LINGERING THICK and heavy in the room, suffocating the conversation, making it nearly impossible to enjoy the meal.

And sure, he'd expected some nerves, perhaps even anxiety from Bristol.

Just not from Keegan.

Try as he might, throughout dinner, he hadn't been able to break it. The conversation lulled on more than one occasion, Bristol pretending to eat, pushing around the beef stroganoff on her plate, while Keegan ate with gusto, going back for seconds, then thirds, always ensuring his mouth was too full to speak.

Kaden thought back to that morning, to his decision that subtle was no longer the way to play this game. He'd changed his mind. It wasn't about being subtle or taking the reins. No, he was convinced it was time to stop playing the game altogether.

Before he could say something to put them both at ease, Keegan piped up with a question that had Kaden looking to Bristol for an answer.

"Tell me somethin'. What happened to that last guy you were datin'? Chuck was it?"

"Charles," she corrected, her attention on her food. "We were … quite different."

"And the one before that?" Keegan asked. "David?"

"Daniel," she said. "Same. Not much in common."

"And the six before that?" Keegan bit out, his tone turning harsher than Kaden had expected.

Bristol's head snapped up, sparks glittering in her light blue eyes. "Is this some sort of interrogation?"

"Maybe."

"No," Kaden stated firmly, glaring at Keegan. "It's not."

"I'm just curious." Keegan's tone lost some of its heat as he leaned back in his chair, picked up his beer. "Figured there was a reason you'd crammed 'em all in this year. Did it work?"

Yeah, they both knew her reasons, but he doubted Bristol would cop to the fact she'd been dodging them at every turn and using a plethora of first dates to do so.

Bristol looked confused. "Excuse me?"

"You heard me. One man after another since January. Seems kinda convenient after what happened between us last Christmas."

"Nothin' happened last Christmas," she countered.

It was Kaden's turn to chime in. "No?"

Those blue eyes swung toward him. "If you're talkin' about the game we played … it was just a game."

"You're gonna have to try harder to convince me."

Bristol dropped her fork on her plate with a clatter. "What is this, Kaden? I thought you wanted to talk about the auction."

He chuckled, grabbed his beer. "Did you now?"

"Yes. Why else would you invite me here? It's not like either one of you has paid me any mind this past year. Not since you walked out of my hotel room *last Christmas*."

He studied her for a moment. If he didn't know better, he would think she was offended that they hadn't pursued her that night. Had she thought they had rejected her? Surely not. The woman was too smart for that. Plus, he'd told her they would be waiting when she was ready.

"Perhaps all those guys you were datin' made it a little difficult," Keegan supplied, the words spoken dangerously low.

Yeah. This was taking a turn in the wrong direction. As much as Kaden wanted to hash this out, he didn't think this was the appropriate way to do so. Bristol was obviously defensive, as was Keegan.

Bristol pushed back her chair, grabbed her cell phone from where she'd placed it on the table.

"Clearly this was a bad idea," she said, looking from one to the other.

"You're damn right it was," Keegan snapped. "Always playin' games, this one." He shoved to his feet, beer bottle in hand.

Kaden sighed when Keegan stormed out of the room. Bristol hadn't gotten to her feet, but he could tell she wanted to. The only thing stopping her seemed to be her surprised reaction to Keegan's outburst.

"What is he talkin' about?" she asked. "Who's been playin' games?"

When she met his gaze, Kaden held it and opted for the truth "You have, darlin'."

Her eyebrows lowered into that V that relayed her confusion. "What are you talkin' about?"

Kaden canted his head to the side. "*That*, Bristol." He jerked his chin in her direction. "That right there's the game I'm talkin' about. You pretend nothin' happened between us."

"I'm not pretending. I'm not the one who hightailed it when things got too hot. If I recall correctly, you and your brother walked out on *me*. Not the other way around." She shot to her feet. "I think I should go."

Holy hell. She *had* taken their gentlemanly gesture as a rejection.

Explained a lot.

Just not all the refuted attempts they'd made for the past ten months.

"Runnin' like usual," he said softly as she passed by his chair.

Her footsteps stopped. "Is that what you think?"

Setting his beer down, Kaden stood, slowly pivoting to face her.

She was standing just a few feet away, so he eliminated some of the distance, holding her stare as he peered down at her.

"How would you explain it?"

"I'm not runnin'." Her teeth were clenched.

"Sure looks like it to me."

"Why? Because I haven't followed the two of you around like a little puppy?" Bristol's eyes narrowed. "I'm not one of your toys, Kaden. I refuse to be."

He laughed, stepped forward until he was practically on top of her. "Toys? Name the last time you saw us with a woman, Bristol."

It was obvious she was attempting to think back on that.

"Months," he said, his voice lower as he pursued her when she took a step back. "That's how long it's been since we've entertained a woman. And that was because you decided to flaunt Barry in our faces."

"Bradley," she corrected.

Yeah, he knew the guy's name. He knew all their names. Hell, he even knew how long they'd stuck around.

And that was the problem.

Bristol took another step back, him a step forward until she was up against the wall. He had to give her props, she didn't attempt to slip away. Bristol held her ground, tilting her head back to stare up at him.

"You remember that night," he said, cupping her face and brushing his thumb over the slight dent in her chin. "You remember the same way we do."

She didn't respond with words, but her increased breaths told him all he needed to know. She did remember.

"And you've been runnin'," he accused.

Bristol shook her head. "No."

He ignored her response because it was a lie. "Why're you runnin' now?"

Leaning in, he brought his lips closer to hers.

"Kaden…"

"Do we scare you?"

"No," she rasped. "You terrify me."

He pulled back an inch. "*I* do?"

"Both of you."

"Why?"

Her response was a shrug.

"We won't hurt you."

"That's not the fear I'm talkin' about, Kaden."

He knew that, but he'd wanted to hear her admit it.

"Can you make that promise, huh?" Her whisper was laced with pain. "That you won't break my heart?"

Because there were no guarantees on anything, he didn't answer. What he wanted to tell her was that she was it for him. Something he'd realized when he'd fallen for her without even trying. Since the day they met, Kaden had been a goner where she was concerned. She was his end game. He would walk through fire to protect her and he would never forsake her. Unfortunately, she wouldn't believe the words even if he spoke them. Actions spoke much louder.

"I should go."

Initially, he had intended to let her simply walk away after, but now that she was here, now that she was this close, he couldn't bring himself to let her go. God only knew if or when he'd ever have this opportunity again, and truth be told, he was growing tired of the chase. He wanted her, had always wanted her. And it was high time they all faced the truth. There was something between them, something worth pursuing if only they could all get on the same page.

"Stay," he whispered, leaning down. "For a little while, Bristol. Just stay."

"It's not a good idea." There was no conviction behind her words.

To prove her wrong, Kaden leaned down until his lips brushed hers.

"I've thought about that night," he softly. "When you kissed me like there was no tomorrow."

A soft whimper was her response.

"Do you think about that night, Bristol? And don't you dare lie to me."

Another whimper. "Yes."

"Did you enjoy it? When we both kissed you?"

"Yes." The word was a breathless moan.

Kaden pressed his lips more firmly to hers, retreated but never enough that his mouth wasn't touching hers.

"Did it scare you at the time?" When he knew she was going to agree, he added, "Be honest."

Bristol shook her head, her lips brushing against his, which resulted in another whimper from her.

He had to admit, he was rather fond of his own self-restraint in that moment. As it was, his cock was like a steel beam behind his zipper, throbbing with an ache he'd battled damn near every night since the one he was referring to. He wanted this woman with a passion that defied logic.

"No, Kaden. It didn't scare me."

"But you wanted more." It wasn't a question.

"Yes."

"Why didn't you say so?"

Her eyes remained on his and he could see a wealth of emotion in them, but she didn't put voice to what she was feeling.

"Trust me when I say it was damn hard to walk away that night." He kept his voice low. "So damn hard, but we did it for you. We didn't want you to feel pressured."

"I didn't."

"So why run now?"

He felt her shrug.

Tilting his head, he remained just out of reach of her lips to see her response. When she leaned in closer, he eliminated the gap, kissing her lightly. Only this time, he licked her lower lip. Once, twice. Another sensual whimper and her hands were on his hips. Kaden wasn't sure she was even aware that she was pulling him closer. He knew better than to tell her.

Instead, he kissed her with all the passion he'd restrained for so long. When her tongue met his, the storm raged, all those suppressed desires roaring full throttle. Kaden pushed her into the wall, his body firm against hers, his hands sliding down to her thighs so he could maneuver her where he wanted her. Bristol was the one who began grinding against his erection, her arms circling his neck, her whimpers and moans growing louder.

He didn't relent because Bristol was finally ... *finally* ... right where he wanted her.

Keegan heard the angry voices coming from the living room, followed by silence, then a few well-placed moans. It was enough to pique his interest, to draw him out of his bedroom.

He stood in the small square space that served as a hall between the two bedrooms, the bathroom and the rest of the house. With his shoulder against the jamb, he watched Kaden and Bristol as they practically inhaled one another. It didn't surprise him to find them like that, Bristol pinned to the wall by Kaden's much larger body, his brother's thigh wedged between hers. Hell, it was a long fucking time coming as far as he was concerned.

If he were one to admit to insecurities, this would be one of those times. Watching his twin with a woman was usually something he had a front-row seat for. The last time he'd been on the outside looking in without being privy to what was taking place had been when he caught Meredith and Kaden at their house, nearly a decade ago. She'd been naked, him fully dressed. Keegan doubted either of them had expected him to come home. Yet there he'd been watching the two of them in a position very similar to this one.

Keegan fucking hated that strange sensation that tingled in his gut. It was fear, he realized. Fear that his brother would leave him behind for a woman when he realized it was a hell of a lot easier to find that elusive happy ever after that way. Kaden had refrained with Meredith. Would he do it again? Or would he simply shove Keegan aside to assuage the need he had for this woman?

Bristol would probably be all for it then.

"What about Keegan?" Bristol asked, her voice a sexy rasp. "He hates me."

No, he didn't hate her, but he didn't like these games she was playing. Not one fucking bit.

"He doesn't hate you," Kaden said, pulling back and staring down at her.

They looked cozy like that. More so than they had when they'd been chatting at the daycare center. There was an intimacy between them, a fire burning, threatening to get out of control at any moment.

Now would've been the perfect opportunity for Bristol to tell Kaden she didn't want the hassle of two of them. It would probably work, too, considering how long Kaden had been pining away for her and the fact Kaden had given up on love everlasting in the past because of Keegan.

As he stood there watching, Keegan waited for the words, waited for his twin to shun him for the first time in their lives. What it was about Bristol, he wasn't sure, but he had the strange feeling she could be the one to come between them. Whether it was because there was something intriguing about her or simply because she'd gotten under Kaden's skin, he didn't know, and he honestly didn't want to think about it.

"I didn't mean to hurt him."

Keegan's eyes narrowed. Why the hell would she think she had?

"What do you wanna do about that?" Kaden asked.

Yeah, what he said.

"I need to talk to him," she said, her arms coming down from around Kaden's neck. "Before this goes any further."

And there you had it. At least she was going to have the decency to ask him to step aside. It was more than he'd gotten in the past.

Keegan slipped back into his bedroom, closing the door silently before dropping onto his bed and staring up at the ceiling. He had no idea if Bristol meant she wanted to talk to him right that moment, but in the event she did, he damn sure wasn't going to be caught spying.

A short time later, there was a soft knock on his door.

"Come in."

Bristol came into the room, her eyes instantly on him where he remained on the bed, hands tucked behind his head. He hoped like hell he looked carefree because that was what he was going for. Damn sure didn't want the little tease to know he'd had a bout of anxiety a few minutes ago.

"Can we talk?"

"About?" he prompted.

She closed the door behind her, stepped closer to the bed, her gaze slowly perusing the space. There wasn't much in there. A bed, dresser, lamp. Considering he was rarely in the space, and only to sleep, Keegan didn't need a whole lot. He preferred to spend his time in the living room, usually parked in front of a video game. Otherwise, they were hanging with family, at the bar, or at the shop.

"I want to apologize," she said softly. "If you thought I was purposely avoiding you all this time."

He huffed a laugh. "Lyin' already, darlin'. Not a good track record with that, huh?"

"I'm not lyin'," she insisted. "It's the truth."

"Your truth, maybe. But from where I'm sittin', you've been runnin' for a damn long time."

Her eyes narrowed, but he didn't wait for her to argue.

"You got what you wanted, Bristol. Kaden's been pinin' away for you for a couple of years now. Why don't you go on back out there and seduce him. You and I both know you want to."

"You are such a … a … a *b*-hole."

His eyes shot to her face. "A *what*?"

"You heard me."

Sitting up, he grinned. "I did. But what language are you speakin'?"

Those pretty blue eyes narrowed more.

"Don't make me repeat it." Her tone had softened, but the gleam in her eye was still sparking.

"Heaven forbid I make you say a four-letter word."

Her hands went to her hips. "I'm tryin' to apologize, Keegan."

"I heard you."

"So you're just bein' ornery because you can?"

Okay, she was hot when she was pissed. Hotter than usual, perhaps he should say.

Deciding on a different tack, Keegan got to his feet, took a step toward her. He knew she expected him to be the fun-loving guy because that was the persona he stuck to. It suited him, made everyone believe he didn't have a care in the world. If he was being honest, it was what he preferred as well. Kept people from asking how he was doing. With a smile on his face, they figured they already knew.

"Why'd you come in here, darlin'?" He took another step toward her, expecting her to back up, but she held her ground, her head tipping back to stare up at him.

She really was pretty. It was in the softness of her face, the roundness of her chin, and the small dent in the center of it. But there was a mix of sexy in there, too. Her long lashes, those pouty lips, and the sleek column of her neck that he wanted to nuzzle.

And he couldn't forget the way she smelled. It had to be perfume, something subtle yet intoxicating. It wasn't flowery or overpowering. It was the perfect mixture and it drew him to her.

"To apologize," she said, her voice soft.

"You're expectin' me to say it's all right? That I don't mind bein' shunned?"

"I'm not the one who walked out that day." Her chin was at a defiant angle.

"What day?"

"The one y'all keep throwin' in my face. If I recall correctly, y'all walked out on me."

"You were drunk."

"So were you."

He grinned. "They don't cancel each other out, you know."

Bristol didn't respond.

"Fine. Say you were pissed that we left you that night, your body aching and hot, eager." Keegan gave in to the urge and touched the dent in her chin, then slid his finger along her jawline. "What's your excuse for all the times since then? And don't tell me you thought we didn't want you. That's bullshit and you know it."

The narrowing of her eyes and the purse of her lips were barely discernible, but he could tell she wanted to argue.

"What's done is done, Bristol." Keegan leaned down, keeping his voice low. "You've said your piece. Why're you still here? My brother's out there."

"What makes you think I only want your brother?"

Such strong resolve for such a sweet little thing. He liked that. A little too much, in fact.

"That's not the case?"

"No."

That was the truth, he could sense it. A nice change of pace for the little daycare owner who'd been stringing them along.

"Prove it," he challenged.

"How?"

"Use your imagination, darlin'."

"I'm not sleepin' with you to prove a point."

"No one said a damn thing about sleep." He leaned down, brushing that sensitive spot behind her ear with his thumb.

When his lips brushed hers, Keegan expected her to stop the charade, to tell him the real reason she was there. That she wanted to pursue things with Kaden, that she needed him to forgive her so she could move forward without a guilty conscience.

He did not expect her to lean into his lips and kiss him, or for her hands to slide up his chest then around his neck. Her fingernails scraped sensually against the back of his head and she was pulling him down to her.

With one simple swipe of her tongue against his lips, Bristol disarmed him completely. He gave in, gripping her hip with one hand, tangling his fingers in her hair with the other, and jerking her closer. The kiss ignited, her soft whimpers spurring him on.

For fuck's sake. Keegan hadn't gotten quite so caught up in a kiss since … hell, he didn't know when. Bristol's mouth was soft and sweet, submitting to his but never surrendering entirely. He fucking loved when a woman knew what she wanted, knew how to coax a man into giving it to her. He never would've pegged this sweet woman as one who could, but … *dayum*.

"Keep it up and I'm gonna strip you naked and bury myself inside you," he warned, figuring that would be enough to scare her away from him.

Rather than pull out of his arms, Bristol whimpered as she leaned into him, their bodies pressed intimately together.

Keegan slid his hand down, lifted her leg so he could settle his hips at the soft apex of her thighs, grinding his rigid cock against her pussy. He couldn't remember a time he'd been quite this out of control. It didn't happen to him. He knew just what needed to be done to seduce a woman and still maintain that safe emotional distance. With Bristol, he was straddling that line, too damn close to the edge for comfort.

"You want that?" he asked, his voice laced with gravel.

"God, yes."

Again, not at all what he expected.

"Then open the door," he demanded. "It's right behind you."

Without an ounce of hesitation, her hand came from around his neck, reached back. A second later the door was opening.

Keegan pressed his forehead to hers, their breaths mingling while he held her lower body right where he wanted her. "Tell Kaden to join us."

There was another whimper as she rolled her hips, the friction against his cock stealing what little air was left in his lungs.

"Kaden," she said loudly enough to be heard through the house.

Although he couldn't see him, Keegan was aware of his brother coming closer, stepping into the room. Kaden's hand brushed his when he gripped Bristol's hip and pressed up against her back. Then she was sandwiched between them, Keegan taking her mouth once more while Kaden moved her hair out of the way to trail his lips over the back of her neck.

They had her right where they wanted her.

The question was, how long would she stay?

IF SOMEONE WOULD'VE TOLD HER SHE'D BE sandwiched between these two tonight, Bristol would've told them they were out of their mind. Despite the fact she'd willingly come over, succumbing to Kaden's invitation, never did she think it would come down to this.

At the same time, she had no desire to stop it.

The opposite, in fact.

They were right. She had been running for the past year, keeping her distance because they scared the bejesus out of her. And it wasn't because she truly believed they'd walked out on her that night. They'd been perfect gentlemen, not taking advantage of her inebriated state. She'd been grateful, but at the same time disappointed.

The passion they stirred in her was something she had never experienced before. She'd known that when she'd kissed them in that hotel room, and she'd remembered it every single day since. But this ... *this* put that to shame because there were now two sets of hands on her, two men kissing her at the same time, touching her, making her burn from the inside out.

Bristol wanted to rationalize it, to assure herself this was a one-time thing, that tomorrow her brain would be back online, and she would be able to move forward with the experience behind her. They would be out of her system once and for all.

Unfortunately, rationalizing anything wasn't going to happen. Not when they were touching her like that.

Keegan's hand slid down so it covered her throat, his thumb and forefinger beneath her ears, tilting her head so he could deepen the kiss.

The man could kiss. Holy moly. She'd thought Kaden's kiss had been lethal, but it was a teddy bear compared to the lion that was devouring her now. Because of his laidback nature, Bristol had figured Keegan would be the gentler of the two. She'd mistakenly believed Kaden would be like a storm coming to a head and if he unleashed on her, she'd be knocked of her feet. Clearly she'd been wrong about both of them.

Not that it mattered. She would take them both exactly as they were.

The only thing she was absolutely certain of: she did not want this to end. Ever.

Bristol sucked in a sharp breath when Kaden's hands slipped beneath her shirt, grazing bare skin as they moved higher, higher. Oh, God. Too much.

"You sure about this?" Kaden asked from behind her, his lips continuing to glide over her neck, sucking on the sensitive skin every now and again.

She nodded, which broke the kiss, Keegan's lips pulling back and giving her a moment to catch her breath. Only, her lungs weren't working because the sensation of Kaden's hands on her was more than she could bear. To distract herself, she looked up into Keegan's eyes, holding his stare for as long as she could, seeing the fire in his eyes, the passion that she prayed he would unleash on her. The only reason she looked away was so Kaden could lift her shirt over her head.

Her knees weakened when Keegan's eyes lowered to her satin-and-lace-covered breasts. The fire in his eyes was still smoldering, but it seemed hotter somehow.

Those steel-blue eyes darted to hers briefly, then back down when he cupped her breasts in his hands.

She whimpered, unable to do or say anything else. The sensation was exquisite, and he wasn't even doing anything.

For a second, she thought nothing could feel quite as good as that, but then there was warm, naked flesh against her back. The heat of Kaden's skin against hers was a shock to her senses, had her dragging more air into her lungs. It was then she realized Kaden had discarded his shirt and now she was leaning into him, allowing him to hold her up while Keegan fondled her nipples through the satin of her bra.

"Remove it," Keegan muttered.

Evidently, he'd been speaking to Kaden because the next thing she knew the clasp was unhooked and her bra was sliding down her arms, then falling to the floor.

Keegan's eyes lifted, meeting hers. He held her there, suspended on a breath as she waited for him to…

He tweaked her nipples, both at the same time.

"Oh, God," she cried, thrusting her chest forward, not caring that she was as wanton as she'd ever been before.

But rather than give her what she so desperately needed, Keegan reached for her arm. The next thing she knew, Bristol was leaning against Keegan, her back to his chest, staring into Kaden's face while he stared down at her topless form.

"Fucking beautiful," Kaden whispered.

"Please…" No, she wasn't above begging. Not right now. Nothing mattered other than the two of them finishing what she'd started.

Kaden stepped forward, his big hands performing the same titillating moves Keegan's had, plumping her breasts, tweaking her nipples. She was staring at his sun-bronzed skin against her much paler flesh, watching, waiting.

But then Keegan's hand curled under her chin, cupping her throat once more. He tilted her head up and back, leaned over her shoulder, and kissed her. The kiss stole what rational thought she had left, sent her body reeling, so when Kaden leaned in and sucked one nipple into his mouth, she came. The orgasm ripped through her with a vengeance, stealing the starch from her legs, her cries of pleasure turning into whimpers when Keegan continued to kiss her.

If Keegan hadn't been behind her, she would've been on the floor.

His mouth slowly separated from hers, but he remained there, staring down at her. "That was so fucking beautiful. We're gonna make you come a dozen more times before the night is over."

Was that a threat or a promise? she wondered.

Or perhaps a little of both.

Chapter Five

WHEN BRISTOL CAME, IT WAS WITH COMPLETE abandon.

Keegan wasn't sure he'd ever heard anything quite so … *carnal*. And completely unexpected.

From where he stood, they were just getting started, yet this beautiful, sensual creature had orgasmed from two mouths being on her at the same time. He wasn't sure how he felt about that, because it left him reeling and more than a little off-kilter.

Not ready to release her, Keegan held her against him and stared down into Bristol's face. Hers was relaxed, her eyes closed, her breaths soft and rapid as she leaned into him. Thankfully the bed wasn't far away because the last thing he wanted was to break the intensity of the moment while they relocated to a horizontal position.

With little effort, he moved them closer then gently eased her down on the mattress before crawling over her and positioning himself beside her, Kaden joining them on her other side. While he wanted to give Bristol time to come down from the hedonistic high, he couldn't. He was completely enraptured, eager to make her orgasm a few dozen more times before this was over, and in order to do that, he couldn't relent.

When Kaden zeroed in on her mouth, Keegan shifted to his knees at the end of the bed, positioning himself between Bristol's thighs. She was still mostly dressed but that didn't matter to him. Right now he wanted to feast on those luscious tits, to see if he could make her come from his mouth alone the way Kaden had.

Leaning over her, he licked one nipple then the other, alternating between the two while she writhed beneath the onslaught. He didn't rush, wanting to ease her back up to that peak once more. Or at least he tried not to rush. It didn't help when her fingers weaved into the longer hair on the top of his head, holding him to her breasts while she thrust her chest upward.

She wasn't what he expected, he would admit. Yes, he'd fantasized about Bristol, but Keegan figured that was more because she'd evaded them for so long. In every one of those fantasies, she'd been sweet, almost innocent. Making love, not succumbing to the libidinous pleasure. With his imaginary Bristol, there hadn't been these sensual moans or the urgent pleas and whimpers. The fictional encounters had always been slow and gentle, and he wondered why he'd thought Bristol wouldn't be capable of passion. Probably because he'd wanted to believe that.

He tended to want what he couldn't have, which made it seem all the more appealing. He couldn't count the number of times they'd gotten a woman between them only for his desire to ebb far too quickly. By judging Bristol, he'd likely been presumptuous in his attempt to protect himself from the potential hurt. His desire for her certainly wasn't diminishing now. He had a renewed sense of purpose, his objective to make this night memorable, to give her what she so desperately seemed to need.

"More, Keegan," she pleaded. "I need more."

At the sound of his name, he lifted his head to find she was once more kissing Kaden while her hand urged his head lower.

Never one to disappoint a woman, Keegan trailed kisses down her stomach while he worked free the button on her jeans, easing down the zipper. He wasn't quite as gentle when he tugged the denim down over her hips. With her wriggling, they managed to get them off, and he took a moment to admire her in the white silk panties and nothing else.

She was a tiny little thing, much smaller than he'd thought. Bristol somehow managed to camouflage her body with the oversized shirts she wore, because beneath was a smaller bone structure and some lovely curves. Which he greatly appreciated. Her breasts weren't overly large, but they were a handful. The indention of her waist gave way to generous hips. He loved her hips, something to hold on to while he drilled her from behind.

He could've stared at her all day, but not right now. As it was, his mouth was watering with the need to taste her, to bury his face between those trim, toned thighs and feast for hours.

Keegan didn't bother removing her panties; instead, he pulled them aside so he could see the glistening folds of her pussy. When he did, her back bowed, her hand reaching for him while her mouth remained fused with Kaden's. He observed the pair momentarily, watched as his brother devoured her mouth while his fingers plucked her nipples. With his eyes on them, Keegan lowered himself to the mattress, shouldering his way between her thighs, and let his breath fan her soft pink flesh.

He gave her a tentative lick to see her reaction and it was exactly as he expected. Bristol's back bowed again, arching up from the bed. When she came back down, her hips were thrust upward, her pussy rising to meet his mouth. Evidently, she knew what she wanted, and he'd be damned if he would deny her.

Settling in for the long haul, Keegan curled his arms around her legs, spreading her wide and holding her in place while he pressed a kiss to her smooth, hairless mound then worked his way along her slit. Alternating between gentle flicks of his tongue and light presses of his lips, he waited until she was moaning softly, her hips gyrating, a silent plea for more.

So he gave her more.

In fact, Keegan feasted on her like a starving man. He worked her clit with his lips and tongue, bringing her to the brink. When he could feel the tension in her thighs, he fucked her with his tongue, pushing in as deep as he could go while she rocked against him. Never did he let her get quite to the point of orgasm. Not because he wasn't eager to hear her come again but because he wasn't ready to stop. Hell, he could've remained right here for the rest of the night, tasting her sweetness, hearing her insistent whimpers.

He kept right on until Kaden's hand slid down between her legs, his fingers pushing inside her. Keegan watched his brother penetrate her for a second before repositioning so he could resume sucking on her clit, the two of them giving her what she was begging for. With Kaden fingering her and Keegan offering an all-out sensual assault on the swollen bundle of nerves, it wasn't surprising when she came this time.

Their names were tumbling from her lips, shouted on a strangled, breathless moan. Not just one name but both, which meant Bristol was right there with them, aware it wasn't just Kaden, not only Keegan who was mastering her body. Both of them.

"Please, Keegan … Kaden!" she cried out. "I need more."

Well, hell. When she asked so nicely…

They gave her more. Keegan took over with his fingers while Kaden launched up off the bed. With the sound of clothes rustling, Keegan positioned himself so his mouth could find hers once more. Part of him expected her to push him away. After all, his mouth had just been buried in her cunt, and some women weren't keen on kissing after the fact.

Not Bristol. Her arms went around his neck, pulling him closer while her tongue dueled with his. To keep from falling on top of her, he had no choice but to remove his fingers from the tight clasp of her pussy, planting his hands on the bed and holding himself over her. He kissed her, long and deep. Tongues, lips, and teeth clashed while her hands began roaming over him.

His shirt was removed, then those deft little fingers moved on to the button on his jeans. It was then that Keegan broke the kiss, lifting his head so he could meet her gaze. He let her continue, sucked in a breath when cool, smooth fingers found his rock-hard cock. She stroked him, their eyes locked together in those few heated seconds before Kaden joined them on the bed.

Feeling a bit unsettled by the intensity of that moment they'd shared, Keegan pulled back, handed her off to Kaden while he got to his feet. He needed a minute, which he spent disrobing completely, getting a condom, rolling it on. He watched the pair of them. Kaden was far gentler with her than Keegan had been but that was generally the case.

Oh, his brother was capable of the same intensity, but he had a better handle on it than Keegan.

And right here, right now, he had a feeling that was what Bristol needed.

SHE FELT AS PERFECT AS KADEN HAD imagined she would. All that smooth, warm skin pressed up against him. Those soft, insistent moans urging them for more. Bristol was everything he'd anticipated and then some. But it was her eagerness that surprised him, her lack of inhibitions. There was no hesitation on her part, not with either of them.

He'd waited for this moment to come, convinced it would eventually. It was the very reason he'd held on despite his brother's obvious resistance to the notion.

No one was resisting now.

When Keegan got up, Kaden had the pleasure of having her all to himself momentarily. After Bristol slipped her panties down her legs, leaving her gloriously naked, Kaden moved over her, fusing his lips to hers, loving the way she kissed him with total abandon, as though this was the only place she wanted to be. Her hands were soft and smooth as they glided over his bare skin, gentle, almost reverent as time slowed momentarily.

"I want to feel you inside me," she whispered against his lips.

He hadn't expected those words to come out of her mouth. Not his sweet, innocent Bristol. But they did and it turned up the temperature within him a few dozen degrees.

Her hand snaked down between his legs, her fingers curling around his cock. It was a light, delicate touch, as though she was afraid she would hurt him.

Kaden grunted, rolling his hips, enjoying the sensation of her smooth fingers on him as he pumped into her hand.

"Fuck, yes," he groaned softly. "Keep touchin' me, Bristol. Fuck…"

She did, her fingers curling around him firmly as he rocked his hips, fucking her closed fist.

When she peered down between them, watching as she stroked him, Kaden kept his focus on her. There was so much hunger in her expression.

Her fingers tightened infinitesimally when she looked up into his face again. "Please, Kaden … I can't wait any longer."

He knew the feeling, but he held off, giving Keegan a minute to return to the bed. Right before he did, Kaden rolled to his back, bringing Bristol with him so that she was straddling his hips.

Keegan tossed a condom his way but, before he could reach for it, Bristol had it in her hand. She tore it open, inched back on his thighs. Goddamn, she was beautiful. Those luscious, firm tits on full display, the dusky pink nipples hardened into points. Her chest was heaving as she rolled the latex over him, her eyes widening as she did.

Yeah, he'd seen that look a few times before. It was usually the first time a woman got a good look at one or both of them. To put it mildly, God had been gracious, generously endowing them in that department. Some would be jealous, but Kaden knew it to be both a blessing and a curse. For one, there were reactions similar to Bristol's now. She was likely wondering if it would hurt when he drove himself hard and deep inside her. More so because of the double action going on in this room.

He wouldn't hurt her. Of that he was certain. It might take a little more time for her body to acclimate, but it would.

With the condom in place, Kaden pulled her back down to him, his lips finding hers once more while he gripped his cock and guided it between her thighs. He hated the presence of the condom, wishing he could feel the silky wetness of her pussy gliding over him. But it was a necessary evil.

For now.

"Lift your hips," he whispered, resuming the kiss.

She did, allowing him to guide himself to the blistering heat of her body. Pushing the head inside her, Kaden moved his hands to her hips, slowly guiding her down on him. He took his time, inching inside her while he maintained the kiss. Their bodies took over, hers rocking against him, his hips lifting to meet her, the slick, smooth walls of her pussy relaxing so he could go in deeper and deeper.

Behind her, Kaden felt the mattress shift, knew Keegan was positioning himself to join them.

Bristol moaned softly, and he had to assume Keegan was touching her, running his hands over her back, her ass, keeping her nerve endings at attention.

They continued like that for long minutes while her body acclimated to the intrusion, her pussy clutching him tightly, the overwhelming sensations dragging the air from his lungs as the pleasure spiked in his bloodstream.

When Bristol pulled her mouth from his and looked down at him, he met her gaze. "We'll be gentle."

"Don't need gentle," she countered, a deep sigh escaping when he pushed his hips upward, filling her almost completely.

She did need gentle, even if she didn't realize it, even if she was so turned on her body burned and ached. He knew the feeling. This was what he'd fantasized about in the dark of night when he jacked off. Her beautiful face peering down at him, the smooth walls of her pussy enveloping him tightly.

When she was moving at a rhythmic pace, he rested his hands on her hips and let her fuck herself on him, taking more each time she rocked backward. It seemed to last for an eternity, but at the same time not nearly long enough before he felt Keegan's finger brush his where his brother gripped her hips.

Dropping his hands down beside him, Kaden watched Bristol's face when Keegan lifted her hips slightly, enough that Kaden's cock slipped from her body. Her eyes widened, a natural reaction when she realized Keegan was now the one filling her tight little pussy.

Her hand landed in the center of Kaden's chest when she leaned forward. "Yes, please. Oh…" Another moan escaped her.

Kaden held her wrist simply so he could maintain that connection and watched as she took his brother deep inside her body. Her lips parted in a perfect O, her eyes closing, her nipples hardening even more. She looked like sex personified, so fucking beautiful, so damn sexy.

"Oh, God, yes," she moaned, her fingers curling so her nails began digging into his chest.

Above him, she began to rock faster, her beautiful tits swaying as Keegan fucked her from behind.

And then it was his turn again, and he was ready and waiting when Keegan dislodged from her body, allowing him to slide in deep.

Bristol's eyes opened, met his, and he saw the acceptance. They would both fuck her, alternating just like this, again and again. It was not traditional by any sense of the imagination, but it worked for them, and based on her moans and the way her fingernails dug into his chest, it was working for her, too.

FUCK, HER PUSSY WAS TIGHT.

It took everything in him to hold back, to give Kaden his turn, filling her, listening to those sexy moans as she gave herself over to them.

As she sat astride Kaden, Keegan moved her hair out of the way, pressed his lips to her neck, tasting the saltiness of perspiration coating her skin.

"We can do this for hours," he whispered, nipping her earlobe. "With us alternating inside you, the frequent stop and go'll allow us to go for much, much longer than if it was only one of us fucking you."

Bristol moaned, turning her head so that her lips were close enough to kiss.

So he did, accepting her weight when she leaned against him, her body rocking as she continued to ride Kaden, who was driving his hips upward, fucking her deeper and deeper with every thrust.

Christ.

"My turn," he said when he pulled his lips free.

Planting one hand in the middle of her back, he urged her forward. Keegan gritted his teeth as he plunged back into the exquisite depths of Bristol's body, pushing in as deep as he could go, enjoying how she sheathed him, milked him.

He couldn't see her face, but he could imagine her expression, especially when they'd first begun to alternate. Keegan had felt her hesitation, but it had lasted only a second, which he took as a good sign. Now that they'd gotten their rhythm, he let himself get lost in the moment, his eyes sliding over the smooth expanse of her back, the curve of her ass, and the way his cock glided into her again and again.

They traded off several more times, alternating not only their cocks but also the pace at which they fucked her. Slow and easy, fast and hard. So incredibly deep.

Before long, Keegan was leaning over Bristol, her body sandwiched between them. When he pulled out, Kaden would glide effortlessly in. Over and over, they continued to fuck her, one then the other, on glorious repeat.

Keegan brushed her hair aside again, kissed her neck, her shoulder. When Kaden pulled out, he pushed in, nipping her with his teeth, grunting from the brutal pleasure that assaulted him.

"So fucking tight," he groaned near her ear. "You feel so fucking good, Bristol."

She cried out and he damn near lost his mind when her pussy clamped down on him like a vise. Her body shuddered as she climaxed, but they weren't finished yet.

Pulling out, he focused on kissing her neck, nipping her earlobe, patiently waiting his turn. It seemed to go on forever, the intoxicating pleasure never ending. It was better than he'd expected, something he feared he could find himself craving.

"Kaden … oh, God … I'm gonna…" Her words died off, replaced by a sensual cry that had Keegan's balls tightening as he imagined his cock was the one her pussy was strangling.

Their movements became more insistent as they alternated more frequently, neither of them wanting to give up the tight clasp of her pussy. They made her come three more times before Keegan met Kaden's eyes over her shoulder, nodded. He wasn't going to last much longer, and he expected Kaden to be right there with him.

Levering himself back up, Keegan waited until Kaden pulled out. When he did, he drove in deep, his hips pumping faster as he gripped her hips, holding her still, letting the earth-shattering pleasure consume him. Once more he conceded to his brother, knowing it wouldn't happen again.

"Fuck!" Kaden hissed, the power in his thrusts jarring Bristol's body.

She cried out both their names, a strangled whimper following. Keegan saw her back muscles tighten, her neck strain as another orgasm gripped her.

"Oh, fuck! Coming," Kaden shouted.

Keegan waited patiently for his brother to come down enough to pull out and then it was his turn. He didn't hold back this time. He kept a firm grip on her hips, holding her still, drilling her hard and fast, deeper and deeper, spurred by her sweet moans and his name falling from her lips.

"Keegan … oh … I'm … I'm … Keegan!"

He felt it, the way her body clamped down on his cock, milking his release from him. A guttural groan escaped as he whispered her name, the sensations tearing through his body stronger than he'd felt in … fuck, maybe ever.

And then it was over.

The three of them were a pile of limbs and racing heartbeats right there in his bed. No doubt he would smell sex for quite some time, and he welcomed it. In fact, he hoped his sheets smelled like her so he could breathe her in for longer.

Only he wasn't supposed to want that. He refused to. It would only result in disappointment. This was sex. Incredible, sure, but that was as much as he was willing to give. Keegan would fuck her a thousand times, but he wasn't giving her a piece of himself. He couldn't.

"You okay?" he heard Kaden ask.

Turning his head, Keegan peered over at Bristol. Her blue eyes were bright, her smile sweet as she glanced between them.

"Never better."

Keegan stared at her, feeling the warmth in his chest as he fought to push it down. No way was he going to fall for this woman.

No. Fucking. Way.

BRISTOL WAS BASKING IN THE POST-ORGASMIC bliss, her head still spinning after the most intense sex she'd ever experienced. As she lay there, Kaden's warm body still beneath her, Keegan's beside them, she wondered if anything could ever ruin this moment.

"Wonder what the parents of your kids'd think if they could see you now," Keegan said, his tone once again curt as he stared at the ceiling overhead.

Yep.

That did it.

Not only because she could feel the distance Keegan was so obviously putting between them but also because he was right. What *would* they think?

Holy crap.

It hadn't occurred to her that she would be the talk of the town if word spread that she'd been mixing it up with Kaden and Keegan Walker.

Feeling far too vulnerable to be lying there naked, Bristol rolled off of Kaden then got to her feet. On her way out of the room, she grabbed her clothes, which were strewn across the floor. It took everything she had not to try to cover herself as she marched naked out the bedroom door and across the small hallway to the bathroom.

Once inside, she closed the door, her hands shaking as she fought to lock it.

What had she done?

How in the world was she ever going to be able to show her face again? She'd gotten caught up in the moment, given in to the overwhelming urges, and had sex with both of them. At the same time.

Images of them sandwiched together flooded her mind. The two of them alternating, filling her while she was overwhelmed by a pleasure so fierce she wasn't sure how she was still in one piece. And she'd loved it. They hadn't made love to her. No, it was far too intense to call it that. Fucking was what it was called, crude as it sounded. They had fucked her, and she had enjoyed every single second.

Her chest heaved, an urge to cry bubbling in her throat, making her sinuses burn. It had been spectacular, but so very wrong at the same time. No one would understand something like this. Hell, she didn't even understand it.

She had to get out of there. Now.

With trembling hands, she yanked on her clothes one piece at a time, ignoring the urge to look at herself in the mirror. She did not want to see what she looked like after that.

Once she was dressed, she swiped her hand over her hair then opened the door. Keegan's bedroom door was closed but she didn't remember closing it. Not that it mattered, she had nothing to say to either of them. Right now she needed to go home, get her bearings, remind herself that this was an experience she'd enjoyed and would remember forever. If she was lucky, no one else would ever know about it, and she wouldn't have to face the judgment of the small town she lived in, those disapproving eyes on her.

Taking a deep breath, she grabbed her cell phone, which she'd left on the small coffee table, and her keys from the kitchen island. She was heading for the door when she heard footsteps.

"Hey."

Kaden.

Swallowing hard, she glanced over at him. He was wearing only his jeans and he looked as well-sexed as she felt. Shame washed over her, had her ducking her head and hurrying toward the door.

She didn't make it before he was there, standing in front of her, blocking the exit.

"I need to go," she insisted. Otherwise it was possible she was going to break down into an emotional mess.

"He didn't mean it," Kaden said softly. "He's bein' an ass. That's what he does when he's worried he might like a woman."

Like.

Not love.

No, Keegan would never love her. She knew that. It shouldn't have bothered her, but it did.

"I need to go," she repeated.

"Bristol."

She took a deep breath, steeled herself for looking into his eyes, then did just that. "What?"

"Don't go. Stay with me tonight."

Her head began an incessant shake. "Oh, no. No, no. Not a good idea. I need to get home."

"I won't beg," he said, his tone shifting to something she didn't recognize.

Narrowing her eyes on his face, she let her shame wash over her. "I don't want you to."

Kaden took a step back as though her words had been a physical slap. When he did, she made a dash for the door, flinging it open and racing out into the night. When she was behind the wheel of her car, she shoved the key in the ignition and prayed the ornery thing would start. It was touch-and-go these days, and the last thing she needed was to be stuck there after her hasty retreat.

Her stomach churned at the thought as she turned the key, sending up silent prayers.

Thankfully, they were answered.

Chapter Six

ON FRIDAY AFTERNOON, THE DAY BEFORE HALLOWEEN, Travis Walker strolled through Alluring Indulgence Resort, nodding at familiar faces, stopping to talk to a couple of their guests.

He usually enjoyed this part of his day, interacting with those who were sneaking in a long weekend, getting away from real life, and indulging in their desires for a little while. This was the place for them to do that, to let their inhibitions go while in a comfortable, discreet environment. Alluring Indulgence Resort was Travis's brainchild, a place he'd designed and built from the ground up. It was a thriving business thanks to the dedication he and his brothers gave the place, one that on any given day he found himself proud to be a part of.

Unfortunately, these days he didn't have much enthusiasm for the one place he loved almost as much as his family. In fact, he didn't have enthusiasm for much of anything. Work kept him busy, but for the first time since he opened these doors six years ago, it didn't make him happy. Nothing did.

Although it pissed him off, his thoughts drifted, the reason for his obsessive anger and his rabid fury taking over: the woman who had kidnapped his child.

It was this very place that had put Travis on Juliet Prince's radar because it was here that she had been abandoned by her husband. Based on what Brantley Walker and Reese Tavoularis had uncovered during their search for Travis's daughter, after a weekend here, Juliet's husband had traded up, found someone who suited him better—younger, prettier, smarter, hornier, he didn't know—and discarded what he no longer needed.

Somewhere in that woman's warped and twisted mind, she'd conjured up the idea that Travis was responsible for the ruination of her marriage. Because of this place, where it all unraveled for her.

Sucked that it happened, but it damn sure didn't excuse what Juliet Prince had done, the pain she'd caused, the terror she had inflicted. Nothing would.

That hadn't been the point of this place. The interactions that went on here weren't meant to be excuses to cheat, yet Travis knew that Juliet Prince wasn't the only person who'd been discarded thanks to those indulgences. He wondered how many people blamed him personally for their ill-fated marriages. She had. Juliet Prince had held Travis personally responsible for her happily ever after going up in flames. The husband had taken their daughter from her, getting sole custody in the divorce. However, Travis suspected that had nothing to do with the new wife and everything to do with the crazy that was Juliet Prince.

Not that he particularly gave a shit about her happiness. In fact, he had to believe she deserved what came to her. Maybe not before, but certainly now. The bitch had traumatized his daughter. Kidnapped her, abandoned her. According to the details that were slowly coming out in therapy, those two days had been hell for Kate. Absolute hell.

But Juliet had also traumatized Kylie and Gage. Travis's wife and husband had been fraught with terror and grief during the ordeal, and he hadn't been able to do a damn thing about it. Something else he would never forgive her for.

Which was the reason Travis was hell-bent on ensuring Juliet Prince received payback.

At his hands.

If only he could find her.

The fact that he couldn't spoke volumes. He wouldn't deny he had more means than most. Money, power, reputation. He had it all and he'd worked damn hard to earn every bit of it. He had connections from the White House down to the criminal underworld, people who would do whatever he needed.

Yet he hadn't utilized those connections, relying solely on his cousin Brantley because he knew, once the Navy SEAL set his mind to something, he would see it through. And Travis needed this kept on the down low. Finding her was a priority, but he didn't need the world to know he had.

So why the fuck hadn't Juliet Prince been found yet? She was one woman. Where the fuck was she?

As that question bounced around in his head, he fought the urge to return to his office, bury himself in his computer. He'd been looking high and low, running searches of his own in an attempt to nail her down. A couple of times he'd been close, but she had evaded him.

"Hey."

Glancing over, Travis saw his husband strolling toward him, that worried expression firmly on Gage's handsome face. It was the same look he'd seen every single day since Kate was returned.

"Yeah?"

"Think maybe we could head out early today? Take the kids to do somethin'?"

"You and Kylie should do that," he told him, continuing to walk so he could greet the other guests who had ventured out of their rooms for the evening.

"We'd prefer if you came with us."

"No can do."

"Why?"

Travis came to an abrupt stop, turning to face his husband. "Because I have shit to do."

"Do you? Or is that your excuse to ignore us?"

Frowning, Travis lowered his voice. "What the fuck are you talkin' about?"

Gage's dark eyebrows lifted skeptically. "You're gonna stand there and pretend you haven't been so completely absorbed with finding that woman that you can't spend an extra minute with us?"

"I see you every damn day," he countered, his ire rising. "Here. At home. You're every-fucking-where I am, Gage. That not enough for you?"

The second those words were out of his mouth, Travis wished like hell he could pull them back, swallow them down. He hated the pain he could see in Gage's eyes.

"No, actually, Trav, it's not," Gage bit out. "But hey, you do you, and I'll take care of the rest."

Travis didn't get a chance to apologize or argue his point, because Gage spun around and stormed off, heading right for the doors leading to the employee parking lot.

He was tempted to go after him but changed his mind. He didn't have the energy to fight with Gage right now. And this thing between them—the temper, the frustration—it would dissipate soon enough.

As soon as Travis found that bitch and put the hell they'd all suffered behind them.

"Oh, my heavens, Bristol, I don't know how much longer we can go on like this," Renee Bridgewater said from her spot at the small table in the daycare kitchen.

"I know." And boy, did she.

For the third time this week, Jennifer, one of her part-time afternoon teachers, had called in sick, leaving them in a state of chaos because they'd been depending on her to show up since Bristol was already down one teacher. It was Friday, so she should've expected it. Fridays were the worst.

Always on time, always reliable Maggie had called in that morning, offering to come in despite her obvious illness. She would have, too, if Bristol hadn't demanded she stay home. No sense getting everyone else sick. She knew Maggie would have to be at death's door before she ever called in, so Bristol had known it was bad. The woman never missed a day if it could be helped.

Unlike Maggie, Jennifer wasn't punctual or loyal. She was the one who called in about three, sometimes four times a month. The young woman lived at home with her parents and had a penchant for going into Austin on the weekends and not returning until … well, until she felt like it. And sometimes she set out for those long weekends early by skipping out on them on Friday, like she'd done today.

Unfortunately, this was the last straw. Bristol needed to be able to depend on her employees, and the other teachers didn't deserve to be overworked and overrun because someone would rather be partying or didn't feel like coming in to work because they were nursing a hangover.

"I'll put an ad in the paper," she promised Renee. "See if we can get someone in here."

Renee nodded. "You should do that, yes. While you're at it…"

Bristol glanced at the older woman, raised an eyebrow.

"I know you're good friends with Kayla, which is why I think she's avoiding talking to you, but that girl would be a great addition here."

Bristol frowned. "Kayla? Kayla Spivey?"

Renee nodded.

"Why would she want to work here?"

"Well, for one, she just got her degree in early childhood education. And two, she's been looking to find a place closer to home."

How in the world did Bristol not know this?

"Why didn't she tell me that?"

Renee shrugged. "Some friends don't like to take advantage."

"She could never take advantage of me. She's one of my closest friends."

"Don't have to convince me," Renee said. "And now you know, so maybe you can reach out to her. I think she'd be a good second-in-command. Someone you could rely on so you can take a day off every now and then. Maybe sneak in a vacation once every three or four years."

A day off? Vacation? Bristol wasn't even sure what that looked like. Aside from weekends, she spent every waking hour here at the daycare. Sometimes weekends too, depending on what needed to be done. And there were definitely times she would've preferred to stay in bed, today being one of them. After last night…

Nope. Not going there.

"I'll call her," Bristol decided.

"And you should still put an ad in the paper," Renee added. "We could use a helping hand around here. Someone to replace Jennifer. Maybe full-time, though."

Two new employees? That sounded daunting to her P and L, but she couldn't deny Renee was right. It would be nice to have enough people there to cover all that needed to be done.

Resigned to doing it simply because Kayla was one of her very best friends and she was bothered that she didn't even realize Kayla had been going to school, she made the call.

A few hours later, Kayla stopped in, surprising Bristol.

After buzzing her into the building, she met her friend in the front office. "Hey, I didn't think I'd see you today. I thought we agreed on next week?"

"We did, I know, but you piqued my curiosity. Couldn't put it off." Kayla walked over to the wide window in the front office that overlooked the main recreation room. "Wow, the place looks fantastic. I honestly had no idea it was this big."

"You've never been here before?" Bristol asked, surprised that she hadn't realized that either.

"Nope." Kayla smiled. "Never really had a reason to, I guess."

"Can I get you somethin' to drink? Water? Juice?" Bristol smiled. "We might still have some coffee left. Made a pot at lunch."

"I'm good." Kayla turned to face her. "You sounded chipper on the phone. What's up?"

"Please, have a seat," Bristol urged, motioning to the chair on the opposite side of the desk.

Kayla's expression turned worried, a frown marring her forehead. "Did I do something wrong?"

Bristol chuckled. "Not at all. God, no, Kayla." She exhaled, let her shoulders relax. "I just thought maybe we could chat."

Kayla merely stared back at her, a deer in the headlights.

Because she knew Kayla would continue to worry, Bristol decided to get right to the point. "Why didn't you tell us you got your degree?"

A hint of pink infused Kayla's pale cheeks, made all the more noticeable by the black hair that hung down to her shoulders.

"It's a … uh … recent development." Kayla slowly lowered herself into the chair.

"I didn't even know you were in school. And that makes me a horrible friend, I will admit."

"It does not." Kayla gave a weak laugh, her eyes lowering, focusing on her fidgeting hands in her lap. "I was taking classes online. It took longer than I wanted, but I got it done. I didn't think it was a big deal."

"It's a huge deal," she insisted. "We should've gone out to celebrate."

Kayla shrugged one shoulder. Always modest, this one.

Although Renee had already told her, Bristol asked, "What's your degree in?"

"Early childhood development. I've been working in a daycare in Round Rock for a while now."

Bristol leaned forward, smiled. "Why didn't you tell me? I would've been thrilled to hire you."

Kayla's eyes lifted and there was the familiar wariness in them. "Because you've done enough to help me. Last thing I want is for you to think I'm a mooch."

Inside those dark gray eyes, Bristol still saw a hint of the woman they'd met years ago, the one who had been abused by a longtime boyfriend. Four years younger than her and a Coyote Ridge transplant since the age of thirteen, Kayla had been brought into their informal girls club a few years ago when they'd all been having margarita night at Moonshiners. That night, Bianca had chased off Kayla's heavy-handed boyfriend and they'd befriended the woman. Since her breakup with that jackass, Kayla had been breaking out of her shell bit by bit. Yes, she was still a little on the shy side, but she'd come a long way.

"Well, I know for a fact you're not a mooch. And I wouldn't be the one doing a favor here. You'd be doing me a huge one."

Kayla's eyebrows dipped down. "How so?"

"I am in desperate need of someone who can help me run this place. Not only a teacher," she explained, "but someone who can assist with the other stuff, too."

Bristol could see the hope glittering in those pretty gray eyes.

"With a degree, the pay's a little better than a teacher," she continued. "And I figure, as we progress, we'll work out compensation according to your job duties."

"You … want me to work here?"

"I do, Kayla. I really, really do." She grinned. "Would you be open to that?"

Her friend's smile formed slowly but it grew wider as her eyes sparkled. "I'd… Oh, God. That would be fantastic. My car's about to crap out on me, but this is close enough for me to walk if I have to." Kayla inhaled deeply. "I can't thank you enough."

"No need to thank me. I should be thanking you. Just let me know when you can start and—"

"Two weeks," Kayla blurted. "I just need to give my notice."

"That's perfect." Bristol opened the bottom drawer in her desk, pulled out the required paperwork, and slid it over. "If you want, you can get started on this before then. I do have to run a background check, as you know."

"Nothing to worry about on that front."

Bristol grinned, feeling genuinely happy for the first time since she woke up that morning. "I look forward to having you here in two weeks. In the meantime, I'm going to see if I can find another teacher to replace the one I need to let go."

She took a deep breath, released it.

Maybe her life wasn't going into the crapper after all.

Two hours later, Bristol was recanting that thought.

At some point between last night's debacle and the stress of today, she had completely forgotten that she'd promised to go to Moonshiners with Bianca. Her best friend had texted to remind her about the pre-auction celebration and made it very clear Bristol was not allowed to back out.

Now, as she was walking to her car, having closed up the daycare for the weekend, Bianca's last text was rattling around in her head. Ever since she'd talked to Bianca a few hours ago and given a noncommittal answer, she'd been checking in to make sure Bristol wasn't planning on holing up in her house and ignoring everyone.

It was exactly what she wanted to do.

Unfortunately, Bianca was relentless when she wanted something, and it seemed she wasn't going to let this go. Which meant Bristol had no choice but to take her friend up on her offer of a night out at Moonshiners.

She only hoped Kaden and Keegan wouldn't be there. She honestly didn't know if she'd survive an encounter with them.

WHEN KEEGAN STEPPED INTO MOONSHINERS ON FRIDAY evening, the place was empty, save for a couple of old cowboys sitting at the bar shooting the shit. An hour after that, the place was packed. There wasn't a table to be had, the pool tables were crowded, the jukebox blared, and conversations rolled through the room at a dull roar.

Just a perfect Friday night in the sticks as far as Keegan was concerned.

He loved coming to Moonshiners because it felt like home to him. Perhaps he wasn't from Coyote Ridge, but the people here sure made him feel as though he was. He especially enjoyed nights like tonight when he'd managed to round up a handful of people. Along with his friends and family there to sit back and chill, he noticed a few single ladies lurking about, which meant the possibilities were endless.

And yes, he was determined he was going to keep an open mind, pretend last night had never happened, and fucking move on with his damn life.

After Bristol had stormed out of their house, Keegan never expected to see her again unless absolutely necessary. And fine, he had been an asshole. But he wouldn't apologize for it. Hell, she'd proven it was true, practically turning green at the thought of the town realizing she was hooking up with two men at the same time. Some women simply couldn't handle the pressure. Bristol Newton was evidently one of them. It was for the best, really. Deep down, Keegan knew nothing would've ever come of that anyway.

And with that, Keegan made a promise not to think on it anymore tonight. It was done and over, the deed successfully completed, and now they could put it behind them.

He would, at least.

"Thanks, Bailey," Zane told the waitress when she delivered another round of beers to the table.

"No problem, boys. Maybe nurse 'em a little longer, would ya?"

"We'll give it our best shot," Keegan assured her, then turned toward Sawyer. "So I've got a question for ya."

"Hit me," Sawyer said with a smirk, tilting his beer bottle to his lips.

"If a new shop were to open up on Main Street, what do you think would survive there?"

"I have no fuckin' clue, man. But I can tell you one thing. Snatch up that real estate and do it fast."

"Yeah?" Keegan glanced at Kaden, smirked.

"You're talkin' about ol' Eddie Schneider's place?" Zane prompted.

"Helluva deal," Jaxson Briggs chimed in. "Considered snatchin' it myself, to be honest."

"Okay," Kaden spoke up. "And your thoughts on an arcade?"

All eyes shifted from one person to the next, as though they were waiting for the punch line.

"You're serious?" Zane chuckled.

"Not my first choice," CJ stated.

The consensus from the peanut gallery was the same.

"Just an idea," Keegan told them.

"Yours?" Zane asked with a grin.

"It might work," CJ said, though there wasn't much conviction in his words. "But I'm not sure the teenagers these days are interested in the same shit we were."

"If it ain't in their Instagram feed, hell, they don't even know it exists," Zane rumbled.

"Anyone else notice how everything's sellin' these days?" Sawyer mused.

Jaxson leaned in, rested his forearms on the table. "Shit, I remember back when Mack was thinkin' about sellin' this place."

Yep. Keegan remembered it like it was yesterday. The whole town had been up in arms thinking their beloved bar would be out of commission, likely converted into a yarn store or some shit. It had been Mack's son doing the pushing, attempting to get his father to turn his back on all of them so Daniel could turn him into someone he wasn't.

Everyone in town knew that Daniel Schwartz had no qualms about flipping Mack's life upside down. According to the rumor mill, he'd been doing it since he came to Coyote Ridge several years back with the excuse he was attempting to have a relationship with his absentee father. Over time, Mack's elation at having his boy around had turned disastrous.

While Daniel never had stuck around for long, he'd jack-in-the-box it about the time Mack was getting back to normal, flip the man on his ear once again. And the dance would start again. Right up until Mack had finally put his foot down, refusing to give in to his son's ridiculous attempts to ruin his life. The bar was now safe, and the town's favorite bartender had up and married the man he'd been in love with. All was right in their world.

Keegan was grateful. He couldn't imagine what his Friday nights would look like if these doors weren't open.

"Are you really thinkin' about doin' it?" Jaxson asked. "Openin' an arcade?"

Sawyer intervened before Keegan could respond. "I figured you'd be givin' a go at the ol' Tucker ranch."

Keegan's ears perked up. "What're you takin' about?"

Sawyer glanced around, frowned. "Ol' Jeremiah Tucker. He's gettin' on up there in years. Ninety-one this year. His kids talked him into movin' to Wyoming with them. He's puttin' the place up for sale."

Keegan leaned in. "Are you serious?"

"Yeah." Sawyer lifted his beer bottle, pausing before it reached his mouth. "I thought you knew."

"Hell no, I didn't." If he had, he would've put an offer in already. "Do you know if it's on the market yet?"

Sawyer shrugged. "No idea. Stop in and talk to my old man. He's got the inside scoop. Been friends with ol' Tuck for years."

Keegan resisted the urge to look at his watch. He knew he couldn't swing by Uncle Curtis's tonight. But tomorrow was a different story.

He glanced over at Kaden, breathed a relieved sigh when his brother nodded his head. They'd go by there tomorrow. Talk to Curtis, maybe talk to Jeremiah Tucker.

Holy shit. A ranch.

Grinning ear to ear, Keegan gulped the rest of his beer. No way could this night get any better.

No sooner did the thought clear his gray matter than the doors at the front of the building opened and everyone's attention swung to the newcomers. A round of greetings erupted, welcoming anyone and everyone in for a good time.

He continued to watch as the bodies dispersed, allowing him to see who had arrived.

"Holy fuck," Keegan muttered under his breath.

His mouth went instantly dry the second *she* walked through the door.

This was, perhaps, the first time he'd seen Bristol Newton dressed up for a night out. The body-hugging, chocolate-brown dress she wore didn't reveal a whole lot of skin up top, but it did more than enough to highlight every single one of her glorious curves. And the short skirt showcasing her sexy legs … Fuck. She'd topped off the outfit with western boots and he was seconds away from swallowing his own damn tongue.

She'd done this on purpose, he knew. She was taunting them, letting them see exactly what they couldn't have.

It pissed him off. After last night...

When her eyes swung over, Keegan met her stare head on. She looked tired. And not at all happy to be there.

Someone nudged his shoulder and Keegan tore his gaze away long enough to glance at his twin, who looked like someone had just run over his dog.

Then Zane elbowed him, leaned in, and chuckled. "Put your tongues back in your mouths."

Too damn late for that.

Chapter Seven

THE MOMENT SHE STEPPED INTO THE BAR, Bristol felt eyes on her, and it had nothing to do with ego. She knew exactly whose heavy-lidded gazes she felt, which was the very reason she was sitting with her back to Kaden and Keegan, who were currently engaging in conversation with a group of mostly Walker men.

Thankfully, her friends surrounded her, chatting and laughing. It was almost enough of a distraction for her not to remember what had happened last night, to ignore the pain that continued to stab somewhere in the vicinity of her heart. After all, she'd promised herself she would put that not-quite-sane encounter with Kaden and Keegan behind her. Forever.

Of course, Bianca was still urging her to bid on the twins at tomorrow's auction, to live a little, her friend continued to say. No way was Bristol telling her that she'd already given in to that urge and it had blown up in her face. Nope. She would be taking that secret to the grave. Hence the reason she was here tonight. If she'd been able to tell Bianca what happened, she knew her friend wouldn't have been so adamant she come. Nor would Bianca continue to drone on about the auction.

And the constant reminder that they would be auctioned off to the highest bidder tomorrow wasn't helping, either. Just the thought of some woman taking them home for a night … she didn't want to admit it, but it didn't sit well with her. In fact, it filled her with insane jealousy, something she had absolutely no right to feel.

"Tell me this isn't just what the doctor ordered," Bianca said with a chuckle. "Chilled wine and hot cowboys. What more could you ask for?"

Chilled wine and a dark room, that was definitely preferable.

"Amen, sista," Adeline crooned.

"Hey," Kayla said in a stern voice, "don't encourage her."

"Yeah, exactly," Jamie teased, mock-glaring at Bianca. "Aren't you married?"

Since Bianca was the only one of the five of them who was hitched to the ol' ball and chain, they took it upon themselves to give her crap as often as possible.

Bristol and Bianca had grown up with Adeline Miller and Jamie Collier, all four of them being roughly the same age and having lived in Coyote Ridge their entire lives. Kayla Spivey was the recent addition to their little group. The five of them chatted endlessly via their group text message and made a point to get together at least once a week, even if it was only for coffee on Saturday morning.

Bianca grinned. "Married but not dead. I'm sure you ladies remember what that's like, right?"

"Don't remind me," Bristol choked out. If she never thought about her ex-husband again, it would be too soon.

As of now, none of them had a good track record when it came to forever and ever amen. Well, except Bianca. She seemed to be doing something right.

"Where is Jake, anyway?" Jamie asked.

"Miami. He'll be back tomorrow night," Bianca said a little dreamily.

Bristol chuckled. Her friend had been married for just over six years now, but you wouldn't know it by talking to her. If Bristol had to guess, the honeymoon period still hadn't ended for those two. Probably helped that Jake was some fancy advertising executive who traveled all over the country. Bianca went with him when she could and when she couldn't ... well, she claimed their time apart only made his homecomings that much hotter. They were certainly still in love.

Then again, that seemed to be the case for most people Bristol knew. Since becoming close to the Walker family, she found herself surrounded by so much love, sometimes it was nauseating. The way the Walkers treated their women... well, to be honest, Bristol often found herself daydreaming about finding a love like that. She envied Curtis and Lorrie the most, hoping one day she would find a love like theirs, one that would transcend time and tragedy.

Granted, her fantasies of happily ever after never lasted long. With a failed marriage behind her, Bristol didn't subscribe to the love-lasts-longer-than-a-day philosophy that plenty of others did. The funny thing was, she didn't have too many standards when it came to men. Unlike her friends, who were always coming up with another prerequisite for their "perfect" man. Everyone knew there was no such thing, but sometimes it was fun to pretend. No, Bristol only preferred they be employed, educated enough to hold a decent conversation, and willing to be friends before they moved on to the next phase. The last one was usually what killed a decent opportunity. The last three guys Bristol had dated had been polar opposites except for one thing: they thought sex was the foundation for a relationship.

Too bad she wasn't into one-night stands. That would be the route she would take if she were. Until last night's debacle, she'd been enduring the sexual drought just fine, thank you very much. Now it looked like the clock was going to reset.

"Did it hurt?" a deep voice bellowed from behind her.

Bristol's gaze shot to Bianca, hoping for some sort of warning as to who it was. She got nothing.

She cautiously turned to see a man standing behind her. He was tall, relatively good-looking, more so if he would've kept his beard trimmed. He wore a black Resistol hat, a buckle the size of Montana, and a gleam in his dark brown eyes. And that gleam seemed to be pinned right on her ... cleavage.

"I'm sorry?" she asked, confused.

He had the decency to look at her face when he said, "When you fell from heaven, sugar? Did it hurt?"

Oh, brother.

Forcing a smile, Bristol turned back to her friends. Unfortunately, they merely stared at her, waiting to see what would happen next. She knew they were enjoying this, probably a little too much.

There was a tap on her shoulder. With a sigh, Bristol peered over her shoulder again. "Yes?"

"Can I buy you a drink?" the man asked, seemingly not at all bothered by getting the cold shoulder.

Bristol held up her wine. "I'm good but thank you."

"Perhaps you'd like somethin' a little stronger," he suggested.

Still wouldn't make me go home with you. Bristol shook her head. "I think I'll stick to my wine, thanks."

Again, she turned back, just in time to see her traitorous friends giggling.

When the man's hand landed on her arm, Bristol found herself jerking away from him, frowning. She hadn't given him permission to touch her, and nothing pissed her off more than a man who couldn't take a hint.

"How about a dance?"

"No, thank you," she said as politely as she could. "I'm not here to dance tonight. Just to hang out with my friends. But thank you for the offer." Her polite tone was quickly fizzling.

Bristol turned and gave the man her back again, hoping she wouldn't have to punch him.

"Persistent, isn't he?" Bianca asked with a fake smile.

None of her friends were amused anymore. The man's ignorant determination had put them all off.

"Can't take a hint, either," Kayla added under her breath.

It was times like these when Bristol wished there was a gay bar in Coyote Ridge. A place a woman could go simply to hang out with friends and not have to worry about men trying to pick them up. That was one thing she loved about hanging around the Walkers. Every one of Curtis and Lorrie's sons was married, so Bristol had the opportunity to relax, chill with friends, laugh and joke without worrying about someone hitting on her.

Not that she considered herself some royal beauty or anything. But it was inevitable around these parts. Figuring the ratio of men to women was somewhere along the lines of four to one, it was almost a given that at least one would hit on her.

"Hey, there's a table opening up. Let's grab it," Bianca stated, taking Bristol's arm and steering her away from the bar. Kayla, Jamie, and Adeline fell into step.

When she realized they were moving toward Kaden and Keegan, Bristol held her breath, prayed Bianca wasn't going to do something to embarrass her.

Luckily, her friend was making a beeline for the table near the wall, a few feet away from the group of men who seemed caught up in what appeared to be a relatively serious conversation. As Bristol slid into her seat, she made the mistake of glancing over just in time to see Kaden and Keegan were both looking her way.

Neither of them appeared happy.

Bristol immediately turned away, glancing over at Bianca and Jamie, who had taken seats across from her. Thankfully, Adeline moved a chair to the end of the table, blocking her view of the twins, while Kayla pulled out the chair beside Bristol.

"Remind me why we came here tonight," Jamie prompted when she got settled.

"Because Bristol needs some adult conversation," Adeline said simply. "Isn't that why we always get together?"

Bristol laughed. It was a brittle sound, but hopefully not noticeable. It was true. She definitely spent more time with the under-five set than anything, which meant adult conversation was lacking in her life. When she wasn't at work, or volunteering to babysit for someone, she was home alone, usually binge-watching whatever television drama was popular. This month, she found herself hooked on *Riverdale*.

It wasn't the most glamorous life, but Bristol couldn't complain. She had a thriving business, lived in a small town she loved, had great friends. She didn't dwell on the fact that she was single. Well, mostly. There were definitely times she got lonely, especially when she thought about her dad. Ever since he'd died seven years ago, Bristol had felt the hole he'd left in her heart and her life.

"We do have one thing to celebrate," Bristol announced, aiming for something positive.

"The auction?"

"Nope."

It was clear Bianca was doing a mental skim to figure it out for herself.

"Kayla's gonna come work with me," she said, purposely not using the word *for*.

"Really?" A grin broke out on Bianca's face. "That's fantastic. What brought that on?"

Bristol could see the blush already creeping up Kayla's neck. She never did want to be the center of attention.

"She got her degree," Bristol announced, wanting everyone to be as proud as she was.

Bianca and Jamie squealed, then there was a round of hugs and congratulations for Kayla. When everyone settled, another round of wine was being brought out and Bristol felt a little lighter than she had.

Bianca cleared her throat. "So, about this auction…"

Annnd then it was gone.

"Ooh." Jamie leaned in closer. "Can I just say, I am so ready for this. I've been saving up."

"Me, too," Adeline said. "For two whole months."

"Did you finalize the list?" Bristol asked Bianca. "Did Cassius agree?"

Bianca's smile was blinding. "He did. I've got all ten."

Jamie gave a dreamy smile. "I know exactly who I'm gonna bid on."

"CJ," they all said at the same time.

Jamie's face flamed red, which made the rest of them laugh.

"Oh, come on. We know you've been moonin' over that man for ages," Adeline teased. "I can tell you, I don't think he requires payment to go out with you."

More laughter ensued.

"And you, Ms. Bristol?" Bianca asked pointedly. "Have you been saving up to make a play for a couple of hot cowboys? Mouthwatering twins, perhaps?"

Hoping she succeeded, she kept a neutral expression on her face. "I will not be bidding. I know it's for a good cause and all, but I'm strapped for cash right now."

"I could always give you a loan." Bianca leaned in. "If it'll help you seal the deal."

"No deal to be sealed," she insisted, bringing her wineglass to her lips.

"Oh, come on, you—"

"Bianca, stop," Bristol bit out, feeling that sudden emotional storm brewing in her chest.

Her friends went stone still, all eyes pinned on her.

She managed a few deep breaths, downed the rest of her wine, and addressed them. "I'm just not interested."

It was written plain as day on Bianca's face: her best friend didn't believe her.

BRISTOL DAMN SURE WASN'T DRESSED FOR COMFORT tonight, Kaden thought as he caught a glimpse of her sitting at the table with her friends. No, she was dressed to kill, clearly looking to draw some attention. The question was, whose attention was she hoping for?

Not theirs, that was for damn sure.

From the moment she'd stepped into the bar, he'd been hyperaware of her. Which was likely how he knew she was avoiding them at all costs. He was tempted to think she was there to torment them, and from the way her glossy pink lips pulled back in a smile as she continued to talk to her friends, she was damn proud of herself.

Forcing himself to look away, he caught sight of Keegan, who continued to glance her way the same as he was. But there wasn't interest or curiosity on his brother's face. More like disdain and … he was tempted to say hatred, but Keegan didn't hate anyone. Well, except the two women they'd thought they were in love with at different points in their lives. Keegan definitely hated them.

What Kaden needed to do was to get Bristol alone, to talk through what happened last night and figure out where to go from here. He was a problem solver, a mediator. Surely with a little coaxing, he could get this thing between them back on track.

Why not now? he wondered. Bristol was here, he was here…

Never one to pass up an opportunity, Kaden started to push his chair back but came up short when Keegan put a firm hand on his forearm.

"Don't you dare."

That was more than hatred he detected in Keegan's tone. It was lethal. Definitely a warning and not a request.

Confused, he stared at Keegan, saw the pain his brother was so desperate to disguise.

"It's done," Keegan stated firmly.

The hell it was. Not if he had anything to say about it, but Kaden knew when to leave well enough alone. They were all still shaken by what had happened, the intensity of last night. That encounter had been more than merely sex. It had been … different. Amazing, sure, but there'd also been a connection he'd never felt before.

They'd never been with a woman who was with both of them at the same time. And he wasn't talking in the literal sense because they'd physically shared every single woman they'd ever been with. Yes, even fucked a woman in that very same manner plenty of times over the course of their lives. But they'd never had a woman as completely committed to both of them the way Bristol had been. Throughout the encounter, she'd maintained a connection with them both, never singling one out and leaving the other behind.

Like he said, it had been different.

And he wasn't willing to let that go. However, leaving it alone for a few days would give them time to cool off.

Kaden settled back into his chair, took a deep drink of his beer.

While he listened to CJ ramble on about shit going down at the firehouse, Kaden kept an eye on Bristol. That outfit she was wearing was enough to turn every cowboy's head in the county. From the chocolate-brown dress to the boots on her feet, she looked like a dessert every straight man wanted to indulge in. It both turned him on to see her dressed like that and pissed him off because he knew she hadn't dressed up for them.

"Hey, cowboy, why don't you go ask her to dance?"

Kaden took a swig of his beer, glanced at Rafe Sharpe, then realized he hadn't been talking to him but rather to his twin.

"I will as soon as you ask the waitress to dance," Keegan countered.

"Is that a dare, Walker?" Rafe smirked, though his eyes had hardened.

"No," Kaden interrupted. "It's not a dare. And you two idiots are gonna sit right there and drink your beers. No makin' fools outta yourselves tonight."

"Too late for that," Jaxson said with a laugh.

"You either, Briggs," Kaden snapped.

A round of laughter erupted. Never failed with this bunch. Kaden was always trying to keep Keegan in line. Add in a few other knuckleheads and it became infinitely more difficult.

"Rumor has it you boys are gonna be up on the auction block with me and Jaxson tomorrow," CJ noted, evidently feeling the tension.

"That does seem to be the rumor," Kaden confirmed, forcing himself not to look over at Bristol.

"Scared of the competition?" Jaxson joked. "We could wager. Which one of us'll bring in the most money."

"You're on," Keegan said. "Most money and the hottest chick."

"You're a pig," someone said.

Keegan snorted and Kaden knew this was a lost cause. His brother was going to act out in an attempt to move past what was going on. He didn't necessarily blame him, but he damn sure wasn't looking forward to the ride. God only knew where it would land them.

His thoughts drifted to one of his recent conversations with Keegan. More specifically, when he'd admitted to Keegan he was still looking for something more than a horizontal romp with a sexy female. As usual, Keegan had shrugged him off. He knew his brother was still hung up on the fact their history with women and serious relationships sucked balls. The two women they'd thought would be love everlasting had turned out to be a waste of time and energy. Didn't mean they were doomed forever, did it?

After all, he considered himself a fairly reasonable man with a good head on his shoulders. He could read people relatively well and he knew when to cut and run. With Bristol, he couldn't help but believe that day hadn't come yet. There was still a chance with her.

Maybe that was wishful thinking, but whatever. Kaden wasn't the sort to let the past dictate his future, no matter what Keegan believed.

Truth was, Kaden had never considered Bristol a one-nighter. How could he? She was too damn sweet for that shit. He'd honestly believed she was looking for something more. Last night's quick escape had told him otherwise, but it wasn't something they couldn't work through.

While Kaden definitely saw potential with Bristol, it wasn't only about him. Never in his life had he thought about settling down without his brother in tow. Most people wouldn't understand, but Kaden had never felt the need to explain it. He had no desire to do so now, either. Not even with Bristol.

More than once since he'd met her, Kaden had fantasized about settling down here in this small town. Every time he did, his thoughts included images of Bristol with them. The three of them. Together. And now he had a serious dilemma. The woman he was falling in love with and the brother he would never turn his back on were at odds with each other.

When the conversation at the table shifted to upcoming events at Alluring Indulgence Resort, Kaden found himself tuning out, his attention drifting over to Bristol.

It was then he realized she was no longer there.

Chapter Eight

WHEN KEEGAN WOKE ON SATURDAY MORNING, IT wasn't with a hangover, thank God. He hadn't stayed out too late, hadn't spent the entire night playing GTA or Forza, but he was still moving slowly. He figured he could attribute it to mood, and he was bound and determined to put his best foot forward.

The first thing he did when he woke up was call Curtis. His uncle had been surprised to hear from him, but not surprised by what he'd inquired about. Then, after a few minutes, they'd agreed that the three of them would stop in to see Jeremiah Tucker after church on Sunday. In the meantime, his uncle promised to call the man to let him know Keegan and Kaden were interested in buying his ranch.

No doubt about it, Keegan was excited about the prospect. It seemed he'd waited his entire life for this opportunity. He damn sure didn't want it to pass him by.

As for why that didn't brighten his day completely, he refused to think about.

Last night, Kaden had been the solemn one, suggesting they go home shortly after he realized Bristol had left. Keegan hadn't noticed. Sort of. He'd tried not to, anyway. But he'd caught bits and pieces of the girl spat that had taken place at Bristol's table. Evidently, her friends were giving her crap about something and Bristol had decided she'd had enough. Shortly thereafter she left.

When his brother suggested they go to her house, make sure she was all right, Keegan had politely declined. Bristol was a big girl; she could handle herself. If she needed help, she would know to ask someone. As far as Keegan was concerned, what they'd had or the potential for what they could've had was over. His fault, of course. But that didn't change the outcome of where they stood.

It was for the best. Keegan could accept relationships weren't his thing. He'd invested too much time in them only to end up being the odd man out. He wasn't willing to risk it again. One-nighters were more his style. Nothing to get hung up on, no one to leave him wanting.

Last night at the bar, Keegan had considered asking Kaden to give the population of lovely ladies some attention, but he hadn't been feeling it, either. So he'd taken his leave when Kaden did, come home, and hit the sack early. Because of that, he'd woken early, which left him plenty of time to psych himself up for…

Oh, right. Today was the auction. *That* was certainly something that would brighten his mood.

They were going to be auctioned off to the highest bidder. To some eager woman if they were lucky. He tried to think about which ladies he knew in the area who were single. There were quite a few, but when he tried to think of his options, there was only one he could come up with. Her name was evidently seared into his brain.

He considered finding paper and a pen, jotting down names of women who would be a viable option as far as distractions went, but decided that was a complete waste of his time. He had much better things to do like…

Fuck.

Midafternoon finally rolled around, giving Keegan an excuse to get out of the house. They decided to come to Walker Park—yes, it was officially named after the founding family—a little early, giving them time to chat with their random family members—aunts, uncles, cousins, even their sister was there—and check out the variety of fun and food being offered by the many people set up throughout, before the festivities got underway.

As soon as they got there, Kaden said something about checking in with someone. Keegan hadn't been paying all that much attention, too taken by the sights and smells of the fall festival. Admittedly, he loved this event although he wasn't sure why. Could've been the haunted house or the trick-or-treaters who were donning costumes and getting candy from the people selling their wares. Or maybe it was the aroma of apple pie and funnel cake that lured him.

The moment he saw Kate with her mom and one of her dads, Keegan's smile returned in full force. He sauntered over, said hello to Kylie and Gage, then gave Kate a light punch on the arm.

When the girl smiled up at him, life was instantly better. He'd been waiting for this day, for Kate to return to a semblance of her normal, smiling self. She wasn't quite there yet, but it was certainly progress.

"Hey," he greeted Kylie and Gage. "Where's Travis?"

He noticed how Gage instantly looked away.

"He had work to do," she explained. "Said he might swing by later."

From her tone, he could tell she didn't believe there was work. Then again, Keegan knew Travis well. The man always put his family above everything else. Or rather, the man he'd known before Kate's kidnapping had, anyway. No one could pretend there wasn't something different about Travis these days.

"Y'all gonna watch the auction?" he asked.

"We most certainly are," Kylie said. "Fully intend to inflate those prices if at all possible. It is for a good cause and all."

"And if it backfires and you end up with a hunky date of your very own?"

Kylie glanced up at Gage. "I have all the hunky dates I need, but we could always use an extra babysitter."

Keegan laughed.

"Well, I'll get outta your hair," he said as he twirled one of Kate's pigtails. "Let you get back to it. Tell Travis I said hey."

With that, Keegan headed off to find Kaden, figuring his brother was already mingling with those gathering for the auction. He immediately spotted him across the way, his brother's gaze swinging his way. Forcing a lightness he didn't quite feel, he headed in Kaden's direction.

From the moment he made his first pass by the stage set up for the event and the surrounding area sectioned off for today's auction, Keegan realized he had died and gone to heaven. Women every-fucking-where and most of them here with one goal in mind. Landing themselves a man for the evening, their eyes on the prize. And two of those prizes being him and Kaden.

He was actually surprised to see such a good turnout. He had no idea there were this many single women in Coyote Ridge. They ranged from probably mid-twenties to, by his guesstimate, mid-seventies, and a good portion in between.

Not that he cared about age or race or size for that matter. Keegan was an equal-opportunity lover and he welcomed any and all. Except for married women. No sense mixing it up with those who were tied down. Relationships might not be his thing, but he still considered them sacred. Do unto others and all that jazz.

Right now any and all included the six women circling him and Kaden, asking question after question, all hanging on their every word. They were almost enough of a distraction for him not to notice the one woman moving through the space, ignoring him like he had the plague.

Keyword being *almost*.

Yeah, he had noticed Bristol as soon as she approached, talking to one of the women she was usually hanging out with at Moonshiners. Kayla, he thought her name was. They had their heads together. Every so often Bristol would gesture toward something or someone. No matter what, she always kept her back to them. A protective instinct, maybe? Afraid if she looked at them even once she'd end up naked and writhing between them again?

The memory of Thursday night continued to play in his head, most notably when Bristol had run out of the room like her ass was on fire and they were the flames threatening to come for her.

It hadn't surprised him one fucking bit. In fact, he had expected it.

Granted, he hadn't been exactly nice when he'd made the comment about what the parents of her students would think. In his defense, it had been about self-preservation. No way was he going to allow himself to fantasize about anything more with this woman. Hell no. Not when she was the queen of distance where they were concerned.

So, yeah, he had said it in hopes she would do exactly what she'd done. Run.

Still, he found himself watching her as she spoke animatedly to a man who had approached her after her friend left to tackle whatever she was tasked with. While the chatter droned on around him, Keegan smiled when appropriate but continued to observe Bristol despite his reservations.

It was as though he was a magnet and her gaze was drawn to his, because it wasn't long before Bristol turned, her eyes searching as though she sensed someone was watching. When she met his eyes across the way, she instantly looked away and not subtly, either.

It pissed him off that he cared that she wasn't paying any attention to them, hadn't except for those brief few seconds. So much so, he turned his attention to the women surrounding him, tried to figure out which of them would be the one sandwiched between them tonight.

Because damn it all to hell, he would fuck Bristol Newton right out of his head if he had to.

CURTIS WALKER STROLLED UP TO JEREMIAH TUCKER'S front porch, smiled as he glanced around.

From where he stood, he could just make out the house his nephew Brantley had bought. If Kaden and Keegan bought this place, they'd be next-door neighbors. For some reason, he liked the idea of that. He could see them having cookouts from time to time, maybe Brantley and Reese pitching in and vice versa. Not a bad setup this would be.

Curtis couldn't remember when his brother Gerald had given this plot of land to ol' Tuck. Probably a good fifty years, maybe. Whenever it was, it felt like yesterday. He still remembered the view of the rolling hills out beyond the back pasture. At the time, it had been unused land. Land that was ripe for running cattle, something they'd heard Tuck was eager to do but had never had the means to do at the time. So, with their siblings' permission, Gerald had gone to Tuck with an opportunity, one that had benefited them all at the time.

Now here they were, many decades later, and Tuck was gearing up for the next phase of his life, which evidently didn't involve a stay in Coyote Ridge.

Curtis hated to see him leave, but he couldn't imagine spending his days away from his own family, so he understood.

As he stepped up onto the porch, he noticed the front door was open, the flimsy screen door the only thing between him and the indoors.

He rapped his knuckles on the worn wood. "Hey, Tuck. You in there?"

"It's open," the old grisly voice called out. "Come on in, Walker."

Smiling, Curtis opened the door and stepped inside. Aside from the underlying stench of cigarettes, the house smelled like dust and mildew, as though it had been closed up for some time. He knew that wasn't the case. Tuck spent all his time here these days, rarely venturing out even on the nights Curtis and his old buddies met up at Moonshiners to shoot the shit and catch up. Health issues, Tuck had told him a while back.

"What brings you by, Walker?" Tuck asked, his gnarled hand curled around a wooden cane as he hobbled toward the kitchen.

"Thought I'd let you know I've got some buyers for your ranch."

Bushy white eyebrows lifted in curiosity. "More than one?"

"Have a seat, Tuck," Curtis told him.

"Got some tea in the fridge," Tuck replied as he detoured to the table. "Maybe you could pour us some."

Curtis nodded, headed for the refrigerator. He noticed a couple of cardboard boxes sitting on the counter. They hadn't been closed up yet, and he could see dishes inside.

"Packin' up, are ya?" he said as he grabbed the glass pitcher, closed the refrigerator door.

"That was Lizzy's doin'."

Curtis glanced back over his shoulder. "Your great-granddaughter?"

"Yep. Last time they were down for a visit, she got excited about the prospect of me movin' up there to be with them."

So she was speeding up the process. It would be good for Tuck to be around love like that.

After filling two glasses with ice, Curtis poured the tea, joined Tuck at the table.

"Now I know your boys ain't got no interest in this ol' ranch, Walker. So who you got in mind?"

Right to the point. That was the way Tuck had always been. Didn't appear time or age had dulled his sharp edges one bit.

"My nephews," he said easily, taking a sip of the tea. A bit sweeter than he expected.

"Tells me nothin'." Tuck grinned, revealing the absence of a couple of teeth. "You got a boatload of 'em."

"Kaden and Keegan. Gerald and Sue Ellen's twins. They've been workin' at the demo company for a while now."

"And they wanna be ranchers?"

"Always have."

For as long as he could remember, Keegan had been talking about running a ranch of his own one day. And as much as he hated to lose them on his own spread, he knew this would be the perfect opportunity for them. Plus, it would help cement them back in Coyote Ridge, where he hoped the rest of the family would soon move back to. Curtis had been working on Gerald for a time now, trying to convince his older brother that he was missed. Now that Gerald's kids were working their way back around, he got the feeling the old fart would be here before too long.

"I'm gonna bring them by tomorrow," Curtis told Tuck. "After church. Let them do the hagglin' with you."

"Ain't no hagglin' necessary, Walker. It's theirs if they want it. Can't ever repay you for what you did for me and mine back in the day. Only right that I return the favor."

Curtis grinned. "I'm not lookin' for a favor, nor do I want repayment. You tell 'em the price, deal with them on it."

Tuck nodded, his gaze swinging to the back door, which was also open. "I'm gonna miss this ol' place, Walker. But it's time. I need to be around my kids and my grandkids. For as long as I've got left." He turned back to Curtis. "But it ain't what it used to be. Needs some work."

"They've got strong backs," Curtis assured him.

"They married?"

"Nope. One day, though."

Tuck grinned. "They young'n's?"

"Old enough to know better. Fine boys, though. You'll like 'em."

Tuck nodded. "I just want it to be in good hands."

"It will be. That I can promise."

Curtis could've easily bought the place himself, found a way to work the land or rent it to a rancher to run cattle. He'd considered it, too, while he'd been waiting for Keegan to bring it up. According to Sawyer, the boy hadn't known it was going up for sale, which explained why Curtis hadn't heard anything from him until this morning.

Now that he had, he knew it was exactly where Kaden and Keegan needed to be. This was where they would settle down, find what they'd spent a lifetime looking for.

It was nothing less than what every man deserved.

BRISTOL REALIZED AS SOON AS SHE ARRIVED at the park for the auction that she should've told Bianca she couldn't make it. No matter how hard she tried not to notice the fact that Kaden and Keegan were surrounded by beautiful, intelligent women, she couldn't stop herself from daring a peek in their direction. Every so often she would catch Kaden looking her way, but never Keegan.

Well, not until a moment ago, and the anger she saw in his eyes was not something she recognized on him. Keegan Walker was the one who smiled and laughed, joked and teased. Rarely was he ever serious, to the point she had wondered if he was even capable of it. After their encounter the other night, she knew there was something dark lurking behind those smooth grins and that jovial laugh. And it appeared their falling-out wasn't doing anything to improve his attitude.

She'd spent last night and most of today doing her best to put the encounter out of her mind, reminding herself time and again that they were now out of her system and she would not be returning for seconds. Not even if Keegan apologized for being rude and she got over the fact the entire town would look down their noses at her.

Nope. She was moving on and no one needed to be the wiser, either. As far as she was concerned, not even Bianca or Rex, her two closest friends, would ever find out the truth no matter how much they pestered her. It was better that way. She would keep it to herself. Last thing she needed was to be the butt of everyone's jokes. The last thing she wanted was pity or those blasted sympathetic looks. She'd lived it once thanks to her ex-husband. Not doing it again.

As she walked through the people gathering together, laughing and talking, no one stopped her to chat. Not even Kaden or Keegan when she slipped past them, pretending to be invisible. Not that she'd expected either of them to come after her. She was the one who had run out on them, like a chicken being chased by a fox. Only she wasn't being chased, and the sad thing was, she sort of wished one or both of them had made the effort. At least then she wouldn't feel quite so much like another notch in their bedpost.

What she needed to do was focus on her one and only task, which was ensuring this auction went off without a hitch. Of course, that required the master of ceremonies to be there, and since Bianca was MIA, Bristol was worried that wouldn't happen.

The auction was scheduled to start in half an hour, and without the mayor there to run the show, Bristol feared it would fall on her. The absolute last thing she wanted was to have to stand there while a dozen women fought over who would get the chance to take home the sexy twins, because that seemed to be the topic of the hour, the very words she heard as she weaved through the gathering.

She was pretty sure all the single ladies in town had shown up. Some married ones, too. The ages ranged from roughly twenty-two to perhaps ninety. No doubt about it, the auction was going to be a success.

And it was a good thing.

Really.

Except for the fact she was running herself ragged trying to keep up. Worst were all the questions she didn't have answers to. Sure, it was an auction and it was fairly straightforward, but there were things Bianca hadn't shared with her. Which, now that Bristol thought about it, was probably her own fault. And now that Bianca was MIA, she didn't have a choice but to tell everyone she would get back to them when she could.

If she had her way, she would man the refreshments from behind a table and leave the mingling to someone else. She couldn't deny she had a way with people, but it wasn't her first choice of things to do.

Yet here she was.

All of the men who would be auctioned off had arrived and they were hanging out with the women, chatting, laughing, and smiling. Though there was plenty of attention to go around, it seemed several women had taken a liking to Kaden and Keegan, including Adeline.

Not that she cared. She didn't.

Really.

Uggh.

Fine. She cared a little. There might be a tiny spark of jealousy deep down inside her, but she was doing just fine ignoring it.

Mostly.

"Bristol?"

Turning at the sound of her name, Bristol came nearly face-to-face with Stephanie Hennessy. Had she known who it was before then, she would've pretended not to hear her. Granted, that was a crappy thing to do considering Stephanie was one of her kids' parents, the mother of Danielle and Danica, six-year-old twin girls who'd been going to her daycare almost since the beginning.

"Mrs. Hennessy." Bristol forced a smile. "It's good to see you." She glanced around, then made eye contact. "I honestly didn't expect you to be here."

Stephanie smiled brightly. "I had to see what was going on in town. This is the event everyone's been talking about."

Yes. Yes, it was.

The way she said *event* was as though it was a dirty word. Bristol would expect no less from Stephanie. The woman thought most things, as well as people, were beneath her.

"I'm surprised to see you working. Is the daycare doing all right? Should I be worried that you'll be closing your doors soon?"

Always flocking to drama, this one.

Bristol laughed. "Of course not. I'm simply volunteering, helping out Bianca."

Stephanie nodded as though considering that. "I didn't realize you knew the mayor."

Then she clearly walked around with blinders on, because everyone in this town knew Bianca and Bristol had been best friends since elementary school.

Bristol merely smiled and said, "I do. Is John here?"

"Oh, no. He's off on business. Has a big client in Los Angeles he's tending to this week."

Bristol didn't bother to tell her it was the weekend and most people were with their families then. The rumor going around Coyote Ridge was that John Hennessy had another woman on the side.

"Well, help yourself to refreshments. Bianca should be here shortly."

"Thank you, dear. If you could let her know I'm here when you see her."

Clearly, she'd been relegated to Stephanie's personal assistant. "Of course."

A sigh of relief escaped her when Stephanie turned and wandered toward a group of women. While she would never let Stephanie know how she truly felt about her and her two spoiled children, Bristol preferred not to have contact with her if she didn't have to.

Needing something to do, Bristol placed several clear plastic cups onto a tray, filled each one halfway with champagne, and then wandered around, urging those who had registered for the auction to take one. She smiled when it was appropriate, laughed at a couple of jokes. It wasn't the most glamorous job in the world, but she didn't mind it.

When she came upon the group surrounding Kaden and Keegan, she cleared her throat, offered champagne. The women mostly ignored her, but she didn't care.

"So, when I win the date with you both, what will that entail?" one woman asked.

"You mean when *I* win the date," Adeline said with a giggle. "I'm hoping there's nothing off-limits. We'll make a night of it."

Bristol felt a strange churning in her stomach. How could these women be so ... forward? Especially one of her friends. She'd never understood it.

Not by choice, Bristol made eye contact with Kaden, noticed the way he was watching her. Unable to resist, she peered over at Keegan. He wasn't looking her way, instead giving his groupies his undivided attention.

Why wouldn't he? He'd pretty much shunned her before their skin had even cooled after the amazing sex. And then he'd opened his mouth and made her feel about two inches tall, spurring her immediate escape. Which had been the right thing to do, she reassured herself. Never mind the fact she'd regretted giving in to her urges in the first place.

"Well, I was thinking when *I* win the date," another woman chimed in, "I'll cook dinner for you both. At my place."

The woman probably had food in her refrigerator. In her pantry, even. Bristol hadn't been to the grocery store in ages.

"Steak and baked potatoes," the woman added. "Big, strong men like you deserve a good meal."

Bristol fought the urge to mimic gagging herself as she turned back to the refreshment table. She still had a couple of cups available, but she needed a moment to catch her breath.

If she was the one who won the date with the twins, she'd hope for a nice restaurant, maybe some wine and conversation. Sleeping with them would be the last thing on her mind. On a first date. *As if.*

Oh, God.

Her face flamed as she realized that was exactly what had happened. Kaden had invited her over, she'd gone, and then...

Oh, crap. What was wrong with her?

A firm hand curled around her arm, tugging her around.

"Oh, my heavens! I'm so sorry I'm late," Bianca blurted, her hair a bit disheveled.

Bristol schooled her expression, forced a smile. "You're late? I didn't even notice."

"I got caught up with a resident. They stopped in at my office to talk about updating the equipment at the park. I told her we could go over it at the next meeting, but she insisted on talking to me now."

Bristol eyed Bianca's hair. "A resident?"

"Yes."

"Where's your husband, Bianca?"

"What?"

Bristol grinned, giving Bianca the knowing eye. "He's in town, isn't he?"

"Maybe."

She laughed, patting her own hair as a signal. "Your secret's safe with me."

There was a rare blush on Bianca's cheeks as she began to finger comb her hair.

Bristol motioned around the area. "As you can see, everyone's enjoyin' themselves. But I think they're gettin' antsy."

"Good turnout. I can only hope they're all gonna dig deep into their wallets."

"I don't think you'll have to worry about that." She had a feeling, like Jamie and Adeline, many of these single women had been saving up for this event.

And she very seriously doubted they were all doing it for a good cause. Selfish reasons probably played a pretty big part.

———————————

KADEN WISHED LIKE HELL HE HADN'T SIGNED them up for the auction.

Had he known that two days before they would've had an erotic encounter with the woman he was in love with, he wouldn't have given this thing a second thought.

And yes, he was fairly certain he was in love with Bristol. Had been for quite some time now. The only thing keeping them apart was insecurity. Keegan's and Bristol's. Which meant Kaden was stuck in the middle, torn by his loyalty and love for both of them. This event was going to end up hurting them all, even if neither of them realized that.

How the hell had they gotten to this place? Two nights ago, for the briefest of moments, Kaden had seen his life laid out before him, that evasive happiness he'd been searching for within his grasp only for it to be ripped away at the last second.

Unfortunately, they were committed to this auction because Walkers didn't go back on their word. And the turnout was good, which would hopefully reap the results the mayor was going for as far as raising money was concerned. What Kaden was worried about was Keegan, because his brother hadn't been the same since Thursday night.

He'd gotten used to being called the moody twin while Keegan had the reputation of being fun-loving and never serious. But what people didn't realize was that they were very much alike, not only in appearance but attitude as well. From the womb, they'd been close. Growing up, they rarely did anything apart. Why it worked out that way, he had no idea, but Kaden had never felt the need to be separate from his twin. The opposite, really.

For the past thirty-seven years, they'd had the same experiences, living life almost as though they were one. Perhaps because of that, he could often feel what his brother was feeling. They'd always wanted the same things, their interests mirroring the other's. And that included the desire to own and operate a ranch one day and to settle down with one woman they would share.

The biggest difference between them was that Kaden had never lost hope that one day they would find that love that would last. Keegan, on the other hand, had sworn it off, hence the reason his brother had treated Bristol so callously the other night. Keegan was only trying to protect himself from heartache. Having been pushed out by the women they'd been involved with before had kept him from opening up to anyone else.

Others would see his insensitive comment as a rejection, but Kaden knew better. He could see it in the way Keegan continued to steal glances at Bristol across the way, his eyes hardly leaving her for a minute. The man was as overwhelmed by her as Kaden, but not willing to admit it.

It would've likely played out better if Kaden hadn't allowed Bristol's abrupt departure to piss him off. Rather than go after her or call to smooth things over, he'd let his frustrations fester. And now they were at that awkward point where apologizing for his brother's rudeness wouldn't go over well.

Not how he'd seen that going.

And here he was, about to be auctioned off to the highest bidder while Bristol looked on. No chance in hell was she going to bid on them, so he was screwed in that department. The most he could hope for was for some little old lady to up the ante because she was looking for some company of the platonic variety. Then again, with the way Keegan had been flirting with the single women, he doubted he'd get that lucky, either.

Screwed.

That's what he was.

Totally fucking screwed.

Two hours later, Kaden learned that he'd been wrong to assume. Turned out, they didn't have the shittiest luck on the planet like he'd suspected. How or why a higher power was watching over them, he didn't know, nor was he questioning it.

Of course, he'd been damned suspicious when their names were called and Gage's numbered paddle had gone high in the air. Considering there were no rules on what could or could not be done on the so-called date, he figured Gage was going to purchase them for manual labor or some shit like that. For a second, he'd been more concerned than if some random woman had won them. Right up until he noticed Gage's oldest daughter, Kate, was the one bidding on them. She'd been sitting on Gage's shoulders, lifting the paddle whenever Gage tapped her knee.

With the help of Keegan spurring the little girl on, they'd brought in the highest bid of the day and landed themselves a McDonald's date with the cutest five-year-old he knew.

Too bad Bristol hadn't stuck around to see it. About halfway through the third guy's bidding, right before Kaden and Keegan were called up to the stage, he'd noticed her leaving after saying a quick goodbye to Bianca. It had pained him to watch her walk away and not be able to go after her.

Then again, he figured it was for the best.

In some regards, they really did have shit luck. But it was nothing a McDonald's playground couldn't fix.

Chapter Nine

KEEGAN WOKE ALONE IN HIS BED ON Sunday morning, a bit surprised to find himself at home. The dream he'd had of Bristol had been so real, so vivid, he'd expected to wake up in her bed, with her in his arms.

Nope.

No Bristol.

Never again.

He didn't know where she was, nor did he care.

If he said it enough, it would eventually be true. That was how it worked.

It was driving him fucking crazy that he couldn't stop thinking about her. Before the night they'd spent together, he hadn't thought about her all that much. Okay. Maybe not nearly as much as this. He'd thought about her, fantasized, even. But this was getting ridiculous. He found himself constantly wondering what she was doing, who she was with. And oddly enough, he wanted to be around her, to see her smile.

Which was utter bullshit.

Why? Why did she suddenly matter?

Thankfully for everyone, Keegan had something that would take his mind off Bristol and everyone else. Something that involved an errand to run after church, one that included a conversation about a ranch. A ranch that, with any luck, would belong to him and his brother in the near future.

There would be no woman responsible for changing his and Kaden's lives for the better. No, that would be credited to chasing their own dream, the one they'd had since they were young.

A ranch.

Right here in Coyote Ridge.

Hell yes.

He wasn't sure life could get much better than this.

Turned out, life could get hella better.

Church had been one of those inspirational moments followed by a short drive to the outskirts of town and an introduction to Jeremiah Tucker, better known as Tuck by his friends. At ninety-one, the man was an absolute hoot. And from what Keegan could tell, he was quite fond of the Walker family, something they'd learned as Tuck took them on a long tour of the barn, the pasture, then back to the house with the help of a dilapidated old golf cart with mud tires that Uncle Curtis had driven.

"Did you know your daddy's the one who offered me this prime piece of real estate?" Tuck said, leading the way into the house so they could have lemonade.

Keegan glanced over at Curtis, then back to Tuck. "He's our uncle."

Tuck grinned, his wrinkled face shrinking as he did. "I'm no dummy, boy. And Curtis ain't the one who gave me the property anyhow."

"Gerald did," Curtis confirmed. "It was the first piece we parceled out."

"How much did you buy it for back then?" Keegan asked, though he knew the question bordered on rude.

Tuck laughed, easing down into a chair at the kitchen table. "The darn fool wouldn't take my money. Not that I had much of it at the time. He insisted it was his way of makin' right for some of his old man's sins."

Keegan had heard plenty of stories about Frank Walker, Sr., and while his kids had turned out to be respectable members of society, the man wasn't known for his sparkling personality.

"Would you mind sharin' what Frank did?" Kaden asked.

Tuck glanced at Curtis, then shook his head. "It ain't worth repeatin'. Just know that we got over it long ago. Anyway. It was mighty nice of your daddy," Tuck said, his eyes taking on that distant look. "And I hate to part with it now, but my kids're right. I need to be with 'em." His gaze shifted to Keegan and Kaden. "Wyoming's a mite cold, but it'll be a nice place to go to die."

Keegan heard the teasing in the old man's tone, but he couldn't bring himself to laugh.

"Unfortunately for you boys, I ain't got the means to pass it back to the Walkers without a price."

"We wouldn't expect you to," Kaden told him. "You just let us know your price and we'll see what we can do."

Tuck shifted forward, pulled an envelope out of his back pocket, then placed it on the table. His gnarled fingers moved it in their direction.

"Keep in mind, this ain't the list price. It's the friends' discount. If it comes down to puttin' it on the market official-like, I'll be askin' market value."

Keegan nodded at Kaden, urging his brother to open the envelope. He watched his brother's face as he did, noticed the slight flare of his eyes before Kaden passed it over.

He held his breath, then took a peek.

The number he saw was far less than he expected based on the research he'd done. Definitely reasonable. Which meant it would come down to whether or not they could get the loan. And come up with the down payment. Couldn't forget that.

"What about the cattle?" Kaden inquired.

"Whatcha see is whatcha get," Tuck answered. "Only ten heads out there. Got that young'n Cassius King takin' care of things. Might I suggest you keep the young man on. Hot-headed on a good day, but a damn fine cowboy."

Keegan figured they'd do well to keep Cassius on. They'd need someone to help out until they got things up and running fully.

"The house'll be cleared out," Tuck continued, "but the equipment'll stay. Includin' the tractor, though I'm warnin' ya, it's seen better days. I'd go and get myself a good mechanic."

"Got that one covered, sir," Kaden said with a smile.

Keegan felt that strange churning sensation in his gut. Anticipation. The thought of owning this place was more than he'd thought possible. Not to mention everything he'd ever dreamed about.

"The information's all there," Tuck said, pointing at the papers. "Got the acreage, square footage, even the profit and loss for the past decade. Some of that's my fault there. Gettin' harder and harder to handle things 'round here and help's not as good as it used to be." He grinned wide. "Or as cheap. But if you're lookin' to buy a ranch to get rich, you ain't in your right mind."

No, Keegan knew most ranchers didn't roll in dough. But it wasn't about the money for him. It was about owning something he could be proud of, a place he could work with his own two hands.

"How long do we have to get the money and all that?" Kaden inquired.

Now Tuck frowned, his eyes lowering to the table. "I hate to put a rush on it, but I need to have everything in order by the end of the week."

A week? Could they even get it all done in a week?

"My grandkids'll be down next weekend to load up the rest of my things. They want me good and settled in before the holiday season rolls in. If we don't have a contract workin' by then, I'll hafta leave it in the hands of the real estate gal. She'll take care of it from there."

Keegan glanced at Kaden, willed his brother to agree to buy this place. No way could they not.

"And don't worry," Tuck continued, "I'm willin' to rent it to you in the interim so you can move in now. No sense lettin' it sit empty when I'm gone."

Well, that was good news. Provided they could get the loan, they could be getting things underway while they waited for it to close.

"Somethin' you should know," Tuck added.

Keegan's attention shifted back to the old man.

"House needs a lotta work. It's livable, but most of the appliances have crapped out, the floors squeak in more places than they don't, some of the plumbin's leakin'. The roof's new though. Had it replaced a few years ago."

"Anything that won't pass inspection?" Curtis asked.

"Doubtful. Nothin' that'd matter to the bank, anyhow."

"Mr. Tucker," Kaden said, his voice low, "we're gonna do everything in our power to get you that contract by Friday. We'll make a trip into town tomorrow, go to the bank, see what we can do."

Tuck glanced between the two of them. "I think this place'll be in good hands if you boys want it."

"We definitely want it," Keegan said firmly.

More than he wanted anything else.

KADEN STEERED THE TRUCK BACK TO THE house, fighting a smile.

"A fuckin' ranch," Keegan said on an excited exhale. "Can you believe it?"

"It's not a done deal yet," he informed his twin. "There're a lot of hurdles to jump through first."

His brother sighed and Kaden felt shitty for taking the wind out of his brother's sails.

"I know. But this is more of an opportunity than we've had in a long damn time." Keegan grinned again. "What time's the bank open in the mornin'?"

"Probably eight."

"So we'll be there at five till. Cool?"

Since Keegan's idea of being on time meant ten minutes late, Kaden had to think his brother was serious about this. Then again, why wouldn't he be? They'd only dreamed about this their entire life.

Kaden didn't bother to answer because the question didn't require one. Regardless of what he said, Keegan would be at the bank first thing tomorrow morning. If Kaden had any hope of making this work, he had to get everything in order before then. Which meant he would have to check into their finances. Luckily for them both, Kaden was the one who had squirreled away money all these years. Not only his own but Keegan's as well. Had he left it to Keegan, they would've had a house full of video games and not a damn thing set aside for their future.

It sure as hell helped that they'd been living with family for some time now. Because of that, and the ridiculously small amount of rent Uncle Curtis had asked for, Kaden had been able to save a large portion of their paychecks. Based on simple math, they definitely had what they needed to get the ranch.

However, he couldn't deny he was excited about the prospect. Question would come down to credit scores, rates, and all that noise.

Not that he would tell Keegan as much. Not yet. Not until they saw everything laid out on paper.

A fucking ranch.

Kaden spent the rest of the day going over the numbers, checking their credit scores, and downloading information from the bank's website. While he sat on the couch with his MacBook propped in his lap, Keegan was reclined in the chair, his Xbox controller in hand, headset covering his ears.

Every so often, Kaden's gaze would lift to the screen and he'd watch as his brother wrecked yet another vehicle.

That was one gene he hadn't gotten that Keegan had. Kaden had never been much into video games. He would play, sure. From time to time he would give in to his brother, pick up a controller to stop the harassment. As they'd gotten older though, the novelty had worn off for him. He suspected the same could be said for Keegan, but for his brother, it was a way to pass the time.

So he sat quietly, continuing to look at their finances, pulling together the documents the bank's website said they would need to get a mortgage, and waited patiently for Keegan to get frustrated enough to quit the game.

"Son of a bitch," Keegan grunted, yanking the headset off his head and tossing it onto the coffee table.

"We need to talk," Kaden said the moment he had his brother's attention.

"If it's not about the ranch, it's not a topic I care to discuss."

Which meant Keegan already knew Kaden was ready to talk about Bristol.

"We can't avoid this forever."

"Sure we can. It's what we do with all the women who pass through our beds."

Kaden stared over at Keegan, his frustration building. "And just how many women do we take to our beds?"

"Not nearly enough, man."

"Keegan, I'm serious."

His brother's gaze swung over. Keegan looked pissed, but that had been what Kaden was going for. He knew Keegan was angry over what had happened the other night, about how he'd reacted. What Kaden didn't understand was why he was so hell-bent on sabotaging a good thing.

"Bristol didn't deserve what you said to her," he said, broaching the subject.

"Yeah, well, I only spoke the truth. You know as well as I do that she can't handle it."

He held on to his temper, knowing it would get him nowhere. "She's important, Keeg."

"Yeah? Well, I thought so, too. Then what'd she do? Ignored us for ten months and then hopped right into bed with us only to haul ass when things got too hot."

Kaden hated that Keegan was attempting to cheapen what they'd shared, but he knew his brother and he knew there was only one reason he would do that. Had it been a run-of-the-mill experience, Keegan would've looked back on it fondly, brought it up a few times before it died a natural death. Something along the lines of: *Hey, remember that hot chick we had sandwiched between us? What was her name? Eh. Doesn't matter. Damn, but I liked the way she screamed.* Or: *What was that girl's name? We should look her up again, see if she wants to get nekkid.*

That was what Keegan did. The encounters they had with women weren't exactly memorable, but they weren't forgettable, either. Except that was exactly what Keegan was doing with Bristol. Putting her in the past as though he needed her to stay there.

Kaden never knew what to expect from Keegan, but he wasn't all that surprised that his brother had written Bristol off. In a way, he understood his reasons, even though he couldn't bring himself to do the same.

That night with her had sealed his fate. It might take time, but he had every intention of getting in her good graces once again and convincing her that, despite evidence to the contrary, they weren't jackasses. And he fully intended to do so with Keegan at his side. They had vowed never to let a woman come between them, and Kaden wasn't about to start now.

But that didn't mean he had to give up the one woman who made sense in their lives, the one he could see a real future with. Bristol was different from Kim or Meredith. Kaden had never been as into them as he'd tried to be, because deep down, he had known they weren't fully on board with the idea of living a life with two men. He had a feeling Bristol saw them as a whole, not as individuals. Which was something else they would have to deal with when the time was right, but first he had to get the three of them back to where they were.

Sooner rather than later would be nice, but Kaden was purposely holding off. No one knew Keegan better than he did, and if he were to move too quickly, it would only set Keegan off. But he wasn't an idiot. He knew Keegan's attitude problem was directly related to that night. More accurately, to what he'd realized that night: that he had feelings for Bristol.

Only something intense and emotional could get Keegan to react in such a rude manner, especially with a woman. Kaden had to suspect his brother was as in love with Bristol as he was.

Question was: would Keegan accept it?

Bigger question: could they convince Bristol?

"WHAT ARE YOU WORKIN' ON?"

Travis looked up from his computer screen, watching as Kylie stepped into his home office. His wife looked tired and perhaps a bit stressed, something he'd noticed was happening quite frequently as of late. He figured he was to blame for some of it, thanks to his obsession with finding Juliet Prince.

"Research." He closed his laptop, pushed back from his desk, and patted his knee, using the distraction as a way of escaping himself for a little while. "Come here."

Kylie strolled over, brushing her hair back from her face before settling on his lap, her head instantly dropping to his shoulder.

"We missed you yesterday," she said softly.

Travis grunted. He didn't know what to say to that. He'd gone and done the one thing he promised himself he wouldn't. He had allowed something else to keep him from his family. He'd managed all these years not to get sidetracked by his business, and here he was, letting some crazy bitch throw him off his game. Unfortunately, he had the feeling it was going to get worse before it got better.

"I finally got Avery down," Kylie added when he didn't say anything.

"She still runnin' a fever?"

"Right at a hundred. Doc said it's an ear infection." She sighed. "I was so scared she was gonna tell me it was strep, and I'd wake up tomorrow to find out the rest of 'em had it."

Travis brushed her forehead with his lips. They'd been through this numerous times before. Both ear infections and strep throat tended to run their course through the kiddos nearly every time one of them came down with them. And it had only been a few days ago when Haden had been running a fever.

"Antibiotics?" he asked.

"Yep. Hopefully she'll sleep through the night."

"Well, you let me and Gage worry about that."

"I don't think I have a choice," she said with a yawn. "I'm so tired." She shifted. "How'd Kate do today?"

Travis relaxed into his chair, curling his arm around her. "Better. I dropped her with Ethan and Beau for a bit. They made her the honorary babysitter. She spent a couple of hours bein' the boss."

"She gets that from you," Kylie said with a chuckle. "Wantin' to be the boss."

Yes, she did. And like him, she was good at it.

"She had a good time with Kaden and Keegan, too," Kylie continued. "They took her to McDonald's. Stayed with her the entire time." Kylie laughed. "You should hear Kate tell how Keegan was climbin' all through that indoor playscape. Guy's a nut."

He was. But Keegan was damn good with kids, and Travis was grateful the twins were there for Kate when she needed them.

"I think she's gettin' better every day," Kylie mused.

According to the psychologist they were seeing, it would take time before Kate felt completely safe again. She didn't seem to have any issues provided one of them was with her, but she still refused to go to school. Luckily, homeschooling was an option for them, and Kylie had spent the past couple of weeks getting it all set up. Until Kate was ready to get back into the swing of things, they would do what was necessary to accommodate. Travis didn't blame his daughter for not trusting the adults who had been responsible for her safety when she'd been kidnapped a few weeks back. Hell, Travis didn't trust the damn school.

Not that it was entirely their fault. Juliet Prince had clearly had one goal in mind when she'd set out that morning. Hurting him had been her objective, and evidently, she would go to any lengths to do so, proven when she'd snatched Kate, then simply vanished. The fact that his cousin had managed to track her down and get Kate back quickly was the only reason Travis hadn't lost his ever-loving mind.

He wouldn't say he was doing much better now. Perhaps he was worse off than he'd been then. Even he would admit he was obsessed, and it wasn't a good look for him. His family was suffering because of it, yet Travis couldn't find his way back from the edge. Not until she was dealt with appropriately.

He hated that he wasn't any closer to finding her than he had been when he first started, but that only made him work harder, putting in endless hours doing research. At some point, she would surface. Of that, he was certain. If only his patience wasn't worn thin. He was pretty sure he was driving his cousin Brantley crazy with the incessant voicemails telling him he needed his help.

Kylie's hand shifted over his chest. "I think I need to take a shower."

Travis kissed her forehead, ready to release her so she could go do that.

Evidently, she had other plans, because she leaned in, her lips grazing his neck. The sensation that tore through his body set him ablaze.

"Shower with me, Travis," she whispered, trailing kisses along his jaw. "Let's escape it all for just a little while."

"Where's Gage?"

"Watchin' *Frozen* with the kids."

Again? Good Lord. They'd seen it at least three dozen times.

Of course, with them engrossed in the animated movie and supervised, that meant they had some time to themselves, which was unheard of these days. With five kids, there was rarely any spare minutes for them to be alone unless they were in bed for the night. Even then it was touch-and-go.

Travis knew better than to pass up an opportunity such as this one.

Shifting Kylie on his lap, he cupped her ass with both hands and got to his feet. Her legs wrapped around his hips as her lips melded to his.

Without breaking the lip-lock, Travis carried her out of his office, through the foyer, up the stairs, and down the hall to their bedroom. With a swift kick, he got the door closed behind him and made his way into the bathroom. Setting Kylie on the edge of the sink, he made quick work of turning on the shower and toeing off his boots before returning to her.

When her arms wrapped around him, there was an urgency in her movements, very similar to the need he felt building inside him. His was motivated by that restless energy. As for hers, he wasn't sure what was spurring it, but he was certainly on board.

"Kylie…"

"Now, Travis," she moaned against his mouth, her hands sliding beneath his shirt, shoving the cotton up high on his chest.

He helped her along, tugging the T-shirt over his head, tossing it to the floor. While he did the same with hers, she ripped at the button on his fly, yanking it open, then tugging the zipper down.

They were a fumble of hands as they hurried to get the other undressed. Once they were both naked, Travis set her on the counter again, holding her right on the edge as he guided himself inside her, pleasure lighting up his nerve endings as the tight clasp of her body sheathed him.

Kylie moaned, her lips tearing free as he pushed inside her, retreated slowly. She leaned back against the mirror, their eyes meeting as he thrust into her hard and deep.

"God yes," she cried out. "Like that. Just … like that, Trav. Make me come."

He didn't know the last time he'd seen her come apart like this, but he loved that about Kylie. She wasn't shy when it came to what she wanted. As time had gone by, she'd become more vocal, more insistent with her own sexual needs, ensuring both he and Gage knew what she needed. And while he could've made love to her a dozen times a day, it was moments like this one when she had him hanging by a fragile thread.

Gripping her hips to hold her in place, Travis thrust into her, filling her. His pace increased, her beautiful tits bouncing with every punishing impalement. The tight clasp of her pussy drove him mad, made his spine tingle, his inevitable release within reach.

"Harder," she pleaded, grabbing for him, her arms wreathing his neck.

Travis lifted her off the counter, spun around, and pressed her back to the door. He held her there, nailing her hard and deep until they were both panting and moaning. His thighs burned with the effort, but it was a sweet heat because he was right where he wanted to be.

"Trav... oh, God..."

Kylie's inner muscles clamped down on him, dragging a ragged groan from his throat as he held on for as long as he could. But when her head fell back, hitting the door with a thud, he knew he was a goner. Her pussy gripped him like a vise, milking him as she cried out in that sensual way she did. He gritted his teeth, drove into her several more times, until holding back was no longer an option. He slammed home as his body jerked and spasmed, filling her in the most intimate of ways.

They were both breathing hard, but Travis didn't move. He wasn't sure he could.

When Kylie chuckled, her muscles gripped him again, making him groan.

"We really do need that shower now," she said, pressing her lips to his cheek.

It was in the shower that Travis took her once more. Because they both had needed it.

Chapter Ten

FIRST THING MONDAY MORNING, KEEGAN DRAGGED KADEN down to the bank. They managed to get there a few minutes before the doors opened, and every second Keegan waited felt like eons.

The giddy feeling, he realized, was more like anxiety than hope. At some point during the night, he'd woken up in a cold sweat, dreaming that the bank had turned them down flat, refusing to give them a loan for the property. With a few callous words, the woman in his dream had dashed all his hopes.

He'd been almost tempted to say fuck it, to tell Kaden he'd changed his mind. Last thing he needed was another letdown. Right now, he wasn't sure he could deal with the bad news.

At the same time, this was his dream. No way could he let his anxiety take him down.

Of course, he was damn good at hiding it, so he plastered on a smile, shoved a nuked breakfast burrito and a mug of lukewarm coffee at his brother, and forced him out the door. To keep from fidgeting, Keegan had driven, managing somehow to not break any traffic laws on the way to town.

Fortunately, the bank wasn't busy at that time of morning, and they'd managed to wrangle a meeting with the bank manager without an appointment. At least, that was what Kaden had told him. Then again, the bank manager—who just so happened to be related to them—was the only other person working besides one teller. There wasn't another soul inside the building, so there weren't exactly people knocking down the door for a loan.

They'd been directed into this office, offered more coffee—which they had both refused—and were now waiting for the manager to appear. It took everything in him not to hyperventilate.

Keegan heard footsteps seconds before a familiar voice said, "I heard it through the grapevine that you boys are lookin' to buy Tuck's ranch."

"We are," Keegan said with a grin, letting some of that repressed hope out in his voice.

And then there were three in the small office, which couldn't have been more than eight by eight if an inch, held little more than a single desk, two uncomfortable guest chairs, one executive chair, a printer, a computer, and now the bank manager, Griffin Walker, one of their many cousins.

"You realize who your neighbor'll be, don't you?"

"Who?" Keegan inquired, glancing between Kaden and Griffin.

"My brother," Griffin said, leaning back in his chair. "Brantley lives next door to ol' Tuck."

"Did you know that?" Keegan asked Kaden.

"I did." His brother grinned. "And I don't think it'll be a problem."

"Didn't figure it would." Griffin glanced between them, his expression shifting to serious. He held that look for several seconds before a grin broke out on his face and he looked at Kaden. "Sorry, man. I tried."

Keegan wasn't sure he understood. He'd heard *sorry*, but it was said with a chuckle. That didn't mean bad news, did it?

"What's goin' on?" Keegan asked, fear once more trickling into his bloodstream.

Griffin leaned back in his chair, his grin widening. "Congrats."

Keegan frowned. "For what?"

"It's yours if you want it."

How the hell could that be possible? They were here to fill out the application, go through the process. All the bullshit Keegan wasn't looking forward to but knew was necessary.

Keegan peered over at Kaden. "What's he talkin' about?"

Griffin chuckled. "You didn't tell him you applied for the loan already?"

"No." Kaden exhaled heavily. "Figured I'd let it be a surprise."

Why that surprised him, Keegan didn't know. That sounded just like Kaden. Always one step ahead, the expected outcome in sight.

"It's ours?" Keegan asked, his gaze darting between the two of them.

"Well, provided the appraisal comes back, which, based on the asking price, I can't imagine it won't." Griffin glanced between them again. "We are lookin' for twenty percent down."

"Twenty percent?" Keegan pulled the paper Griffin laid out toward him. "Holy shit."

That was a lot of damn money.

"We're good for it," Kaden said, his voice oddly reassuring.

"We are?"

Another laugh from Griffin as he stared at Kaden. "I take it you're the money man."

"I have to be. Otherwise, we'd own stock in Xbox and not much else."

Keegan probably should've been offended by that, but he couldn't bring himself to care. The ranch was theirs.

"It's my understanding Tuck's movin' to Wyoming with his kids," Kaden said. "There gonna be a problem with him signin' the papers from there?"

"We'll get it all worked out. I will need to get his John Hancock on a few things so we can get started processing the paperwork, but I've already talked to him. I called him up yesterday when I saw the application come through. I'll meet with him this afternoon, get things underway."

"What do you need from us?" Kaden asked.

While his brother and his cousin chatted it up, Keegan continued to stare at the paper in front of him. The one that had his and his brother's names as the buyers for Tuck's ranch. He was grateful Kaden was there to take care of the details, because he wasn't sure he could do much of anything besides stare.

Theirs.

The ranch was…

He felt a little light-headed.

"Hey, Keeg? You all right?"

He honestly didn't know, but he nodded anyway.

Two hours later, Keegan was doing his best to stay focused on the work he had before him, but his attention span was for shit. The only thing he could think about was what they needed to tackle first when they moved in. His goal was to get the ranch up and running, but he knew the house needed some work. Griffin had told them the earliest they'd be able to close on the place was thirty days from now.

Thirty days felt like an eternity.

"I was thinkin' we'd take Tuck up on his offer to rent the place while we wait for closing," Kaden said from beside him.

Keegan's head snapped up. "Are you readin' my mind?"

Kaden's brow furrowed. "What? You just said thirty days felt like an eternity."

Had he?

Well, hell. Now he was voicing his thoughts aloud.

"So we move when? Next weekend?"

A laugh sounded from his brother. "I was kinda thinkin' we could give him a hand packin' his stuff. That way his grandkids don't have to do it all in a weekend. After work. A little each day."

"Yeah," he agreed. "Give us a chance to get eyes on what needs to be fixed."

"And for me to get a grasp on finances. Figure out how we'll handle the lot of it," Kaden noted. "Why don't we stop by after work? Talk to Tuck. Give you somethin' to look forward to."

Keegan grinned. Yeah. And until then, perhaps he could get his head back in the game.

AFTER WORK, KADEN HAULED HIS BROTHER OVER to Tuck's place. Turned out, the old man was happy to see them. Then again, he figured Tuck would've been happy to see pretty much anyone. It was a good thing he was moving to be closer to his kids. The man was clearly lonely and living out here all alone was a big reason why.

Tuck accepted their offer to help pack, but rather than let them get down to it, Tuck had kept them busy, showing off pictures of his kids and grandkids, his great-granddaughter. The man was proud, no doubt about it.

By the time they were able to get out of there, they'd both been starving, so they stopped in at the diner, ate without a whole lot of conversation. Kaden had considered asking Keegan if they could stop by Bristol's on the way home, but he held off. Last thing he wanted was to ruin Keegan's good mood.

Didn't mean he wasn't going to attempt to talk to her. Ever since he'd gotten the approval for the loan, there was only one person he'd wanted to share the news with. Of course, they'd called their parents, filled in their siblings, and got word to Curtis, but he didn't get the opportunity share his good news with Bristol. Why it seemed to all come down to that, he couldn't explain, but it pained him that she wasn't going to be part of it.

Kaden knew it wasn't a good idea to go talk to Bristol without informing his brother, but he had to. He could no longer sit back and let that incident go without a discussion. And he seriously doubted either of them were going to take the lead, so it was up to him to attempt to make amends.

He waited until Keegan went to his room for the night, then slipped out of the house. He figured if his brother heard the truck start up, he could come up with a lie on the fly. Hungry, thirsty, whatever. Then again, he doubted Keegan would notice. The man had been in his own little world since Griffin informed them they got the ranch.

It only took a few minutes to make his way over to Bristol's. She lived in the same area as their cousin Brendon, a neat and tidy little neighborhood comprised mostly of 1950s ranch-style one-stories. There were a few houses that still had their Halloween decorations up, but for the most part, the lawns were neat and tidy, security lights on on a few, the rest dark.

When he pulled up to her house, nerves took over. What would he do if she slammed the door in his face? Told him she never wanted to see him again? At the moment, they were in limbo. Once he went to that door, he would know exactly where they stood. Did he really want to hear her thoughts on the matter?

He decided he did, forced his body to move. Getting out of the truck was the easy part. Convincing his hand to knock was something else entirely. Kaden stood on her front porch for the better part of a minute before he got up the nerve.

Instead of opening it, Bristol shouted through the door. "What do you want, Kaden?"

Well, at least she was home and she'd made the effort to look out. Although, he was surprised she'd been able to tell them apart in the dark, but hey, if his parents could, why couldn't she?

"To talk."

"There's nothin' to talk about."

"You know there is, Bristol."

"I'm not in the mood right now."

Christ. He hadn't anticipated it going this way. At the very least he'd expected to see her. For whatever reason, he needed to see with his own two eyes that she was all right. After she'd slipped away from the auction, he hadn't seen her. For the first time in a very, very long time, she hadn't gone to Curtis and Lorrie's for dinner yesterday. Now she was relegating him to a conversation through the door.

"Please open the door."

"No."

"Bristol…" He took a step closer so he could speak without shouting. "Let me in so we can talk."

"Go away. I have nothin' more to say to you or your brother."

Kaden leaned his forehead against the door and closed his eyes. "Please. You have to let me apologize."

"What? You're sorry we slept together? Well, so am I. No apology necessary. It cancels itself out, Kaden."

His stomach twisted in a knot. He damn sure wasn't sorry they'd slept together. Hell, if he had his way, she would've been in his bed every night since then and every night going forward. He'd played this game for so long, Kaden was tired of waiting. He was ready to get on with his life now and he wanted Bristol to be part of it.

"Would it make a difference if I told you I love you?"

There was no response. Not right away. And that hurt. Like a fucking arrow in the chest.

"I'm not giving in on this, Kaden, so you might as well leave." This time her voice wavered, like perhaps she was crying.

Goddamn, but she was stubborn.

"I'm sorry," he finally told her. "I'm sorry for what Keegan said. I'm sorry that he can be an ass. But I'm not sorry for what happened. All three of us wanted it. Hell, I *still* want it."

"Yeah, well, Keegan made it clear that he doesn't."

"No, Keegan made it clear that he's scared, Bristol. That's what he does when he gets scared."

A mirthless laugh resounded inside. "Scared? Of what? Does he think I expected a marriage proposal after one night?"

No, the opposite. That you don't *expect it.*

Kaden didn't say that because he wouldn't do that to Keegan. His brother's insecurities were rational even if they were misdirected.

"Just go, please." Her voice was softer. "I need some space from the two of you."

Space.

They'd given her space for a long damn time now. If they gave her more now, he knew without a doubt Bristol would find a way to completely eradicate them from her life. But what other choice did he have? He couldn't make her want him.

"All right," he heard himself saying. "I'll go. If you ever need anything…"

She didn't respond, so he decided to leave it at that.

Unfortunately, like Keegan, he'd been burned, too. And a man could only grovel so much.

Chapter Eleven

One month later
Friday, December 4, 2020

THE MONTH OF NOVEMBER FLEW BY FOR Keegan.

Then again, he'd been so damn busy, most of the time he hadn't known what day it was. He'd looked to Kaden to direct him where to go and when to be there. To the shop, church, Curtis and Lorrie's for Sunday dinner. They'd had Thanksgiving there, too, along with Eve, Quinn, and Wesley, who'd all managed to be in town for the holiday. The rest of the time he'd spent working on the house, fixing what needed to be fixed.

Thankfully, Cassius had decided to stay on and work, and maintaining the few remaining cattle Tuck had left behind and giving them the lay of the land. Although Cassius was little more than a kid himself at twenty-five, he was a damn hard worker like Tuck had said. And yes, he was ornery and short tempered but oddly enough, Keegan realized he liked the guy.

After they'd gotten Tuck packed up and loaded into the U-Haul his granddaughter Erin had rented for the long trip to Wyoming, they hadn't wasted any time. They spent their days at Walker Demo, the evenings and sometimes late into the night at the ranch. The goal had been to get the house livable so they could move in, work on it in their spare time. It took another week and a half after Tuck left for that to happen, but they'd bought some new appliances, fixed the leak in the bathroom plumbing, and hauled one of the beds from their place over temporarily. With running water, a refrigerator, a bed to sleep in, and the closing paperwork to make it theirs signed on the dotted line, they'd started on the real work: renovating the entire house from top to bottom.

It was a painstakingly slow process.

Wouldn't have been, of course, if they'd hired someone to do the work, but Keegan wasn't willing to relinquish that to anyone. He wanted to make a mark on the first house they owned, and their blood, sweat, and tears was one hell of a way to show their dedication.

So now, on another glorious Friday afternoon, after putting in a long day, Keegan stared out the passenger window as Kaden drove from the jobsite back to town, heading to their house.

As the scenery passed him by, Keegan's brain ran through the day, mentally checking to make sure there wasn't something he needed to take care of. He'd woken up in time for breakfast at the diner for the first time that week. Usually his nights were too long, and it was all he could do to drag his tired ass right to the shop. This morning he'd been invigorated, although he couldn't quite pinpoint why. He figured it was his desire to stop moping about, allowing his thoughts to continuously drift where they didn't belong. Not that he was succeeding at the latter but he was damn sure trying.

Once they'd gotten to the shop, he'd worked on some engines and got the news that Autumn would be bringing on a couple of people to help drum up new business. After they'd gossiped about that with Ethan for a good hour, they'd pushed out some equipment. Their final task of the day had been personally delivering a piece to one of the jobsites.

"D'you hear?" Kaden said. "That building on Main Street finally sold."

No, he hadn't heard. Then again, he hadn't been paying attention to much of anything going on in town. "What's it gonna be?"

"A spa."

The words traveled through his headspace, then took root. He glanced over at Kaden. "A spa? Like…?" He couldn't think of what they did at a spa.

"Manicures, pedicures, massages," Kaden supplied.

"Oh, right." He laughed. "Who the fuck would rather go to a spa over an arcade?"

"Women, Keeg. Women would prefer a spa to an arcade."

"If you say so." He wasn't buying it, but it really wasn't his problem, either. He had his ranch, so he had no hard feelings that someone else had purchased that building.

"You up for a night out?" Kaden prompted when he turned down the dirt drive that split their front pasture.

"Where?"

"Moonshiners."

It wasn't like him to have to think on it, but that was exactly what he did.

"Keeg? I know you're—"

"Yeah, I'm up for it," he decided just so his brother couldn't start up with him again.

Keegan had no desire whatsoever to get into this with him. Every time Kaden had attempted to talk for the past month, it was always about Bristol. Everything in his brother's orbit seemed to revolve around the woman although they'd had no interaction with her during that time. Keegan blamed Kaden for the fact that he couldn't stop thinking about her, either. Kaden's fault because he was always trying to fucking talk about her, about the shit that had gone down between them.

And damn it all to hell, Bristol was invading his brain day and night, no matter how hard he tried to exorcise her from his mind. For the past few weeks, Keegan had done little more than think about that night they'd spent in his bed, the three of them. Try as he might, he couldn't seem to get those images out of his head. Twice he'd actually talked Kaden into hooking up with another woman only to back off at the last minute. He tried to tell himself it was because Kaden's heart wasn't in it, but he knew better. His wasn't, either.

It had taken some time, but he'd finally recognized the emotion.

Regret.

He fucking hated himself for letting Bristol slip away, but now that a month had gone by and they hadn't said so much as three words to her in that time, Keegan accepted there was no salvaging it.

So Keegan had taken to shutting down Kaden's attempt to psychoanalyze the situation, and he fully intended to continue doing so. Eventually one day he would forget all about Bristol Newton and his life would get back to normal again. In the meantime, he would continue focusing on what was important: moving on with his life.

"It's high time we got back in the game," he said now. "Friday night ... bound to be some feisty cowgirls lookin' for a good time."

His brother sighed. "Not interested."

"Well, why the hell not?" There was no heat in his tone. It would've required effort.

"You don't think about what might've been?" Kaden asked.

Hell yes. "No. Why would I? Not like it's a possibility." He turned his attention out the window, watched as they neared their house.

"I'm gettin' tired of the games," Kaden said softly, pulling the truck to a stop in front of the house.

"No one's playin' a fuckin' game," Keegan snapped, although he had to look away because he knew Kaden was hurting. Had been since that night. Bristol was the one woman Kaden hadn't moved on from. He'd known for some time that his brother was thinking she could be the one. For both of them.

And then Keegan had gone and fucked that all up.

"You're never gonna be ready, are you?" Kaden asked.

Keegan sighed, pushing open the truck door. "I didn't say that."

"Then what *are* you sayin'?" Kaden asked, storming up behind him as Keegan headed into the house.

He honestly didn't know. He'd long ago shifted away from thoughts of happily ever after. It made a hell of a lot more sense to live in the moment. It was easier that way.

"Keegan, talk to me."

Spinning around, he faced off with his brother. "She's not gonna give us the time of day, Kaden. You saw her that night. Completely uninhibited. But the fuckin' minute it was over, she was havin' regrets."

And so was I.

"You were a dick to her," Kaden snapped.

"Yeah? Why's that? Because I spoke the truth? You know it as well as I do. No way would she be caught dead with the two of us. Not in public. Is that what you want? To be some woman's dirty little secret?" Keegan felt his anger rising. "Because I don't. I've played that role too many times. I won't do it again."

"You didn't even give it a fucking chance," Kaden bit out.

No. No, he hadn't. "It wouldn't've mattered if I did."

"You're wrong."

No, he most certainly was not. Bristol was a firecracker in the bedroom; she'd proven that in just one short encounter. Quite possibly the best lay he'd ever had. But keepin' it in the bedroom … not his style.

And even if Bristol did come around, it wouldn't have been long before Keegan disappointed her. Or worse, offended her. She was the sort of woman who needed tender loving. And that wasn't Keegan. He wanted a woman who liked to walk on the wild side, one who'd get down and dirty in the backseat of his truck, let him tease her in the dark corner of a bar, use his fingers to make her come while everyone else was doing their thing. Hell, he'd be surprised if Bristol Newton would let a man kiss her in public, much less finger-fuck her in a dark booth.

He knew for a fact she damn sure wouldn't let two of them do it, so none of it fucking mattered.

"I'm done worryin' about Bristol, Kaden. We haven't heard from her for a fucking month. I'm sure she's forgotten all about us."

And if he tried really fucking hard, hopefully Keegan would eventually forget about her, too.

Several hours later, they were sitting at a table at Moonshiners, drinking beer and listening to Travis Tritt croon from the jukebox.

He'd managed to wrangle a couple of their buddies into joining them, and it would've been a damn good night if it hadn't been for the fact *she* had come here tonight.

Yep. They'd been there for all of an hour when Bristol strolled in with two of her friends. Bianca and Jamie. The three women had secured a booth on the far side of the room, minding their own business, laughing and talking. And while they did that, Keegan had been in the perfect position to see Bristol clearly. The other two women were blocked out by CJ's big head, but it didn't matter. Keegan didn't care to see them anyway.

Not that he cared to see Bristol, either, but for some fucked-up reason, he had an unobstructed view of her talking with her friends, smiling that million-megawatt grin, and turning down every man who attempted to come on to her.

Oh, lookie there. Number five was strolling up, pausing to be polite and...

Keegan watched as Bristol looked up at the man, smiled sweetly, then motioned to her friends while she shook her head. His lip-reading skills weren't exactly tuned, but Keegan was pretty sure she *thanks but no thanks*'d him.

Would she turn Keegan down if he asked? Brush him off like lint on those tight-ass jeans she wore?

It was an interesting conundrum he found himself in. Not once in his life had he ever had a problem mixing it up with the ladies, nor had he ever worried himself over it. He'd always had the gift for sweet-talking. Add that to his decent appearance and he hadn't done too bad.

He'd also never treated a woman with disrespect. Partly because his parents had instilled manners into them from the day they took their first breath, and partly because he wanted to ensure a repeat was always an option. One never knew what situation they might find themselves in.

Yet there was one woman in the world who he'd treated badly. He was man enough to admit—at least to himself—that he'd dumped all his past pain and heartache at Bristol's feet, holding her responsible for the sins of those who'd come before her. Unlike the women in his past, Bristol hadn't stuck around to face his wrath. Which he figured was the very reason he thought about her endlessly no matter how hard he tried not to.

And there she was sitting not twenty feet away right now.

He wanted to ask her to dance and he had no fucking idea why that was.

As he was contemplating an asinine move, the perfect opportunity presented itself when Bianca called it a night, leaving Bristol and Jamie alone at their table.

The bright red bow on the opportunity-of-a-lifetime package came when CJ asked Jamie to dance and she said yes, which left only one sitting at that table.

"Where're you goin'?" Kaden asked when Keegan got to his feet.

"I'll be back," he assured his twin.

Without hesitating, he started toward Bristol. When he approached, she was tucking her cell phone into the dainty little purse she was carrying and pulling out her keys.

He cleared his throat to get her attention.

No, he wasn't expecting a smile, so he was only mildly disappointed when he didn't get one.

She turned her attention back to the table, to the glass of what looked to be vodka with soda and lime she'd been nursing for the past hour. "What do you want, Keegan?"

"Care to dance?"

She didn't bother looking up at him when she said, "No. I don't."

Usually he could take a hint, but for some reason his feet wouldn't move to carry him away from her table. He remained where he was, staring down at her, willing her to look up.

When she finally did, he held her gaze, ensured she saw he wasn't going to take no for an answer. Not happily, anyway. "Dance with me, Bristol."

There was a flash in her eyes, and he was fairly certain it wasn't disdain. In fact, he was pretty sure she liked that he wasn't trying to butter her up with sweet words and bullshit.

Holding out his hand, he waited for Bristol to take it. She hesitated for long seconds, which only made it sweeter when she relented. When her small fingers grasped his, Keegan felt heat travel through his entire body. An image of this woman naked, sandwiched between him and his brother, writhing and crying out their names, was nearly enough to have him missing a step. Luckily, he'd long ago learned how to walk and fantasize at the same time.

They made their way past the tables to the small dance floor. Turning to face her, Keegan took one of her hands in his, the other moving to her hip. Without effort or thought, they began to two-step, a dance that was as natural as breathing. Because of the height difference, Bristol had to move in close, a plus as far as he was concerned.

Keegan felt the tension in her body, the jerkiness of her movements but he pretended not to. After a few minutes, she seemed to relax a little, her hand softening in his.

Brantley Gilbert gave way to Luke Combs on the jukebox, the slower song giving Keegan the opportunity to pull Bristol in even closer. Her hair smelled like lavender, a sweet scent he knew he'd be smelling in his dreams.

Neither of them spoke for the longest time, not until Keegan became aware of her staring up at him as they moved.

"What's on your mind, darlin'?" he asked, peering down as he firmed his grip on her hip and resisted the urge to pull her in even more.

"Nothin'."

"Liar."

The tension was back, her body stiffening. Keegan didn't stop moving, continuing around the dance floor with her keeping up.

He stared down at her, waiting for her to look at him again. She finally did.

Were those tears in her eyes?

Just the thought of her crying made his heart clench in his chest.

"Bristol…" Forcing his feet to stop, Keegan held her stare as he cocked his head to the side.

"I need to go," she said, making a feeble attempt to pull away.

Keegan held on. Not too tight, not enough to force her to stay but enough to let her know it was where he wanted her.

"Why're you doin' this?" Bristol whispered.

He stared down at her. "Doin' what?"

"Actin' like we're just gonna pick up where we left off."

"Why wouldn't we?" It wasn't the wisest thing to say, but hey, when a man was awestruck, words weren't the most important thing on his mind.

"It's been a month, Keegan. A *month* since I've so much as talked to you. And if I remember correctly, you were more than happy to be rid of me."

He pulled her into him, lowered his head in an attempt to settle her. He didn't like how near to the surface those tears appeared to be. "I don't recall you showin' up on our doorstep, either."

"Darn right I didn't. And I won't. No matter what, I won't ask you for a damn thing."

That comment took him by surprise. Not only the words but the tone.

He stared down at her, saw her blue eyes glistening until a single tear finally spilled over. It was nearly his undoing, those damn tears.

But he should've known Bristol wouldn't let anyone see her cry. She quickly ducked her head, and it only took a minute before she'd pulled herself together, stepping back from him.

"Bristol…"

"No." She shook her head as though to punctuate the word. "I … I…" She took a deep, steadying breath. "I don't have the energy for this right now, Keegan. I'm not willin' to go back to playin' your stupid game."

"My game?" He couldn't believe she'd accused him of playing, much less laid all the blame at his feet. "If I recall correctly, it was your game and I didn't bother playin'." He stepped in closer, lowered his voice. "Yet you still ended up in my bed."

She jerked back as though he'd slapped her.

Before he could elaborate on the matter, a gruff voice sounded behind him.

"Mind if I cut in?"

Keegan forced his attention to the cowboy who'd interrupted. "Actually, I do."

"Why don't we let the lady decide." The man's hardened gaze shifted to Bristol. "Now that you've added dancin' to tonight's festivities, I figure you owe me one."

Because he was in tune with her body language, Keegan saw Bristol tense, knew she wasn't interested in dancing with the man, which was why he was taken by surprise when she stepped away from Keegan and right up to the asshole.

"Sure," she said, not bothering to look Keegan in the eye as she moved away from him.

Keegan felt a shocking possessiveness coil in his gut when the man put his hands on her. He didn't like the way the guy pulled her close, as though he had every right to do so. Even when Bristol attempted to put space between them, he would step in, closing the distance once more.

"What the fuck?" Kaden hissed when he moved to stand beside him, their arms touching.

Damn good question.

STICKING AROUND WHILE BRISTOL DANCED WITH THAT jackass was about as fun as a root canal, yet Kaden refused to leave until she did. Not only because he knew she was doing it for their benefit, or because the thought of her leaving with that dick made him sick to his stomach, but more so he wanted to ensure she left safely.

Just call him Saint Kaden.

Of course, waiting meant watching the dipshit do his best to talk her into leaving with him. Not for coffee or a late dinner, of course. No, this guy'd been raised in a doghouse somewhere, because Kaden overheard the fool asking her to go out to his truck so they could make out. Seriously. The son of a bitch was failing miserably but he was either too drunk or too stupid to realize it.

And Kaden had a front-row seat to the pathetic action. Lucky him.

He considered asking to cut in, but being rejected by her in such a public way wasn't high on his list of things to do. She'd shunned him once, completely brushing him off after he'd told her he loved her. Last thing Kaden wanted was another dent in his ego. Rather than try, he waited. Eventually, his patience paid off.

"I'll walk you out," the dumb shit offered Bristol when she finally pulled away from him.

"No, thanks. I'm good."

"Not a problem," the man assured her. "Just gives me more time to talk you into breakfast."

"It's too early for breakfast," she said, clearly not realizing what the man was proposing.

"Perhaps we can fill a few hours another way," he suggested, the two of them passing right by Kaden.

Whether it was because he willed her to or purely by chance, Bristol glanced over at him, their eyes meeting. He hoped like hell she saw his disappointment, his hurt, not to mention his concern. He still wasn't sure what the hell had actually happened or how Keegan ended up dancing with her. Whatever transpired between them hadn't ended well, and Keegan hadn't been forthcoming with details when he'd asked, either.

She looked over at Keegan before passing them on her way to the exit. No sooner had her new friend pushed open the door, motioned her outside than Kaden was on his feet, marching after her at a fast clip. He heard Keegan right behind him along with a few choice curse words from his brother.

With a sigh, Kaden followed the not-so-happy couple, stepping outside, hoping like hell his twin didn't do something stupid like beat the fucker to a pulp. It wasn't that Kaden wasn't interested in throwing down in the parking lot, but admittedly, he wasn't keen on the idea of going home with unnecessary scrapes and bruises. Or more importantly, putting Bristol in the middle of it and risking her getting hurt.

Kaden stopped on the wooden porch of the bar, watched the pair as Bristol was attempting to get her car door opened. The man had leaned against it, making it impossible for her to get past him.

"Come on, honey. What's one night? Just the two of us? Beneath the stars."

"Oh, for fuck's sake," Keegan grumbled. "I'm gonna beat his ass if he doesn't move on."

"I'm good," Bristol told him. "But thanks for the dance. Now if you don't mind."

Surprisingly, the guy moved away from the car, opened the door as she slipped inside. Perhaps he wasn't as dumb as he looked.

"Maybe tomorrow night," the man stated. "You. Me. Dinner. My place."

Because she was in her car, Kaden couldn't make out her words, but based on the idiot's grimace, she'd once again rejected him.

"Fine." He stepped back, shut her car door a little too hard. "Not like you're the last woman on earth."

And even if this fool was the last *man* on earth, Kaden had a feeling the guy would've still struck out.

"Come on," Kaden told Keegan, nudging his shoulder. "Let's get home."

Keegan shook his head. "Wait till she pulls out. I wanna make sure he doesn't follow her."

Well, now. If that wasn't an interesting change of pace. Keegan worried about Bristol. And outwardly showing it.

Interesting.

Conceding, Kaden crossed his arms over his chest, waited for Bristol to start her car while the guy headed in the opposite direction. She made two attempts before the engine sparked to life, but it lasted only a second before it died on her.

From his position, he could see her frowning, the yellow glow from the sodium lamp shining down into her car. Bristol gave it two more tries but the *click-click-click* a pretty telltale sign it wasn't going to give in.

Keegan was off the wooden porch and heading her way before Kaden realized what he was doing. He motioned to Bristol as he neared. A second later, she was out of the car with her phone in her hand.

"Need some help?" Keegan offered, his tone curt as he moved toward her.

Like he didn't want to help.

Right.

Clearly Bristol hadn't realized they'd come out, because her eyes widened as they focused on Keegan then darted over to Kaden.

"Happens all the time. It won't start. I'll just call Bianca, see if she'll come get me."

Keegan glanced back at him. "Bring the truck around. We'll jump it."

If it was what Kaden thought it was, jumping it wouldn't help. But who was he to intervene?

Figuring his brother had a plan, Kaden made his way to the truck. By the time he pulled it around, Keegan had the hood of Bristol's car propped up, shining the flashlight on his cell phone at the engine.

Kaden made quick work of grabbing the jumper cables from the toolbox in the bed before joining Keegan.

Ten minutes later, they were in agreement that her alternator was bad, and the battery would no longer hold a charge.

"What does that mean?" Bristol asked when they explained the situation.

"Nothin' major," Keegan assured her. "Little pricey, but won't take much to change it out, get a new battery along with it. We'll get it towed to the Walker Demo shop tomorrow. Fix it right up."

Bristol shook her head. "You don't have to do that."

Kaden urged her toward his truck. "Of course we do."

"I can call a mechanic," she told him, her eyes sad.

Keegan cocked an eyebrow. "You've got two right here. Why pay someone when we can knock it out for free?"

Kaden held his breath, prayed WWIII didn't break out between these two. It was obvious they were both harboring a grudge, but the situation prevented them from being outwardly hostile about it.

He hoped.

Bristol didn't say a word and Kaden waited for her response. He recalled the last conversation he'd had with her. It had been through her front door when she refused to talk to him. The night he'd told her he loved her. He hadn't made any more attempts at conversation since, despite the fact he'd seen her around town numerous times since.

Her pretty blue eyes bounced back and forth between them for a moment. She looked incredibly sad and more than a little wary.

"Curtis and Lorrie would insist," Kaden told her when it was clear she was still debating. "In fact, they'd have our hides if we didn't do it."

There was real concern in her eyes. Or was that regret?

"As long as I can pay for the parts," she finally said.

Knowing she wasn't going to relent, Kaden nodded. It was late and he wasn't in the mood to argue.

"We'll give you a lift to your place," Kaden told her.

Not exactly in line with the fantasies he'd had as of late, but hey, you win some, you lose some.

While she grabbed her purse and locked up her car, Kaden stored the jumper cables back in the toolbox, then the three of them piled into Kaden's truck. Much to his dismay, Bristol had gotten comfortable in the back seat. He would've preferred she sat up front with him, but when Keegan offered, she had refused.

"You know, my dad was a mechanic," she said absently as Kaden was pulling the truck out onto the main road that led away from town.

Yes, Kaden knew that. He knew quite a bit about her, actually.

"That was his life," she continued. "The only thing he loved in this world."

Kaden peered at her in the rearview mirror.

"Besides me, of course," she added with a sad smile.

"Sorry for your loss," Kaden said.

Because it was such a small town, the ups and downs of someone's life were pretty much fair game. He knew her father had passed away many years back, knew she lived alone in the house she'd grown up in. If the rumors were true, her mother had abandoned them when Bristol was young, but that was all he'd heard.

"Thanks." Her gaze shot to his in the mirror. "I still miss him. Your parents are in El Paso, right?" she asked, her voice coming across somewhat stronger.

Idle chitchat. That was what she was going for. As though they were fucking strangers.

Kaden gritted his teeth, focused on driving.

"They are," Keegan answered.

"When's the last time you visited?"

"It's been a while," Kaden told her. "But they're comin' down for Christmas."

"Is it hard to be away from them?"

"We get back there as much as we can," Keegan explained. "At least once every couple of months. Since Ethan and Beau had the babies, we've had to cut down on the number of trips. They understand."

"Now that you've got the ranch, I guess you won't be traveling too much, huh?"

Kaden wasn't surprised she knew about the ranch. Small towns and all. But he did sense the curiosity in her tone.

"Not anytime soon," Keegan stated, his eyes shooting over to Kaden. "A lot to take care of."

"Congrats, by the way," she said softly.

"Thanks."

Kaden pulled into her driveway, put the truck in park, and stared at the house. He wasn't getting out if he didn't have to. And he didn't give a shit if it was rude.

This brief interaction was just about more than he could handle.

"Thanks for the ride home."

He nodded. "You're welcome. We'll check in with you tomorrow. About the car."

"I'll walk her up," Keegan said softly before opening his door.

As he sat in the truck, he watched Keegan escort her up to the porch and wished like hell he had the nerve to talk his way into her house and right into her bed.

Because, of course, he was certifiable.

Chapter Twelve

BRISTOL COULD FEEL TEARS COMING ON EVEN as she beelined it for her front porch. While she appreciated Kaden and Keegan driving her home and offering to help with her car, she couldn't be around them right now. Not if she expected to keep it together.

What had she been thinking letting Keegan talk her into a dance? Worse than that, though … what had she been thinking dancing with some stranger? It had creeped her out, but at the time, it had been the only way she could keep from breaking down into an emotional mess, something she'd been battling for a couple of weeks now.

As she approached her front door, she was hyperaware of Keegan walking beside her. She could still smell him, that intoxicating scent that was unique to them. It was cologne, she knew. Nothing overpowering, but enough to tie her up in knots at the memories the scent evoked.

"You okay?" he asked when they stepped up onto her porch.

"Fine," she muttered, fumbling for her keys inside her purse. Thankfully it was a small purse, or she would've risked breaking down in her attempt to find them.

"You really should replace that bulb," Keegan said, nodding his chin toward the porch light.

"Yeah. I know. It's just…" Shoving the key in the lock, she turned it. "It's just one of many things that I need to do around here."

"I can do it if you'd like."

Oh, God.

Why did he have to be so … nice? He wasn't supposed to be nice. Keegan was supposed to be pissed off at her, angry over the events of the past. She wouldn't do well if he was nice to her.

Bristol swallowed past the lump forming in her throat. "Thanks, but no."

"It's not a problem, Bristol. It's not safe for this light to be out."

Again, *why* was he being nice to her? After what they'd been through…

"It's all right," she whispered. "I'll…"

Oh, hell.

The tears were coming and there was nothing she could do to stop them.

Not wanting him to see the epic meltdown she'd been holding back, Bristol shoved open her front door and raced inside, heading right for the bathroom. There was no time to argue with him, and slamming the door in his face seemed incredibly rude after they'd driven her home.

"No, no, no," she muttered, pacing the small space as she fought to regulate her breathing. Her stomach was twisting, her chest felt tight, her sinuses were burning as she fought to contain the tears.

Bristol turned to stare at herself in the mirror, something she'd done constantly these past few days.

As she looked into her own eyes, the tears continued to well.

"Bristol?"

Oh, God. Now Kaden was inside, too.

"Are you all right?"

No. No, she was most certainly *not* all right.

But she would be.

Eventually.

Maybe.

"Go back out there, thank them, and send them on their way," she told the woman in the mirror as she gripped the pedestal sink until her knuckles were white. "Lie. Tell them you just had too much to drink. They'll believe it."

"Bristol."

The tone was harsher—Keegan's—and filled with concern.

"Either you come out or we're comin' in."

Oh, crap. She could actually picture them busting down the door. Then she'd have just one more thing that needed to be replaced in this house, and on top of everything else, she—

Bristol shrieked, jumping nearly a foot off the ground when a fist started pounding on the door.

"You can do this," she told her reflection. "You can."

She took a deep breath and turned around, reaching for the doorknob. A small smile formed when she realized she hadn't even locked it. They could've simply turned the knob and walked in on her.

Bristol shoved her hair back from her face, straightened her spine, and opened the door.

"Sorry about that," she said without looking at either of them. "I had to pee."

"Do you always talk to yourself when you pee?" Keegan asked, clearly skeptical.

"Only sometimes. When I've had too much—" Nope. Not going to lie.

For one, it was wrong. And two, if they honestly believed it, they could use it against her later.

Without looking back at them, she headed for the front door.

"Thanks again for bringin' me home. If you can't figure out what's wrong with the car, I'll just have someone else pick it up." She opened the door, stood there staring out into the night. No way would she risk looking at either one of them. "Just let me know."

Silence.

No footsteps, no nothing. Their response was complete silence.

Which meant she had to look back to see what they were doing.

When she did, she saw them standing nearly shoulder to shoulder, arms crossed over their chests, watching her as though she might break into a million tiny pieces.

Truth was, she wasn't so sure she wouldn't.

Kaden dropped his arms and moved toward her. Rather than back away from him, Bristol stood her ground, focused on her breathing. She could probably face off with Keegan with less risk of falling apart because with him she could draw from the well of anger that boiled inside her. Unfortunately, he remained where he was.

She lowered her gaze, studying the hideous mauve carpet.

"Bristol…"

"Hmm?"

Kaden's warm hand curled around her cheek, his thumb sliding beneath her chin, gently tipping her head back.

It was a childish move, but she closed her eyes so she didn't have to look at him. Only way to save herself.

"Talk to us. Did somethin' happen?"

"No. Of course not. I'm just tired." That much was true. She was exhausted. Both mentally and physically.

His fingers brushed her cheek. Just a light graze that made her chest clench painfully tight.

Do not fall apart. Do not fall apart.

"You should really…" Bristol breathed in and out a few times, slow and steady. Holding back the sobs although they tore at her chest. "You should go."

His hand firmed on her cheek and she opened her eyes.

Stupid, stupid, *stupid* move on her part, because the instant she saw the concern on his handsome face, the tears spilled over.

The next thing she knew, Bristol was in his arms, her face buried in his shirt. Every ounce of emotion she'd bottled up for the past month boiled over. Between her broken heart and the news she'd learned just a couple of days ago, it was a wonder she hadn't lost it sooner.

The fact that Kaden didn't bombard her with questions helped, but it wasn't enough. The emotional chaos chose to use this outlet now that it was available. She clung to him, holding on tight, scared to let go. This was where she'd wanted to be for so long now and here they were.

"I'm sorry, Bristol. So fuckin' sorry."

Keegan.

He was behind her, his hand warm on her shoulder, his words spoken softly near her ear.

A sob ripped through her. Did he not know he had the power to break her? He was *not* supposed to be *nice*.

"Come here," Keegan whispered, the torment in his voice too much.

She cried harder, then spun around and slammed her head into the brick wall of his chest, throwing her arms around him. There was nothing for him to apologize for. What had happened that night … well, it had happened. And there was nothing they could do to change it. Nothing at all.

But she wasn't losing it over what happened all those weeks ago. Did it hurt? Absolutely. She'd spent the past five weeks in a daze, going through the motions, focusing on putting one foot in front of the other and ignoring the pain in her chest brought on by the jagged pieces left of her heart. It wasn't easy, but she was managing.

Or she had been.

"We need to talk about that night," Kaden said softly from behind her. "If for nothing else, we need closure."

Closure?

Bristol didn't want closure. It was too late for that.

"That's not…" She fought to level her breathing, releasing the death grip she had on Keegan's shirt. "That's not what this is. I mean, yes. It is, but it isn't. I…"

Crap. How in the world was she going to explain this?

"Talk to us," Keegan insisted, his big hands gripping her shoulders and shifting her back.

Bristol swiped the tears away with the backs of her knuckles then with her fingers.

You have to tell them, Bristol. They deserve to know.

Rex's words rang in her head and they helped to calm the storm. She'd needed someone to lean on, and since he was her oldest and dearest friend, she'd gone right to him although she swore she wouldn't. Not only had Rex listened and consoled her, he'd also encouraged her to talk to Kaden and Keegan. It was her intention to do so, but she hadn't yet figured out that plan.

But here they were. What better time than the present, right?

She managed to take a step back, feeling a little steadier. When she looked up at them both, she swallowed the tears that threatened to come.

Rex was right. They did deserve to know. She just didn't think now was the right time to tell them. Maybe tomorrow. When she was calmer. When she'd gotten some sleep. When...

"I'm..." What she meant to say was *I'm better now, thank you.* What came out was, "I'm pregnant."

They cast quick looks at one another then their attention returned to her. Kaden stepped forward, cupped her face, and said the one thing she never, ever, *ever* would've predicted he would say.

"Please tell us that's a good thing."

Yep.

More tears.

If KEEGAN HAD EVER BEEN AT A loss for words, he couldn't remember it.

Right now ... well, hell, he'd be hard-pressed to tell someone his full name and birthdate.

Pregnant.

He'd always wondered how some guys reacted to instances such as this. An accidental pregnancy. Unplanned at the very least because, yes, there was always a risk, but seriously. They were always safe. Always. Whenever he'd thought about what might happen if some woman sprung that sort of news on him, he'd always felt a little queasy.

So why not now?

God, he had no fucking clue.

He knew he should've been freaking out, probably backing up to the door, asking for a do-over, because there was no way this could be possible. They'd had sex once. One freaking time and they'd used condoms. Of course, there was always the possibility one of the condoms had broken. He had no idea because he'd been so pissed off that night, he hadn't bothered to pay attention.

Pregnant.

"Let's sit," Kaden said to Bristol, leading her over to the ugly flower couch.

Sit. Yes. Probably a good idea.

Before he could guide her down, Bristol spun around to face Kaden while Keegan stood there, still dumbfounded.

"That's it? That's all you have to say?" She sounded incredulous.

"What would you like us to say?" Kaden asked, his tone a bit surprised but still calm.

"I don't know." She glanced his way. "What about you?"

Him?

What about him?

He didn't know his own fucking name.

She must have recognized his confusion because she tacked on, "You're not gonna ask if it's yours?"

"If it wasn't, would you be tellin' us this?" he asked because, you know, that seemed logical.

"Well, no."

Keegan shrugged and he felt a little better. "Then there's your answer."

Her gaze bounced between them. "You have nothin' else to say? Not 'how did this happen, Bristol?'"

"Seems pretty self-explanatory," they said at the same time.

Bristol's eyes were wide, her shock evident.

Keegan knew how she felt. He was shocked at his own response, too.

"But it was only one time," she argued, as though they'd brought this news to *her* doorstep.

Keegan realized his brother was simply staring at her.

When she looked at him as though expecting some sort of rationalization, Keegan said, "I didn't pay all that much attention in sex ed, I'll admit, but what I do recall is that it only takes once." He lifted his eyebrows. "Am I wrong?"

"Well, no," she bit out. "But we used condoms."

"Which are only ninety-eight percent effective," Kaden challenged.

What he said. And if they took into account they were both fucking her at the same time, pulling out repeatedly, two times one divided by ninety-eight percent, carry the... Oh, who the fuck was he kidding? He didn't know the math for that. But it actually wasn't all that difficult to believe that this could've happened. After that one amazing, incredible night...

Bristol huffed and eased down onto the couch, drawing Keegan from his wandering thoughts.

Kaden took a seat beside her, but Keegan remained on his feet. He wasn't sure sitting was a good idea just yet. For one, his hands were shaking, and he was a bit out of sorts. Not from the news, though. Which was really fucking odd. He should've been panicked or at the very least defensive. He was neither. More like nervous because what he said to her from this point forward would have to make up for what he'd done before. As much as he wanted to pretend he'd doubted whether she would stick around, he knew deep down it was all him. His own insecurities, his fears ... they'd gotten the best of him and he had royally fucked shit up.

But this ... this could be his second chance.

"When did you find out?" his brother asked.

"Earlier in the week. But I went to the doctor yesterday. Just to, you know, confirm it."

"Then why were you drinkin' at the bar?" Keegan wondered aloud, then shook his head when he realized that came out like an accusation.

"It was Sprite," Bristol said, waving off the question.

Well, that made sense.

"I didn't know how I was gonna tell you," she said softly. "I definitely didn't plan it to go like this, but I knew I had to. I went out tonight to try to get my head on straight, hoping to spend some time with my friends before I had to broach the difficult subject." Bristol looked at each of them. "They don't know, by the way. My friends. I haven't told them yet. Well, no one but Rex. I needed someone's perspective and he's my oldest and dearest friend. I trust him."

Rex knew? Before they did?

"He said I needed to tell you, that you deserved to know."

Keegan noticed the way she continued to say *you*. Not *y'all*. She was speaking to them as though they were one.

Keegan did some simple math in his head. "That makes you, what? Four weeks along?"

"Five." Bristol glanced between them. "I went to the doctor to be sure. He wanted to do an ultrasound, but I asked him if we could wait. Until next week. I ... uh ... I figured I would tell you by then. That way, in case you wanted to go with me..."

Admittedly, Keegan knew more pregnancy terminology than he should, but that was because he was around when Zoey was pregnant with Ethan and Beau's triplets. He'd heard more than his fair share of details during that experience, so he knew an ultrasound was some kind of x-ray thing the doctor did to see the baby.

"He said we could do a DNA test if you want," she continued. "I wouldn't blame you. I mean, I haven't been with anyone else. Certainly not since you and ... well, it was a really, really long time before that night."

"How long?" he asked, more for his own curiosity. He liked the idea that Bristol hadn't been with any man but them in quite some time.

Her eyes narrowed.

"I didn't mean it like that," he said defensively, tacking on a smile.

"That's his alpha caveman comin' out," Kaden explained. "The idea of no man touchin' you and all that."

"Ah." There was a barely there hint of a smile. "Anyway, if you want, we can schedule to get—"

"It's not necessary," Keegan told her. "I doubt there's a chance they can determine exactly which of us is the father."

Her eyes locked on his. "I wasn't ... I didn't..." She sighed. "I guess I'm a little screwed up, because in my head, you're both the father. I mean, what we did ... how we did it..."

"And the fact we're identical twins," Kaden noted.

"Yeah. That, too."

The three of them were quiet for a moment.

"I know we didn't leave things on the best of terms, but I figured you'd want to be part of the baby's life," she said softly.

"We want to be part of your life," Kaden corrected. "And the baby's."

When Bristol looked up at him as though looking for him to say something, too, Keegan thought for a brief moment that he might cry. And he didn't cry. Ever.

He was the reason they were at this point.

Not the pregnancy. That was the three of them together.

But it had been his irrational response to her that had sent her running and kept them apart for the past five weeks. There was no doubt about it, he'd been miserable since that night, since he'd opened his big fucking mouth and shot his chances with her all to hell.

"That's not what I'm askin' for," Bristol said, her eyes on him. "I told you earlier, I won't ask anything of you, Keegan."

He had no idea what he could possibly do to earn her forgiveness, but Keegan didn't want her to do this alone. Nor did he want to only be part of the baby's life. Like Kaden, he wanted to be part of hers. The three of them, together.

When his brain gave his legs direction, they actually worked, carrying him closer to her. He shoved the cheap brass coffee table out of the way and eased down to his knees in front of her. With her sitting on the couch and him kneeling on the floor, they were almost the same height.

His intention had been to beg her to give them a chance, but as soon as he was that close, he couldn't resist the urge to kiss her. So he pulled her to the edge of the cushion, settled himself between her thighs, and fused his mouth to hers. To his relief, she didn't push him away, didn't act surprised. In fact, Bristol kissed him back, their tongues doing a slow, sensual slide, hesitant at first but quickly gaining speed.

Keegan's entire body hardened in that moment. More so than it had when he'd danced with her a short time ago. There was no tension in her body now. Bristol was pliant, her arms wreathing his neck as she inched closer until she nearly fell off the couch onto the floor. Not that he would've allowed that to happen.

"Kaden…"

"Right here, darlin'," he whispered, bumping Keegan with his knee as he moved closer to her.

Because he was inclined to share everything with Kaden, Keegan released her mouth, then observed as Kaden picked up where he'd left off.

"We should take this slow," Kaden said when they came up for air.

Always the cautious one, his brother.

But he was right, they really should take—

"Or not," she said, reaching for Keegan again.

Okay, yeah. What she said.

This time the kiss was explosive, a clash of tongues and teeth, the two of them attempting to make up for lost time. Keegan surged to his feet, Bristol's legs wrapped around his hips.

"Bedroom," he rumbled against her mouth.

Her arm moved and he assumed she was pointing out the way, but he wasn't paying any attention, so he started walking anyway. He took the short hallway off the living room, grateful it was the right direction, and ended up in an empty bedroom.

"Other one," Bristol said with a raspy laugh before kissing him again.

He made it to the other room, flipped on the light, and was glad to see there was a bed.

Nothing fancy, just a mattress and box spring, and not very big, but a bed, nonetheless.

Besides her, it was the only other thing they needed.

Chapter Thirteen

WHEN SHE HAD COME OUT OF THE bathroom earlier, Bristol had planned to send them on their way. When she was alone, she would've shored up her nerves and prepared herself to address the situation with them tomorrow. Or the next day. Within a week, for sure.

She had not intended to blurt out the news she'd been carrying around for the past few days. Ever since she'd broken down and taken a pregnancy test on Tuesday, Bristol had been a mess, but she'd managed to hold it together. Even after she'd made an appointment and the doctor confirmed what the little plastic stick had told her—yes, she was definitely pregnant—she hadn't cried, hadn't panicked.

But just one sympathetic look from these two and she was a goner.

However, she hadn't expected that little revelation to result in Keegan carrying her to her bedroom, Kaden just a few steps behind them.

As much time as she had spent ignoring them, pretending she didn't want them with a passion that made absolutely no sense, she had expected it would take some time before they could make it back around to even being friends. The idea of being lovers again … that honestly hadn't crossed her mind.

But here they were, and not being with them wasn't something she wanted to think about. She needed this connection because she'd missed it, missed *them*.

When Keegan set her on her feet, she dropped her arms, straightened her shirt. And when Kaden came around to join them, she turned to face him. Looking up, she saw the heat in his blue-gray eyes, the hunger that matched her own. But there was something else, something more.

Would it make a difference if I told you I love you?

She could still hear his words from that night. She'd replayed them over and over in her head for weeks now, always changing the ending. In none of those fictional scenarios had she turned him away the way she had in reality. That had been the final nail in her heart, the one that had splintered her into pieces. However, they were a package deal, and with the way Keegan had treated her, Bristol had known it wouldn't work. She hadn't wanted to get her hopes up.

And here they were.

Her second chance.

This was what she wanted, what she'd been thinking and dreaming about since the first and only night they'd been together. Longer. Even before that, Bristol had always known deep down that she would fall for them if she allowed herself to.

"I'm sorry," she whispered, doing her best to keep the tears at bay. "For turning you away."

"It's in the past."

Maybe, but it was still something they would have to move beyond.

In true Kaden fashion, he was gentle when he cupped her face and brushed his thumb over her cheek. His eyes implored hers, the intensity making her feel naked although she was still fully clothed.

"Tell us what you want," he said softly, cupping both sides of her neck.

"I don't wanna tell you," she answered. "You already know."

He continued to stare at her, the heat of his body warm against her front while Keegan moved in behind her. Her knees weakened when Keegan's big hands cupped her waist.

"Then how 'bout we tell you what *we* want," Keegan suggested.

Yes. That was a fantastic idea.

Bristol found herself nodding.

"No more games," Kaden stated softly.

"No more excuses," Keegan added.

Kaden spoke again. "We're gonna take this one minute at a time."

Clearly they'd given this some thought.

Then Keegan. "The only people who matter are the three of us."

"This isn't temporary," Kaden said. "We're all in this together or we're not in it at all."

"I'm in," she said, her voice stronger than she'd expected.

"You're never gonna wonder just how much we want you, Bristol," Kaden whispered.

"Startin' now," Keegan added.

How he did it, she wasn't sure, but in a move nearly too swift to process, Kaden swept her right off her feet, lowering her to the bed, coming over her, his mouth finding hers. And in that moment, Bristol lost herself in him. The entire world faded away, centering on this man's mouth moving against hers, his tongue lapping at hers, his hands gently caressing as he shifted off of her, lying at her side.

The bed dipped, another warm body joined them, and then Bristol was looking over at Keegan. His eyes were intense, but his mouth was gentle when he leaned down and sealed it to hers. But those gentle lips firmed, his body hardening, their need and hunger seeming to align.

Keegan's kiss was hot, demanding, and exactly what she expected from him. She moaned, unable to hold it in, because kissing them, as odd as it was to be kissing two men, was exquisite. As mind-numbingly perfect as it had been the first time they were together. Similar, yet uniquely different. She felt alive again and she didn't want the feeling to end.

When she couldn't bear it any longer, reaching for them, eager to touch and explore, she found Keegan pulling back. They each took one of her hands, lifting her arms upward, over her head.

"Don't move," Kaden whispered, leaning in and kissing her lips.

As much as she wanted to touch them, she was curious as to where this was going, so she left her hands where they were, watched them both intently.

"Do you trust us, Bristol?" Kaden asked.

It was in his eyes that she saw so much. More than she ever expected to see, and this wasn't the first time. The way he looked at her, she'd always felt like the only person in the room when he pinned his gaze on her. And here, in her bedroom, it felt decidedly more intimate, like a connection had been made.

"Yes," she whispered, nodding her head as though he might not understand the word and she desperately wanted them to continue.

She sucked in air when she felt a warm hand slide beneath her shirt, spanning her stomach. It was sinfully erotic because she knew it wasn't Kaden's hand touching her, but it was his face she was looking at.

It was intense, this feeling, knowing she had the attention of both of these ridiculously hot men, seeing the hunger in their eyes, hearing the rasp of their breaths. She had relived that night in Keegan's bed over and over again, never believing she would find herself with them again, but here they were. That night had been the most intense, the most erotic night of her life. She wanted to relive it again and again. Tonight, tomorrow night. For the foreseeable future. And it seemed they were intent on giving it to her.

"This isn't only about sex," Kaden said.

"Although there's gonna be a lot of that goin' on," Keegan added. "We've got a lot of time to make up for."

She glanced over at him, sucked in a breath when Kaden leaned down and kissed the underside of her arm.

"Is that what you want?" Keegan asked.

Again, the sensation of looking at one of them while feeling the other was erotic, had her breath lodging in her throat.

Bristol's entire body trembled, her hips jutting up from the bed. She needed to be touched. Somewhere, everywhere. It didn't matter. She was coiling tightly, her body poised to explode, and she needed them—one or both, she didn't care—to do something about it.

And she needed it *now*.

"All you hafta do is say yes, darlin'. It's that easy," Keegan said.

Did he not understand there wasn't anything easy about this? When she said yes, because she most definitely would, there was the potential that they would run roughshod over her heart. There was no doubt in her mind she had already fallen for them both, her heart as invested as her body.

"Say yes," he urged.

"Yes," she mumbled. "God yes."

Keegan's masculine groan had her body catching fire, the way his lips sealed to hers, his tongue gliding so easily into her mouth. Bristol moaned, opening to allow him entry, her tongue joining the mix. She inhaled his intoxicating scent knowing she was doomed. One word. One single word had no doubt altered the course of her life even if she didn't know how much yet.

Before she was ready, Keegan pulled back. His stormy blue eyes scanned her face once again as his thumb brushed her cheek. "I hope you're ready for us, darlin'."

She wasn't. That was a given.

"Because there's no runnin' from this. Not anymore."

KADEN WAS TEMPTED TO THINK HE WAS dreaming. Only his dreams never quite made it this far. Not when this sexy woman was the leading lady in them.

Truth was, when he saw Bristol at Moonshiners tonight, he'd considered hightailing it out of there. After all, he had spent the past month trying to come up with a foolproof plan that would get her back into their bed for the rest of their days. Only she wouldn't so much as talk to him, so he'd never been able to solidify a plan of action. Not even a one-sided way to get the two of them to hash out this thing between them.

It had pained him not to be able to figure it out, because Kaden was the one who took care of those things. The details.

Of course, Keegan being Keegan, he simply walked up to her and asked her to dance. That was his brother's MO. As though the last time they'd been together hadn't blown up in their faces.

But that was Keegan. He was the risk taker, the one who didn't look before he leaped. Kaden didn't operate like that. He wanted a plan, a path to follow, a decision to be made. Without those, he felt as though he was flailing, the ground yanked out from under him.

Only because he hadn't yet had time to figure out the best route to take had Kaden followed his twin's lead. And here they were. In Bristol's bed because Keegan had made a move, and Kaden was grateful he had. As usual, his brother's timing was impeccable.

She was pregnant.

Even the thought had Kaden's heart squeezing tightly, his hopes once again soaring. This was quite possibly the best news. As though the universe had been on his side all along and now they had something that would tie the three of them together.

He glanced down, watched as Bristol rolled her hips, her chest thrusting upward. He wanted to see her naked, to watch her writhe and moan, all those sexy curves on display, eagerly awaiting his hands, his mouth, his tongue. That night was forever etched in his mind and he wanted another one to add to the collection. And a few hundred more to go along with it.

Fuck. This was going to be over before it started.

"You have a problem with any of it so far?" Keegan asked Bristol, his lips trailing along her jaw.

"No." The rasp in her voice had Kaden's cock jerking behind his zipper.

"We're not runnin' out when this is over," Kaden told her. Told both of them, really.

"No more runnin'," she agreed softly, her body still undulating.

Her blue eyes darted to his face, rolling back when Keegan sucked the skin of her neck.

"Please, Kaden … Keegan," she whispered, her back bowing, her need growing to the point she could no longer hide it.

Kaden placed his hand on her flat belly, slid his fingers downward, dipping them beneath the waistband of her jeans. She had far too many clothes on.

Bristol sucked in a breath, making the denim gap, his fingers sliding lower. He loved the silky-smooth feel of her skin.

"Unbutton them," he instructed, wanting to be sure she was aware of the direction they were headed.

Pulling his hand back, he let it trail down her thigh, gliding gently over her toned legs. He watched the movement, distracted only when her fingers quickly freed the button on her jeans, then lowered the zipper.

"Push 'em down." He let his whiskered chin brush her cheek. "But not off."

Now it was his turn to hold his breath, because fuck, this woman was hot. He'd known she would be, if and when she'd ever let herself go, and she had proven it to them once. He wanted her to prove it again, wanted her to show him just how much she'd missed this.

Kaden could feel her eyes on him as she lifted her hips and shimmied her jeans down over them. He watched as she revealed a sexy pair of silky turquoise panties.

Yep. Blue was his new favorite color.

"Fuck," Keegan whispered, the bed shifting as he pushed to his feet.

Kaden moved, claiming Bristol's mouth once more because he couldn't resist tasting her. He swallowed her soft moans, loving the way she had ignored their request to keep her hands above her head. Now her hands were curling around his head, holding him to her as though he might possibly think about leaving.

"Oh, God," she cried out, pulling her mouth from his.

Kaden lifted his head, glanced down her body to see Keegan at the end of the bed. The man had wasted no time.

While Kaden's view was obstructed, he got the gist of it based on the way Keegan held her legs perpendicular to her body, her toes toward the ceiling. The jeans, pushed down to mid-thigh—still hindered her ability to move, and based on the way she was swirling her hips, she wasn't too happy about that.

"You like that?" Kaden asked Bristol, leaning over her and watching the ecstasy contort her beautiful features.

"Yes … oh, God, yes."

"My turn," Kaden demanded. It wasn't like him to take over, but since he hadn't had the pleasure of licking her pussy the last time they were together, he felt it was his due.

A soft chuckle sounded from Keegan, but then they were trading places so that Kaden was pushing her knees in close to her chest with one hand, tugging her panties aside with the other. His tongue glided between her smooth pussy lips, spread wide because of the position.

The fact that she shaved or waxed was a turn-on like no other. Not simply because there was no hair to contend with but because it meant Bristol had been anticipating this. He knew for a fact she hadn't slept with another man—aside from them—in quite some time despite the fact she'd been flaunting dates earlier in the year. Gossip ran like wildfire within the small town of Coyote Ridge, and he would've heard about any trysts even if he hadn't witnessed her with another man. It was the only reason he'd been able to refrain from pursuing her relentlessly these past couple of years.

Bristol's hips bucked, her back bowing as she tried to get closer to his mouth. He wished he could see her face, that she could watch while he reveled in her sweetness.

He pulled back, said, "Take off her jeans."

And yes, he was well aware that he'd taken control this time unlike last time. But that was the way it worked. They didn't battle for dominance when it came to sharing a woman. They worked in tandem, and right now, Kaden needed to be in control.

When Keegan took hold of her legs, Kaden once again tugged her panties aside and resumed licking and teasing while his brother's movements jarred her body. And when he finally had the denim off, Kaden decided the panties had to go, too.

When that feat was accomplished, Bristol's feet returned to the mattress, this time her knees falling open. She was completely bared to him and he was pretty damn sure he'd died and gone to heaven.

Goddamn, she was beautiful. The way she lifted her head to observe, her eyes flaring when he would spear her with his tongue before suckling her clit.

"Time for the shirt to go," Keegan whispered, staring down at her.

It took some effort because Bristol continued to writhe, but the lightweight sweater finally came off, revealing a matching turquoise bra. As much as he liked it on her, he wanted it off. Keegan evidently had other plans, because rather than remove it, he tugged on the cups, freeing her breasts so that the lovely pale flesh toppled over. Keegan lowered his head, taking one hardened nipple between his lips, sucking gently.

"Oh, God." Bristol squirmed beneath the onslaught, Kaden devouring her cunt, Keegan focused on her tits. Her soft moans grew louder the longer they worked her over until she was panting and groaning, chasing that elusive release.

Kaden focused all his attention on her, wanting to build her up higher before he sent her over. But when he heard his brother's voice, he knew Keegan was going to get her there faster by saying those dirty words she seemed to be fond of.

"Come for us," Keegan growled softly. "Come all over his face, Bristol. Let me hear you."

And when she did, when Kaden's mouth tormented her until she fell over that cliff, he was filled with an emotion he couldn't name.

And to think, they were just getting started.

WHEN BRISTOL FINALLY LET GO, FLYING APART as Kaden suckled her clit, Keegan damn near came in his fucking jeans.

Although it wasn't something they bragged about, Keegan and his brother had been with numerous women over the course of their lives. They'd lost their virginity when they were sixteen to a woman who was well over the legal age. She had introduced them to a world of sexual exploration that had only confirmed their desire to share one woman between them.

And over the years, they'd pleasured many, taken what was freely offered, and enjoyed the no-strings-attached lifestyle.

So this was a first for him.

Not merely because they'd verbally stated this wasn't a one-night thing, nor was it only about sex. No, words were merely words. What he felt for this woman … truthfully, it surprised him. He'd never wanted the *more* that came along with an intense bout of sex. But deny it as he might, with Bristol … he'd come to want more a long time ago even if he'd given up on any hopes of that coming to fruition.

Now that he had her right where he'd dreamed of her being again, he was eager to explore this further, see if there was a chance for that *more* he'd been missing. But first, he wanted to make up for lost time, to lose himself in her again.

After ridding her of her bra because, *come on now*, she looked damn good naked, Keegan watched Bristol's face, the contentment he could see. It gave him hope. Kaden joined them once more and then they were both watching her, that sexy, dazed expression on her face. Her eyes were closed, her mouth open, her chest still rising and falling rapidly, as though that had been the most intense orgasm of her life.

"So, I was thinkin'…" He waited until she looked at him. "You got any board games we can play?"

Bristol's eyes opened wide, making him laugh.

"What? You've got a phobia or somethin'? Allergic to Monopoly?"

Her brows formed a cute little V. "After … *that*, you wanna play a game?"

"Don't you?" he teased.

What he wanted to do was make her comfortable and it seemed to be working.

Considering they hadn't talked to her in weeks, Keegan wasn't sure what to expect. A short time ago, she'd been in tears, and now she was that uninhibited free spirit he remembered from their first night together. Was it that easy? Could they move forward, put the past behind them without some long, drawn-out conversation to go along with it?

Not that he was complaining. Keegan had never been the one for talking. Not with women. He'd never had anything to contribute. Sex was sex. It had nothing to do with love.

But didn't they need to nitpick everything that had gone wrong so they could ensure it went right in the future? That was what a relationship entailed, did it not?

Feigning a casualness his body was most definitely belying, Keegan rolled to his back, tucked his hands beneath his head. If talking was necessary, he was willing to put forth the effort because this was important. Bristol was important.

"So whaddya wanna do now?"

Bristol giggled and to his utter surprise, she was sitting up, then she was straddling his hips, leaning over him, her hair falling down around them both.

"Are you tellin' me you're bored, Keegan Walker?"

He smirked. "What if I am?"

Her eyes flashed with mischief and he laughed.

The bed moved and he felt Kaden's arm against his, his brother having taken up the spot she vacated.

When it came to sex with a woman, they'd never had to plan how it would play out. They were so in tune with one another, it just worked. A couple of women had been put off by that, but Keegan had never thought much of it. No, they didn't touch each other because … *eww*. However, to be intimate with a woman the way they were, it required they be comfortable around one another. And they were. Ultimately, it was about the woman's pleasure, not their own. They derived theirs from pleasing her.

Sliding his hands up Bristol's thighs, Keegan let her smooth skin tease his palms. When she didn't stop him, he ventured higher, his thumbs caressing the crease where her thighs met her torso. Bristol sat up then, inhaling deeply as she stared down to watch his hands move over her.

For a brief moment, he had a mental image of her pregnant, her belly round with their baby. He had never given that much thought, but the idea was a major turn-on.

When she looked up, her gaze shifted to Kaden, and then in a move that surprised him, she repositioned so that she was straddling Keegan's right thigh and Kaden's left.

That was an interesting turn of events, not to mention a highly intoxicating move on her part. Most women didn't quite understand how to include them both at the same time. But that didn't seem to be a problem for Bristol. In fact, it was something she was damn good at. If he didn't know better, he would've said it was natural.

"Touch yourself," Kaden instructed, his voice laced with gravel.

Her eyes darted between their faces momentarily, but then her hands began wandering up over her hips, her belly, pausing to cup her beautiful tits.

Keegan was enraptured, watching as she tweaked her nipples, sighing as she did.

"Lean forward," Keegan stated.

She did.

"A little more," Kaden added.

Bristol shifted forward and he was aware she was being careful because her knees were in prime positions between their legs.

"Keep comin', darlin'," Keegan said with a smile.

Then she was leaning forward, her hands on their shoulders to brace herself as her hair fell down in a silk curtain once more.

When Kaden lifted his head to suckle her breast, Keegan mirrored his brother's movements, licking her other distended nipple until it hardened into a tighter point. Bristol moaned and sighed, leaning down lower as they feasted on her, sucking, licking, nipping. Before long, she was grinding her sweet pussy along their thighs, while Keegan's cock was trying to fight its way out from behind his zipper.

Keegan was entirely focused when Bristol moved, her body tilting because she'd shifted her hand, tugging at his T-shirt while he still had a mouthful of her firm tit.

He took the hint, releasing her before jerking the cotton upward, over his head, and onto the floor. She must've given Kaden the same signal, because he performed the same move, both of them eventually shirtless beneath her. He missed the warmth of her against his lips when she sat up, her gaze trailing down their chests, lower.

When her palm flattened on his stomach, sliding upward, the sensations took over. He loved that she touched them at the same time. Although Bristol came across as a sweet, innocent woman, Keegan suspected deep down, there was a wildcat eager to break free. She spent so much of her time playing for an audience, all those parents who trusted her to care for her children. At some point, she had disregarded her own needs, ignored her own desires in order to ensure she maintained that trust.

Keegan fully intended to be the one to take her on that trip to the wild side, to show her things she'd never imagined, never quite fantasized about. The taboo if you would.

Bristol's movements halted, her head lifting, her gaze meeting first his, then Kaden's. He could see something in her eyes, knew she needed something, but it was imperative that she tell them. The last thing they ever did was make assumptions when it came to interactions such as this. It was easier to take cues from a woman, to let her set the pace.

Keegan knew once they learned more about what she wanted, what she needed, it would be different, but until then, they had to leave it to her to decide where they went from here.

Turned out, she didn't disappoint.

Chapter Fourteen

BRISTOL HAD NEVER FELT QUITE THIS POWERFUL before. And lucky. Yes, that was a good word for it. Not because she didn't think she was worthy, but because laid out before her were two delectable men who drew her attention like no one else.

While their first encounter had been hot and definitely the most intense sex she'd ever had, Bristol never got the chance to visually feast on them the way she wanted to. The first and only time they'd been together, she'd been at their mercy. Now they were at hers. So this time she had every intention of taking her due from them.

Because *seriously*. So. Freaking. Hot.

Never in her life had she met a man, much less two, who could bring her damn near close to drooling. From the arches of their dark eyebrows, the not-too-narrow blades of their noses, those scrumptious lips, to the scruff that lined their jaws and chins... They were exquisite male specimens.

And don't even get her started on their bodies. Lord have mercy, she'd never seen so much lightly-bronzed skin covering ripped and toned muscle, the perfect amount of hair on their chests, the delicious trail that dipped into their jeans.

The jeans she was hoping would come off sooner rather than later.

What thrilled her the most was how powerful and sexy she felt because they seemed to be waiting for her to make a move, as though she could control these two delicious men with a simple touch or a mere glance. Only, she wasn't sure what she wanted because when you were presented with a feast, how were you supposed to know where to start?

Hmm.

Should've been an easy question and perhaps it would've been if Bristol wasn't feeling a tad overwhelmed by it all. So much so, she was confused about which direction to go next. Her body was aflame. It didn't matter that she'd survived an orgasm that had shattered her into a million pieces before she'd been drawn back together. She still felt empty inside and she longed to be filled, to be consumed.

Because she sensed they had far more patience than she, Bristol decided to go with the easy request. "Please just ... touch me."

They glanced at each other briefly and then they were sitting up, their lips grazing her shoulders, hands cupping her breasts, her ass. It was overwhelming in the best possible way.

"Lean back," Kaden urged.

Bristol planted her hands behind her, one on each of their knees, bowing her back. Once again, they were lapping and laving at her oh-so-sensitive nipples, drawing her into their mouths, igniting nerve endings she didn't even realize she had.

She'd never been all that fond of her breasts. They weren't big but they weren't small, and yes, they were surprisingly sensitive. Sometimes too much so, but Kaden and Keegan seemed to know exactly how much pressure to apply with their lips and their teeth, how much suction was necessary to tighten that invisible line that went from her breasts to her clit.

All thoughts about the past, the future slipped away on a breathless moan. Nothing mattered except for this moment, right here, right now.

"Please," she whimpered, her sex clenching with the desperation she could feel building inside her. If they didn't do something, she feared she was going to explode.

"Tell us," Keegan encouraged. "What do you need, darlin'?"

She considered that momentarily as she panted. "The jeans have to go."

They wasted no time shifting her aside, getting to their feet, and ridding themselves of their remaining clothes. Their movements were so in sync, she wondered if they even realized how truly identical they still were.

When they were reclined on the pillows once more, Kaden said, "And now?"

"You," she told them, hoping they understood it was in the general sense. "Inside me."

It was obvious they were aiming for casual, but a rough groan escaped both of them at the same time, the sound in stereo, making her swoon. She loved that she could do that to them, that they seemed as hot for her as she was for them.

She only hoped they had condoms because she didn't. Why would she? Bristol hadn't intended to have sex with anyone; therefore she hadn't felt the need to buy any only for them to expire tucked away in her nightstand.

But wait. Did they need condoms?

"I'm clean," she blurted, realizing how much she wanted to feel them inside her without the barrier.

Kaden stared into her eyes as he sat up once again as everything seemed to slow down.

The intensity, the heat of the moment was still there, but there was something else, too.

"We are, too," he said softly, his eyes so warm.

She believed him. More importantly, she trusted him. The man had told her he loved her. Before, anyway. He had always put her first and Bristol knew he wouldn't lie.

"We … uh … don't need condoms," she said, feeling her face flame. "If, you know, y'all are okay with it."

More masculine groans sounded, and she took that as approval.

There was movement then, Kaden getting to his feet while she toppled over onto Keegan. He rolled her onto her back, his upper body coming over hers as their lips melded. She kissed him, lost in his exquisite taste, the delectable way he played her mouth, teasing, taunting, promising so much more. He kissed better than any man she'd ever kissed before. Save for Kaden, that was. Then again, she hadn't kissed all that many men in her life.

Just when she thought things were heating from simmer to boil, Keegan lifted his head, staring down into her eyes.

The look on his face stole her breath. His stormy blue eyes were bright, his jaw tense. He held her in his gaze as he cupped her face with one hand, his thumb lightly brushing along her jaw. He took a breath, let it out, and the words that followed made her heart squeeze.

"I'm so fucking sorry, Bristol."

The words were spoken so low she knew they were meant only for her, and for whatever reason, that hit her right in the solar plexus.

"Me, too," she replied, her voice just as low.

Their gazes held and she hoped he understood her silent request for them to start anew. Life was too damn short for them to hang on to the pain and anger from that one overwhelming night.

And then his mouth was on hers once more.

Keegan groaned as he rolled so she was atop him once more, his work-rough hands gliding over her back, sliding down, cupping her ass, and jerking her against him.

The hard ridge of his erection pressed intimately against her sex, teasing her. While she ached for him to fill her, she didn't let that stop her from grinding herself along that thick ridge, seeking the friction that would douse the blaze consuming her.

Because she feared she would combust if she didn't do something, Bristol took the reins, breaking free from his lips, trailing her mouth down his jaw, his neck, his collarbone. She ventured lower, licking and kissing his warm skin, inhaling the sexy male scent that went right to her head. The light dusting of hair on his chest tickled her nose, made her body pulse with need.

She had to shift lower, inching backward until she was straddling his shins, his thick, hard cock bobbing proudly before her.

From there, she was left with only one option.

While he was naked and laid out before her like a feast, Bristol remained frozen, her eyes locked on the long, thick stalk of flesh between his thighs. The sight brought back the memories of that night, the exquisite way they'd taken her at the same time. She'd never experienced anything quite that amazing.

"Bristol."

Her eyes shot up to Keegan's face. She could see his concern, figured she better do something to ensure he knew she was all right. She reached for his cock, wrapping her fingers around him. He was hard as steel, smooth as silk. His groan sent a frisson of heat through her.

They both watched her hands as she stroked him. Down, then up. Slowly. Bristol was both fascinated and terrified, eager and hesitant. Thankfully, her need won out, because the next thing she knew, she was leaning down so she could press her lips to the head of his cock, licking lightly.

Another groan, then his hand reached for her, sliding over her head in a touch that was both reverent and desperate.

"Ah, fuck," Keegan groaned low in his throat when she opened her mouth around him. "Oh, shit, Bristol. Baby…"

She took him in deep, her lips wrapping around him, sliding downward. She couldn't even get half of him in her mouth, but he didn't seem bothered by it. Bristol curled her fingers around the base of his cock, stroking him in tandem with her mouth while he rocked his hips.

Part of her couldn't believe she was doing this. She thought she would never experience the same sort of pleasure they'd given her that night. Bristol had even had regrets that she hadn't had a chance to explore them more.

Now she was desperate to explore them both, to spend the rest of the weekend … hell, the rest of the month, right here in this bed getting to know them on the most intimate of levels.

If only.

AROUSED. EXHILARATED. EAGER.

Those were all words Kaden would use to describe himself as he watched as Bristol took Keegan's cock between her lips, sliding her mouth over him. For a second, he would've sworn he could feel the silky glide of her tongue along his flesh as though she was doing the same to him.

Glancing at his brother, he watched Keegan's face contort with pleasure, his eyes rolling back as he tangled his fingers in Bristol's hair, hips gently rolling as he pushed deeper into her mouth.

They were a sight, that was for sure.

And while he wished her mouth was on him, Kaden wasn't jealous. He'd never been jealous of Keegan. For whatever reason, this worked for them. It wasn't about who got the most attention, more so about what the combination of the two of them could do for her.

While Bristol explored his twin, Kaden stepped back to observe. It was something he'd always enjoyed. He couldn't explain it, but he felt the same now as he watched Bristol. She was naked and beautiful as she pleasured his brother, her soft moans and Keegan's grunts and groans the backdrop to the sexy interlude.

Rather than join them and risk interrupting, Kaden stepped up to the end of the bed, right behind Bristol. Because she had worked her way down Keegan's long legs, her ass was right there, in the perfect position for his hands to roam. It was all he could do not to grab her hips and thrust deep inside, to sate the growing ache inside him.

As it was, Bristol was paying him no mind, seemingly oblivious to the fact he was there with them, but the instant he touched her, Bristol moaned, wiggling her butt, shifting farther back in invitation.

She definitely knew he was there and that knowledge warmed him another few degrees.

Unable to resist, he slid his hands over her soft, smooth skin, gliding up her spine, pausing at her neck then working his way down and around so he could cup her breasts, trailing his lips between her shoulder blades. Encouragement came from her eager moans and the way she rocked back against him. He wanted to touch her everywhere, to taste her again and again. It wouldn't be enough, he knew. It would never be enough.

Leaning forward, he pressed his chest to her back, propping himself up with one fist on the mattress while sliding the other between her thighs, seeking the heat of her.

Bristol paused what she was doing, shifting her legs wider, her back arching. "Oh, God. Kaden…"

He fucking loved when she said his name. It was a reminder that she was aware of who was with her. That it was them pleasuring her, bringing her to new heights.

Kaden slipped one finger inside the tight clasp of her pussy, teased her as she pushed herself upright, forcing Kaden to stand as he continued to finger her slick pussy.

"Don't stop," she pleaded, pressing back against him, grinding her hips down as he fingered her.

From over her shoulder, he could see Keegan watching her, the heat in his gaze as he observed. Keegan took up where Bristol left off, stroking himself while he watched the show, and for a second, Kaden felt as though he could see Bristol through his brother's eyes.

"Please, Kaden… Oh, God, yes."

He gave her what she requested, pushing two fingers into her tight sheath while she ground her hips downward, taking his fingers in deep.

"More," she bit out, her tone bordering on urgent. "I need more."

So he gave her more. Planting his palm on her back, he urged her down to the bed then situated her so she was in her original position, kneeling over Keegan.

"Suck him," Kaden instructed, his voice edged with lust.

"Oh, yeah, baby," Keegan grunted. "Suck me, Bristol. Just like that."

Bristol whimpered when Kaden shifted her knee, effectively spreading her legs wider.

Looking up at Keegan over Bristol's head, he met his brother's gaze, nudged his chin forward, urging Keegan to shift back a bit.

His brother did, the move allowing Bristol to lean forward more, providing a better angle.

And then he was right where he wanted to be, sliding his cock along the glistening seam of her sex, her slickness coating him, easing his way as he glided over her clit until she was moaning softly, a sexy sound that had his cock jerking.

Fuck.

He grunted from the sensations of her bare flesh against his. He couldn't remember the last time he'd gone without a condom. Years, he knew. And there was nothing like feeling a woman's silky heat on his shaft. More accurately, this woman's.

Once more he met Keegan's gaze so his brother knew what to expect, then he gripped Bristol's hip with one hand, his cock with the other as he pushed the head into the blessed heat of her body. Slow. So fucking slowly he entered her, her inner muscles clasping tightly as he worked himself deeper.

He was pretty sure he stopped breathing as he gripped her other hip, pulling her back as he stroked into her, deeper, deeper still.

Heat rolled through him, from the head of his dick up through every inch of him, the pleasure making his head spin.

Bristol stopped moving, allowing Kaden to control her movements. Another moan escaped her as she arched her back, her knees spreading wider, offering herself to him.

"God yes." She bowed her back more, pushing her ass toward him, taking him deeper without him having to move. "Kaden … oh, God."

Fuck. Just hearing her say his name was more than he could bear.

"More?" The word was ripped from his throat, the pleasure nearly unbearable.

"Yes. Please."

He retreated slowly, lurched forward, driving in deeper, his brain turning to mush as the blistering heat of her pussy enveloped him. She was so fucking tight, so fucking wet. Kaden rocked his hips, her inner muscles clenching around him, strangling his cock in the most exquisite way. He knew it was only a matter of minutes before he was going to come. Hell, he wasn't even sure he could wait long enough to make her come first.

"Look at me," Keegan urged, reaching forward and tipping Bristol's chin up. "Watch me while he fucks you."

Bristol's upper body lifted as she propped herself up with her hands, the shift in position causing her pussy to clamp down on him.

Kaden gripped her hips, pulling her back as he impaled her, driving forward until he bottomed out inside her. He admired the sleek line of her back, all that smooth ivory skin while he fought to control his breathing, fighting the sensations that tore through him. His gaze trailed lower, observing the way his cock disappeared into the heaven of her body and he damn near lost it.

Several more times, he let the slick walls of her pussy squeeze him as he thrust in and out, her juices easing his way. Then he began to move, faster, harder, deeper. She met him thrust for thrust, this hellcat taking all he could give her, his name falling from her lips even as she maintained eye contact with his twin.

Kaden bit the inside of his cheek, staving off his release because he wanted to feel her pussy lock on him when she came. He fucked her with a fury he'd never known before. Hard, fast, again and again, sweat dripping down his forehead as he watched his cock tunnel into the sweetest pussy he'd ever known. The next time he was inside her, he would be beneath her. Like the first time. He would be the one making eye contact, letting her see him as he became one with her.

When Bristol cried out his name on a long, throaty moan, her pussy squeezing him, it triggered his release, an orgasm so powerful it damn near knocked him off his feet.

He pulled out, stumbled back, and before he could right himself, Bristol was impaled on Keegan, a cry of ecstasy escaping.

It was all he could do to walk around to the side of the bed and fall into it, but it was all that was necessary. The next thing he knew, Bristol was leaning over him, her mouth seeking his as she whimpered. Although he couldn't see beyond the fall of her hair, he knew Keegan had taken over, was fucking her from beneath, filling her to overflowing. All the while, Bristol tried to maintain the kiss until her body was being jarred too much.

When she lifted her head, he cupped her cheek, maintaining eye contact, watching her expressions flitter across her face as Keegan brought her to climax twice more before his twin came with a bed-rattling groan.

KEEGAN WAS CONTENT TO LIE IN BRISTOL'S darkened room, his big body hugging the edge of the queen-size mattress, the sexy woman who'd blown his mind a few minutes ago snuggled up at his side.

Unlike the last time he'd found himself like this, he didn't panic, didn't open his big fucking mouth and say something stupid.

No, he just remained there, catching his breath and letting his body return to its normal state. That had been incredible, there was no denying it. As good as, if not better than their first night together. It was good to know he hadn't been imagining the chemistry between them.

Bristol moved closer, her hand sliding over his chest, her fingers brushing his neck.

"You awake?" she whispered.

"Yeah."

Her soft sigh wasn't quite as content as he would've hoped it would be after that, but he did his best not to read anything into it.

"I need for us to keep this between us for now," she said.

Keegan tensed and she pulled away immediately, pushing up to look down at him.

"It's not bad," she added quickly. "Just until I can figure out how to deal with it."

"It?"

He watched her face, hated that he saw something very similar to regret there.

"This relationship."

There was movement on the other side of the bed. Kaden was evidently awake.

"And the baby?" Kaden asked. "Are we supposed to keep that quiet, too?"

For once his brother didn't sound like the easygoing, laid-back man Keegan knew him to be.

"For now, yes."

"We can't tell our family?" Keegan knew he sounded pissed but that was because he was quickly inching in that direction.

Bristol leaned in, her lips brushing his. "Just for a little while. Please. I know it won't be easy, but…"

He waited for her to explain.

She didn't.

"It's not what you think," she tacked on, kissing him again, softly, slowly.

Oh, it most definitely was.

And Keegan wasn't sure whether he should be thrilled or worried that she was willing to seduce him in order to get what she wanted.

Chapter Fifteen

TRAVIS WOKE EARLY ON SATURDAY MORNING. BEFORE the sun, before even the kids had woken.

He'd spent last night in his recliner, having stayed up late with Kate, watching a movie until she fell asleep in his lap. At that point, he'd relocated her to her bed and headed for his own. Before he'd gotten his bedroom door open, he'd heard the sounds coming from inside. Kylie's sexy moans, Gage's raspy grunts.

Rather than interrupt their stolen moments, he'd gone back downstairs and settled in to think. He'd obviously fallen asleep.

To avoid waking the rest of the house, Travis tugged on his boots and headed for the resort. He had a shower in his office, which he took advantage of, changing into a spare set of clothes he kept there.

Now, he was sitting at his desk, finalizing the resort's guest list for this year's New Year's Bash. It was late notice, but he knew a lot of their guests thought of this place as a spur-of-the-moment indulgence, somewhere they could sneak off to when that coveted invitation appeared in their mailbox. Rarely did anyone ever decline the invitation.

Last year they had forgone doing anything for the resort in lieu of making it a family affair. The Walkers had descended on the resort for Christmas, making it impossible to plan for a resort celebration, so this year, Travis was dedicating the holidays to the guests, making up for lost time, so to speak.

Not necessarily because he felt he owed the guests anything. No, this was personal. Selfish, he figured was a good description. Until he found Juliet Prince, he was no good to his own family. Hell, he could hardly look his daughter in the eye knowing he had failed her. Epically. And until he brought that woman to justice, proved to Kate she was safe once again, that she didn't have to be held just to fall asleep, Travis knew he had to stay focused.

He reviewed the final name on the list, added one more for good measure, then shot the email over to Sawyer, who would handle ensuring the invitations went out. On Monday, of course. When normal people worked.

Travis had just hit send when his cell phone buzzed on his desk.

He glanced over at the screen. It was home calling, which meant Kylie since Gage preferred text as his method of communication.

"Hello."

"Hey." Her voice was warm and concerned. "You slipped out early."

Leaning back in his chair, Travis closed his eyes. "Yeah. I've got stuff to do here."

"You gonna be there long?"

"A while. Why?"

"We were thinkin' we'd take the kids over to your parents for a little while."

"I'm sure they'd like that."

"So we'll see you…?"

"I need a few hours. I'll text you when I'm finishing up."

"Okay."

He could hear the disappointment, but Travis ignored it. He owed Kylie as much as he owed Kate. He knew his wife worried endlessly about that woman still being out there. They were all losing sleep over it.

"Talk to you later."

"I love you, Travis," she said softly.

"Love you, too." He disconnected the call because it was pointless to express his feelings over the phone.

He half expected Gage to stroll in, to smile and tell him to give up for the day. That's what his husband did. Gage kept Travis's spirits up, motivated him to do what needed to be done, ensured he was involved in every aspect of their family life because Travis was often so focused he lost track of time.

But Gage wasn't going to come in, he wasn't going to make an attempt at seduction to get Travis to do what he wanted him to do. In fact, he wasn't even sure Gage ever wanted to talk to him again. They hadn't spoken much in the past week. Aside from sleeping under the same roof, though not necessarily in the same bed. They'd been alternating staying with Kate because she continued to have nightmares, which meant their physical interactions had been limited as well.

It would get back to normal. Eventually. Once he found Juliet Prince and she ended up behind bars or in the ground—his preference was for the latter because his hatred for her was so intense.

Until then, Kylie and Gage could hold down the fort. They were used to this from him. Travis had never pretended to be anything other than what he was. He had a single-minded focus at times, and they knew it was better to simply leave him be until he got it resolved.

And it would be resolved.

Soon, he hoped.

BRISTOL WOKE TO HER CELL PHONE RINGING and Kaden tapping her on the arm.

She took the phone he offered and blindly tapped the screen to answer.

"Hello?"

"Oh, thank Christ," Rex rumbled.

"What?" She rubbed her eyes, yawned. "What's wrong?"

"Why is your car at Moonshiners?" he asked, his gruff tone thick with concern.

Bristol forced her heavy lids to open, peering over at the clock. "Oh, my God, Rex. It's six thirty. On Saturday. Why are you callin' me?"

"Shall I repeat the question?"

Sighing, she relaxed against the warm body she was curled up against, holding the phone to her ear. "Don't worry. My car broke down. I got a ride home."

"Christ, woman. I was scared to death. Who drove you home?"

"Kaden and Keegan."

"Kaden and Keegan?"

"Shall I repeat the answer?" she mimicked.

His tone softened. "Did you tell them?"

"I did."

"And?"

"It's all good," she assured him. "Now, if you don't mind, I'm gonna call you later. After I get some sleep."

With a grumble, Rex disconnected the call.

Bristol smiled when Kaden took the phone from her hand. She snuggled in and drifted back to sleep, hoping she could find her way back to that sexy dream she'd been having.

When she woke the next time, the sun had brightened her bedroom. The first thing she noticed was that she was alone in her bed. No Kaden, no Keegan.

And no clothes.

She listened, attempting to hear noises coming from the other room. Aside from the heater blowing softly from the ceiling vents, Bristol heard nothing else.

It appeared her sexy twins had vacated the premises.

Since there was no note on the nightstand, she reached for her phone, checking to see if maybe they'd texted.

A smile pulled at her mouth when she saw there was a text from Kaden: *Sorry we left, but I didn't want to wake you. Got your car towed. Gonna be a few days to get the part. We'll bring Keegan's truck by so you'll have something to drive in the meantime. Text us when you wake up.*

Sighing, she rolled onto her back and stared up at the ceiling. She really wanted to text him back and tell him it was fine, she didn't need a vehicle. It was the truth. She'd been a bit overdramatic when she said she could walk into town if she needed to, although she was perfectly capable. However, it wouldn't be necessary because she knew Bianca would give her a ride anywhere she needed to go.

So why didn't she?

"Because you want to see them," she whispered.

Because she wanted to be with them, she acknowledged.

And there you had it. Bristol knew it was the most idiotic thing she'd ever done, but she wanted to see them, wanted to spend time with them. She had missed them and these last weeks had been filled with so much regret, she'd hardly slept, barely ate.

It probably wouldn't have been so hard but Bristol had spent the past few years immersed in the Walkers' world, mixing it up with their family, and that included spending a lot of time with Kaden and Keegan around. To not have that...

Needless to say, she hadn't been having a good time. To the point she was an emotional wreck, riding a roller coaster of ups and downs, never realizing that it was her hormones that were in an uproar. It wasn't until early last week when she started feeling queasy. That was when she did the math, realizing she'd missed her period.

Please tell us that's a good thing.

Bristol could still hear Kaden's words, the hope that had been in that one single sentence. Honest to God, she hadn't known what to expect when she told them, but it hadn't been for either of them to accept it so easily. In fact, she was sure they'd come to terms with the news far easier than she had.

Not that she wasn't happy. She was.

Even if they weren't willing to be part of the baby's life, Bristol had always wanted children and she considered this a blessing. As far as raising a child as a single parent, Bristol saw no problem with that. After all, she'd been raised that way. From the time her mother skipped out on them, her father had been her sole provider and she'd turned out just fine.

But for them to want to be a part of it...

She felt the warmth fill her chest, emotions churning in her gut. Tears sprang to her eyes, but she smiled because they weren't sad tears. They were hopeful ones. Kaden and Keegan would make amazing fathers. They were two of the greatest men she knew. They loved their families, they were great with kids, quick to smile, the first to joke and tease, as well as the first to offer a hug when someone needed it. At their core, Kaden and Keegan were exactly what Bristol had always hoped to find in a man.

But that was where the problem lay. They were two men. The same but vastly different, yet still two. And while, sure, she had fascinated about what it would be like to be Kylie in a Travis and Gage sandwich, Bristol wasn't sure she was as strong as Kylie, didn't think she'd have the ability to deal with the gossip and rumors that would most certainly go around about her.

In the same sense, she wanted to be strong and independent like Kylie Walker-Matthews. She wanted to hold her head high and not worry about what others thought of her. Most importantly, she wanted to let her wild side free. She'd never been able to do that before, always maintaining the sweet, polite facade so as to ensure she fit in wherever she went. Bristol wasn't the sort to speak her mind freely, determined to always be politically correct and never ruffle feathers. Sometimes it was a curse, others it was a blessing.

Keegan had been right on the money that first night when he made that statement about what the parents of her students would think. She had a business to worry about, right? The last thing she wanted the parents of her kids to think was that she was some hussy who liked to mix it up with multiple partners. She was terrified of what might happen when it came out that she was pregnant with their baby, and she still didn't know how to go about dealing with it.

What she did know was that she wanted to keep seeing them. Just on the down low for now. While they hadn't seemed entirely pleased by her request, their lack of argument made her believe they would respect her wish. Hopefully she'd be able to get past her hang-up sooner rather than later. After all, she wouldn't be able to hide her pregnancy forever. Eventually she would start showing.

As for right this very minute…

Bristol wanted to spend time with them.

Grabbing her phone, she tapped out a message to both of them in a group text: *If you haven't eaten, I could make something for lunch. You know, as a thank you.*

She sent the text and felt her face flame. She hadn't meant it the way it sounded.

She quickly added: *For my car. To thank you for my car. Not for ... you know.*

Within a minute, she received two responses, at the exact same time: *We'd love to.*

Her heart skipped a beat. Was that how they did everything? Together?

Now that she thought about it, when one was around, the other was usually close by. In fact, she didn't think she'd ever been to a function when only one of them was there. Were they that close? Was that why they were into sharing women?

Funny. Bristol had never really thought about it, though she'd been around the twins enough to have picked up on certain nuances. She'd always considered Braydon and Brendon inseparable, but she knew that wasn't true. Though she'd heard rumors that they'd shared women in their younger years, they'd opted for separation when it came to their families.

She thought about all the times she'd been around Kaden and Keegan, how they interacted with one another. They finished each other's sentences as though they'd had the exact same thought. It was almost eerie, yet oddly fascinating at the same time.

Kinda like their first night together. They'd been so in sync, if it hadn't been for the intermittent pausing so they could alternate, she would've considered them one.

Realizing she could get lost in her thoughts and find herself pressed for time, Bristol forced herself out of bed. She made a beeline for the bathroom.

It took half an hour, but she managed to shower, dry her hair, and apply makeup. Another ten minutes to figure out what to wear before she was making her way out of her bedroom, her mind already going through the list of lunch options. She'd made it across the living room when she heard the deep rumble of an engine out front.

After hurrying to the window, she peeked through the blinds to see Kaden parking his truck behind Keegan's, the two of them getting out.

Her heart fluttered. "Oh, Lord."

What had she been thinking?

Keegan had been expecting a nothing-special sort of day. The kind of Saturday spent getting his chores out of the way and then parking it in front of the television, video game controller in hand. It was how he used to pass the time most weekends, because what else was he going to do? Perhaps it was a tad pathetic, but he didn't much care.

Only, it hadn't started as a nothing-special sort of day.

He'd woken up in Bristol's bed, which made it ... well, pretty extraordinary right off the bat.

Keegan hated that he'd left without waking her, but they had chores at the ranch that couldn't be ignored, so he'd woken Kaden and they'd slipped out just before dawn.

Then Bristol had offered an invitation to lunch and his entire day was suddenly on a new course. He was no longer considering which room they would tackle for renovations or which video game he would conquer, because he was damn sure not the kind of guy who would pick a video game over a woman. He'd seen those videos online where the woman greets her man while he's playing a video game. She's supposedly buck naked behind the camera because it was all about seeing his reaction. One guy—the smart one—tossed the game controller in his pursuit of his woman. The other ... well, the other was simply a jackass, because *come on.* Seriously. What the hell kind of guy could resist the temptation of his woman? Especially if she went to the effort to capture his attention?

Needless to say, Keegan's online teammates were on their own if his woman were to greet him like that.

His woman.

Their woman.

He couldn't believe he was actually thinking of Bristol as theirs, but there was no way he could deny it. As far as he was concerned, he was in the same place Kaden was. She was their end game.

Even if Bristol did want them to keep it a secret for the time being. He could respect that. For a little while, anyway.

Rather than let his insecurities get the best of him, Keegan had decided he would be the man she needed him to be, the one she could and would love the same as she loved Kaden. He would not be the one to keep distance between them. Not this time.

So, here he was, waltzing up the short path to Bristol's front door while scanning the neighborhood.

Not far from the heart of Coyote Ridge, it was one of the older parts of town. Because Brendon and Cheyenne lived just a couple of streets over, Keegan knew the houses had been built sometime back in the fifties. Most were the single-story ranch, well maintained from the roof down to the manicured lawns. He could see signs of the holidays. A couple of blow-up snowmen sitting in the yards, lights strung from the eaves.

It was then he wondered if Bristol was the sort to decorate for the holidays. Considering she worked with kids all day, he would peg her for the sort to participate in the various traditions, if for no other reason than to appease the little ones. If Keegan had a house in a neighborhood like this, that would be what he would do. He would go all out for every holiday, just for the kids.

He smiled to himself. Neighborhood or not, he would soon be putting up Christmas decorations. Next year, for sure. For their own child to see.

Stepping to the side, Keegan waited while Kaden rapped his knuckles on the front door.

A minute later, the sound of a lock disengaging was followed by the squeak of the front door as it opened.

"Hey," Bristol greeted, smiling up at them. "I didn't realize you were on the way."

"You offered food," Kaden said as though that was all they needed to drop everything and run. In all fairness, it kinda was.

"Come in." She stepped back, gestured them inside.

Because they'd come over in the middle of the night, been blindsided by the news of the pregnancy, fallen into bed with the sexiest woman on the planet, and slipped out before dawn, Keegan hadn't had a chance to really give the house a good once-over. He didn't have the same problem now. And yes, the house was as closed off as he'd thought it was. Then again, that had been the style back then, each room separated and individualized.

What really surprised him was the decor. The furniture was dated, as though it had been with the house since it was built. The flowered sofa had seen better days, as had the mauve carpet, the blue and green wallpaper border along the ceiling, and the brass and glass coffee table that he'd shoved aside last night.

Had he been inclined to learn anything about Bristol based on her house, Keegan would've failed miserably. It felt more like a house for an older man than a thirty-one-year-old woman.

As he followed Bristol toward the kitchen, he noticed the cheap, plastic-framed pictures on one wall did not match at all with the oversized farmhouse clock on another.

Then it dawned on him. This house had originally belonged to her grandparents, passed down to her father when they died. Her father had moved his family in, vacating the small farmhouse he'd been renting previously. And by the looks of it, this was still her father's house, despite the fact he'd passed on years ago. Bristol clearly hadn't updated anything since then. As though she was expecting him to come back at any moment, maybe fall into that ugly blue recliner, grab the clicker, and watch some tube.

"I'm sorry," she said when they stepped into the kitchen. "I didn't have time to put anything together."

She made a beeline for the refrigerator.

Keegan met Kaden's confused look. He didn't need to hear his brother's question to know he was wondering why she was so nervous. She certainly hadn't been last night.

"When I texted you, I had just gotten up," she explained, her head halfway in the refrigerator. "Then I had to shower and get ready. I was about to make coffee, but I heard you pull up."

Kaden moved toward her, took her arm, and pulled her back. "Why don't you take a seat and leave the preparations to us."

Bristol stared up at him, horrified. "You want to—"

"Cook for you," Keegan supplied, taking her hand as Kaden passed her off. "Yes, we do. So you just sit back and chill."

Rather than deliver her to the kitchen table, Keegan pulled her to a stop.

"Right here." He patted the countertop.

When she didn't move, Keegan smiled.

"I promise, we don't bite, Bristol," he assured her. "Not even in the light of day."

"And we won't burn your house down," Kaden promised. "I'm rather good in the kitchen."

"And I know when to stay outta the way," Keegan admitted.

Her pretty blue eyes bounced between the two of them. It took a moment, but she finally smiled, then hopped up onto the counter.

"Okay. I'll sit here. You two can do your thing."

"You want us to start that coffee?" Keegan asked.

"That would be amazing. And yes, it's caffeinated though I should probably have decaf." Her gaze bounced between them as she rambled on. "I read that too much caffeine's not good for the baby. I usually have a couple of cups in the morning, a couple in the afternoon but now I'm limiting myself." She gripped the edge of the counter as though gearing up to jump down. "Maybe I should make it."

Before she could move, Keegan put a hand on her thigh, leaned in. "You sit. We've got this."

Bristol's breath hitched, stirring that temptation to kiss her.

For a moment, just an infinitesimal amount of time, Keegan considered it. Leaning in, brushing her lips with his. He could practically taste her, the memories of last night flooding his brain. He wanted to kiss her again, to strip her bare, to sink into the heavenly warmth of her body. God, how he wanted to. Of course, if he did that, they'd miss lunch and, in her condition, she needed to eat.

So he refrained.

While Kaden went to work on the coffee, Keegan did an inventory of the refrigerator, then the pantry.

"You can learn a lot about a person by what you find in their kitchen," he told Bristol as he scanned the contents, finding little to nothing that would make a decent lunch. Or any meal for that matter.

"What does my refrigerator tell you about me?" she prompted.

Keegan peeked around the door, smiled at her. "That you don't eat at home often."

Bristol giggled. "If you're insinuatin' I don't have food, then you're wrong."

Holding up a container of yogurt, he waggled it. "This expired two months ago."

Her eyes widened in horror.

Keegan chuckled, then snatched all the stray containers and tossed them into the trash.

"I haven't been to the grocery store in a while," Bristol admitted. "I've been busy."

"Don't worry," Kaden said, "if you look in our fridge, you'll find a six-pack of beer."

"No, you won't," Keegan told him. "Drank that last week."

"Okay, fine," Kaden said with a smirk. "Then you'll find a jar of pickles and some bologna."

"Nix the bologna, too," Keegan told him. "Ate that before we went out last night."

Bristol laughed and he realized she was finally relaxing.

Turning to face her, he leaned against the refrigerator. "Based on my assessment, we've got two choices."

"Which are?" Kaden prompted.

"Either we Door Dash it, or we go to the diner." Keegan looked at Bristol. "So, which will it be?"

He already knew the answer, but you couldn't blame a guy for trying.

Chapter Sixteen

"In," Bristol blurted almost immediately. "We ... um ... we should eat in."

Kaden glanced over, watching as she began fidgeting, her gaze bouncing rapidly between them as though she was afraid they might disagree.

"I can order it," she quickly added. "Since, you know, it's my address and all."

She was far too nervous. Why? he wondered. Because she thought they might want to be seen in public with her? They'd already agreed to keeping a low profile for the time being. Was it really that big of a deal? Enough that she went into a panic at the thought of them wanting to take her out to lunch?

He let that thought slip away because he did not want to go there right now. They were on even footing, back to where they were supposed to be, and the last damn thing he wanted was for this to become a pissing match between Keegan and Bristol the way it had been before.

Plus, Keegan had managed to put her at ease when he'd poked fun at what she had in her refrigerator, and Kaden didn't want to miss the opportunity to have her relax a little around them. Not to mention, Kaden had really been looking forward to a little alone time with her since she made the offer of lunch.

So, they argued over whether to order fried chicken or sandwiches—chicken won out—then relocated to the living room while they waited for the meal to be delivered.

"I love what you've done with the place," Keegan said, a teasing hint in his words. "So very … retro."

Kaden's back stiffened as he watched Bristol, curious as to whether she would take offense to the comment.

A strangled laugh came out of her as she stared at him. "Do you know you're the first person who's ever called me out on it?" Her gaze swung around the room. "I figure if I wait long enough, it'll all come back in style."

"It's possible," Keegan agreed. "I mean, record players are a thing again. I'm just not sure green, blue, and mauve were ever a good combination to begin with."

Kaden knew Bristol had a sense of style because the daycare had a modern yet rustic flare that somehow suited her personality. This place… He seriously doubted anyone would've guessed Bristol Newton lived here if it had been on a test.

"My parents did some updates when we moved in after my grandparents passed. But my dad never updated anything after my mother left us," she explained. "This place is still as she left it, and truth is, I hate it, but I haven't gotten around to doin' anything about it. Well, other than clean out my father's bedroom. Bianca insisted I do it because it would help ease the pain of him being gone. It took me about three years to get around to it, but it's empty now."

"Do you plan on stayin' here?" Kaden asked.

"First person to ask me that, too," she muttered, her gaze swinging through the room. "I've given it a lot of thought. More so right after my dad passed. It was hard to be here, but at the same time, I felt a connection to him so I moved back in. I don't know what I'll do in the long run. I've considered sellin' it, but real estate's not cheap, nor is it readily available in Coyote Ridge. And honestly, it's a comfortable place. Needs some updates, probably a new air conditioner."

Kaden wouldn't tell her as much, but he was already wondering how they should approach her moving in with them, which of the other bedrooms would become the nursery. From the moment she'd told them she was pregnant, he'd known that was where she belonged. Then again, he'd thought the same thing before he found out she was having their baby.

"Well, the first thing you need to do is update the television," Keegan told her, reaching for the clunky remote.

He clicked it on, the three of them staring at the blank screen.

"I don't have cable, but I did invest in Apple TV, so I can stream whatever I want, though I haven't messed with it in a while."

"You mean that thing's new enough to have HDMI input?" Kaden asked.

She chuckled. "No, but the one in my bedroom is."

"I don't remember a TV," Keegan said with a smirk.

Bristol blushed.

Yeah, the television hadn't exactly been important when they'd been in that room.

Instead of going down that rabbit hole, Kaden shifted on the uncomfortable couch, smiled. "You're not here much, are you?"

"Only on the weekends. Weekdays I'm at the daycare from five in the morning to roughly seven in the evening. On a good day, I can sneak out at six. Now that Kayla's there, I'm hopin' I can start alternating times with her so I can have a few hours to myself during the week." Bristol smiled but it was weak. "What about y'all? How's the ranch comin' along? Word around town is you're doin' a gut job on the place."

"Not quite that extensive. Mostly cosmetic," Kaden explained. "We've been doin' what we can for the past few weeks, bits and pieces here and there."

He didn't mention it had kept them busy while she had been ignoring them.

"I take it you don't miss Kaleb's old house?"

"Not even a little," Keegan answered.

"Only because it's in better condition," Kaden said.

Bristol smiled, clearly catching their contradicting viewpoints.

Kaden noticed there was a lingering tension in the air. Almost like Bristol was expecting them to pounce on her at the first opportunity. If she wasn't fidgeting, she was repositioning, her gaze never settling on one place for long.

Then it dawned on him. This was the first time they'd really sat down to have a civilized conversation, just the three of them. Generally, they were around others when they chatted, usually crossing paths at Curtis and Lorrie's.

Of course, Bristol's anxiety ratcheted up a few notches when silence settled between them. For the life of him, Kaden couldn't come up with anything to say. Thankfully, she finally did.

"Did you see they're buildin' a spa on Main Street?"

Keegan chuckled. "A spa. We'd been tossin' around the idea of buyin' it. You know, before we learned the ranch was available."

Bristol smiled. "Really?"

Kaden shook his head. "No. We weren't tossin' it around." He nodded toward Keegan. "He was."

"Whatever." Keegan grinned, turned his attention to Bristol. "We'll let you settle the debate."

Bristol's blue eyes widened. "What debate's that?"

"We batted around ideas on what might work there."

"Such as?"

Keegan shrugged. "Vape shop, thrift store, sandwich shop."

Kaden grinned when Bristol didn't seem impressed.

"Yarn store?" Keegan's grin widened. "Maybe one of them overpriced pet stores dedicated to pamperin' your pooch."

"Tell her what you were *really* thinkin'," Kaden urged.

Keegan's chin tilted up. "Arcade."

Kaden glanced her way, relaxed somewhat. "What are your thoughts?"

"Old-school arcade? Like Pac-Man and Centipede? Or you talkin' monster televisions hooked to PlayStation and Xbox?"

"Definitely old-school," Keegan said quickly.

"Skee-Ball?" Bristol asked.

Keegan's grin widened. "Sure. Why not?"

"If it was yours, what would *you* put in there?" Kaden inquired.

"Good question. We've got a bookstore now. And a bakery."

"Plus the toy store," Keegan added. "Have you been in that place?"

Bristol nodded. "Once. To check it out. A little too new-age for my taste. An arcade, huh? I'm not sure it would've lured in the teenage crowd, but you would've gotten us old folks in there all the time." She smiled sweetly. "But good thing for the women of Coyote Ridge, a day spa's exactly what we need."

Kaden made a mental note to see about getting her a gift certificate to the place when it opened.

"So, how did you come to buy the ranch?" Bristol asked, sounding surprised. "I didn't even know Tuck was sellin'."

Kaden was the one to respond. "He moved to Wyoming to be with his kids and grandkids."

"Wow. I guess I thought he'd always be part of the landscape. Kinda like the Walkers."

"He's gettin' up there in age," Keegan explained. "Got some health issues. His kids wanted him closer to them."

Kaden watched as she tossed around the information.

"That's hard work," she finally said. "He runs what? Thirty head of cattle out there?"

"At his high point, yeah, thirty was about where he was," Kaden told her. "Right now, there're ten out there. Once we get settled, we'll figure out what we can and can't handle."

"What about Walker Demo? Working a ranch is a full-time gig."

"It is," Keegan confirmed. "We plan to let Autumn know we'll be goin' to part-time. Won't leave her in the lurch."

"Is that what you wanna do?" she asked, again looking back and forth between them. "Be ranchers?"

"What we've wanted for as long as we can remember," Kaden admitted.

A knock sounded on the door and Bristol shot to her feet like someone had fired a pistol in her ear. So much for thinking she was beginning to get comfortable.

"I think she's scared of us," Keegan whispered when she carried the food into the kitchen.

Kaden stared after her, though he couldn't see her because of all the damn walls separating the space.

He wasn't sure *scared* was the right word, but they certainly made her nervous. Then again, he was feeling a bit twitchy himself. You could've knocked him over with a feather when she texted to suggest lunch. Now that he was here, Kaden couldn't help but think this was a bad idea.

"You gonna hold down the couch?" Keegan teased. "Or you comin' to join us?"

Hell, he hadn't even realized his brother had left the room.

AFTER THEY ATE, AS SHE CLEARED THE table of the old plastic plates her father had favored, Bristol wished she'd taken the time to make a few upgrades to this place. The fact that Keegan had called her out on it had cemented the fact she truly was stuck in the past. Probably one of the reasons she didn't have people over.

Of course, there wasn't a damn thing she could do about it right now. It was bad enough she'd made the offer to fix them lunch only to realize she didn't have any food in the house. Seriously, who did that? Certainly not a good host.

"Why don't you let me handle that?"

Spinning around, Bristol inhaled sharply when she noticed Keegan standing directly behind her.

Before she could argue, he took the plate out of her hand, carried it over to the sink.

"I'll get to it eventually," she assured him. "The dishwasher doesn't work, so I'll wash them by hand."

Something she would surely have to fix before the baby arrived. There would be more dishes to contend with then.

"What's wrong with it?" he asked, his gaze dropping to the dishwasher.

She giggled uncomfortably. "No idea. It hasn't worked for years." Bristol took a step back, looked past him. "Where's Kaden?"

"He got a call. Stepped outside."

Nodding as though that made sense, Bristol gripped the hem of her sweater, rubbed it between her fingers. Yep, she was feeling a little antsy.

"Do we make you nervous?" he asked, coming to stand in front of her.

"What?" She forced a smile, tried not to fidget, then lied through her teeth. "No. Of course not."

Keegan tilted her chin back using one finger, his gaze raking over her face.

"Okay, fine. Yes." She smiled up at him. "A little."

"Why's that?"

"I honestly have no idea," she admitted.

"Do we scare you?" He gently rubbed her cheek.

Bristol shook her head. Funny how that simple touch, the lightest brush of his finger on her skin, warmed every cell in her entire body.

For so long, she'd tried to convince herself she had no real interest in Kaden and Keegan, but she had always known it was utter crap. In fact, she'd somehow managed to fall in love without any effort at all. They made it pretty easy. Well, when Keegan wasn't getting defensive and being rude, of course.

But he'd apologized for that already and Bristol was bound and determined to leave that behind them. No sense dredging up the past, not moments like that one. It would only get in the way of their future. Whatever that might be.

Right now she would live in the moment because the moment was all they had. Tomorrow would be a new day, with its new set of obstacles and issues. Today was where she needed to be. With Kaden and Keegan.

The truth was, Bristol had been looking for an excuse to explore more of what they were offering ever since that night at Alluring Indulgence Resort last Christmas. Only she hadn't had the nerve to approach them. And yes, she'd managed to evade them at every turn, but that was due more to fear than lack of interest.

It wasn't like it was a rational fear. Certainly not anything ominous.

No, Bristol had worried all along that she could so easily fall for these two men. And it had happened without her even realizing it. They were men she admired, men she enjoyed talking to, men who made her laugh.

Bristol lost her train of thought when Keegan's lips brushed hers.

"Where'd you go?" he whispered before kissing her a little more firmly as he stepped in close, his hand resting lightly on her hip.

"I'm right here," she said with a smile, allowing her hands to slide up his chest, around his neck.

He pressed his lips to hers before his tongue joined the mix, sliding sinfully against hers.

The man could kiss, she'd give him that. He somehow managed to own her mouth by coaxing her, not dominating. It was a heady thing, really. Something she found impossible to resist.

"Bristol…"

Heat engulfed her from head to toe when Keegan's hands slid down her back, cupping her butt. When he pulled her in closer, she suddenly felt light-headed. Not necessarily a good thing considering they were still standing in her kitchen. She got the feeling he could have her naked in two seconds flat without ever touching her clothes. The man was that potent.

Keegan shifted, his stubbled jaw rubbing lightly over her cheek. She could feel his warm breath against her skin, and she was almost positive her knees were turning to jelly.

"I want to taste you again," he said softly against her ear. "Right here. I want to sit you on that counter and lick your pussy until you beg me to make you come."

Oh, God.

Goose bumps broke out on her arms, made her scalp tingle. She'd never been with a man whose thoughts were spoken so freely and with such eroticism.

"Keegan…"

"Let me, Bristol. Let me have you for dessert."

Refusing seemed like a stupid thing to do.

When he went to step back, she grabbed his arm, forced him to stay where he was. Well, technically, she didn't force him to do anything. Keegan had a good eighty, maybe ninety pounds on her. All muscle. He was far stronger, so if he'd wanted to drag her along behind him, it would've required little effort on his part.

"Are you saying no?" The rough gravel of his voice scraped her nerve endings to life in the most sensual way.

"No." She sighed. "I mean, no, I'm not saying no."

The next thing she knew, Keegan was working her leggings off, her panties being dragged down with them, and then he had her perched on the countertop.

But he didn't drop to his knees and put his mouth on her. Oh, no. Clearly he wasn't finished, because he managed to rid her of her shirt and bra, too, leaving her completely naked, her bare butt on the cold laminate countertop while his hot mouth was on hers once again.

Their mouths melded, tongue gliding against tongue, hands roaming, his on her breasts, hers on his back, as Bristol's heart began to beat harder, faster, her need ratcheting up with more speed than she'd thought possible.

"Keegan … please."

"I love when you beg."

Bristol chuckled because he would say something like that.

And then he was kissing his way down her body. She tried to recline but the upper cabinet was in the way, making it impossible for her to move. But Keegan didn't seem to mind. He squatted down, his warm breath fanning her most sensitive parts as he placed her feet so they were sitting squarely on his shoulders, the position making it impossible to close her knees.

She should've been embarrassed, being naked in the kitchen, his face between her legs, but she wasn't. This was liberating. All her life she'd been prim and proper. And sex with her previous partners had always been missionary and boring. But that wasn't because she wanted it that way, it was because no one had ever shown her any other way. People saw her as sweet and innocent, and sure, for the most part maybe she was. But that didn't mean her desires didn't run hot, that she didn't want a man to do unspeakable things like this.

"Oh, God." Bristol moaned when Keegan's tongue lapped at her.

She slid her fingers into his hair, which was just long enough on the top for her to get a handful. She held him there, unable to move because of the position while he worked her into a frenzy with his mouth. Bristol dropped her head back and let the sensations overwhelm her. Her skin tingled the more he teased and tormented, but Keegan never allowed her to reach that pinnacle, always pulling back at the last second.

When her frustration began to rise, she opened her eyes. And that was when she realized Kaden was standing on the opposite side of the kitchen, watching her. He wasn't focused on what Keegan was doing, but on her. Those steel-blue eyes seemed darker, his expression revealing nothing. But still she could see the heat and the hunger etched on his masculine features.

God, he really was a beautiful man.

A beautiful man who enjoyed watching, she realized.

"Oh, God!" she cried out, holding Kaden's gaze as she came from that thought and the exquisite exploration of Keegan's tongue.

And then Keegan was on his feet, blocking her view of Kaden, so she turned her attention to him, kissing him when his mouth descended. She could taste herself on his tongue and that alone did crazy things to her. Something else she'd never done until them.

When he pulled back, Bristol gripped his wrists, not allowing him to go too far.

"Damn, woman," he whispered softly. "Do you know how much I want you?"

Oh, she had some idea.

"Right here," she demanded, reaching for the button on his jeans.

Keegan watched her, his heavy-lidded gaze locked on her face while she freed his cock, shoving his jeans down as much as she could.

She sucked in a shocked breath when Keegan jerked her hips toward him, bringing her to the very edge of the countertop even as he pushed deep inside her.

And then his arms were banded around her and hers around him as she held on for dear life. His thrusts were slow, and impossibly deep. A leisurely, sinful glide that shocked her with its intensity.

He felt so. Freaking. Good.

Keegan was taking it slow and she welcomed the pace, the sensual way he slid in and out.

Bristol lifted her head, met Kaden's gaze where he still remained on the other side of the kitchen. She wanted to include him, but she got the feeling he was content with what was going on. And since she knew once would not be enough, she turned her attention back to Keegan.

He growled softly in her ear, her name spilling from his lips as he continued to stroke himself inside her. He must've decided their movements were too hindered because Keegan's hands slid under her thighs and he lifted her, still lodged inside her to the hilt.

She threw her arms around his neck, held on tightly, and waited for what came next.

CHRIST ALMIGHTY.

The woman was going to be his undoing.

When Keegan situated himself in one of the kitchen chairs, allowing Bristol to straddle him while he continued to impale her on his cock, he thought he was going to lose his mind. She sheathed him, tight and wet and so fucking hot… It was all he could do not to fuck her senseless, to rut like a wild animal and chase the release that was waiting for him.

But this wasn't one of those wild encounters that left him breathless and tired. No, this was … some would probably call it making love because it was gentle and reverent and still so fucking hot, he thought he might spontaneously combust.

When he realized Bristol's legs weren't quite long enough to give her traction, Keegan gripped her hips, pulled her in, his cock sliding deeper into her then pushing her back only to do it again and again.

In this position, he could watch her face, see those sexy breasts as they swayed unbidden in front of him. He loved the way her neck arched when she tipped her head back, those dusky pink nipples that pebbled into tight little nubs. And those sexy moans that were driving him mad.

Keegan was aware of Kaden standing just a few feet away watching them. He'd known the minute his brother had returned, knew that Kaden was content to watch because that was something they both enjoyed. And he could only imagine how hot Bristol was from his position, the slight curve of her waist, the flare of her hips, the way her back muscles shifted beneath all that smooth skin.

And that gave him an idea.

"Turn around," he instructed Bristol. "Let Kaden get a better view."

Her blue eyes sparked with fire and heat. Bristol was eager as she got to her feet, pivoting to face away from him. Keegan gripped her hip and guided her back down so she was sitting on his cock once more, only this time, Kaden had a perfect view of her perfect tits.

He inhaled sharply as her slick heat engulfed him once more, the walls of her pussy milking him as he sought the one place he wanted to be. Inside her. For eternity.

Wrapping one arm around her rib cage, he held Bristol back against him, pumping his hips upward, fucking her from underneath. That lasted a few minutes before she was the one to change positions, planting her hands on his knees and leaning forward. The woman blew his mind as she began lifting and lowering on him, using her arms to leverage herself up before dropping back down.

Fucking hell. She was going to blow his damn mind if she kept that up.

The slow, wet glide of her pussy along his shaft had sparks igniting along his spine. He knew it wouldn't be long before he came from the sheer ecstasy of being inside her. The lack of latex was mind-blowing, giving him the ultimate experience, nothing muted even the slightest.

Bristol whimpered, her head falling back, her hair brushing his face. Then she was leaning back against him once more, reaching for his head.

"Make me come, Keegan. Oh, God … please…"

"My pleasure, darlin'."

Keegan moved then, urging her to her feet. He would've bent her over right there, but the height difference would've proved impossible for him, so instead, he regrettably dislodged from her body, spun her around, lifted her once more, and set her back on the countertop. It was the perfect height for what he wanted, allowed him to slide deep inside her.

So he did.

From there, he proceeded to take them both straight up that mountain, higher and higher, until cresting it became inevitable.

"Come for me," he commanded through gritted teeth, surging his hips forward, fucking her harder, faster.

"Yes … yes … yes!" Bristol cried out, her arms locking around his neck, her body tightening, her pussy clamping down on him until he was coming with a guttural cry of his own.

Chapter Seventeen

ON SUNDAY MORNING, BRISTOL WAS UP EARLY, a smile permanently planted on her face. Not only because she'd spent the night with Kaden and Keegan once again but because she had plans this morning, something she looked forward to, because these days, it was such a rare thing for her and Rex to carve out time to hang out.

Now, as she sat at a table in the Coyote Ridge Bakery, Bristol felt her nerves ratchet up when the bell over the door jangled. She looked up to see Rex Sharpe, her best friend from early childhood, walking her way. He looked good, like always. Tall, dark, and handsome, Rex had a slight resemblance to Curtis and Lorrie's sons. That was because Rex was Lorrie's sister Adele's son, carrying on the Jameson bloodline.

Bristol had known him since they were little, living next door to one another. Despite the fact she'd moved after her grandparents passed away, her father trading the rented little farmhouse for a permanent residence in town, they'd still gone to the same schools, remained friends through the years. Rex was one of the few people in her life she could depend on completely to be there when she needed someone. And she did the same for him. Always had, always would.

She'd stayed by Rex's side through all the hell he'd lived through. Somehow they'd remained friends for their entire lives, and while she enjoyed hanging out with her girlfriends, Rex was the one she went to for advice on the most pressing issues, those that would truly alter her life. He was the one who urged her to put her early childhood degree to good use and open a daycare. He was the one who had talked her into keeping the house she was living in rather than staying in the crappy apartment she'd rented when her marriage failed. He always gave it to her straight, and this was one of those times when she needed a straight shooter.

"I got you a chocolate muffin," she informed him when he joined her at the two-seater table. The Coyote Ridge Bakery was small, but it was the perfect place to have coffee on a Sunday morning. Most of the town's residents were over at the church, and while Bristol respected their right to congregate in the house of worship, it had never been her thing.

"Just don't tell Jack," Rex said with a grin as he slid into the seat across from her. "He's got a thing for those chocolate croissant things. He'd be pissed if he knew I was havin' chocolate for breakfast and he wasn't."

Bristol tapped the small white box sitting on the table. "I got him somethin', too. My way of sayin' thank you for him lettin' you out this mornin'."

Rex looked at the box and the warmth in his eyes was something that still shocked her. She knew it was all for Jack Cunningham, Coyote Ridge's very own claim to fame, a highly coveted graphic artist and Rex's husband. From the story Rex told, Jack had accidentally ended up in their small town and Rex had managed to keep him here indefinitely. They were happy and she was happy for them.

"How is Jack?" she asked, hoping her rioting nerves would settle with some mundane chitchat.

"Good. He just finished up one of his graphic novels. Said his agent is all kinds of happy." Rex grinned. "I have no idea what that means, but as long as he's smilin', I guess I am, too." He took a sip of his coffee. "But I know you didn't bring me here to talk about my husband."

No, she hadn't. Considering she spent more time hanging out with Jack than Rex, she didn't need to inquire about his well-being. She already knew.

But still.

"Bristol?"

Crap.

She sat up straight, squared her shoulders, and met Rex's brown eyes head on. "I told them."

"You mentioned that." He took a sip of the coffee she'd gotten for him. "How'd they take it?"

"Like it was no big deal." She said this with exasperation because she still couldn't believe they'd taken her surprise announcement in stride, as though it was every day they learned they were going to be fathers.

"Doesn't surprise me."

Bristol frowned, lowered her voice. "They didn't bat an eye, Rex. Who *does* that?"

"Men who love you, that's who."

Love.

Her belly fluttered at the word.

She'd spent the entire day with them yesterday and today she was already missing them. They had no plans to see each other, but she was holding out hope that they would because … well, because she was pretty sure she was addicted and now she wanted another fix.

"They've stayed the night," she told him, ensuring she was keeping her voice soft enough that others wouldn't overhear, "the last two nights."

Although she appreciated the fact he didn't freak out at the news, it didn't help that Rex sat back, exhaled, and continued to stare at her, his dark brown eyes assessing. She knew what he was doing. Rex was trying to see right into her soul, to figure out what she was thinking. Oh, he would ask her outright when he was good and ready, but he always did this. Probably because he knew it would make her squirm.

"How'd it happen? They approach you at Moonshiners? Or did you corner them?"

Bristol went on to explain how she'd gone out with Bianca and Jamie, then how Keegan had asked her to dance, not really giving her a way out, and how her car hadn't started.

"They drove me home," she told him. "Probably would've left but I…" Bristol exhaled heavily. "I broke down. I couldn't hold it in anymore."

She still remembered the horrified look on Keegan's face when she sobbed before escaping to the bathroom to hide out.

"We had a rational conversation when I told them I was pregnant."

"You didn't expect that?"

Bristol shrugged. "I didn't know what to expect." She still didn't. "They stayed the night, left early, then came back when I invited them over for lunch yesterday."

She felt her cheeks heating from the memories of what they'd done throughout the day.

"And?"

"And what?"

He grinned. "How was it? The sex."

A flash of heat stole over her, partly from memories of that night, partly because of her embarrassment of the subject. "Amazing."

Rex chuckled. "Any regrets?"

"Not a one," she admitted.

"That's a good thing." He picked at his muffin, smirked. "Better than sex with just one man?"

"Amazing," she whispered, repeating her original answer. "Oh, my God, Rex. I won't lie, I've dreamed about the day, never thought I would be back in that situation. Then suddenly there I was, two hot cowboys…"

Crap. Her gaze swung around, ensuring no one was paying attention to her.

They weren't. Thank God.

"And you didn't run 'em off after?"

"Nope." She was proud of that fact.

"It's about damn time. Glad y'all got it figured out. They've been sniffin' around you long enough."

Bristol laughed. "They have not."

"Oh, honey, they most certainly have." He leaned in. "I have no idea what happened last Christmas, but there were a coupla times I thought they'd burn this town to embers. Especially when you were datin' that ol' city boy a few months back."

She wanted to tell him he'd lost his mind, but Bristol knew exactly what he was talking about. One morning, she had invited Timothy to breakfast here in Coyote Ridge. Because the town lacked options, they'd settled on the diner. Of course, Kaden and Keegan had decided to come in that morning, had taken a booth not too far away from where she'd been. Right in her line of sight. It had been awkward to say the least. There she was, trying to have a pleasant conversation with a pleasant man, and those two sexy men had been sitting right there, staring at her.

"Where are they now?" Rex asked.

"Church. Then they have some errands to run."

"So it's official? Y'all are what? Officially datin'? Y'all gonna go to Curtis and Lorrie's for dinner?"

Bristol shook her head. "I'm not ready for that."

"For what?"

She swallowed hard, knowing this was the part she was having a difficult time with. "I don't think I'm ready for anyone to know about us."

Rex looked away.

"You think that's wrong of me? To not want it to become public knowledge?"

His dark brown eyes returned to her face and there was disappointment in his voice when he said, "You do you, Bristol."

She felt a tad defensive, spurred by his tone. "What does that mean?"

He didn't speak right away, choosing to drink his coffee, staring out at the cars lined up out front.

"Sittin' in the closet … it's not all it's cracked up to be."

Sitting in the… Bristol frowned. What was he talking about?

"Sooner or later, someone's gonna figure it out. Then what? How will you handle it then? Small town, Bristol. Word's gonna spread and then you'll be left defendin' yourself. For what reason? Because you don't want someone else to look at you cross for bein' who you are? For lovin' who you love?"

Bristol stared at him, wide-eyed. She wasn't sure she'd ever heard him speak so much at one time, much less on a topic that was so deep.

Then again, this was a man who'd spent a good chunk of his life in the closet, something the LGBTQ community still had to contend with on a daily basis.

"Not bein' accepted," Rex said softly, "it sucks. But not everyone's gonna look down their nose at you. What're you gonna do when the baby's here? Hide the truth from it, too?"

"No. Of course not."

"So why start now?"

She started to answer, but he kept going.

"Do you love them, Bristol?"

She met his stare, held it for a few seconds. "Yeah. I do."

"So why not embrace it? Jump right on that train and ride it. God knows you deserve some happiness."

He'd been saying that for a long time. Rex was one who had known her ex-husband and he hadn't been a fan.

"And I say fuck those who think it's their place to judge."

She frowned.

"I mean no disrespect, but ever since Baxter, you've changed. Buried that wild streak I know you've got. It's still there, still revved. Just because you pretend otherwise doesn't make it so."

Her gaze shifted to the table. "I'm not wild anymore."

"Liar." He shook his head and smiled. "Remember that girl who went searchin' for the biggest stick she could find? She was bound and determined she was gonna give my old man the beatin' he deserved the next time she saw him." Rex met her gaze. "I remember that girl. God, you had an attitude back then. Didn't take shit from anybody. I admired that about you. Hell, I'd go so far as to say I thought it was hot."

Bristol chuckled. "Whatever."

"If I'd ever been into chicks, you'da been my girl and you know it."

She felt herself blush.

"That girl … she's still in there, Bristol. But you only let part of her out. You're fierce when it comes to your business and your independence. You'll defend those who're important to you, but you won't defend yourself. When it comes to what you think others'll think about you … you hide in your shell. Don't you think it's time you let that girl out? Let her stand up for herself rather than let others beat her into submission?"

She smiled because Rex was always calling her out on her crap. He was the one person she couldn't lie to. He knew her too well. He'd been with her through thick and thin. Besides Bianca, he was the only other person who had stood by her side when she'd found out Baxter had been cheating on her. He was the one person who'd threatened to shoot off his kneecaps if he didn't leave her alone when Baxter decided he wanted to work things out. Rex had also been right by her side when her father died, taking care of her, making sure she wasn't alone. She loved him like a brother.

"Hey."

Lifting her head, she met his dark stare.

"Ain't no one judgin' you. This is your life. You live it how you want to. It's too damn short to ignore what matters. And no matter what you tell me, I know they matter to you."

They did. More than she wanted to admit, even to herself.

But Bristol wasn't naive enough to believe they were ready to settle down. Pregnant or not, she was not expecting anything from them.

"What's on your mind, doll?" Rex asked, his voice soothing, his concern evident.

She sighed. "I don't know."

"Talk to me."

"It's crazy, Rex. Right now, I know it's just sex, and oddly enough, I'm okay with that. In fact, that's what makes it hotter."

"Then what's the problem?"

"There's not one," she said, laughing. "And *that's* the problem."

Rex's deep rumbling laugh had her smile amping up.

"What do I do now?"

"You ride," he said simply. "What else can you do?"

"And what happens when I get in over my head? When I fall so deep I can't dig myself out?"

Because it would happen; she knew that for a fact. Kaden and Keegan made it far too easy to love them. She was already head over heels.

"Do you want more now?"

"Maybe." She honestly didn't know. "I mean, I'm not gettin' any younger, Rex. I always thought I'd have kids by now, so I consider this a blessing. Truly. But that doesn't mean they'll feel the same. It was an accident. A happy accident, but ... you get it. And yes, they took the news well. Better than I would have. But we haven't talked about it since."

"Then talk about it," Rex said as though it was that simple. "If they don't bring up the subject, you need to. Figure it out. Nine months isn't a long time."

"Eight," she said with a quick smile. "Only eight more."

"Next thing you'll be countin' down in weeks."

"Because that's how it's done," she said in defense.

He grinned, took a sip of his coffee, then nodded, his lips pursed. "Like I said, it's your life. Don't waste it sweatin' the small stuff. Go along for the ride. See where it goes. You never know. Those boys might surprise you."

Bristol didn't have to tell him they already had. She was fairly certain it was written all over her face.

"WHERE'RE WE GOIN'?" KEEGAN ASKED WHEN KADEN turned the truck in the opposite direction of the ranch after leaving the church parking lot.

"The shop," he told his brother.

"For?"

"I need to get the part ordered for Bristol's car."

"I thought you did that yesterday."

"Nope. Meant to, got hung up."

More accurately, he'd gotten distracted by the sexy little daycare owner. Even now, Kaden would've preferred going to her house, climbing back into bed with her, and spending a lazy Sunday doing nothing. A lot of naked nothing. And he might have if it didn't feel like that was all they were doing.

"You check the spark plugs and all that?" Keegan asked.

"Nope."

"We can give it a quick once-over," Keegan told him. "Then what's on the agenda for the day?"

What he *wanted* to do was spend time with Bristol. What he *needed* to do was focus on the house. They'd made strides in getting things repaired, even begun to renovate some. He needed to give it his undivided attention if he expected them to ever finish it.

His thoughts drifted to the ranch, only this time, he superimposed Bristol into the picture. She would look good there, he realized. Living with him and Keegan. Married. Some kids running around.

Yeah, he knew he was moving fast where the future was concerned, but he honestly didn't care. At this point in his life, what did he have to lose? He'd spent the past couple of years attempting to get close to this woman. Now that he was, he didn't want to waste a minute. All that taking-things-slow shit didn't appeal to him in the least. Nor did the hiding part. Perhaps it would have if he hadn't been doing exactly that since the first day he met her.

"We need to get an order placed for flooring," he told his brother, pulling himself out of those wayward thoughts.

"You decide on which wood you're gonna go with?"

He shook his head.

"Then I suggest you close your eyes and point," Keegan said with a chuckle. "'Cause it ain't gonna get done if we can't get it ordered."

Yeah, yeah.

"Right now," he told Keegan, "we'll get a better look at the car, see what else's needed. In the meantime, we'll let her keep yours." No way was he leaving her without a vehicle.

"Good plan."

Kaden parked the truck in front of the mechanic shop, grabbed the keys from the center console, then got out.

"I didn't know Ethan was workin' today," Keegan said as they passed the big black Chevy parked directly in front of the door.

Kaden hadn't been aware of it either. And since he knew Beau's mother tended to watch the little ones after church on Sundays, he figured a knock on the door was necessary before they barged in and got an eyeful of husband and husband going at it.

He rapped his knuckles on the door, waited. There was no answer and he knew that could mean one of two things: Ethan and Beau were busy, too caught up to notice the knock. Or Ethan was there alone, had his headphones in, and was working away.

It was a crapshoot as to what they were going to walk in on, but Kaden figured he didn't have much of a choice.

The keys weren't necessary because the door was unlocked, so he opened it, listened. When there were no moans or groans to greet them, Kaden stepped inside.

The good news was, Ethan was working, not indulging. Didn't look as though Beau was there, but Kaden could see Ethan's expression, knew the man's brain was hard at work.

"Hey, man," he said, projecting his voice to be heard over the music in Ethan's ears.

Either hearing them or sensing them, Ethan turned, tugged the earbuds out.

"Hey." Ethan planted his hands on his hips. "What're you doin' here?"

Kaden nodded at the newest vehicular resident. "Bristol's car crapped out on her the other night. Told her we'd give it a look, see if we can get it fixed. You?"

"Travis just left. We were talkin' about Autumn. He wanted to know how she's doin'."

Kaden leaned against the car. "What'd you tell him?"

"That she'll do." He grinned. "Unless, of course, she makes it her mission to overload us more than she already has."

Keegan laughed. "She does know how to ramp up business, don't she?"

"Thank God she's not afraid to get her hands dirty," Kaden added.

Autumn had spent quite a bit of time in the shop, helping out. As it was, the woman was probably more knowledgeable about engines than either of them.

"No shit." Ethan grabbed a tool, turned back to what he was doing. "I hate to see Reese move on, but she's doin' a damn fine job. I was actually surprised she was interested."

They'd never really talked about Ethan's cousin and Kaden was curious. "Yeah? Why's that?"

"Big corporate type," Ethan said, head halfway under the hood, "couple of degrees. I didn't figure she'd want anything to do with Coyote Ridge again."

Kaden didn't know the reason behind that, but he suspected it had something to do with her ex. From the bits and pieces he'd picked up on, they had separated nearly a year ago, although neither had moved forward with divorce proceedings until recently when Autumn officially filed.

"How's Reese doin', anyway?" Keegan asked.

"Good from what I can tell. I ran into him at the diner the other day," Ethan said. "They're inundated with cold cases from across the state."

Reese Tavoularis was a good guy. He'd been running Walker Demolition since his return from the air force a few years back. After their older brother Jared got married and moved to Dead Heat Ranch, the place had been in limbo for a bit. Jaxson had filled in for a while, but he said he wasn't suited for an office job. That was about the time Reese was looking for employment.

It was interesting how things worked around here. It was like a puzzle. Every now and then there would be a hole that needed to be plugged and a piece would be moved in. Sometimes that piece would shift to a different puzzle, fitting perfectly into another gap, and another would seemingly come along.

Not that their world was perfect. Not by a long shot. There was always one issue or another arising, but when it came to family, there was someone there to help out along the way. Kaden and Keegan had fallen into that role on numerous occasions. After all, it was how they had landed this job at Walker Demolition.

Speaking of their job...

"Hey, E, we need to chat about somethin' important."

Ethan stopped what he was doing, standing tall and wiping his hand on a rag. "You're leavin' to go live the high life on the ranch, huh?"

Kaden could feel Keegan's eyes on him. He hadn't yet discussed this with his brother, although they both knew it was inevitable. The ranch would require more time than they had while maintaining full-time here.

"That's the plan. We haven't talked to Autumn yet," he tacked on. "Wanted you to hear it first."

Ethan nodded. "I figured as much, so I've been puttin' out some feelers." He smiled. "Turns out, Beau wants to come back part-time. He's worked out a deal with his mom to watch the kids a few hours a day so he can get outta the house."

"I heard a rumor that Ryan Brehm's lookin' for somethin'," Keegan added.

That seemed to perk up Ethan's ears. "Yeah? Who'd you hear that from?"

"Brehm," Keegan said with a chuckle.

"I guess that speaks to the validity of the rumor." Ethan laughed. "I'll reach out to him."

"We won't run out on you," Kaden promised. "We're here until you've got the help you need."

"I hate to see you go, but I get it."

Kaden knew Ethan was telling the truth. This was where Ethan wanted to be. It'd been his legacy all along, probably one of the main reasons Travis came up with the idea in the first place. And this place suited Ethan. He'd be the first to admit he wasn't much of a people person and he preferred his solitude. This gave him both of those things.

Kaden was sure there were plenty more folks in Coyote Ridge looking for jobs. A couple of good heavy-equipment mechanics, perhaps a couple of ranch hands.

The fact that things were changing again wasn't lost on him.

AFTER CHATTING IT UP WITH ETHAN FOR a good half hour, they let him get back to what he was doing while they did a full inspection of Bristol's car.

"Man, I think this ol' dinosaur needs to give up the ghost," Keegan told his brother. "Damn thing's clingin' to life as it is."

Hell, he figured the only thing going for it was the fact that there were so few miles since Bristol didn't do a whole lot of driving. Then again, it was a Honda, and while he wasn't a fan, he knew it would likely last longer than most. If they were lucky, the only thing it would need besides a new alternator would be a tune-up.

They spent another thirty minutes doing a rundown on it only to find a variety of things that needed to be fixed or replaced altogether, including, as they'd suspected, the alternator and battery. Plus an oil change, some transmission fluid. That was the bare minimum. New brakes and some new spark plugs would go a long way, too.

"We'll get the parts ordered," Kaden said, his head still ducked down near the engine.

"I'm in no rush to get my truck back," he told Kaden. Most of the time, Keegan let his brother drive him around. It was easier that way. "You wanna let her know? Or shall I?" Keegan grinned. "I noticed the heated text messages between you two this mornin'. She prompted it, huh?"

Kaden stood tall, wiping his hands on a rag. "I didn't expect it, honestly."

Keegan hadn't either. When he'd seen the sexually charged back-and-forth between Kaden and Bristol, he'd been more than a little surprised to see Bristol had been the one to instigate it.

"I like this side of her," he admitted.

"It's interesting," Kaden noted. "Just seems…"

"Polar opposite? An about-face? Not at all like her?"

Kaden smirked. "I was gonna say a distraction."

Yeah, that, too. Like Bristol was trying to keep them preoccupied so they didn't have time to think about the important things. Like the fact they were having a baby.

"Not a bad thing, per se," Kaden added. "I just hope she's not doin' it for our benefit."

That was a good point. However, Keegan didn't get the feeling she was playing this up for them. When it came to Bristol, he didn't see anything fake about her. She was ... simple. And he didn't mean that in a bad way. In fact, he appreciated it because there wasn't a lot of undercurrent where she was concerned. That, or they hadn't had time to stir it up yet.

And to think, Keegan had thought she was a prude.

"She goin' to Curtis and Lorrie's for dinner?"

"Nope."

Keegan frowned. "You asked her?"

"I did." Kaden did not look happy.

Keegan thought back to Bristol's request that they keep this quiet for a while. He couldn't help but wonder how long she intended, because there were people he was eager to share the news with. Their mom and dad were going to be over the moon that they were going to be grandparents.

Keegan shoved off the thought. It wouldn't do any good to remind himself that he was once again some woman's dirty little secret. Maybe Bristol didn't see it that way, but she wasn't on their end of this. It sucked.

"I was thinkin' we'd head over there," Kaden suggested. "Hang for a couple of hours before we head back to the house and get to work."

"No can do. I told Sawyer and Kennedy I'd stop by, watch the kiddos for a bit. They wanted to make a trip down to Cabela's for somethin'. Sans little ones. They'll be back in time for dinner. But you should go over there. Spend some time with her one-on-one. See how she reacts to that."

Kaden nodded and Keegan could see the concern in his eyes.

"It's fine," Keegan told him. "I'm not worried about Bristol pickin' you over me."

And that much was true.

He was more concerned that she would pick neither of them in an effort not to tarnish her reputation.

Then again, they'd yet to spend any one-on-one time with her. While she seemed more than content to have the two of them together, there was no way to know how she'd feel after she spent time alone with each of them. It was possible she'd find herself reserved again, wishing for the one-on-one that was normal for most relationships. It had happened to them before, women who had been all about the tag team until they got some individual attention. At that point, they'd flocked to one or the other, deciding they would rather forego the threesome. Keegan wasn't willing to go that route on a permanent basis and he knew Kaden wasn't either. It was the one thing neither of them had to question. If they found a woman who preferred only one of them, it wouldn't work.

And while this thing with Bristol seemed to be moving into the serious category, Keegan knew the same would go for her. If she decided it was one or the other, not both, they would have to figure out a new plan.

All or nothing, that was how it was meant to be.

Chapter Eighteen

WHEN BRISTOL WOKE UP THAT MORNING, IT had been with a hum beneath her skin. She couldn't explain it exactly, but it was almost like a steady current of adrenaline was streaming in her blood. Even through coffee with Rex, it had been there, silently wreaking havoc.

It was them, she realized. Kaden and Keegan.

They made her feel different. Made her feel … strong and sexy in a way no one ever had before.

Bristol kept waiting for the feeling to wane, to go back to being the insecure daycare owner who lived her life for the kids who were in her care. Truth was, that was all she'd lived for these past few years. The routine, the monotony, it had become her safe haven. Ever since Baxter had dumped her for Betsy McTitface or whatever. And holding onto the familiar had been what soothed her soul after losing her father. She'd gotten used to it.

Some might even call it a rut.

But Kaden and Keegan stirred something inside her, and she was beginning to crave that feeling like a drug. They'd sparked it that first night they'd kissed her at Alluring Indulgence Resort, again after their first night together in Keegan's bed despite the undesirable ending. It was still there, even now, after these last painful, lonely weeks she'd spent trying to get over them. Now she was wondering if perhaps she was turning over a new leaf.

In fact, she'd been a bit feistier than she'd ever been before, hence the text messages that had transpired between her and Kaden earlier in the day. It had been a bold move on her part to instigate what she assumed was referred to as sexting. Yes, her face might've flamed a few times from embarrassment, but she hadn't wanted to bury her head in the sand indefinitely afterward.

Now, as she sat on the ugly flower couch in her living room, Bristol debated as to whether she should call Bianca. For whatever reason, her conversation with Rex had her wanting to get someone else's opinion. Not because she disagreed with him, more so because she could see his point.

And that worried her. She didn't want to be the girl who cowered and hid from the rest of the world.

She had just made up her mind to call Bianca when her cell phone rang.

Bristol snatched it up, hit the talk button, grinning as she did. "I was just about to call you."

"Uh-huh. I've heard that before," Bianca grumbled.

"No, seriously." Bristol twisted on the couch, propping her head on the armrest, extending her legs. "What's wrong? Why do you sound upset?"

"I'm not," Bianca said, and Bristol could hear it for the lie that it was.

"Did Jake go out of town again?"

"Mm-hmm."

"Aww. Why didn't you go with him?"

"Town council meeting's this week," Bianca said sadly then perked up quickly. "But I heard it through the grapevine you've been passin' the time with a hot cowboy."

Bristol frowned, a strange squeezing sensation in her chest. This was her biggest fear realized. "What?"

"Havin' breakfast with Rex?" Bianca snorted. "I see how it is."

The relief that slammed into her was overwhelming. It took a moment for her to catch her breath, but she managed to do so without cluing Bianca in to the panic that had nearly taken over.

"Are you havin' breakfast with other hot cowboys that I don't know about?" Bianca asked, her tone shifting to prodding mode.

Bristol knew if she didn't say something, Bianca would harass her until she did, and that always resulted in Bristol telling more than she cared to.

"I'm gonna tell you somethin'," Bristol said, her tone stern. "But you have to promise to not tell a soul. Not even Jake."

"Your secret's safe with me."

"I'm serious, Bianca. No. One."

"Jesus H. Christ. Who do you think I'm gonna tell?"

Bristol took a deep breath. "I did it," she blurted.

"Did what?"

"I had sex with Kaden and Keegan." The words were shot out of her mouth like a rocket.

There was silence on the other end of the phone.

"Bianca?"

"I'm here. Just ... processing."

"Processing what?"

"Okay, fine. I'm fantasizing."

Bristol laughed, relaxing a bit.

"Tell me everything. And I mean every single detail."

Bristol laughed. No way would she tell her everything, but she could certainly give her the highlights.

"Start with the when," Bianca demanded. "When did this happen?"

"Friday night." She only felt a little bad that she was leaving out the previous encounter. No reason to share that now. Bianca would only get butt-hurt that she hadn't revealed that sooner.

"And? How was it?"

"It was ah-mazing. Absolutely, undeniably the best sex I've ever had in my life."

"That tells me nothing. I'd already expected as much. Give me details."

"Well..." Bristol felt her face warming with embarrassment. "Let's just say, I learned the reason for that saying 'hung like a horse.'"

It was definitely a crude thing to say, but it was also something Bianca would expect. Her best friend had always been hung up on size. To hear her say it, her husband, Jake, had been blessed by the gods where girth was concerned.

"Big?"

"Huge, Bianca. I mean, I thought they would hurt me."

They both laughed and though Bristol realized how crazy it sounded, it was the truth.

"Any DP action?"

"No." She wasn't sure she was quite ready for that yet. Not to mention, if and when she ever decided to go that route with them, she was never going to share those details with anyone. She loved Bianca and all, but come on, there were some things better left unsaid. "But I did have sex with both of them."

She honestly couldn't believe she was spilling her guts like this. "It was … incredible."

"Bristol? Is it just me, or do you sound … happy?"

"I'm not sure what it is, but I feel different."

"You know it's okay to put a name to it. There's nothin' wrong with bein' happy."

"And there's nothin' wrong with some great casual sex," she countered because she didn't want to discuss her happiness, or the future. Her friend was well aware of the fact Bristol no longer believed in the fairy tale, or any sort of happily ever after. It didn't exist.

"That's what this is? Casual sex?" Bianca didn't sound convinced.

"Of course." What else could it be? "And I'm gonna ride it out for as long as I can. No harm, no foul, right?"

"If you say so."

"I do. It's all good, Bianca. I promise."

"Does that mean they'll be accompanying you to the winter carnival?"

Oh, crap. She'd forgotten all about the carnival, which was next weekend.

"Bristol?"

"I … uh … I don't know yet," she said softly. "We're takin' this one day at a time."

"Oh, come on. I am dyin' to see the look on everyone's faces when they see you arm in arm with a couple of smokin'-hot cowboys."

"Bianca, you can't tell anyone," Bristol blurted, her panic setting in. "Seriously. I don't want anyone to know."

She was met with silence again.

"Bianca?"

"I'm here," her friend replied. "Why? Why don't you want the world to know you're happy?"

"Because it's... No one'll understand. I'd prefer we kept it quiet. Please."

"For how long?"

Bristol shrugged although she knew her friend couldn't see her. "I don't know."

"And if it gets serious?"

Can't get much more serious than having a baby together.

"I'll deal with that if the time comes. Until then, I just ... I wanna enjoy them all to myself for a little while."

"Good for you."

She wasn't sure any of this was good. Honestly, Bristol hadn't been dwelling on the notion others would find out. She'd managed to shove that panic down at least temporarily. Locked up here in her house, where no one could see her, that was easy to do. Once she was back at work tomorrow, no doubt she would be wondering who else knew the truth.

"You can't tell anyone, Bianca," she repeated. "Not even the girls."

"I won't. Sheesh. You act like I can't keep a secret."

Depended on the secret, Bristol knew.

A knock sounded on her door, drawing her attention. With the phone to her ear, she got to her feet, padded over, and looked out through the security hole.

"Oh, crap," she muttered, sitting up quickly.

"What's wrong?"

"Kaden's here."

Bianca laughed. "Then I'll be letting you go now. Have fun! Don't do anything I wouldn't do."

The call disconnected and she was left standing there, feeling stupid. She peeked out once more, saw Kaden still standing on her porch, his Stetson on his head.

With a deep breath, she pulled open the door and smiled brightly.

His smile was instant, but it faded just as quickly when his gaze dropped.

Well, crap.

He shifted, presumably to block anyone else's view of her from the door. As it was, she was wearing only her panties and a thin tank that barely reached her navel. Truth was, he was lucky she was wearing that. Bristol wouldn't say she was a naturalist, but she did have a penchant for wandering naked around her house. It was one of the benefits of living alone.

"May I come in?"

She stepped back out of the way, gesturing him inside.

"DO YOU ALWAYS ANSWER THE DOOR LIKE that?" Kaden asked when Bristol closed the door behind him.

"No," she said quickly, a hint of pink rising to her cheeks. "In my defense, no one usually comes to my door, so I'm not forced to open it while I'm barely dressed."

"Do you usually hang out at home"—he nodded his chin toward her lack of clothing—"like that?"

Please, please, please *say yes.*

Bristol peered down at herself then back up at him, more pink infusing her cheeks. "If I'm bein' completely honest, I'm a bit overdressed for a casual Sunday."

"Really?" Intriguing.

Then again, it was a bit warm in her house. Was that because she was barely dressed? Or was she barely dressed because it was hot?

Kaden peeled his coat off, handing it to Bristol when she held out her hand. She turned and hung it on a tall, skinny coat rack like his parents had had back when he was a kid.

"I thought you had things to do today," she said, changing the subject.

"I do. But I wanted to see you. Figured maybe we'd spend some time together. Alone."

She was staring up at him, her blue eyes flashing with what looked like desire. "Where's Keegan?"

"He went to help out Sawyer and Kennedy. Watch the kids for a bit. So you've got me all to yourself for a while."

His thoughts flashed back to Bristol and Keegan in her kitchen yesterday. Kaden had walked in and found her naked with his brother's head between her legs. It had been a shock in one of the best possible ways.

"Well, come in." She stepped back, gestured toward the couch.

Kaden couldn't take his eyes off her. "So, you like to walk around your house naked?"

"You don't?" she countered.

"Not usually, no."

"I guess that's one of the benefits of livin' alone. I don't have to worry about someone catchin' me in my birthday suit."

Rather than sit down, he turned to face her, eyes still traveling down her sweet little body. "I'd like to see that birthday suit."

Honestly, he hadn't meant to say the words out loud.

"That can be arranged," she replied, her voice raspy.

His gaze lifted to her face.

Definitely desire in those pretty blue eyes.

Unable to resist, Kaden stepped forward, closing the space between them. He cupped the side of her face, tilting her head back as he leaned in and kissed her.

When he pulled back, they continued to stare at one another. It was then the heat turned into something more potent. A firestorm blazing between them, electricity sparking as it arced. Not that it was a new thing. It had been there for as long as he could remember. The only difference was that Bristol was no longer pretending otherwise.

"For fuck's sake," he grumbled, reaching for her again as he crushed his mouth to hers.

Bristol kissed him back, her arms sliding around his neck, holding tightly when he lifted her off the ground, his hands filled with the soft, rounded globes of her ass. He hadn't intended for things to go this direction, but it seemed the universe had another plan for him. Perhaps wanting her for so long had altered his ability to be a gentleman in her presence.

He didn't bother attempting to make it to the bedroom; instead, Kaden took her down to the lumpy couch, settling himself over her. He loved the way her thighs cradled his hips, as though he was right where she wanted him.

"Woman," he breathed roughly, "I don't know what the hell it is you do to me."

He could feel her smile against his lips. "The feelin's quite mutual. But you're wearin' too many clothes."

"I thought we were gonna talk," he teased.

"Talkin's overrated." Bristol moaned, arching her back to press into him. "Clothes, Kaden. Get them off."

Kaden was all for it but getting her naked seemed more important right then. It took little effort to relieve her of her panties and that thin tank that had covered very little. She took the liberty to remove his hat, setting it on the coffee table while he let his lips trail down her sweet-smelling skin.

He had half a mind to hold back, to engage her in a little light conversation. *How's the weather? How're you feelin'?* That sort of thing.

Of course, her nipples pebbled, and his train of thought went right out the window.

"Do you have any idea all the dirty things I've wanted to do to you?" he muttered, trailing kisses to her taut nipple.

"Tell me," she murmured.

Lifting his head, he met her gaze, surprised by her request. "You want me to tell you?"

"Well"—she grinned—"provided you can show and tell at the same time."

He licked her nipple.

Bristol moaned, arching her back. "Kaden, I don't know what's goin' on here, but I feel like I'm gonna go up in flames."

He didn't know either, but he felt the same overwhelming intensity. It was a desperate hunger, a driving need to possess her in every possible way.

Ducking his head, he took her nipple between his lips, flicking his tongue over it briefly before moving to the other.

"Have you ever had your tits fucked before?" he asked.

Bristol moaned. "Oh, God … Kaden."

He paused his assault on her flesh. "Yes or no, Bristol?"

"No," she breathed out roughly.

"Squeeze 'em together," he instructed, lifting his head to meet her gaze.

Bristol did as requested, her hands plumping her breasts. They weren't big, but they weren't small, pretty much perfect as far as he was concerned.

Kaden leaned down, pressed a kiss to her chest, then dragged his tongue along the valley between her breasts. "Right here. This is where I want my cock."

Another moan as she began rocking her hips.

He flattened his palm on her ribs, pushed his middle finger between her tits, working his way through the tight fit, imagining his cock tunneling between the warm, smooth flesh.

"Slidin' between your tits, your sweet little tongue swipin' over the head…" Fuck. It was possible he was going to come from simply talking about it.

Before he got too sidetracked, Kaden repositioned her so that her head was on the armrest while he moved back so he could venture lower. He had other things in mind right now, important things. Kaden dipped his tongue into her navel, licking gently, feeling her stomach muscles contract against his ministrations.

"And this sweet little pussy." He groaned, nuzzling her flesh, inhaling her musky scent. "Put your foot up there," he urged, nodding toward the back of the couch. "Spread your legs so I can see how pretty it is."

A sharp inhale preceded Bristol's movements, but she did as he requested, propping one foot on the back of the couch, the other moving to the coffee table. It opened her wide, gave him an unobstructed view of her slick, pink flesh. She was so wet she glistened.

"Do you know how good you taste?"

"Kaden ... please."

"Please what?"

"Lick me."

Yeah, there was no resisting that, so he did as she requested. He dragged his tongue from her slick entrance to her clit, back down again, swirling around her opening, dipping inside. He teased her lightly, never giving her quite enough, loving the moans and groans, the way her fingernails dug into his shoulders as though that might make him give her what she needed.

Using his thumbs, he fondled her labia, holding her open while he tongue-fucked her. She tasted like ambrosia and he knew she would become his addiction. Maybe she already was and that was why he couldn't stop thinking about her.

When she began a rhythmic rocking against his tongue, he switched, circling her clit, sucking her into his mouth, flicking the tiny bundle of nerves. He could feel it pulsing, knew she was close. He didn't push her over the edge, instead maintaining a steady pace, wanting to prolong her pleasure for as long as possible.

She appeared to have other plans, because her fingers twined in his hair, jerking him forward as she ground her clit against his mouth. She came with a shudder and a beautiful cry, her body trembling. He wanted to make her come again, but the hand in his hair tugged, urging him back up her body. Kaden moved, finding her mouth with his, sealing their lips, letting her taste her sweet essence on his tongue.

"My turn," she whispered. "I want to taste you, too."

Kaden lifted his head, again shocked by her boldness but not disappointed.

He lingered a little longer at her mouth before forcing himself to his feet. With her help, his clothes disappeared and then she pushed him back down to the couch. To make room, he shoved her coffee table out of the way with his foot, allowing space for her to go to her knees between his legs.

And then Kaden was captivated, completely enthralled as Bristol took his cock in her small hand, fisting him despite the fact her fingers didn't quite touch. There was no hesitation on her part when she lapped at the precum pooling at the tip, her tongue dancing over the head, gliding down his shaft. She worked him like a pro, but he sensed her vulnerability. She was attempting to assume to know what he enjoyed, and she was nailing it perfectly, but he could tell she wasn't as sure of herself as she pretended.

That was one of many things he loved about her. Yes, he was getting used to this bold version of her, but being able to sense his Bristol beneath that sexy new facade eased the tension he hadn't realized had been growing inside him. As much as he loved this wild side, there was no denying it was her softer, sweeter side he'd always been drawn to.

Kaden let his palm rest on her head, urging her to take more of him but not forcing her. "Such a sweet mouth," he mumbled, wanting to encourage her. "God, yes, Bristol. Baby ... ahh ... take more of me."

She did, going down on him until he felt the head bump the back of her throat. It sent an electric spark through him, but he managed to stave off his release.

"You're gonna make me come," he warned, forgetting all about his eagerness to fuck her beautiful tits. "Keep it up, sweet girl, I'm gonna come down your throat."

She moaned, and it sounded a hell of a lot like encouragement.

"Is that what you want?" His fingers tightened in her hair. "You want me to come in your mouth?"

She nodded, never slowing as she began bobbing up and down, her small hand fisted around the base as she stroked in time with the exquisite suction of her mouth. Then her hand did this gentle twisting thing around his cock and he saw stars.

"Oh, fuck..." Kaden grunted, his back pressing into the couch, his hips thrusting forward.

He came so hard he felt the throbbing in his forehead.

"ALL RIGHT, LITTLE DUDES, YOUR PARENTS ARE gonna be home soon," Keegan informed the two boys currently hiding out in the blanket fort they'd built in the living room.

Well, technically, Keegan was the one who'd built it, and it was some damn fine architecture if he did say so himself. Clean lines done in maroon and cream cotton (a couple of throw blankets), awesome wood base (made from kitchen chairs, of course) and the most comfortable floor he'd ever sat on (pillows from the couch). Granted, he doubted Kennedy would be all that happy to see her many couch cushions, as well as a couple from her bed, being used as floors and walls in their imaginary kingdom. Never mind the fact that Buster, the family's cocker spaniel, had taken a liking to the fort, curling up inside and taking a nap.

"We don't wanna come out!" Brody shouted.

Being that he was two, Keegan had expected such a response.

"Hey, Matthew, you think you can help me here?" Keegan asked, keeping his tone level. "I was thinkin' maybe we could do somethin' really cool for your mom and dad."

One head peeked out, then the other.

"What did you wanna do?" Matthew asked.

Having just had his fourth birthday a couple of months ago, Matthew was a little easier to reason with. And Keegan had learned that Brody tended to do exactly as his older brother did.

"For starters, I wanted to see if we could get those pillows back on the couch. But I wanna see if we can make 'em crooked. That way your mom and dad'll fall in when they sit down."

One big grin formed, then another.

It was probably wrong of him to play them that way, but Keegan knew that was the game. If they thought they could pull one over on their parents, they were all for it. He'd been the same way at that age.

Come to think of it, he was the same way now.

Keegan grinned at the thought.

It took a good twenty minutes for them to deconstruct the blanket fort and get the pillows back where they belonged. It was Matthew's idea to put the pillows from his parents' bed at the foot of the mattress instead of the top so they would have to sleep upside down. Matthew's logic, of course.

As for the couch ... well, the cushions were most definitely crooked, but he figured Sawyer and Kennedy would live. After all, Keegan's babysitting services were free of charge. He had to get his recompense somehow.

An hour later, Keegan was strolling into Curtis and Lorrie's two-story farmhouse, lured by the aroma of roasting meat and the delicious scent of fresh-baked cornbread.

His first stop was over to Lorrie to plant a hello kiss on his aunt's soft cheek.

"Would you mind adding a few place settings to the table?" Lorrie asked, smiling up at him. "We've got a few additional guests comin' this evening."

"Of course. Mind if I ask who?" Keegan grabbed three more plates and three sets of silverware.

"Frank and Iris," she said pleasantly. "And they're bringin' their grandson, Eric."

Keegan had been seeing quite a bit of his Uncle Frank these past few months. He wasn't sure why that was, but he was glad for it.

He set out the extra plates and silverware in various spots reserved for those who dropped by unexpectedly. After delivering the additional settings to the enormous dining room, Keegan returned to the kitchen.

"How'd your afternoon go with Brody and Matthew?" Curtis asked, stepping into the room.

"Good." He smiled. "Blanket fort."

Curtis shook his head in that disbelieving way, a big grin forming on his aging face. "I talked to your daddy today."

"Did you?"

"Said they'd be comin' down for Christmas this year."

"Yes, sir, he promised us they would," he told his uncle. "I tried to get 'em down for Thanksgiving, but Mom was excited to spend it with her brother."

Keegan's father was the oldest of the Walkers as well as the only one who had settled down outside of Coyote Ridge. They'd been begging their parents to simply move here, but there was always one reason or another why they couldn't. Considering his other brothers and his sister were finally relocating, he figured there weren't going to be too many more excuses they could use. Perhaps the lure of some grandkids of his own would get his parents here.

From that point onward, there wasn't a whole lot of in-depth conversation taking place at the weekly meal. Curtis and Lorrie's kids soon descended, bringing along all the grandkids until the house was packed full. Keegan answered all the questions directed his way: *How's life on the ranch? You get the floors done yet?* then asked some of his own: *How're things with the kids? How's work? Anything new you want to brag about?* That sort of thing.

He was busy chatting it up with Braydon and Brendon when Kaden walked in. The first thing Kaden did was seek him out, their eyes meeting across the room. It was just something they did. Since they'd been old enough to go separate ways, they always found their way back together. Not only was Kaden his twin brother, he was also his best friend.

Kaden offered a clipped head shake, an answer to his silent question: Did Bristol come with you?

Keegan couldn't deny he was disappointed not to see Bristol on his brother's arm. He thought for sure Kaden could sweet-talk her into joining them. Didn't seem to be the case.

Last but not least, Frank and Iris arrived with their grandson, Eric, and surprising them when Reese and Brantley were right behind them.

"Welcome, welcome," everyone greeted, dragging the newcomers into the fray.

Once dinner was finished, Keegan and Kaden made their exit after saying their goodbyes.

"We goin' home?" he asked his brother, waiting for Kaden to tell him how things had gone with Bristol. He'd managed not to hound him for the past couple of hours, respecting her wishes for them to keep their interactions a secret for now. If he'd so much as brought up her name, someone would've overheard, and they'd never hear the end of it.

"Yeah."

"And Bristol?"

Kaden glanced over at him from behind the wheel. "Said she was tired."

"That why she didn't come to dinner?"

Kaden grunted, which Keegan knew was a sign that he wasn't happy.

Unable to hold back any longer, Keegan asked what had happened.

He listened as Kaden told him about his arrival, finding her scantily clad, the two of them getting busy on the couch.

That was the thrilling part.

The not-so-thrilling stuff came after that.

"I invited her for dinner; she declined. Said she's not ready for anyone to know about us, then tacked on the part about bein' tired," Kaden said.

Keegan's teeth clamped together, but he fought back the anger. "She say how long she expects that to last?" He looked over at Kaden. "I do plan to tell Mom and Dad about the baby. It's only fair."

Another grunt from his brother.

"You know, I fuckin' knew that—"

"Keegan, don't," Kaden barked. "Let it go."

He glared at his brother. "What?'

"You heard me. Let it go for tonight. Don't let it get to you. Not yet."

A little fucking late for that.

Keegan's temper had always had a flash point, and it appeared Bristol Newton knew exactly how to set it off.

But he managed a deep breath, reminded himself that this was new for Bristol. If she needed a little time, he could give it to her. Not much, but a little.

Chapter Nineteen

ON MONDAY AFTERNOON, TRAVIS HAD MANAGED TO steal a few minutes alone in his office at the resort. He'd spent the better part of the morning dealing with a personnel issue. Evidently, the new sous chef at the hotel's restaurant was beginning to wreak havoc on the head chef, the two of them going nose to nose once every couple of days. Having grown tired of the bickering, Travis sat the two men down and basically told them to cool their shit or they were both out on their asses.

He didn't have time for petty bullshit, and he didn't have any qualms letting them know that.

Now as he sat at his desk, he was reviewing the updated RSVPs for the New Year's Bash. Sawyer was keeping him apprised of the changes as they came in.

His office door opened, drawing his attention.

"Someone mentioned Brantley was here," Gage said when he stormed into the room. "Why didn't you tell me?"

Travis looked up, studied his husband's face. It wasn't the words he'd said that had his hackles rising but the way he said them. As though the thought of him talking to Brantley left a bad taste in his mouth.

"He was givin' me an update on the investigation," Travis told him, leaning back in his chair and getting a grip on his temper. "You got a problem with that?"

Gage walked over, planted his palms on Travis's desk, and leaned toward him. That stony expression remained firmly in place. "We agreed we'd let the FBI deal with this."

"No," he countered, "*you* agreed."

"Goddammit." Gage stood tall. "This shit has to stop, Travis. This obsession with findin' her … it's got to stop. We've got a family to take care of. A family you've played no part in since the day Kate came home."

"Excuse me?" Travis felt his face heat, his ire rising. He fisted his hands. "I'm home every goddamn night, I tuck my kids into bed, see them when they wake up. Kate spends much of her day up here with me, right here in this office. Don't you fucking dare tell me I'm not doin' my part."

"Yeah? And what about me and Kylie? You opposed to sleepin' in our bed now?"

Travis gritted his teeth, glared back at Gage.

His husband had him there. Initially they'd been alternating in their bed because of Kate. As time had crept by, Travis found himself putting distance between them. Mainly because of shit like this. The tension that was growing made it impossible for Travis to sleep, so he'd reverted to staying at work late, then spending the nights in the recliner or on the couch.

"I get it," Gage continued. "Not a minute goes by that I don't think about those horrifying days when we didn't know where Kate was, when we feared the worst. It pisses me off, too, that the woman responsible for upending our lives got away and no one's any closer to finding her. But our kids, our wife, they deserve our full attention, not for us to be distracted and distant."

"They?" Travis crossed his arms over his chest. "A second ago it was about you and Kylie. Which is it, Gage? Am I ignorin' my kids or am I ignorin' you? Because I damn sure don't hear Kylie complainin'."

"Because you're not there," Gage shouted. "You don't see it."

Travis launched to his feet. "See what?"

"The way she cries herself to sleep," Gage bit out. "Terrified that you're gonna do somethin' stupid, that you're gonna end up behind bars for the rest of your fuckin' life."

"So what if I do?" he shot back. "At least y'all will be safe. No one'll have to look over their fuckin' shoulder. We won't have to keep the kids locked in the goddamn house. She's still a threat, Gage."

"No, she's not. Not to us."

"You're fuckin' delusional if you believe that. Fuckin' delusional."

A knock sounded and they both turned to the door to see Kaleb standing there, staring back at them.

"Everything okay?"

"Fuckin' peachy," Travis snapped.

"Oh, yeah. Just fuckin' peachy," Gage grumbled then turned back to Travis. "I'll see you at home or I won't. I suddenly don't really give a fuck."

Travis swallowed hard, watched as Gage stormed out of his office, nearly plowing over Kaleb in the process.

"You wanna talk about it?" his brother offered.

"What do you think?" Travis dropped back into his chair. "Shut the fuckin' door, would ya?"

Thankfully Kaleb didn't try to push his way into the conversation. The door closed, leaving Travis alone with his anger and his pain.

Fuck Gage. Fuck him to hell and back.

Gage was wrong. The kids weren't safe. Kylie wasn't safe. For as long as Juliet Prince was out there, they had to remain vigilant, on alert at all times. Which meant Travis had to leave it to Gage and Kylie to hold down the fort while he continued his search. He would find her.

Of all people, Gage should understand why Travis was hell-bent on finding Juliet Prince, erasing her from the face of the earth. The bitch could've shoved her hand through his chest and ripped his heart out and it wouldn't have hurt any worse than the day she'd stolen Kate out from under their noses. And he'd watched Kylie and Gage suffer the same way, the pain they'd endured when they had no idea where Kate was, what was being done to her.

Travis had been helpless. Completely fucking helpless because his heart had been shredded, making it impossible for him to do what needed to be done. And the longer she was out there, the angrier he got. He knew it was consuming him, but he didn't give a shit. He had one goal.

Find her.

Eliminate her.

He'd be damned if he allowed her to destroy his world again. His or anyone else's.

"IS IT JUST ME, OR DOES HAVING an early dinner make us older than we are?"

Rex Sharpe looked at his husband and smiled. "You call it an early dinner; I call it a late lunch."

"Well, that certainly makes it sound better." Jack slipped his jacket off and hung it over the back of his chair.

"Hello, gentlemen," Rachel greeted when she approached the table.

"Workin' tables tonight?" Rex asked as he flipped open the laminated menu.

"Someone's gotta do it. Plus, we're slow this evening."

"It's still early," Jack said with a chuckle. "Only old people come in at this time, right?"

"Old people and you," she teased. "What can I get you to drink?"

They ordered their usual sweet tea for both of them and Rachel headed for the kitchen to get them.

"Why do you bother looking at the menu?" Jack asked. "We both know you're gonna have the special."

"Maybe I like lookin' at it. You never know when they might get somethin' new."

Jack gestured toward the menu with his chin. "When's the last time they updated that thing?"

Rex had no idea, but he figured it had been years, maybe decades. The diner had always had the same items on their menu. For as long as he could remember, anyway.

When Rachel returned, she set down the glasses in front of them, then pulled out her notepad. "Special, Rex?"

With a smile at Jack, Rex grinned. "Yes, ma'am."

"And you, Jack?"

"I like to mix things up," he said, holding Rex's stare. "I'll have the—"

"Chef salad, no croutons, extra egg, ranch dressing?"

Jack's gaze swung up to Rachel and he frowned. "Really? I'm that predictable now?"

"Not as predictable as this one." She motioned toward Rex with her pen. "I'll get that in for you. Be back in a bit."

When she left, Rex laughed at Jack.

"I can't believe I'm predictable." Jack pulled the menu toward him. "I'm gonna have to find something else I like for next time."

Rex leaned back, relaxed. It was the first time they'd been able to get away from the B and B in a month, and he knew they were going to have to make a change soon. As much as he loved the place, they needed some time away from there. As it was, they lived and worked within those walls, venturing out regularly, but not for long periods of time. Usually for supplies, only one of them at a time so someone remained behind to take care of the guests should they need something. And a rare night at Moonshiners or a meal at the diner was not what he considered time away. Rex wanted a real vacation with Jack. A honeymoon, maybe.

"Are you opposed to hirin' someone to manage the B and B?" Rex asked.

Jack's eyebrows shot upward. "You mean we might actually be able to leave town for a weekend? Hmm. I don't know."

Rex laughed.

"You have someone in mind?"

"Bailey Weber," he said without even thinking.

"Bailey? Moonshiners' waitress Bailey? Bakery Bailey?"

"One and the same, yes."

"She interested?"

"She mentioned it to me, so yeah, I'd say she's interested." Rex glanced down at the table. "Not the manager gig, no. I think she's lookin' for a maid position. Part-time."

"And that'll help us how? I mean, besides I won't have to clean toilets anymore." His eyes widened. "Wait. I won't have to clean toilets anymore."

"I was goin' to be persuasive," Rex told him. "I think she'd make a good manager. While she takes care of the guests, deals with meal prep and the like, we can do the manual labor."

Jack pouted. He *actually* pouted. "You know how I feel about manual labor."

Yes, he did. Jack was a bit spoiled, no doubt about it.

"It's not a done deal," Rex said with a sigh before taking a sip of his tea.

"Speaking of done deal," Jack said. "You never told me how your breakfast with Bristol went. She doing okay?"

Rex frowned for a moment. "What does that have to do with 'done deal'?"

"Nothing." Jack flashed a smile. "Just needed a segue."

Rex shook his head. "She's doin' good."

Jack canted his head to the side and Rex knew he was trying to read his mind. He had purposely not told his husband about the details of that conversation because Bristol asked him not to. Or rather, she threatened bodily harm if he told anyone she was pregnant.

"That's all you have to say? I need gossip, Rex. You know that."

That was something Rex had learned about Jack after they were married. The man craved gossip. Granted, he probably should've figured since Jack wrote graphic novels. He was intrigued by fiction and what better to base it on than real life?

Jack leaned forward, lowered his voice. "Spill. Now."

"What do I get if I do?"

His husband's left eyebrow popped up, which was his way of seducing him.

And he'd be damned if it didn't work. It always worked.

Rex sighed as though he was put out. "She's pregnant."

"Bristol's pregnant? Oh, my God."

"Jack. Damn it. Keep your—"

"Bristol's pregnant?" Rachel asked, staring down at them with two plates in her hand. "Holy moly. That's big news."

Son of a bitch.

EVER SINCE KADEN LEFT BRISTOL'S HOUSE YESTERDAY evening, more than a little disappointed that she had refused to go to Curtis and Lorrie's for dinner, he had been thinking about her. More accurately, he was trying to determine the best way to broach the subject they were clearly avoiding.

Their relationship.

Specifically, what it meant for the three of them as well as the baby.

Rather than get frustrated the way he had last night, he figured it made more sense for them to talk this out. Which was why he'd proposed dinner tonight. Originally his offer had been for her to come to the ranch, but she had politely declined without giving him a reason.

But he knew. Oh, yeah. He definitely knew.

She was avoiding being seen with them.

Evidently she hadn't given much thought to the fact she was driving around town in Keegan's truck, or that both of their trucks had been parked at her house overnight. More than once.

But heaven forbid, if someone saw her at *their* house, rumors could start.

So here he was.

"I know you might not believe this, but I do have food," Bristol said when Kaden carried a bagful of groceries into her house on Monday night.

"I believe you," he said with a grin, "but I doubt you'll have the stuff for steaks and baked potatoes."

"And what if I do?" she shot back, her eyes glittering.

"Well, if you do, then…" He glanced around, considered it. "I'll be your sex slave for the night."

Her eyebrows rose slowly, eyes glittering with interest.

"But if you don't, you have to be ours."

Bristol laughed, her cheeks growing pink. "Where's Keegan?"

"He dropped me off. Ran to the store to grab a six-pack."

"I'll have to be sure to stock beer in the future," Bristol said sweetly.

Because he had missed her despite his frustrations, Kaden took a moment to greet her appropriately. And his version of appropriate consisted of a long, lingering kiss that ended up with her perched on the countertop, him standing between her thighs. He was surprised to see she was wearing pajamas—which appeared to be a sweatshirt and a pair of tiny shorts—although he'd warned her they would be stopping by.

Right before he put thoughts of dinner behind them and dragged her to the nearest flat surface, Kaden pulled back.

"So, do you?" Now it was his turn to lift his eyebrows in question, waiting for her to confirm her deny.

She was breathless. "Do I what?"

"Have steak and potatoes?"

"I … uh…"

She blushed again and he knew what he'd find when he looked in her pantry. Pretty much the same as before. Nothing.

"Fine. You win. I haven't been to the grocery store yet." Her gaze swung over to the stove. "Nor do I have a workin' oven. It's been broken for a few years."

"No worries." He patted her thigh. "Keegan's stoppin' by our place to get his grill."

"I thought you said he was gettin' beer."

"He is."

"Y'all are goin' through a lot trouble for steak."

He met her gaze, held it. "It's worth it, Bristol."

What he didn't say was that she could've made it easier on all of them if she'd just agreed to come over to their place for dinner, but he didn't want to start an argument.

Half an hour later, Keegan arrived. Kaden had gotten the steaks marinating and the potatoes prepped for the microwave.

While he got the indoor grill set up on the counter, Keegan greeted Bristol similar to how he had earlier. The two of them were lip-locked for a few minutes before finally breaking apart.

He saw the way Bristol's eyes glittered with heat, and he suspected she was waiting for him to remember that she was their sex slave for the evening. Not that he had forgotten. Hell, they could've endured the apocalypse and he would've still remembered.

Kaden figured it was a good time to share the news with his twin. "She's our sex slave for the night."

Bristol gasped.

"Is that right?" Keegan's full attention was on her.

Bristol shot him a look that said she was more than a little embarrassed by his delivery of the news.

"What? You took that bet, darlin'."

"What bet?" Keegan inquired.

He let Bristol explain what happened and how she'd managed to get herself in that position.

"You wanna cook?" Keegan asked when she finished. "Or shall I?"

Kaden understood what his brother was really asking. *Do you want to get started with her now or shall I?*

"I'll cook," he offered.

"Very well."

Keegan reached for Bristol's hand, tugging her along as he led the way over to the kitchen table. He pulled out a chair, dropped down into it, then patted his knee in invitation.

Bristol waited for him to set his beer on the table before she got situated on his lap.

While he flipped the steaks, Kaden watched them, watched the way Keegan ran his hands along the smooth expanse of her bare thigh.

To his surprise, his brother didn't strip her bare and have his wicked way with her.

In fact, he got the feeling Keegan was holding back for a reason.

Because he didn't want it to get awkward, Kaden opted for conversation.

"You ever get another teacher hired?" he asked, glancing over at Bristol from his position at the countertop grill. Yesterday she had mentioned that one of her part-time teachers had decided to stay home with her kids, leaving her to fill the position.

"I did not." She sounded disappointed. "We've done a couple of interviews, but I wasn't impressed. I've got a few more later this week, though. So I'm keepin' my hopes up."

"I'll come work at your daycare," Keegan offered, taking a pull on his beer. "I can chill with the kids all day, then sneak off with you while they're down for their naps."

"I'm not sure I could afford a distraction the likes of you. Nothin' would ever get done."

"I'm okay with that," he told her, nuzzling her neck as he pulled her into him. "Damn, you smell good."

Bristol moaned when Keegan pressed his lips against her skin.

"Perhaps dinner should wait," Keegan said, obviously speaking loud enough for Kaden to hear. "Maybe we should just feast on you." Keegan slid his hands beneath Bristol's sweatshirt. "She's not wearin' a bra," he announced.

Kaden wasn't sure why he liked that, but his cock jerked behind his zipper.

"Fucking hell," Keegan rumbled as he lifted the sweatshirt higher.

Kaden grabbed his beer, leaned his hip against the counter, and watched.

"Hold this up," Keegan told her.

Bristol gripped the sweatshirt, holding it high enough to keep her breasts visible. From the way she was sitting, Kaden could see the lovely pale globes and her pretty pink nipples, and his mouth watered with the need to taste her.

"Turn toward me," Keegan instructed.

Kaden had expected her to shift her torso toward Keegan, but Bristol evidently had other plans, because she got to her feet, straddled his thighs, then lifted her sweatshirt again.

"This is nice," Keegan mumbled, pressing his palms against her back as he pulled her toward him, letting his breath fan her nipple. "So fuckin' nice."

Suddenly Kaden wished Keegan was the one cooking dinner. Why had he offered again?

Kaden's view was blocked from the action, but he got the gist. He knew Keegan was teasing her nipples, laving her breasts. He had to satisfy himself with the sounds of Bristol's pleasure, those soft moans that escaped her even as she pressed her chest toward Keegan in an attempt to get closer.

"Take it off," Keegan muttered.

No hesitation on her part. Bristol discarded the sweatshirt, tossing it aside before her hands cupped Keegan's head, holding him in place while he feasted on her once again.

They remained like that for long minutes, driving Kaden absolutely batshit crazy. Somehow he managed to focus on the steaks, not wanting dinner to burn.

"Dinner's ready," he finally announced, hating to break up their little party.

Releasing Bristol's nipple with a resounding *pop*, Keegan sat up.

"Don't bother gettin' dressed," Kaden told her, delivering two of the three plates to the table. "I like you topless."

When he stepped back, Keegan helped Bristol to her feet so she could sit in the other chair.

"I'll do my best to keep my hands to myself," Keegan said, reaching for his beer.

"I won't," Kaden told her when he took his seat.

"Promise?"

"Oh, yeah."

Her giggle had his chest feeling tighter than it had in a long damn time.

And that wasn't a good thing, he realized.

NEVER IN HER LIFE HAD BRISTOL EATEN dinner naked.

Well, not when there were other people around, anyway.

And fine, she wasn't completely naked. She still had on her pajama shorts although they weren't doing much good at all. Especially not when Kaden and Keegan were taking turns sliding their big hands beneath the wide openings and between her legs, their fingers finding her clit, doing wicked hot things to her while she tried to eat. As one might imagine, it was futile to attempt, and she would've given up trying long ago, except they seemed intent on ensuring she had dinner. While one would torment, the other would feed her. By the time she had convinced them she couldn't eat another bite, her entire body was aflame, and she was on the verge of climax.

Only they weren't letting her come. They would work her right to that razor-sharp edge then pull back just before she went careening over. It was both frustrating and exciting. Made all the more so by the heated look in their eyes as they watched her intently.

"I think it might be time for dessert," Keegan suggested.

Before she could tell them she would be forgoing dessert, she realized he wasn't talking about ice cream. He was talking about her.

Without fanfare, Keegan stripped her pajama shorts off, then hoisted her up onto the table the instant Kaden had cleared all the dishes away.

"Now this I could do every night," Keegan whispered, his hands sliding over her thighs, pushing them wide.

Above her, Kaden leaned over, cupping her breasts in his warm hands, kneading her flesh until she was moaning in earnest. She was overwhelmed by sensation as Keegan's fingers began teasing her sex, gliding through her slit, circling her clit. It was too much but, at the same time, not nearly enough. No matter how much she begged and pleaded, they maintained a steady pace, caressing her with only their hands.

"Please, Kaden … oh, God, Keegan. I…" She tried to thrust her hips upward. "More. I need more."

"You want my mouth on you, darlin'?" Keegan's sexy baritone washed over her.

"Yes. Please."

"Mmm. You asked so nicely."

She cried out when his warm breath fanned her pussy. She couldn't see what he was doing, but she didn't need her eyes. He licked her repeatedly, slowly tormenting with his wickedly skillful tongue, building her up once more.

It was all Bristol could do to endure. They assaulted her with overwhelming sensation, taking her to new heights. And the fact that there were two incredibly hot, sexy men focused solely on her made it impossible to ignore a single second of their wicked ministrations.

"Please…" she whimpered, dangerously close to imploding. "Make me come, Keegan."

He growled, the vibrations sending shockwaves through her. But it was when Kaden pinched her nipples and Keegan thrust two fingers inside her while sucking her clit that she felt herself skyrocketing. Her insides coiled tightly then exploded in heat and light, the most intense orgasm of her life leaving her panting and boneless.

Thankfully, they were there, carrying her out of the dining room and into her bedroom. They both joined her on the bed, Kaden crawling over her. At some point he had disrobed, his naked body sliding sensually against hers.

Although she was still reeling from the shock of so much pleasure, Bristol wanted more. She needed to feel them inside her. One, both, she didn't care as long as neither one of them left her.

Kaden was watching her, his eyes roaming over her face as though he was attempting to read her mind. She could've told him she only had one thing on it and that was to have him inside her. Now.

But she refrained from speaking. There was something else in those blue-gray eyes, something that sent a chill down her spine. He looked … not exactly happy despite the desire she could feel coming off him in waves.

Was he angry? Had she done something wrong?

Her nerves began to jangle wildly, insecurity threatening to choke her. Before she could ask him what was wrong, Keegan finally joined them, sliding onto the mattress beside her. With firm fingers, he turned her head to face him, his lips gentle as they fused to hers. It was during that passionate exploratory kiss that Kaden slid deep inside her. He went slow, giving her body time to adjust. All her nerve endings came alive when he began rolling his hips, penetrating her slow and deep. All the while, Keegan continued to kiss her.

Within minutes, she was once again riding that sensual high, hanging on by her fingernails as Kaden's deep, rhythmic thrusts took her to the edge again. Her whimpers were muted, but they both seemed to understand what she needed because Kaden didn't stop; he continued to make love to her until there was no turning back.

Bristol tore her mouth from Keegan's as she cried out in sheer ecstasy, the orgasm coursing through her in a blaze of warmth followed quickly by Kaden's deep, rumbling groan.

But they weren't finished, nor was she.

Keegan traded places with Kaden, taking up position between her thighs. Bristol stared up at him, maintaining eye contact as he pushed inside her. She could see the strain on his face, knew he was holding back.

Bristol pulled her knees toward her chest, changing the angle of penetration, allowing him to go in impossibly deep. She saw the way his eyes glazed, hooded as he watched her face, never looking away.

She reached for him, sliding her left hand over his thigh while using her right to grip Kaden's arm, anchoring herself between them as Keegan began to thrust into her. There was no lovemaking this time. He drove into her hard, fast. How he knew what she needed, Bristol wasn't sure, but she didn't question it. She gave herself over to the intensity.

"Keegan…" She was so close, and she wasn't sure she was going to survive it this time. It was too intense, too—

Bristol screamed out his name, her head falling back as her body tightened and then shattered once more.

Some time later, she didn't know when, Bristol awoke in her darkened bedroom. She was between them, her head on one shoulder, another spooned behind her. She tried to listen to them breathing, to see if she could determine who was who, but in this state, they were identical. She had no idea which was Kaden or which was Keegan. She could've let her hands roam, find those various scars that told her who was who, but it didn't matter. They were here with her. Both of them.

For the first time in her life, Bristol felt safe, cherished.

And irrevocably changed.

Try as she might, she hadn't been able to avoid it. Years had passed while she had kept her distance, but it hadn't mattered. It had all been wasted time because she had fallen anyway.

She was in love with Kaden and Keegan, and she knew that hiding it from anyone was going to become infinitely harder, but she wasn't ready for anyone to find out.

Not yet.

Not until she had a plausible explanation, one that wouldn't make her fodder for the gossip mill.

Until then, she wanted to keep it just between them.

KADEN HEARD BRISTOL'S BREATHING CHANGE, KNEW SHE was awake.

He shifted closer, his hand sliding up to cup her breast as he remained on his side, facing her.

Her soft murmur was both sweet and sexy, a bit of encouragement as he drew her closer.

When she leaned toward him, he cupped her face and found her lips with his own. They remained like that, lips gliding, tongues melding, hands roaming.

This was perfection for him. Bristol in his bed, his brother behind her. The three of them together. Almost didn't matter that it wasn't his house, wasn't his bed.

He'd never truly understood why this was what he was looking for but it felt right. He felt complete in that moment, never wanted it to end, although he knew it would have to come morning. The sun would rise, the day would begin, and life would get back to normal. It was unfortunate that time was a measurement of all things, but he knew that it didn't matter that he'd fallen in love with her so quickly.

The difficult part was going to be in getting Bristol to see that this wasn't something that should be hidden from the world.

Kaden didn't want to live in the dark, didn't want to hide what they had. He wanted everyone to know how lucky they were to have this woman, to love her, to cherish her.

But he'd sensed it tonight almost from the moment he'd stepped in the door.

Bristol was going to make this about sex. In doing so, she could purposely keep the deeper feelings out of the relationship.

Or so she thought.

Bristol moaned softly, her hand sliding over his chest, her nails digging in as a sigh escaped her.

It was then he felt the mattress rocking, knew Keegan had moved up behind her.

Kaden thumbed her pebbled nipple, sucked on her tongue. She was turned on, her breaths becoming more labored.

"Oh, God, yes," she moaned, her knee rising as she lifted her leg.

Kaden kissed her again, keeping her close while Keegan slid inside her from behind. The two of them kept her there while Keegan loved her intimately, their bodies rocking, Bristol's against his.

Yes, this was what Kaden wanted. He wanted Bristol right there between them every night for the rest of their lives.

Pulling his mouth from hers, he watched Bristol's face in the darkened room, the way her eyes closed, her mouth opening on a moan. He peered at his brother over her shoulder. Blue-gray eyes identical to his own opened, staring back at him, and Kaden could see it there, too. They were on the same wavelength in that moment. What Keegan felt, Kaden felt and vice versa.

This.

This was what they'd dreamed about for a lifetime. Another chance for a happily ever after.

If only he could ensure the two of them didn't jump the gun, didn't send Bristol into a panic, perhaps everything would work out the way it was meant to.

Chapter Twenty

"IT'S ONE THING FOR YOU TO SNEAK outta the house before we can even say goodbye, but it's somethin' else entirely when you don't come home."

Travis looked up from his computer, watched as Kylie strolled into his office, her eyes bright with what he assumed was anger. If her tone was anything to go by, she was certainly pissed.

"I don't sneak," he told her, turning his attention back to the computer. "And how the hell do you know I didn't come home last night?"

"Because I waited for you, dammit!"

Okay. He hadn't expected that.

Truth was, Travis was starting to feel like he was on the outside looking in. And it was true, last night he hadn't gone home. Instead, he'd snagged one of the empty rooms, caught a few hours of sleep so he wouldn't risk waking the kids when he came in. It had happened earlier in the week, and he'd spent what few hours he could've slept trying to get Maddox settled.

"Travis."

Releasing a frustrated breath, he sat back in his chair, closed the laptop lid, and ignored the report he'd gotten from Jessica James that morning. The instant it had come in, his heart had skipped a beat. She had an unconfirmed sighting of Juliet Prince somewhere in California. Nothing that would warrant him hopping on his private jet and heading out, but more than he'd gotten in months now.

"This has to stop," Kylie said firmly.

"What might *this* be?" he prompted, watching her closely. "You gonna waltz in here and tell me I'm obsessed, too?"

Kylie didn't respond, but she didn't have to. He saw the answer in her eyes. For the past couple of weeks, Kylie had been walking on eggshells around him, no doubt on edge after getting an earful from Gage. She thought he was acting crazy, too.

There was no denying that cut deep. As deep as it did when Gage had thrown it in his face. Looked as though both the people he loved, the ones he expected to have his back no matter what, had turned on him.

And yeah, maybe that was part of the reason he hadn't gone home last night.

"I don't have time for this, Kylie," he bit out, reaching for his laptop.

Before he could raise the lid, Kylie's hand landed on it, keeping it closed. "We're gonna talk about this."

"From where I sit, looks to me like you and Gage have it covered. There's not much I can say, now is there?"

"I want you to find her," Kylie bit out.

Shocked by the anger in her tone, Travis sat back, stared. "What?"

His wife sighed, standing tall and planting her fists on her hips. "I'm with you on this, Travis. I get where Gage is comin' from, and yeah, I'm worried you're gonna go off the rails. God knows you've done it before. But I want her found. I want her to spend the rest of her natural life behind bars for what she did to my daughter." She exhaled sharply, her voice wavering slightly. "Hell, there are times I imagine my hands wrapped around her throat, squeezing until her eyes bulge out and she chokes on her last breath."

Travis was on his feet when tears sprang to Kylie's eyes. He could feel her tension, knew this was as hard on her as it was on him. And Gage, too. They were all suffering because they didn't have closure for the horrific event that had rattled the foundation of their lives.

"Christ," he muttered, enfolding her in his arms, pressing his lips to her forehead. "I'm sorry, baby."

"Don't be sorry," she sobbed, sliding her hand over his chest, leaning into him. "I don't want you to be sorry for being who you are, Travis. I love you. Not in spite of you bein' hardheaded and sometimes single-minded to the point of distraction but because of it. I know you want to protect us."

More than anything. That was his sole position in life, the man who protected his wife, his children, his husband.

"But we have to keep moving forward," she said, her voice a tad calmer, her arms coming around his waist to hold on to him. "We have to keep livin' our lives. You can run this investigation in the background, but you can't devote all your time to it. The kids can feel the tension. Kate's asked me numerous times if you're still lookin' for that bad woman."

Some of his anger drained away. "What do you tell her?"

"I tell her, yes, of course you are. I'm honest with her. I tell her that neither of her daddies will stop until that evil woman's in jail where she belongs."

Travis felt the emotion bubbling in his chest, the heat in his sinuses. Every time he thought about what Kate went through, he fought to hang on, not to lose it. He hadn't been there to protect her, hadn't stopped that bitch from traumatizing his daughter, his entire family.

When Kylie began to pull back, Travis released her, schooled his expression because it would do no good for Kylie to see him at less than his best. Not now.

"Gage is hurt," she said, meeting his gaze.

"Because I won't stop. I know."

"No." Kylie took his hand, squeezed it. "Because you're doin' this solo. You're not keepin' him in the loop."

"To protect him," he rationalized.

"He doesn't see it that way. Think about it, Travis. Gage wants to protect you, too, and this is his way of doin' that. He needs you." Her eyes implored him. "And he needs you to need him."

Travis took a deep breath, stepped away from Kylie, and paced the floor.

"Let him help," she pleaded. "He needs to feel included where you're concerned, Travis. We both know that."

He turned to face her. "Where is he now?"

"At home. He's takin' the kids to daycare, then he's bringin' Kate here. I told my sister I'd help her with a few things in the spa. Then I was gonna take Kate home with me."

Travis nodded. "All right. I'll talk to him when he gets here."

She walked over to him, her soft hand cupping his cheek as she stared up into his face. Travis could feel her pain, her worry. It was etched in her face and he hated that he'd done that. That he was responsible for all of this.

"I love you," she whispered. "More than life itself, Travis. We all do."

He continued to stare, his heart squeezing in his chest.

"But you have to let us take care of you, too."

He knew that. How could he not? They reminded him of it over and over again.

In fact, that was how they reined him in when he…

When he did shit like this.

Two hours later, Travis gave up on waiting for Gage. His husband never showed, instead taking Kate for breakfast. Just the two of them.

And to add insult to injury, Gage didn't respond when Travis texted him.

It was no less than he deserved.

Friday evening, after putting in a long day and getting far too little sleep this past week, Kaden had one more thing to deal with before he could go home and possibly lose himself in a bottle for the first time in … years.

Yeah. That was exactly what he was going to do. So fucking what if he had a hangover tomorrow. Right now, he didn't really give a shit.

"Where're we headed?" Keegan asked from the passenger seat, his eyes pinned on him.

"Need to stop by the office, talk to Autumn before we head home," Kaden explained.

"Fine. But after that, we're goin' to the lake."

Kaden peered over at his brother. "*What?* Why?"

"Because Bristol agreed to go with us."

Shocked, Kaden managed to keep half his attention on the road. "She did?"

"Well, to be fair, I kinda made it non-negotiable. Told her we needed some fresh air."

"And she agreed?"

"To going out in public? No. But I assured her we'd go somewhere secluded and no one would be the wiser."

Kaden exhaled his disappointment.

"Fine," he said, shifting his attention back to the task at hand: relaying their official resignation to the boss.

He'd been putting this off, but he knew it was time to make the leap, to put in their notice at the demolition shop and shift to taking over the ranch duties full-time.

Kaden wasn't exactly sure why he'd been waiting to tell Autumn. Perhaps he'd thought he would have more news to share than merely a resignation. Something along the lines of, *hey, not only did we buy a ranch, but we're also havin' a baby and gettin' married.* Unfortunately, they hadn't gotten anywhere in that regard.

Nope. No coming out to anyone yet. Bristol was still insisting they keep things quiet for the time being, and Keegan seemed entirely content with that, though Kaden wasn't sure why. Probably had to do with the fact they were getting laid multiple times a day. Morning, night, whenever they were with Bristol—always at her house—the three of them were rarely clothed.

And the more encounters they had, the more he noticed Bristol settling into this routine of seduction. She'd gotten good at steering him away from conversation. Almost as good as Keegan. Kaden had caught on to her ploy, and he'd made the decision that they would be having a heart-to-heart in the very near future. Which meant he wanted to have the rest of their shit in order, so they'd have something to present her with.

Yes, something along the lines of marriage and a future together.

Maybe tonight. At the lake. He couldn't imagine there would be any seduction on Bristol's part. Not when there was the chance someone might see them. It would be the perfect opportunity to chat openly, on neutral ground.

With a plan for later taking root, Kaden pulled up to the office, a single-story, two-room building that housed a couple of desks, a kitchenette, and a bathroom. Considering it was rarely occupied, it didn't make sense they'd have much more than that.

He noticed another car in the parking lot, which was little more than a dirt section worn down by years of tires rolling over it.

"Holy shit," Keegan said as they climbed out. "Nice car."

Yeah, it was. A 1969 cherry-red Chevy Camaro. Damn nice.

He had no idea who it belonged to, but knowing Keegan, they'd befriend the owner and likely be getting an up-close glimpse beneath the hood.

Because he didn't know who was on the other side of the door with Autumn, Kaden knocked before opening it then stepping inside when they were summoned by a "Come in."

"Hey," Autumn greeted from her spot at her desk.

Sitting in a chair across from her was a pretty black woman whose smile was both bright and genuine but had nothing to do with them. Oh, no, that smile was all for Autumn.

"We can come back," he told her quickly.

"No. Come in." Autumn stood, as did her friend. "I'd like you to meet Charlotte Miller. Charlie, meet Kaden and Keegan Walker."

Kaden offered a hand, smiled.

When she faced him head on, he amended his earlier description. Charlie Miller wasn't merely pretty. She was strikingly beautiful, but he wouldn't have been able to pinpoint exactly why if asked. Her shoulder-length black hair was board straight and angled around her long, narrow face. Her brown eyes were so dark it was hard to tell the pupil from the iris. She wore little makeup, but what she wore accentuated her high cheekbones and her long lashes. She was tall, probably just a few inches shy of six feet, but the short-heeled boots had her hitting close to the mark. The clothes she wore seemed tailor-made to fit her trim, athletic body.

"Nice to meet you," he greeted kindly, noticing the sideways glances Autumn was stealing of Charlie.

"Likewise. I've heard a lot about you." She shook Keegan's hand. "Both of you."

"Good, I hope," Keegan replied.

Charlie's smile widened, her dark eyes glittering with mischief. "Mostly."

"Charlie's the newest member of Brantley's task force. She's a Taylor police officer."

"Oh, yeah? How'd you find Brantley?" Keegan inquired.

"He found me, actually," Charlie said easily. "I previously worked on a task force with Sebastian Buchanan. Apparently, I impressed him."

Kaden didn't know Sebastian Buchanan—known as Baz to those around there—all that well, but he'd met the guy, seen him around a couple of times. More importantly, he'd heard good things about him from Brantley and Reese.

"Well, welcome to Coyote Ridge," Kaden said in response.

"Thanks." Her dark eyes cut over to Autumn. "I'm lookin' forward to bein' here."

There was something in Charlie's tone that was familiar. It was appreciation, he realized.

"Well, I should get outta your hair," Charlie said, smiling over at Autumn. "I'll talk to you later."

"Lookin' forward to it," Autumn replied, sounding oddly smitten.

"Nice to meet you both," Charlie said on the way out the door.

"Likewise," Keegan called out. "Next time you're in town, maybe we can get a look under that hood."

"Keegan," Autumn said, obviously gearing up to chastise him for coming on to the woman.

"Absolutely." Charlie peered over at Autumn. "And if I'm lucky, I'll get to take this one for a spin."

Without another word, Charlie was out the door.

"You know she's gay," Autumn told Keegan when the door closed behind the other woman.

"And?" Keegan looked at Kaden then back to Autumn, his confusion evident. "There somethin' wrong with a gay woman ownin' an awesome car?"

Autumn's eyebrows popped. "Car?"

"Nineteen sixty-nine Camaro?"

Autumn spun around and tugged the blinds down to peer outside. A very impressed "Holy shit" followed.

Keegan laughed. "She thought I was hittin' on her."

"Well, in *her* defense," Autumn replied, "it's not a farfetched idea."

"Guilty."

"What brings you boys by?" she asked, returning to her chair and motioning to the empty ones across from her.

Kaden sighed as he took a seat. "We're here to officially give our notice."

Autumn glanced between them as though waiting for the punch line.

Kaden went on to explain about the ranch, their need to be there full-time so they could get the place functioning how they needed it to in order to support them.

"Figured it was best to let you know sooner rather than later," he stated.

He could tell she wasn't exactly thrilled with the news. "How long do I have you for?"

"Tomorrow's our last day," Keegan said, deadpan.

Kaden had to smile when Autumn's eyes rounded like saucers.

"For as long as you need us," Kaden told her. "We've already let Ethan know. He mentioned Beau wants to come back part-time. Figured we'd do the same." He nodded at Keegan. "We'll alternate hours so you'll have one full-time person. At least until you're at the point you don't need us anymore."

He could practically see her brain working, likely turning over images of people who might be a good replacement in her mind.

"Well…" Autumn sat up, pushed her shirt sleeves back and put her elbows on her desk. "I have to ask this."

Kaden waited.

"Is it somethin' I did?" Her gaze bounced back and forth between them. "Because I'll change. I will. I swear to you."

She was dead serious.

"What?" Kaden stared back at her. "We… No…" He shook his head, tried to come up with a better explanation. Came up with "Uh…" instead.

Keegan laughed.

This time Autumn was the one to grin.

Kaden breathed a sigh of relief when he realized she was fucking with him. "I will get you back," he promised.

"I look forward to it." She leaned back again. "And I'm truly happy for you. Both of you. Assuming this is something you can afford to do."

"Our parents are investing," Keegan blurted. "Said they wanted to get in on the action, so to speak."

Kaden held his tongue. He didn't feel the need to explain that even without their parents' money, they could hold their own for a while. He had been saving money for a good majority of their lives with this specific end goal in mind.

"This is somethin' we've wanted our whole lives," Keegan explained. "When the opportunity arose, we had to jump on it."

"Gotta do what you love," she said. "Otherwise, life ain't worth livin'."

No. No, it certainly wasn't.

Two hours later, not long after the sun went down, Kaden was behind the wheel again, this time heading for the lake.

When Keegan told him this was the plan, Kaden admitted he was a bit hesitant. It wasn't their normal outing when they were with a woman. And while he had nothing against the lake, he wasn't sure it was an appropriate way to spend time with Bristol. She wasn't simply some woman who was looking to slake her lust with them, so suggesting a romp in the bed of the truck seemed disrespectful.

Turned out, he was wrong to worry. Bristol seemed completely at ease with their outing. At least after they'd left the town proper, where no one could see her riding with them.

Her reaction was simply another in the list of things he hadn't expected from her.

"Come on, darlin'," Keegan summoned when Kaden backed the truck up near the water.

"Where're we goin'?" she asked, turning to look out the back window.

"Nowhere."

When she turned back around, her eyes met Kaden's. She smiled and that sexy grin had him forgetting all his good intentions, wanting to be just as wild as Keegan in that moment.

"I'll grab the blankets," he told Keegan as the two of them hopped out of the truck.

While Kaden dragged their emergency blanket out from under the back seat and grabbed the two additional ones they'd brought from the house, Keegan lowered the tailgate. Kaden could hear Bristol giggle, figured Keegan had lifted her up and tossed her into the bed of the truck. By the time he joined them, he had some catching up to do. Keegan was standing, while Bristol was seated on the tailgate, her legs curling around Keegan's hips, their lips locked together, Keegan's arms wrapped around her, holding her to him.

Yep, they were in over their heads here.

While Keegan and Bristol made out like teenagers, Kaden stepped up into the truck bed, dropped the blanket, then joined the action, moving to sit behind Bristol. The move had Keegan stepping back before hopping up onto the tailgate beside them.

"Do y'all do this often?" Bristol inquired.

"What? Bring women here to make out?" Keegan teased.

"No," Kaden answered. "We haven't been to the lake since … probably not since early summer."

"At the Memorial Day festival?" Bristol giggled.

"Yeah. Actually." Kaden smiled. He loved to hear her laugh.

Bristol relaxed back against him, her hands resting on his knees.

It was funny but Kaden appreciated moments like this. When nothing was going on, the only thing they had to do was sit there, listening to the frogs and the crickets, watching the moonlight beam down on the glassy surface of the water. His brother was with him, the girl they wanted to spend time with. Not many moments compared to this one, when time seemed to stand still and all their worries remained somewhere behind them.

Bristol shivered, so Kaden wrapped his arms more tightly, letting her absorb his warmth.

"Why'd your family move to El Paso?" she asked, her thumbs brushing over his knees.

"We didn't move," Keegan answered. "It's where we were born."

"But your dad grew up here, right? He's Curtis's older brother?"

"Yep," Kaden responded. "He was in the military—Army— met our mother while he was at Fort Bliss. She grew up in El Paso. They decided to settle down there and raise a family."

"Do you like it better there?"

"Not better, not worse," Keegan stated. "Each has its own perks."

"So what brought you here? To Coyote Ridge?"

"Family," Kaden told her.

"Our parents brought us down here every year for holidays. Sometimes we found it hard to leave," Keegan added.

"Since we were teenagers, it's been the plan," Kaden said softly. "Buyin' a ranch here."

"I've never lived anywhere but here." Bristol sighed. "Never wanted to."

Kaden understood the feeling. While he wasn't married to any one small town, there was something about Coyote Ridge. Although he missed some things about home, he wanted to stay here. To raise a family here.

After a few minutes of silence, Keegan hopped down, walked around to the cab of the truck. Kaden heard the soft whir of the window motor as his brother opened the one in the back glass. A few seconds later, music spilled out. "Withdrawals" by Tyler Farr was what was playing.

Keegan returned, only he didn't sit, he stood in front of Bristol, between both of their legs. When she looked up at him, Kaden watched his brother's expression, noticed the heat, the desire, but there was something else. Keegan felt what Kaden did. Maybe he had all along and he'd simply been pretending otherwise, protecting himself from heartbreak as he was so good at doing. Regardless, Kaden could see it in the way Keegan's hand brushed her cheek, his head lowered.

When Keegan kissed her, Kaden realized this was going in a direction he'd hoped it wouldn't. At least not until they'd had a chance to talk. However, it looked as though his twin wasn't interested in chatting. Based on her soft moan, neither was Bristol.

Knowing he would be left out if he didn't join in, Kaden pressed his chest against her back. The soft moan she emitted said she approved, but it was the way she leaned into him, trying to get closer, that had his body hardening, his cock throbbing.

Unable to resist touching her, tasting her, Kaden brushed her hair aside, leaned down, pressed his lips to her neck. He sucked and licked while his hands slid beneath her sweater, gliding up her silky-smooth skin, cupping her breasts. More moans escaped her, mixing with the music playing softly in the truck.

"Please," Bristol whimpered, leaning into him, arching her back. "Touch me, Kaden. Don't stop touchin' me."

"Are you cold?" he whispered.

"No."

Neither was he. Funny how the chill in the air seemed to disappear completely as their body heat increased.

"Lift up your sweater," he instructed, nipping her earlobe.

When she did, Kaden tugged down the cups of her bra, plumped her tits in his hands, and felt his brother's chin brush his fingers when Keegan leaned down to take her nipple into his mouth.

"Oh, God," she sighed, tilting her head so Kaden could continue gliding his lips over her neck.

She was so damn hot, but he'd expected no less. For the past couple of years, he had watched Bristol. Yes, she was good at hiding all the heat and spark beneath her cool demeanor, but he had always suspected it was there. He wondered what had prompted her to take on the role of caretaker, the woman who would do anything for others but rarely did anything for herself. She did it so well, he doubted she even realized how much she neglected her own needs, her own desires.

And yes, he understood she was using this as a distraction, a way to avoid the pressing issues. These two were good at that. They'd rather be making out than talking. As much as it bothered him, there was no way Kaden could resist being a part of it.

When Keegan stood tall, Kaden straightened, their eyes meeting over her head. Kaden tried to get a feel for what his brother's intentions were. They had to be careful with Bristol. This wasn't some woman they intended to pleasure and send on her way. What happened between the three of them mattered. It mattered more than anything else as far as Kaden was concerned. He'd spent so much time aching for her, but it went further than mere lust. He wanted a future with Bristol, and the easiest way to fuck that up was to take things too far in a situation that she didn't find comfortable. Regardless of how willing she was in the moment.

Keegan nodded and Kaden managed to relax. They were on the same page. Keegan was on to her, too, knew she was acting different than usual. It wasn't necessarily a bad thing, but it often backfired. Those reckless moments had to be reined in eventually, and that was usually accomplished by being slammed with overwhelming regret.

However, it appeared Bristol had plans of her own, proven when she turned in his arms, straddling his thighs, her arms wreathing his neck as she brought his mouth to hers. No way could he resist her, so he fused his lips to hers, slowing her down in the process, taking control with Keegan's help.

"I'm burnin' alive," she whispered against his mouth. "I don't know what y'all do to me, Kaden, but … I feel like I'm gonna go insane if you don't touch me."

There was a desperation in her tone, a plea that he couldn't ignore.

Did he like that she wasn't eager to get back to her house behind closed doors? Yes. Truth was, he was similar to Keegan in that he enjoyed the riskier side of things. He merely refrained from taking too many chances. He left that to his brother because Keegan was the reckless one, not him.

But it didn't mean he was a prude.

It took some effort, but Kaden managed to move backward, sliding farther into the bed of the truck, onto the blanket. He brought Bristol with him, never breaking the kiss. He relished the way her hands snaked beneath his shirt, roaming over his back. Her fingers were soft and cool against his overheated skin, her body pliant. He could've spent the rest of his life right here, in the bed of his truck, this woman in his arms.

When Keegan tapped his shoulder, Kaden eased down onto the blanket, bringing Bristol with him. It wasn't the most comfortable place to lay out, but with her so hot, so eager, discomfort was the last thing on his mind. In an effort to include Keegan, he rolled so Bristol was on her side, her leg curled around his as though she didn't want him to move away. God, he'd waited so damn long for this, to have her wanting him the same way he wanted her. They were so close, but he sensed she wanted to be closer. He understood her need because he felt it, too. Kaden wanted this woman with a passion that rivaled all. When she began grinding against his thigh, he knew what she needed, knew the best way to give it to her.

Kaden pulled his mouth from hers, urged her onto her back while he began unbuttoning her jeans, lowering the zipper. Keegan was on her other side, his mouth sealing to hers while they inhaled one another. With his brother's help, they got her jeans down to her knees, her panties going with them. And then their fingers began to explore her tender folds, teasing, the two of them working in tandem to bring her the pleasure she sought.

Bristol pulled back from Keegan, her back bowing, eyes closing as she writhed so beautifully between them. And when they each dipped two fingers inside her at the same time, she came with a beautiful cry that Kaden knew he would be hearing in his dreams for days to come.

Chapter Twenty-One

SATURDAY NIGHT FOUND BRISTOL SITTING ON HER couch with her Kindle in her hand, an attempt to get lost in some fictional romance. Unfortunately, she continued to reread the same page over and over, her thoughts drifting to the encounter last night in the bed of Kaden's truck.

She still couldn't believe she'd done something so risqué. And she'd done her best to dissect it, to figure out how they'd gotten her distracted enough that it didn't matter that they were outside. But try as she might, she couldn't place the blame squarely on them. Bristol had been the one to practically jump Kaden's bones, begging and pleading for him to touch her.

She breathed in a choppy breath as memories flooded her. Their hands on her, their fingers *in* her. They'd brought her to orgasm with only their skilled fingers. More than once, at that.

Her body heated and she smiled.

The knock on her front door startled her out of her daydreams, had her hopping to her feet.

She exhaled with relief as she marched through the house, hoping against hope that it was Kaden and Keegan because she hadn't seen them since last night. After they'd returned to her house, they had come up with some excuse as to why they couldn't spend the night, and she'd pretended to be okay with it. And today they hadn't made plans to do anything, but if she was lucky, that would change.

The truth was, she missed them. She might've gotten used to not sleeping alone in her bed.

Without bothering to look, she yanked open the door. "Well, I did not expect——" Bristol stopped, stared, frowned. "Bianca. What are you doin' here?"

Her best friend's eyes narrowed.

Was that … anger making them brighter?

Without waiting for an invitation, Bianca marched right into the house, leaving Bristol no choice but to close the door and face her friend.

"I told you I couldn't go out tonight," she said quickly.

Bianca glanced around as though she hadn't been there before then settled her gaze on Bristol.

Oh, yeah, her friend was definitely perturbed.

"Why didn't you tell me?" Bianca asked, her words soft but laced with something. Hurt, maybe?

"Tell you what?"

Bianca's stare shifted to disbelief. "Are you serious right now, Bristol?"

"What? I don't know what you're talking about." It was the truth, even though she suspected her best friend had figured out she was spending all her spare time with Kaden and Keegan and she was here to give her crap about it.

Bianca took a step forward. "When did you find out?"

"Find out what?" she asked, her tone reflecting her growing frustration.

"That you're pregnant!" Bianca bit out.

Bristol inhaled sharply, took a step back. "How…? How did you find out?"

"Word travels. And I can't believe I wasn't the first person you told." Her eyebrow lifted. "Well, after Kaden and Keegan, that is."

Bristol was pretty sure this was what a panic attack felt like. Her chest was tight; air felt like sand coating her lungs as she tried to draw it in.

"Nothin' to say to that?" Bianca asked, hands going to her hips.

She couldn't speak. Her mind was already running a marathon, attempting to figure out how she was going to manage this crisis. She was going to be the talk of the town. No doubt by Monday there would be concerned parents pulling kids out of the daycare. Who could blame them? They didn't want some irresponsible woman in charge of their children. God. And Stephanie Hennessy. That woman was going to have a field day with this, probably spread the news far and wide just to hurt her.

"Did they tell you?" Bristol demanded when she could form words.

"Who?"

"Kaden and Keegan." Bristol ground her molars together. They'd promised. They'd sworn to her they wouldn't tell anyone until she was ready.

The liars.

Tears sprang to her eyes, welling up and spilling over.

"Hey." Bianca was instantly in front of her, pulling her in for a hug. "It's gonna be all right. You know we're all here for you, right? You don't have to do this alone."

Pulling back because she didn't want to be coddled right now, Bristol swiped the tears with her hand.

"How could they?" she muttered, marching to the kitchen. "They promised."

"So it's true? You're pregnant?" Bianca asked, her voice a tad softer than before.

Bristol turned to face her. "Who did you tell?"

Bianca frowned. "No one. God. I just heard."

"From who?"

She could tell Bianca didn't want to tell her, but Bristol waited her out.

"Rachel," Bianca finally said.

"Rachel? At the diner?" Bristol spun away. "Oh, my God. Oh, my God."

Panic set in again.

"They told her," she bit out. "They told everyone. How could they do this to me? They promised."

"Okay. Calm down." Bianca's hands settled on her shoulder. "Bristol, it's gonna be all right. Take a breath."

"It's not!" she shouted. "It's not gonna be okay! How can it be? I'm screwing twins. I'm gonna be the girl everyone looks at, the one everyone's whispering about."

Oh, yeah, she was pretty sure she was going to be sick.

Violently ill.

"Sit," Bianca snapped, shoving Bristol into one of the kitchen chairs and then pushing her head down between her knees. "Breathe, Bristol. Calm. Down."

Easy for her to say.

Her head popped back up. "I have to call them."

Bristol was on her feet, stomping toward the living room where she'd left her phone.

She found Kaden's number first, hit the button to make the call.

"Yeah?"

His gruff tone had her pausing for a moment.

"It's Bristol," she told him, sure he hadn't recognized who was calling.

"I know. What do you need?"

Her heart was in her throat. He'd never been curt like that before. Not with her. That was something reserved for Keegan.

Shit. Maybe she'd gotten their numbers mixed up.

"Kaden?"

"Yeah. What do you need, Bristol?"

"Why'd you do it?" she blurted, ignoring the concern niggling at her brain. "Why'd you tell people? You promised me you wouldn't."

"What are you talkin' about?"

"The baby? Half the town knows now."

Okay, so that was not something she knew for a fact, but it did help to drive home her point.

"I didn't tell anyone," he said firmly. "You asked us not to. No. Amend that. You *told* us not to. So we haven't."

"Keegan did then," she insisted.

"We haven't told anyone. Not even our fucking parents, Bristol. What's goin' on?"

Tears sprang to her eyes.

How could this be happening? No one was supposed to know. Not until she figured out how to deal with it herself. Not until she was certain she could handle the curious stares and all the questions that would no doubt arise when people found out she was pregnant, and she didn't know who the father was because she'd slept with them both. At the same freaking time.

"I can't believe y'all did this to me," she whispered, her chest aching. "You promised."

"We didn't do this," he snapped, his anger apparent. "Maybe it was someone else you told."

"I didn't tell anyone else!" Bristol took a deep breath. "I've gotta go."

She hung up the phone, not wanting to hear him deny it anymore. No one else knew that she was pregnant. No one—Except…

"Oh, God." Bristol fumbled for the chair and took a seat. "Rex knows."

Bianca was still standing in her kitchen, staring at her like she'd lost her mind. It was a good possibility she had.

"You told Rex but not me?" Bianca looked … apoplectic at that realization.

"No. I mean, yes. I told him. I needed his perspective."

"Right. Perspective." Bianca turned toward the door. "Now I know exactly where I fit in around here."

"Wait," Bristol called out.

"No. I've said my piece. I'm done."

"You can't be mad at me!" Bristol insisted, shooting to her feet and stomping into the living room, where Bianca was reaching for the doorknob.

"Can't I?" Bianca spun around. "I've spent the past month trying to figure out what's goin' on with you. We all have. We've been there for you, damn it. And you were keeping this secret from us. I thought we were best friends, Bristol."

"This isn't about you."

Bianca gave a curt nod. "Clearly. It's all about you. Just like it's been for a really long time." She sighed. "Like I said, I'm done."

With that, her friend walked out of the house, leaving Bristol to stare after her.

An hour later, Bristol was lying in her darkened bedroom, eyes swollen and scratchy but wide open. Try as she might, she couldn't sleep, her thoughts continuing to drift to Kaden and Keegan. To being seen with them in public. The stares the looks.

No doubt about it, she would be slated as the town slut.

For the first time, she was grateful her father wasn't around to see it. Heaven forbid he find out his daughter was a trampy whore who spread her legs for more than one man at a time.

Her chest tightened, her stomach lurched. What had she done? That one night, her lapse in judgement, it was going to taint the rest of her life. She would have to explain not only to those who knew her but also to her child that she was not the woman she'd prided herself in being. Bristol had spent her life attempting to set a good example only to screw it up.

And to think, she'd somehow managed to overcome Baxter's betrayal. For the longest time, she'd gotten sympathetic glances from everyone she knew, everyone feeling sorry for the girl who couldn't keep her man happy.

A sob tore free and she rolled over, hugging her pillow tight to her chest.

What made it worse was the fact that she wished Kaden and Keegan were there, holding her, assuring her, helping her through this.

But they weren't here and she seriously doubted they would be ever again. Not after the way she handled things. Her reaction to people finding out she was pregnant ... it was inexcusable.

Bristol's stomach lurched again and she breathed in deeply. Slowly. In, out.

She honestly didn't know what was worse: the town finding out or her losing Kaden and Keegan for good.

Both were enough to keep her stomach in chaos.

"WHAT THE HELL WAS THAT ABOUT?" KEEGAN asked, joining Kaden in the kitchen.

"She accused us of spreadin' the news about the baby," Kaden told his brother as he stared at the refrigerator, debating on whether he was going to have a beer or something harder. Right now, the latter was looking damn good.

"To who?"

"Accordin' to her, the whole town." Kaden could still hear the fear in her voice, as though someone finding out was the end of the world.

"We haven't even told Mom and Dad yet," Keegan stated firmly. "And trust me when I say I've been damn close to callin' them about a dozen times."

Yeah. Kaden knew the feeling. They were the first people he wanted to share the news with, but out of respect for Bristol, he'd refrained. Well, that and he'd been hopeful they would attend the sonogram with her so they'd have some first pictures of the baby to share with their parents. However, if word got around before...

"We're gonna have to tell 'em now," he told Keegan. "If word spreads to Eve, she'll go straight to them first."

Keegan sighed. "I was hopin' to wait until we saw the sonogram. Figured we could give the details. You know Mom's gonna ask."

Yes, she would. She would want to know the expected due date, the sex of the baby. All that good stuff. Just thinking about it had Kaden's chest warming. They were having a baby with Bristol. It was probably stupid, but the idea of it made him hopeful.

"We have to go talk to her," Kaden decided.

"Then what're we waitin' for?"

Twenty minutes later, Kaden pulled his truck into Bristol's driveway directly behind Keegan's. Bristol was still driving it because they hadn't gotten around to fixing her car yet, although the parts had come in midweek. It was on his list of things to do, but he'd been caught up in other things this week. Like work, renovations, his overwhelming thoughts about their shaky relationship with Bristol. He'd procrastinated because he knew her car gave him an excuse to talk to her if it came down to it.

Kaden hoped like hell it didn't come to that.

He wasted no time getting out of the truck, heading for her porch. Keegan stared up at the burned-out light bulb while Kaden knocked on the door.

"I just changed that," Keegan muttered. "I think she's got a loose wire."

Probably. The entire house needed work.

When he heard the deadbolt unlock, Kaden took a single step back, waited until Bristol opened the door.

He didn't give her a chance to greet them or to send them away before he said, "Can we come in?"

She looked like she'd been crying, but he pretended not to notice, walking inside when she gave them room.

"Were you asleep?" Keegan asked, closing the door behind him.

Kaden wasn't normally rude, but right now, he wasn't interested in making small talk. He was still trying to pick himself up off the floor after she'd blasted him with her phone call.

"Why do you think someone's spreadin' the news about the baby?" Kaden asked, turning to face her.

Bristol was fidgeting with the hem of her oversized sweatshirt. "Bianca told me. She came over. She's really mad at me." Tears glistened in her eyes. "Not that I blame her. I didn't tell her because I wasn't ready to deal with it. Once she knows, it makes it more real."

"You understand it's real regardless of who knows."

"Yes," she said sharply. "Of course I know that."

Well, the tears dried up fast.

Planting his hands on his hips, Kaden faced off with her. "What exactly do you want from us?"

Confusion wrinkled her forehead. "What do you mean?"

"Are we in a relationship? Or is this just sex for you?"

"You know what?" Keegan cleared his throat. "While y'all hash this out, I'm gonna get another light bulb."

Kaden never took his eyes off Bristol, ignoring his brother as he made a beeline for the kitchen.

"It's not just sex, Kaden. I don't operate that way. That's *your* MO."

Ah. So she was insecure about them. Made sense. But he knew that was only part of the problem.

"Not since you," he told her.

"Right."

Now she was accusing him of what? Messing around with other women?

"I get that you're insecure, but Bristol, there's no reason for that." He took a step toward her. "We're committed, have been all along."

"You have, maybe," she said, her eyes cutting to the kitchen. "But you can't claim *we* on that one. We were all there that night."

Yes, they were. And he was well aware of what happened.

"That's in the past." And it needed to stay there.

"And what if I can't get over it?"

Kaden stared at her, shocked by that statement. "You've seemed pretty damn over it up to this point." Taking another step closer, he kept his eyes on hers. "Or was that your way of placating us?"

Her eyebrows lowered.

"What were you gonna do? Keep up the ruse until the baby was born?"

"It wasn't a ruse," she said softly, her head tilting back to maintain eye contact.

"A distraction, then?"

"No."

He closed the remaining distance between them, leaned his head toward hers.

"Then let's quit playin' this game, Bristol. It's time to move forward. To deal with the future. Move in with us."

Bristol's eyes widened, her mouth falling open. "What?"

"I love you. I want to spend the rest of my life with you. But that's not news to you, is it?"

She didn't answer, so he continued, "Do you love us, Bristol?"

"Kaden…"

Pulling back, he met her gaze.

It was in those light blue eyes that he saw both confusion and remorse. It was enough to have him stepping away, his gut churning.

He realized she was having second thoughts.

"You can't answer that, can you?"

Bristol swallowed, licked her lips, still looking uncertain. "It's just ... too soon, don't you think?"

Too soon? She really wanted to play that card? After they'd spent a fucking year chasing after her, she thought that the future was too soon?

"I thought we were havin' fun," Bristol stated.

Kaden nodded because his throat was closing up now. No words could escape because he realized he'd done it again. He had leaped too far ahead, found himself in the deep end of the pool. This time by his damn self.

"You two all right?"

Kaden looked over at his brother, back to Bristol. Without a word, he turned and walked toward the front door, then continued right out into the night.

"WHAT'D YOU SAY TO HIM?" KEEGAN ASKED, his gaze cautious as he approached her.

"Nothing," she lied easily. "One minute we were..."

Okay, so she couldn't lie to Keegan. For one, there was nothing she could say that would rationalize the conversation that had just taken place. Kaden had taken her completely off guard.

Her move in with them?

How had they gone from this intense sexual relationship that was just starting up to ... moving in together? She could count on one hand the number of times they'd had sex. Okay, maybe two hands. And one foot.

Whatever.

It was so ... sudden.

Sure, they were having a baby together, but ... well, women had babies all the time. A lot of them were single women. Having a spouse wasn't a requirement for the role of mom. They weren't ready for that sort of commitment. Merging their lives into one, that was ludicrous, right?

"Bristol?"

She wanted to scream. She wanted to cry. She wanted… Bristol wanted to go to sleep and wake up so she could do this day all over again. It was not going the way she would've expected. Not by a long shot.

It'd only been a week since they'd started talking again. And fine, they'd spent the night together a few nights, and yes, Bristol enjoyed those moments. But she hadn't been expecting things to progress quite so quickly.

"Bristol?"

"Hmm?" She looked up, met Keegan's concerned gaze.

"Where's my brother goin'?"

"I don't know." And that much was true.

"What happened?"

"We were talkin'." More like arguing, but whatever. "Then he mentioned me movin' in and I might've reacted badly, but it doesn't change anything. I mean, he's movin' too fast, right? Don't you think?"

Keegan didn't look away and she saw it in his eyes. It was the same thing she'd seen in Kaden's. They were on the same page. They were thinking about a future but neither of them had bothered to clue her in on it?

"I don't understand how we got here," she said softly, holding his gaze. "I thought … I thought we were goin' slow."

"Any slower, Bristol, and we're goin' in reverse." There was heat in his tone now, frustration, maybe anger. "Is this temporary for you, Bristol?"

She frowned. "What? No. I … I don't know."

His dark eyebrows shot upward, his surprise obvious.

Move in with them? Then what? Would they want to get married? How the heck did that even work? Polygamy was illegal in Texas, right? Maybe everywhere? How had they gotten here? How—

A wave of heat hit her, but not the sensual kind. It was enough to have her stepping back, leaning against the wall, trying to draw in breath although her lungs felt constricted.

"Bristol? What's wrong?"

"There's not enough air," she said. "It's too hot in here."

The next thing she knew, Keegan was leading her down the hallway, into the kitchen. He urged her into one of the kitchen chairs, put his hand on her shoulder, and rubbed gently.

When the hot flash faded, Bristol breathed through the queasiness, her hand to her stomach.

Keegan squatted down, put his hand on her knee. "Is it the baby?" There was real concern in his voice.

She didn't want him panicking, so she attempted a smile. "Yes and no. Just morning sickness. But, you know, it's not relegated to only the morning. At least not for me. It happens all the time. Day, night…"

She realized she was rambling, so she stopped.

Keegan stood, walked away. When he returned, he passed over a bottle of water. "Here. It's cold."

She took it from him, took a sip, let the chill soothe down her throat then rolled the bottle along her wrists. It took a few minutes, and the nauseous feeling subsided.

"When's the last time you ate?" he asked.

"Lunch. It was late though. I had a peanut butter sandwich." Bristol took a deep breath.

"What Kaden said, Bristol…" Keegan stepped closer, placing his hands on her knees and crouching down in front of her again. "If you haven't realized it already, Kaden doesn't say things he doesn't mean. He's the thinker, the planner. He works through something until he knows the possible outcomes, then he proceeds with an end goal. With that said, it might not look like it from the outside, but he's as vulnerable as the rest of us. He just does a damn fine job of hidin' it."

Unlike him, she knew. Keegan was the one who resorted to snide comments. Not Kaden.

"We just started seein' each other," she said as an excuse.

"Officially, sure." He lifted her chin with his finger, forcing her to look at him. "But we've been doin' this dance for a long damn time. There's only so much foreplay necessary before the Big Bang."

"So eloquent."

"I have my moments." His eyes glittered briefly. "But I'm serious."

"Is it because I'm pregnant?"

"It's because it's inevitable. The pregnancy, Bristol, that's just a bonus. Was it unexpected? Damn straight it was. Would we do it differently if we could? Sure. Would we go back and change it if we could? No. Things happen for a reason."

She swallowed hard, stared into his beautiful face. Who would've thought Keegan could be the rational one?

"If you don't feel the same, we need to know."

"I haven't thought about it." It was mostly true. A couple times, she'd let her fantasies run wild, imagined a life with the two of them. But no sooner would they appear than she would shove them back into the little box in her mind. Bristol didn't look to the future. Anytime she did, it never worked out well for her.

"Well, you need to."

She nodded because she knew that was what he expected.

Keegan stood tall. "I need to go find Kaden. I need my truck."

Bristol retrieved the keys from her purse, passed them to him. "I'll go with you."

His eyes were hard when they met hers. "No. It's somethin' we need to work out on our own."

The ache in her chest stole her breath. This was emotional though, not morning sickness. The thought of not having these two men in her life now that she did … Bristol wasn't sure she could even fathom it.

Forty-five minutes later, Bristol was still pacing her house. Into the kitchen, back to the living room. Around and around she went. In her hand? Well, that would be her cell phone.

At least two dozen times she'd started to dial Kaden's number, but she didn't. She couldn't.

The only thing she could do was hear Rex's words ringing in her ear. The last time she'd talked to him, he'd basically put her in her place. And in doing so, the butthole had managed to build up her spirits.

Remember that girl who went searchin' for the biggest stick she could find? She was bound and determined she was gonna give my old man the beatin' he deserved the next time she saw him. I remember that girl. God, you had an attitude back then. Didn't take shit from anybody. I admired that about you. Hell, I'd go so far as to say I thought it was hot.

Bristol did remember that girl. She'd been fierce. And Rex was right, she'd taken shit from nobody.

But then life happened. She married Baxter, divorced Baxter. And her dad died. She'd been alone for so long, it was easier to keep her head down, not rock the boat, so to speak. And after a solid year of seeing all those sympathetic gazes locked on her after Baxter claimed she was frigid and that was the reason he'd said adios, Bristol hadn't wanted to risk it again. It wasn't true. He was just a butthole.

"No," she said aloud. "He's an asshole."

The word was so foreign on her tongue that it made her smile. "Asshole. Asshole. Asshole."

Bristol stopped pacing and tapped her phone screen, pulled up her contacts. She found the one she wanted and dialed.

"Hey. I know you're probably busy, but do you think we could meet for coffee tomorrow?"

Chapter Twenty-Two

AFTER LEAVING BRISTOL'S, KEEGAN HEADED FOR MOONSHINERS. It was the one place he knew his brother would go for an escape and it was exactly where he found him.

The place was packed, half a dozen cowboys playing pool in the back, the stools lining the bar all filled. Rafe was behind the bar tonight, working to fill orders, giving Mack a rare night off.

To his surprise, rather than sidled up to the bar, Kaden was sitting in a booth in the back, alone, nursing a beer. From where he stood, it appeared his twin was intensely focused on the woodgrain in the tabletop. Keegan knew that wasn't the case. More than likely, Kaden was lost somewhere in his head, probably coming to understand Keegan's reasons for avoiding relationships for so long.

They never worked out.

Keegan sympathized with his brother. To a degree, anyway. However, he could also see the rationality behind Bristol's response. Kaden had clearly surprised her with his proposition, and she hadn't been able to process in time to mask her initial reaction. It happened.

Wow. Look at him being all rational and shit. Someone should probably write down the date because it didn't happen often.

As he approached Kaden's table, Keegan waved off the waitress. He wasn't going to stay long, and he wasn't in the mood to drink tonight. He was exhausted, both body and mind. So much had transpired in the past week and the upcoming ones didn't show signs of slowing down. For now, he wanted to keep a clear head.

And wasn't that an interesting turn of events? Rational and level-headed. He had to smile because seriously. They must've been in some sort of alternate universe.

Kaden looked up, glanced around, then looked at him again. "Where's Bristol?"

"I left her at home," he said as he eased into the booth across from Kaden. "I don't think she's feelin' well."

Kaden frowned, concern making his brow furrow. "What's wrong with her?"

Keegan shrugged. "I'm sure she'll be fine. Probably just a bit overwhelmed."

"I didn't mean to say it."

He didn't have to ask what *it* was.

"No?" Keegan wasn't sure he bought that. In fact, he was pretty sure his brother had been holding that in for a while. Anyone who knew Kaden knew he was ready to settle down, had been for a long time.

Kaden glared back at him. "What? Did you think I was out to sabotage this?"

He chuckled. "Of course not. That's my job. But you sprung it on her pretty fast, don't you think?"

"No," Kaden grumbled. "I don't."

He wouldn't. Because in Kaden's mind, they'd been with Bristol since the night at Alluring Indulgence nearly a year ago. That had been when the dance officially started. The past year had merely been them two-stepping in the right direction. And yes, that included the frequent steps back they continued to take.

"You're tellin' me that's not where we were headed?"

Keegan leaned back in the booth, considered it.

"It doesn't fucking matter," Kaden said, evidently not needing Keegan's response. "We'll have to figure out where to go from here."

Because Bristol was pregnant. He knew that was what Kaden was referring to. And that would mean Bristol would be part of their lives indefinitely, if for no other reason than because they weren't going to *not* be part of their child's life. No, they hadn't planned this, and no, it wasn't how Keegan had seen it going, but that didn't mean he wasn't happy about the idea of becoming a father. Hell, he'd honestly never thought they'd get to this point.

"Are you sayin' it's over completely?" Keegan prompted, wanting to ensure they were on the same page because he got the feeling this was just Kaden being ornery, something Keegan had mastered.

Kaden cast him a shuttered look. "It was bound to happen," he said softly, once again peering down at the table. "Too much is goin' right in our world."

And there was another twist. Unlike Keegan, Kaden was the glass-half-full sort. Always looking on the bright side while Keegan was the one waiting for the other shoe to drop. And while Keegan had gotten good at pretending he didn't have a care in the world, they both wore their emotions on their sleeves. Kaden was merely good at not blurting it out at the slightest provocation.

Until tonight.

"I won't apologize," Kaden grumbled.

"I'm not expectin' you to," Keegan told his brother. "We were gonna have to address it sooner or later."

"I told her I loved her."

Yeah, Keegan had heard him mention that. "When?"

"Before." Kaden kept his eyes on the beer bottle in front of him. "I went to her house a couple of days after the auction. Tried to apologize."

Ouch. Keegan could only assume it hadn't gone well otherwise they wouldn't have lost an entire month with her.

"She wouldn't open the door. It was an idiot move on my part."

But it didn't make it any less true. Keegan knew Kaden had fallen in love with Bristol a long time ago. Probably one of the reasons Keegan had fallen in love with her. In his mind, a woman who was good enough for his brother was good enough for him because Kaden was the good twin, the one who deserved all the happiness in the world.

"Do you love her?" Kaden asked.

Keegan hadn't expected the question, but his answer was easy. "Yeah. I love her."

"Do you think she's right? It's too soon?"

"No." Keegan leaned forward, resting his elbows on the table. "And I don't think she believes it, either."

"Sure sounded convinced to me."

"It hasn't been that long, Kaden. Hell, we spent one weekend with her and that's pretty much it."

His brother's head snapped up. "It's been a fuckin' year, Keeg. We've put our entire lives on hold so I could moon over her for a fuckin' year."

Keegan swallowed his surprise. He had not expected Kaden to accept responsibility for it.

But they both knew it wasn't all Kaden's fault.

"If I recall, I didn't put up much of a fight."

Kaden glared at him. "Maybe you should have. Then we wouldn't be in this fuckin' mess."

Ouch again. And now they were getting down to the blame game.

Because he wasn't interested in playing, Keegan slid out of the booth, got to his feet. He glared down at Kaden. "I'll see you back at the house. Don't you dare drive drunk."

A grunt was the only response he received before he strolled out of the bar, waving at Rafe on his way out.

Keegan considered going back to Bristol's to check on her but decided against it. He had too much to do right now and he needed sleep. They were currently undertaking a huge project with the house. Before Bristol had told them she was pregnant, they hadn't had a deadline. Now that there was a due date, wasting time wasn't something they could afford.

Keegan had been home for an hour when his cell phone chimed.

Figuring it was Rafe texting him from the bar to tell him Kaden was too drunk to drive home, he sat up in his bed, snatched his phone.

The screen came to life, but it wasn't Rafe who had texted him. Nor was it Kaden.

The text was from Bristol and it was sent to both of them.

I overreacted and I'm sorry. I know that doesn't make it okay, but I wanted you to know. Maybe we can get together tomorrow. To talk.

Keegan's chest constricted.

And now everyone was surprising him. The last thing he expected from Bristol was an apology. In fact, he'd been waiting for the Dear John text, not a request to see them. She was like Keegan in that regard. They were both quick to make decisions—good or bad—and by sharing them with everyone else, it made them official.

As far as Keegan was concerned, this was a good thing. It meant there was still hope for them.

As he lay on his bed, he stared up at the ceiling and smiled.

Who woulda thought?

TRAVIS HAD CONSIDERED SLEEPING AT THE RESORT again tonight. No doubt about it, not going home was easier. He wouldn't risk dealing with Kylie or Gage, getting into an argument, upsetting the kids. In a nutshell, they were better off if he stayed here.

Only Travis didn't want to stay here. He wanted to go home.

No, he *needed* to go home.

He needed the comfort he could find with his husband and wife, the love he got from his children. He wasn't this man, the one who stayed away from them because he was out of control.

With those good intentions, Travis dragged his tired ass home. Granted, it was going on two in the morning, so technically he had spent most of the night there, and he was sure Gage and Kylie would see it that way, too. But if he was lucky, they were asleep, and he wouldn't have to deal with it until morning. And if not…

If only he could bring himself to care.

He hated that feeling. Hated it so fucking much.

Having spent the better part of the day waiting for a confirmation that they had in fact found Juliet Prince, Travis felt every single one of his forty-two years. Plus a couple of decades to boot.

He was tired. So fucking tired. Mentally, physically, emotionally. This constant state of chaos wasn't something he was familiar with. Travis knew how to remain level when things went haywire, but these past couple of months had taken their toll on him. And he had only one person to blame.

Himself.

When he pulled into his driveway, he shut off the truck and sat there for a few minutes staring up at the big house. It had been Gage's house at one time, brought back to its former glory by his wife's perfectly manicured hand. This house had actually been what brought them all together. Gage had found out that Travis had been married—and never divorced—to Kylie, and in an act of revenge, Gage had lured Kylie here by using the house as the carrot.

It had worked.

Over the years, they'd managed to fill that house with life and love…

Travis's chest tightened.

The house was dark, all the lights off except for the one on the porch. There were security lights around the house that would come on if someone or something got close enough, but there was nothing out there now.

As he stared, he felt that familiar storm brewing, the emotional turmoil twisting him up on the inside. Those people inside the walls of that dark house were his to protect, his to love, and he'd failed them. And in his attempt to make it right, he was failing them again.

The constriction on his heart grew more intense until a sob tore out of him, tears following not long after.

He was fucking it all up. He knew he was, but he didn't know how to stop the spiral, how to pull himself back from the ledge. He'd depended on Gage to do that for so long, and in his quest to protect his family, Travis had hurt the man he loved.

He gripped the steering wheel with both hands and let the tears fall because there was nothing he could do to keep them at bay. He didn't even attempt to stop them when the front door opened and Gage appeared as though summoned, as though the man could feel Travis's pain.

Travis swallowed although his throat was tight, watched as Gage strolled down the steps, heading toward Travis's truck. He wasn't sure what he expected, but it wasn't for Gage to walk around to the driver's door, to open it.

"Come on," Gage said softly. "Let's go inside."

Travis stared over at him, not bothering to hide his tears. Kylie and Gage were the two people in his life he'd never had to hide from, so it was natural. As was the pained look on Gage's face at seeing those tears.

Gage's long, strong fingers curled around Travis's wrist. "Come on, Trav."

He let his husband lead him into the house, although he barely remembered the walk.

Another sob tore at his chest, nearly taking him to his knees, but Gage was there.

Gage was *always* there.

"I'm sorry," Travis whispered, staring into those brown eyes that had taunted him all those years ago. "So fuckin' sorry."

Gage pulled him close, palmed the back of his head, and held him. He was warm and smelled so good, so familiar.

Like usual, Travis clung to him, scared to let go because, if he did, there was a good chance he'd splinter even more.

"I love you," he whispered, breathing in, taking Gage's familiar scent deep into his lungs.

"I know." Gage's strong arms tightened around him. "I love you, too, Trav. Always will."

He had needed to hear that, more than he would ever be willing to admit. Travis wasn't one to show weakness, but he was as human as everyone else. He hurt like everyone else.

He would blame the chaos on what happened next, how he found Gage's mouth with his own. He kissed him like there might not be a tomorrow, and to his relief, Gage kissed him back. They both succumbed to the onslaught, to the passion that flowed freely between them. It didn't matter that they were in the living room or that they could make enough noise to wake the house. Nothing mattered except the sparks they ignited when they kissed.

"I need you," Travis breathed against Gage's lips. "Need you so much."

Gage gripped Travis's head in his hands, pressed their foreheads together. "Do you?"

"Yes." He tried to tilt his head to bring their mouths together, but Gage held him back. "Christ, yes, I need you, Gage. I've always needed you. Don't you get it? Don't you get that you're the one I lean on? The one I look to to hold me up when I'm falling over? You, Gage. It's always been you."

Gage's hands tightened on his head, his voice a guttural rasp when he said, "You pushed me away, Travis."

Oh, fuck. He could feel Gage's pain as if it were his own. He heard it in Gage's voice, and it tore at him.

Although he couldn't move closer, Travis did have the use of his hands, so he slid them beneath Gage's T-shirt, forced it up, and waited for Gage to release him. That worked because those strong hands released him, allowing Travis to rip the shirt up and over Gage's head. Before it hit the floor, Travis had Gage up against the wall, nose to nose.

"When I push you, it's because I need you to push back," Travis ground out, keeping his voice low. "I fuckin' needed you to push back, dammit."

Travis didn't let Gage speak. He kissed him instead, their lips slamming together, tongues battling as the emotional storm stirred the chaos.

And then he was tearing at Gage's clothes, shoving the flannel pajama pants down to his ankles, gripping the steel-hard length of him in his hand.

"I fuckin' need you," he bit out again. "Right. Now."

"Then take me," Gage challenged. "If I'm what you need, show me."

Oh, fuck.

"I will," he warned. "Right here."

Gage's brown eyes glittered with challenge and Travis accepted it.

With rough hands, he spun Gage around, roughly shoved him against the wall, biting his shoulder in the process.

This wasn't the first time they'd engaged in this emotion-driven battle of wills. It had happened plenty of times before and would happen plenty more. Travis had come to think of it as his anchor, what he needed to regain his footing.

Gage.

Always Gage.

Leaning against Gage's back, Travis reached around and stroked Gage's cock with one hand while he fumbled with the button on his own jeans. It took a few minutes, but he managed to get the denim down to his thighs, out of the way enough that his cock was free.

"Spread your legs," he demanded, breathing against Gage's ear.

Gage didn't hesitate, widening his stance, his hands planted on the wall.

Travis guided his cock along the crack of Gage's ass, pushing and prodding, his dick anxious for the blistering heat he knew he would find.

He had enough mind to pause, to use his own saliva as lubricant before he took a single step back, jerked Gage's hips toward him, and drove in deep and hard.

They both groaned.

Right there in the living room, just one floor below all those sleeping in the house, Travis fucked Gage. He used his husband's body to calm the dragon that had been unleashed, used it to drown out the noise in his head.

"I fuckin' needed you to push back," Travis said through clenched teeth, his emotions getting the best of him.

"I know." Gage grunted, reaching back and gripping Travis's thigh.

He didn't push him away, didn't pull him closer, just held on.

While Kylie was his shelter in the storm, Gage was his lifeline, the one he depended on to reel him in when necessary. He hadn't realized how out of control he truly was until he realized Gage wasn't there to catch him.

"I need you," Travis whimpered, biting Gage's shoulder, trying to hold on as he continued to slam his hips forward again and again.

"You've got me, Travis. I'm not goin' anywhere."

A sob tore free because he had needed to hear that more than anything. The thought of losing his family ... it wasn't something he could accept but he knew he put them through so much. Especially at times like this when he couldn't keep himself under control.

Travis stopped moving, lodged to the hilt inside Gage while he breathed in, out, in again. He took a moment because the storm wasn't raging anymore.

He dislodged from Gage's body, tugged his jeans up so he could walk, then took Gage by the arm and led the way to his office. Once inside, he closed and locked the door, flipped on the light, and began removing the rest of his clothes.

"On the couch," he said, not looking at Gage while he retrieved the lubricant from the top drawer of his desk.

When he joined Gage, he was calmer, more focused. Enough to realize that he needed this man more than his next breath.

So he took him again, this time slower, deeper. With the lights on. Face-to-face.

Travis took his time sliding in deep, retreating slowly. Their gazes remained locked, so much being said without a word spoken. And when he knew Gage was close, Travis heaved himself up, using Gage's shins for leverage as he began pumping his hips faster.

"Stroke yourself. I want you to come with me."

He saw the flash of heat in those dark brown eyes and it was a solace that he'd been missing for too long now. Sex might not be the answer, but for them it was what soothed, the current that connected them.

"God, baby," Travis groaned, his hand gripping Gage's legs tighter. "I'm gonna come. Fuck." He groaned and growled, fucking Gage harder, faster while he watched Gage's hand piston over his cock, stroking in rhythm to Travis's thrusts.

When it became too much, when his release barreled down on him, Travis ground his teeth together and waited. And when Gage's eyes slammed shut and his cock erupted, Travis threw his head back and groaned, doing his level best not to wake the entire house with the energy he released.

Completely spent, he fell forward, crushing Gage beneath him as he sought the man's mouth with his own. The kiss was gentle, reverent, Gage's hands warm and reassuring as they slid over his back.

"I'm sorry," Travis whispered. "So fuckin' sorry."

Gage wrapped his arms around him and held him close, giving Travis the time and privacy he needed to let the rest of the emotions drain out of him.

He had no idea how long they remained like that, but he didn't move until Gage said, "Let's go to bed."

"Where's Kylie?" he asked, pulling back from Gage and scrubbing the tears away with his hands.

"She's there waitin' for us."

A few minutes later, after a quick shower for both of them, Travis was in their bed, too, spooned up to Kylie while Gage was pressed up against his back. It didn't take long for Kylie to find him in the dark, turning so she was facing him.

And then there he was, right where he needed to be.

At least for a little while.

Chapter Twenty-Three

BRISTOL WOKE EARLY ON SUNDAY MORNING, FEELING a little worse for wear after tossing and turning most of the night. But she was alert and that was all that mattered as she washed her face, brushed her hair and dragged on clothes. The text she'd been hoping for came right before she woke up, letting her know to go to the diner for her coffee date, so she called for an Uber and had them deliver her there.

When she arrived, she found the popular town restaurant was relatively empty, most people in Coyote Ridge still warm in their beds, tucked beneath the covers to catch a few more hours before they ventured off to church or relaxed on their day off.

"Hey, Bristol," came the voice from the back corner, followed by a wave.

She smiled and headed that way.

"I hope I didn't drag you out too early," Bristol said by way of greeting.

Kylie Walker-Matthews watched her approach, a brilliant smile on her pretty face. "It was a … uh … a good night, so no. Not too early."

Bristol slipped off her coat, laying it in the seat and sliding in. The waitress made a quick pass by the table, and Bristol considered ordering coffee just to keep up the ruse but changed her mind at the last second, going for orange juice instead.

Kylie was watching her intently as a slow smile formed.

"You're pregnant," the other woman said, her voice so low Bristol barely heard her.

Evidently, her wide eyes must've given her away because Kylie chuckled.

"Who told you?"

Kylie nodded toward the empty coffee mug in front of Bristol. "It was the first thing to go when I was pregnant with my babies. Hardest thing, too."

Yeah, Bristol had a feeling giving up coffee was going to be easy in comparison to what was looming in her future.

"Is this a good thing?" Kylie asked, taking a sip from her mug.

"Yes."

"You sound certain."

"I am. About the baby, yes. That's the easy decision."

Kylie observed her, those cornflower-blue eyes scanning her face. "So I take it you didn't ask me here for motherhood advice."

Bristol shook her head then thanked the waitress when she brought her juice.

"Can I get you something else?"

"Oatmeal, please. And fruit," Kylie said easily. "For both of us."

"Sure thing."

And then they were alone again, and Bristol knew she had to get on with it or she would lose her nerve.

"How'd you manage it?"

Kylie didn't ask what she was referring to, and Bristol had to wonder if the woman had been asked that question more than this one time.

"Love."

Bristol waited for her to elaborate. She didn't.

"I don't understand."

Kylie leaned forward. "What's difficult about it? Love can get you through anything. If it's real, if it's strong, nothing else matters."

That wasn't what she was hoping to hear.

She'd spent most of the night trying to predict what Kylie's answer would be and she'd hoped for some sort of elaborate plan to skirt all those knowing stares she would no doubt get when she ventured out in public with Kaden and Keegan. If she ventured out. Right now she wasn't sure they were even going to give her the time of day. Neither one of them had responded to her text last night.

"Kaden and Keegan?" Kylie said. "They're the fathers?"

Swallowing hard, Bristol nodded. She'd known Kylie would figure it out. Considering how much time Bristol had spent with the twins over the years, talking, laughing, flirting, it wasn't that much of a leap to figure out she had feelings for them. Certainly not for the Walkers who'd seen them together so often.

"Do you love them, Bristol?" Kylie held up a hand before Bristol could respond. "It's a simple question. Yes or no. Do you love them?"

God. When limited to only a one-word answer, it was pretty easy to respond.

"Yes. But it's—"

Kylie cut her off with a wave of her dainty hand. "That's a start. Now look around and tell me who in here is starin' at me."

A little confused by the odd request, Bristol did as Kylie requested simply because she was curious. No one was paying them any mind. Then again, there were only a few tables that were occupied.

"They don't care," Kylie said, leaning forward. "Sure, you're gonna get a few who're curious. I mean, come on. What woman isn't gonna wonder what it's like to be sandwiched between two smokin'-hot men?"

Bristol felt her cheeks warm.

"And yes, take it from me, there are a few who'll be wondering exactly that, a couple even ballsy enough to ask." Kylie grinned. "But I can guarantee you, there are more who are wondering how much easier it must be because we can split the household chores three ways."

She couldn't help it, she laughed, but it was strained. "It's the ones who'll think I'm easy that have me worried," she admitted.

Kylie rested her elbows on the table. "For the sake of argument, tell me whose opinion matters most to you in this town."

"What do you mean?"

"Okay, let's do it this way." Kylie became animated when she spoke. "I'm going to never get out of bed again when … who … looks down their nose at me?"

"No one." Bristol frowned. "I mean, no one has that sort of power over me."

"Oh, come on." Kylie huffed. "There's got to be someone."

Because Kylie seemed to want an answer, Bristol tried to think, came up with nothing. "There's not."

"But you're worried about *someone* passing judgment."

Bristol took a sip of her juice, nodded. "Fine. The parents of my kids. I doubt they'll all be okay with me bein' with two men."

Kylie's eyebrows dipped low, as though she was considering Bristol's response. "Why's it their business? Are any of the parents of your kids gay?"

"Of course."

"And there's at least one of them who's transgender."

Bristol nodded. "Yes."

"And you never thought twice about letting their kids go there, did you?"

"Of course not."

"So why're you discriminating against yourself?"

"I'm…" Wow. She hadn't thought of it that way.

"How many kids are on the waiting list for your daycare?"

"Um … I don't know offhand."

"But there are some?"

"Yes." She'd been blessed in that regard. It also helped that she was the only licensed daycare center out this direction.

Kylie's face changed instantly. "So what's the problem?"

"You make it sound so simple."

"It is." Kylie leaned back when the waitress brought their oatmeal and fruit. "If you love them and they love you, it'll be easier than you think. You just have to give it a chance."

Bristol stared down at the oatmeal. "I might've screwed that up already."

"Doubtful."

She looked up at Kylie. "How can you be sure?"

"Because I've been around these past couple of years, Bristol. I've watched the three of you. I've seen the way you look at them when they aren't looking and vice versa. There's something worth pursuing there. You just have to want it."

"I do," she admitted.

"Then stop makin' excuses."

That was one thing she admired about Kylie. She didn't beat around the bush.

After she finished her breakfast with Kylie, Bristol had a few more things to do before she could go home.

Her first stop was Bianca's.

As she walked up the twisty path that led to the cute little house her best friend lived in, Bristol remembered when Bianca and Jake had bought the place. For whatever reason, Bristol had always thought Bianca would be the sort to want a monstrous Victorian mansion, something as big and grandiose as her personality, so it had been a complete surprise when Bianca had bought this little two-bedroom bungalow.

But oddly enough, it suited Bianca with its rustic charm and down-home sweetness. Even the white rocking chairs on the front porch.

Taking a deep breath, Bristol knocked on the door, waited. Of course she feared Bianca would ignore her, but she knew she had to do this. After her conversation with Kylie, Bristol had realized that Bianca was right. Bristol had been making herself the center of the universe. Everything she did, everything she said, how she treated the people she loved, it all revolved around how she wanted others to see her. And since that was in direct contradiction to what she really wanted, she understood how she had hurt so many people in her quest to keep a low profile and not rock the boat, so to speak.

She was going to make amends.

Bristol heard the knob rattle, the deadbolt disengage, and then the door was opening.

Bianca looked flawlessly beautiful as usual. Her silky brown hair falling over her shoulders, her teal blue eyes highlighted with minimal makeup. Yep, despite the early hour, Bianca was up and dressed, ready for church.

"Can we talk?" Bristol asked before her friend could turn her away with the excuse she had somewhere else to be.

Bianca's gaze scanned her face and then she was stepping back, motioning Bristol inside.

When the door closed behind her, Bristol spun around and faced her friend. "I am so, so, *so* sorry, Bianca."

No sooner were those few words out of her mouth than Bianca was lunging forward, arms coming around her. Bristol was returning the gesture, hugging her best friend tightly, both of them suddenly spilling over in both words and tears.

"I'm so sorry, Bristol."

"No, I'm sorry."

"I shouldn't have been so mean."

"I shouldn't have kept it from you."

"I'm sorry I was a jealous bitch."

"I'm sorry I told Rex before you."

"I didn't mean what I said."

"I didn't mean to hurt you."

They talked over one another, blubbering uncontrollably until they began laughing.

When they pulled back, Bristol was swiping the tears away with her hands while Bianca made a mad dash for tissues.

"I wish I could blame it on the hormones," Bristol said with a watery laugh, accepting the tissues Bianca passed over.

"Me, too."

Bristol's brain came to an abrupt stop at those two words and she stared at her friend. "What?"

Bianca was nodding, staring at the tissue in her hand, a smile pulling at her lips.

"Are you sayin' what I think you're sayin'?"

More nodding, more staring, but now Bianca was strangling those poor tissues.

"Bianca?"

When her friend looked up, there were more tears, followed by a wide smile. "I'm pregnant, too."

Bristol was pretty sure her heart stopped then kick started once more, a giddy excitement filling her chest. "Seriously?"

Bianca nodded again and another sob escaped.

And once more, they were hugging it out, laughing and crying. But now they were happy tears.

Bristol finally pulled back, stared at her friend.

"You didn't tell me," she said softly, though it wasn't an accusation.

"I just found out."

"How far along?"

"Seven weeks."

"Oh, my God!"

Bianca's face lit up. "I know!"

Once more, they threw themselves into each other's arms, giggling and laughing, the world finally right again.

At least for the two of them.

Bristol still had a few more apologies to hand out, but with this bond once again strengthened, she knew she could do just about anything.

FUCKING HANGOVER.

Kaden knew better than to drink whiskey. It never ended well for him.

"Mornin', brother," Keegan greeted a little too loudly when he joined Kaden in the kitchen.

Kaden could do little more than grunt.

There was clacking and clanging as Keegan rummaged through cabinets looking for God only knew what. Kaden figured he wasn't really looking for anything, just doing his damnedest to make as much noise as possible. After all, it was nothing less than what Kaden always did to him.

"You take anything for it?" Keegan asked.

He grunted again, knowing his brother would understand it for the yes that it was.

"Good. Now you're gonna have to get over it because we've got a lunch date."

Kaden frowned. "With who?"

"Bristol."

He sat up straight, staring at Keegan as his brain processed the words. "What? When?"

Keegan lifted his arm, stared at his make-believe watch, and said, "Half an hour."

"When did this happen?"

"She sent the text last night." Keegan frowned. "You didn't get it."

Kaden grunted again. "Phone died. Left it in the truck."

"Well, then I'm Santa Claus this mornin', huh? 'Cause we have a lunch date with a very sexy, very apologetic little daycare owner." Keegan strolled by, plunked a bottle of water down on the table in front of him. "But you might wanna take a shower, man. You stink."

"Fuck off."

"Oh, and brush your damn teeth," Keegan called out as he left the room.

Despite the throbbing in his skull, Kaden smiled. Not because Bristol had invited them to lunch—well, not *only* because of that— but because he must be stuck in some alternate reality because seriously. Keegan telling him what to do. When's the last time that happened?

Half an hour later and right on time, Kaden was walking up the path to Bristol's door, a few steps behind Keegan, who was whistling while he walked. Fucking whistling.

If he didn't know better, Kaden would think Keegan was having fun with the fact that Kaden was suffering. Granted, he might've been laying it on a little thick at the moment because his headache had subsided somewhat. He wasn't sure if it was the hot shower, the strong coffee, or the magical ibuprofen, but something was doing the trick.

And not a minute too soon, because Kaden had been forced to ride with Keegan so they could pick up Kaden's truck from Moonshiners, where he'd left it last night when he called for an Uber to get him home. Keegan insisted that Bristol needed one of their vehicles and he damn sure wasn't going to leave her hanging.

That reminded Kaden that they hadn't gotten Bristol's car fixed yet. Maybe they could get to that later today.

Keegan knocked on the door, waited. A few seconds later, it opened and there stood the absolutely most stunning woman Kaden had ever laid eyes on. She was dressed in a short, lightweight sweater and a floor-length flowing skirt that he'd never seen before. Her hair was shiny and straight, and she had makeup on. Not a lot, but enough to highlight her beautiful features. She looked so good, it took a minute for him to get with the program.

"Hey," she greeted softly when he walked past her into the house.

"Somethin' smells good," Keegan said, glancing around the living room.

"Before you get too excited, I didn't cook," Bristol said quickly. "Trust me when I tell you, that's not somethin' you want me to do. But I did DoorDash it. Found a great barbecue place and ordered a few things."

Kaden turned to face her, knowing he needed to apologize for his behavior yesterday. He had no right to be such an ass to her.

"Bristol, I am—"

She was in front of him, her hand over his mouth before he could finish the sentence. "Not yet."

Kaden frowned as she lowered her hand, her blue eyes glittering. In fact, she looked like she was glowing. Not literally, of course, but there was definitely something different about her. She actually looked … happy.

"I get to apologize first," she said softly. "But I need for the two of you to go into the kitchen."

Kaden cast a quick look at Keegan, who offered a shrug.

Then they were in the kitchen, he and Keegan sitting in the small breakfast area while Bristol stood at the end of the table

"What's different in here?" Keegan asked, looking around the space.

Bristol motioned behind her. "I've cleaned off the countertops."

Sure enough, they were empty. Her toaster oven was no longer there, as well as whatever knickknacks he'd seen. He couldn't remember what they were, but he did know there had been some.

"We're using paper plates today," she announced. "Because I've packed up all the dishes."

That got their attention. At the same time, they said, "Packed?"

That glow dimmed momentarily as Bristol stared back at them. Kaden could see the uncertainty on her face even as she squared her shoulders.

"Perhaps I've jumped the gun," she said quickly, her gaze swinging back and forth between them. "But I've donated the majority of my stuff to the church. I mean, the furniture and whatnot. I didn't think we'd need it."

We?

"I know I've been impossible this past month and definitely this past week and I am so sorry," she continued. "Neither of you deserved that. I'd like to blame it on hormones, but we all know better than that. I was a coward."

Kaden could only stare at her, her words, spoken in that raspy twang that he loved, bounced around in his head as he attempted to make sense of them.

"It took me screwin' everything up to realize how much of a chicken I was being. And I don't wanna be that girl." She stood taller, straighter. "I'm strong, independent, and I don't back down. At least not when it comes to the important things."

Kaden realized he was holding his breath in anticipation.

"Considering the two of you are the most important things in my life, you deserve so much better."

"Bristol, you—"

She held up her hand, cutting Keegan off before he could finish. Kaden held his tongue, too.

"And I want to be what you deserve," she said softly. "I love you. Both of you. I probably have for a really long time now. First as friends, now as more. And I refuse to be the one to screw that up. If, you know, I haven't done that already."

"What are you sayin'?" Keegan asked, getting to his feet and stepping toward her.

Kaden feared he would crumple to the floor if he tried to stand, so he remained where he was.

"That I'm sorry. That I love you. That I want the three of us—" She paused to put her hand on her belly. "*Four* of us ... to share a life together. I've been stuck in the past for too long, scared to make a ripple in the pond. I've gotten so used to routine, to the mundane, I didn't dare think there could be more for me out there. And then I met the two of you and I was"—Bristol smiled—"smitten."

Kaden swallowed hard, stood, then took a tentative step toward her to see if he'd remain upright.

He did. That was good.

He took another. And another.

Bristol tipped her head back to maintain eye contact as they both approached her. "If the offer still stands, I'd like for us to move on with our lives. Together."

"Everything?" Kaden asked.

Bristol nodded. "Everything. Movin' in together, marriage if you want it." She smiled shyly. "The whole nine yards."

"Christ Almighty, woman," Keegan groaned, pulling her into him as he hugged her tightly.

Kaden waited patiently while Keegan kissed her, a passionate endeavor that took far longer than Kaden wanted it to. But then his brother was stepping back and Kaden was stepping up to her. He pulled her into his arms, hugged her tightly, and let the emotion roll through him. He was shaking, he knew he was, and figured Bristol realized it too. But if she did, she didn't say anything.

"I love you," he whispered in her ear. "I've always loved you."

She made a sound, something like a half sob, half laugh, and he held her tighter, grateful when her arms banded around him.

"Do you mind if I make a call real quick?" Keegan said, watching the pair as they continued to embrace.

"Who're you callin'?" Kaden asked, keeping one arm around Bristol as they turned toward him.

"Mom and Dad." He watched to see Bristol's reaction.

She simply smiled and Keegan would almost say she radiated. It was surreal. He had never seen her look quite so happy.

Kaden glanced down at Bristol.

She nodded.

Pulling his phone out of his pocket, Keegan pulled up their parents' phone number. He dialed, putting it on speaker. It rang endlessly before finally going to voicemail.

He hung up, tried their father's cell number.

Same thing.

For fuck's sake. They were ruining his moment.

Last but not least, he called their mother's cell number.

"Well, it's good to hear from you," Sue Ellen said by way of greeting.

"I've got you on speaker, Mom."

"Do you?" She sounded pleased. "And?"

"Could you do the same? That way Dad can hear?"

"How do you know he's here?" she teased.

"Because you're in the car, Mom. We can hear it. And we all know you don't drive and talk on the phone."

She made a *pfft* sound.

"Okay. You're now on speaker. What is this news you have, Keegan?"

Keegan leaned up against the counter, crossed his legs at the ankle, and looked directly at Bristol.

Her eyes widened and there was a hint of panic on her face, but it didn't last long.

"Hello, Mrs. Walker. This is Bristol Newton."

Keegan's chest swelled. He honestly hadn't known if she would hold true to her word. But this was the strong, independent woman she had just claimed to be. It filled him with hope.

"Bristol? Oh, my. It's so good to hear from you, honey."

"Thank you, Mrs. Walker. Kaden's here, too. And yes, we've got news."

There was silence on the other end and Keegan imagined his mother holding her breath.

Bristol looked up at him, then over to Kaden. The instant she opened her mouth to speak, Keegan talked over her.

"We've got a question to ask first. Hold on, Mom."

Keegan set the phone on the counter and went to one knee at the same time Kaden did, right there in Bristol's outdated kitchen.

Bristol choked out a laugh which made him smile.

He'd always figured he would have some big speech prepared when he proposed to a woman. Something that reflected how he felt about her, all the promises he wanted to make, the future they would share, but as he stared up at her, emotion clogged his throat, making it impossible to speak.

He couldn't believe they were here, at this point in their lives.

"Marry us," Keegan rasped, swallowing past the lump in his throat.

It was then he realized he hadn't even phrased it as a question. Oh, well.

"We want to spend the rest of our lives with you, Bristol Adrienne Newton," Kaden tacked on.

From the phone on the counter, Keegan heard his mother's gasp, but he was too focused on the tears that sprang to Bristol's eyes. His chest squeezed and for a brief moment panic flared.

"We have a ring," he said quickly. "But it's just not here right now."

"I have it," their mother shouted, as though they couldn't hear her clearly. "They left it with me for safekeeping."

"It belonged to our grandmother," Kaden explained.

"My mother," Sue Ellen clarified.

Keegan rolled his eyes, smiled. "She gave it to us and said one day we'd meet the one woman who would deserve it."

"She was very proud of that ring," Sue Ellen called out. "It outlived both of her husbands."

Bristol frowned.

Kaden laughed. "Mom, that makes it sound like she was married twice."

"Oh, sorry." Sue Ellen giggled. "No. She was married to twins."

Bristol's eyes widened and a tear slipped out.

"Marry us," Keegan repeated.

Bristol started nodding as more tears fell. "Yes. Of course. Yes."

Sue Ellen squealed, and Keegan heard their father clear his throat. If he had to guess, his old man was fighting tears of his own. Gerald always was an old softie.

"We're gonna have to call you back, Mom," Keegan said in the direction of the phone.

"Oh, don't bother, honey. We'll see you tonight at Curtis's."

Keegan and Kaden got to their feet, glanced at one another, frowned.

"You're here?" Kaden asked.

"Last night when Keegan called," Sue Ellen said, "I figured it was a good time for us to come down, check out the real estate."

"You're *movin'* here?" Kaden asked, his voice reflecting his shock.

"Figured it's about time. I've got a future daughter-in-law to get to know and a grandbaby to prepare for."

Kaden's gaze swung over to Keegan, his eyes wide.

Oops. He might've left that part out.

"I had to," he muttered, looking between Kaden and Bristol. "I didn't want them to hear it through the grapevine."

"It's okay," Bristol said, stepping up to him and wrapping her arms around his waist. "It's more than okay."

"We'll see y'all tonight," Kaden told Sue Ellen.

"We're lookin' forward to it," Sue Ellen replied before disconnecting the call.

"I love you," Keegan said, peering down at Bristol when she pulled back.

"I know."

He smiled at that.

"Have you known all along?"

She grinned. "I had my suspicions."

Bristol stepped out of his embrace and over to Kaden. "So, which room should we start on first? I've got a lot to pack up."

When Kaden looked up to meet his gaze, Keegan smiled at his brother.

It had taken a lifetime, but they'd finally gotten to the place they'd always imagined they would be, and damn if it didn't feel good.

Chapter Twenty-Four

BRISTOL EXPECTED TO FEEL OUT OF PLACE at Curtis and Lorrie's. She was used to being here on most of her Sunday evenings for dinner, playing with the kids, hanging out with the wives, laughing and joking, getting her adult-time fix while getting some face time with the little ones outside of the daycare.

Tonight she hadn't been certain how they would treat her, not only because she was with Kaden and Keegan but also because she'd been absent from these meals for so long now. But she should've known it would be business as usual.

No one seemed to notice the fact that Kaden had walked her in the door, hand in hand. Or that Keegan had been on her other side, his arm around her shoulder.

For some reason, being with them was as natural as breathing. Even in public, as it turned out.

Probably had something to do with the fact she'd wasted so much time worrying about it, fretting over something she didn't have control over. If someone didn't like how she lived her life, well, they could shove it where the sun didn't shine. Bristol wanted to be that strong, independent girl that Rex had known when she was younger. She deserved to be that girl. And Kaden and Keegan deserved to have that woman at their side, not some withering flower.

Yes, she'd been incredibly nervous to see Gerald and Sue Ellen, her future in-laws. She'd met them before, of course, but never as Kaden and Keegan's fiancée. Sue Ellen greeted her with a huge hug and a "welcome to the family" whispered in her ear. It brought tears to Bristol's eyes, but she fought them back as best she could.

But the hardest part was when she came face-to-face with Wesley, Quinn, and Jared.

Her future brothers-in-law tried to act stern in the beginning, but they must've sensed her nerves because they gave up quickly when their sister, Eve, joined in and stood shoulder to shoulder with Bristol.

"Stick with me, honey. I know how to keep 'em in line."

That prompted some good-natured ribbing between the siblings, Kaden and Keegan joining in the fray. At that point, Bristol had escaped to the kitchen to see if she could help Lorrie with preparations.

"It's about time," Curtis said when he came over to congratulate them after Gerald proudly announced the news to the entire clan. "Welcome to the family."

"Thank you." Again, more tears threatened.

"Officially," Lorrie amended. "Because you've always been a part of the family."

Yep. Tears were powerless against Lorrie. They fell unbidden, stopped only when Curtis presented her with a handkerchief.

And that was how it went for a good half hour. Everyone was congratulating them, excitement filling the air when Kaden proudly announced their additional good news: they were having a baby. Kylie, Zoey, and Eve took it upon themselves to start planning the wedding, promising they would get with Bianca so Bristol's matron of honor could lead the charge.

After dinner, the kids were rambunctious as usual, even those who hadn't had a nap. The only one who seemed somewhat somber and quiet was Kate. She knew Kate would come around when she was ready. Her parents were doing everything they could, and Bristol was praying for the best. Tonight, Bristol had planned to simply greet Kate and maybe give her a hug, but the little girl had other plans.

"Miss Bristol? Would it be okay if maybe I helped babysit the baby when…" Her brows furrowed. "Is it a boy or a girl?"

"We don't know yet," she admitted.

"Well, it doesn't matter. I like boy and girl babies. Do you think I could maybe help babysit?"

"Of course you can. Anytime your mom and daddies say it's okay."

She smiled and Bristol saw the little girl she'd known for so long behind the grin. Yes, Kate would definitely be making her way back. Sooner rather than later if they were all lucky.

Of course, the good times always came to an end. A lot of little ones to put to bed, parents who were hoping to catch up on some TV time or to go to bed themselves.

"We're gonna head out," Kylie said, stepping up to Bristol for a hug. "And don't think you're off the hook."

"For?"

"We figured we'd give you a reprieve. Next Sunday we'll be giving all three of you crap, so be prepared."

"Well, thank you for sparing me tonight," she said, realizing she was truly grateful but at the same time looking forward to being part of the family.

"No worries. Now be good. We'll see you first thing in the mornin'."

"I'll be ready and waitin'."

Before Travis, Kylie, and Gage could get their kiddos to file out the door, Kaden and Keegan were urging Bristol that way, too. She managed to get in a goodbye to Gerald and Sue Ellen, then Curtis and Lorrie, but that was about all she got before Keegan had her by the hand and was practically dragging her to his truck.

"In a hurry?" she teased.

"I haven't had my wicked way with you yet today." He opened the passenger door for her. "Can you blame me?"

No, she really couldn't. She felt the exact same way. Some alone time with both of them was exactly what she needed.

And to top it all off, having watched Keegan at dinner, the way he interacted with the kids… it had warmed her heart just as it did anytime she saw him with them. There was no denying the man had a way with the little ones. And heaven knew, Bristol had always had a thing for men who were good with kids.

Not that she was really thinking about that now, and certainly not when Keegan reached over and took her hand, linking their fingers as he steered the truck toward her house. The movement felt intimate, a sweet gesture she would've expected more from Kaden than from Keegan. They were vastly different in that regard. Kaden was the sweet one, the twin who thought things through, had a logical answer to nearly everything, while Keegan was the rambunctious, mischievous one, the twin who had a quick quip and liked to debate regardless of whether he was right or not.

She loved them both immensely and for those very reasons. And many, many more.

Bristol couldn't not think of sex when she was around them. She wanted to see them naked, laid out before her. More importantly, she wanted to feel once again the overwhelming intensity of having their sole focus on her.

"What's goin' on in that pretty little head of yours?"

Glancing over, Bristol smiled, loving the dark rumble of Keegan's voice along with the sexy smirk that seemed readily planted on his face at all times.

"I want to see you naked," she blurted, keeping her eyes forward, knowing full well her face was turning a brilliant shade of pink.

"Is that right?" Keegan chuckled. "Were you thinkin' right now? Or could I wait until I get you in the house?"

Bristol laughed. "I'm sure I can wait."

They were quiet for a few minutes, Keegan driving, her hand engulfed in his. Even that little touch had her body warming immensely.

As they were turning into her neighborhood, Keegan glanced over at her and she realized she was staring at him.

"What's on your mind, darlin'?"

Shifting her attention out the window, she said, "I was thinkin', maybe we could … uh … try somethin' new."

"New?"

"Yeah. You know, somethin' I haven't tried before."

She looked over despite her face flaming. She had never been this bold. Ever.

"And what might that be?"

Bristol swallowed hard and managed to push the words out. "Double penetration."

He peered over at her again. "You ever been fucked in the ass?"

Heat swamped her. Partly from embarrassment, partly from desire spurred by those dirty words.

"No," she admitted, though the word was spoken on a breathless whisper.

Keegan's eyes glittered. "Oh, for fuck's sake."

Needless to say, they made it to the house in record time.

WHEN KADEN PULLED INTO BRISTOL'S DRIVE BEHIND Keegan's truck, he wasn't at all surprised to see they'd already disappeared inside the house. Hell, he'd only been a few minutes behind them, but if he knew Keegan, his brother already had Bristol stripped. Perhaps even laid out on the nearest flat surface.

The thought gave him pause, had him stopping on the front porch.

He smiled as he reached for the door handle, wondering if this was how it would be when they got her things moved over to the ranch. Would he come home to find Bristol and Keegan doing their own thing? Or vice versa, Keegan coming home to find them?

He sure as hell hoped so.

From the front porch, he heard Bristol's squeal followed by her sexy laugh as it faded off deeper into the house. He opened the door and stepped inside, closing things up behind him and flipping the lock for good measure.

"What's goin' on in here?" he asked as he stepped into Bristol's bedroom, stopping in the doorway as Keegan was hopping on one foot in an attempt to get his boot off.

"She wants me nekkid," Keegan offered, moving on to the other boot.

"In fairness, I want you *both* naked," Bristol clarified.

"Yeah?"

She glanced his way and he could see the glimmer in her light blue eyes. Yeah, she was feeling feisty again, he could tell. He liked that about her.

He reached for her arm, pulling her against him as he peered down into those glittering eyes.

"I love you," he whispered before brushing his lips over hers.

There was no hesitation in her responding, "I love you, too."

God, that was what he'd longed to hear.

"She's got a request," Keegan announced when he came over to join them.

"That so?"

"Why don't you tell him."

Kaden noticed the way Bristol's cheeks were turning a brilliant red. Redder than he'd ever seen before.

"Tell me, darlin'."

"DP," she whispered.

Just those two letters from her beautiful lips had the ability to harden his body from head to toe. His cock jerked in his jeans.

"She's never had a cock in her beautiful ass," Keegan supplied.

Kaden saw her face redden more, but she was still watching him, her eyes glittering with what he could only assume was desire.

"You're sure?"

She nodded, then inhaled sharply when her body came into contact with his, and he couldn't resist leaning in and kissing her once more. But he didn't linger, figuring these two had already set the mood and slow wasn't on the menu. Instead of consuming her, Kaden released her mouth, then turned her to face away from him, pulling her back to his chest so Keegan could enjoy the show. Kaden let his hands roam down the front of her before reaching for the hem of her sweater and dragging it up and over her head, tossing it to the floor where Keegan's shirt was.

It was quick work to rid her of her bra, leaving her topless, her bottom half covered by that sexy floor-length skirt. But it, too, had to go, so he dipped his fingers in the waistband, then pushed it down her hips.

"Son of a bitch," Keegan groaned, his gaze trailing downward. "You're tellin' me you had no panties on the whole time we were at dinner?"

"You little minx," Kaden whispered against her ear as his hands slid down to cup her bare ass while his brother moved toward them.

"Anyone ever tell you you're a tease?" Keegan asked, curling his finger under her chin and tilting her head back.

"Not a tease," Bristol countered. "A promise."

His brother laughed, then dragged Bristol away, his arm banding around her waist as he lifted her off the floor. Her throaty laugh had Kaden's cock throbbing. There in front of him, Keegan tossed Bristol onto the bed, then followed her down. Only he didn't stay down for long, flipping their positions so that he was underneath her, his head at the bottom of the bed.

"Sit on my face," Keegan told her. "And make sure you're facin' Kaden when you do."

Stepping forward, Kaden offered himself up so she could brace herself as she straddled Keegan's head. Her hands gripped his shoulders as she moaned softly. Her eyes were hooded, her mouth open in a perfect O.

"Ride his face, baby," Kaden urged, leaning in and kissing her, swallowing all those soft, sexy moans.

Their tongues dueled, her breathy moans muted as her hips gyrated. Kaden filled his hands with her firm breasts, kneading them before tweaking her nipples.

She pulled back, inhaling sharply. Her head fell back on her shoulders as she cried out, her muscles tensing, nipples pebbled into beautiful points. Kaden took a step back, admiring how hot she was when she came with Keegan's head buried between her thighs.

It wasn't until Bristol's head came to the level, her blue eye sparkling with desire, that Kaden got with the program. He was shucking his jeans when she climbed off of Keegan, crooked her finger at him, beckoning him to her.

Didn't have to tell him twice.

Kaden moved around to the side of the bed, waited as she turned toward him. She grabbed for him then, pulling him down onto the bed with her.

"You realize we're gonna take you at the same time," he said, watching her face to read her expression.

Bristol nodded.

"Not like the first time," he clarified. "At the *same* time."

"I'm ready."

He believed her. At least, he believed she thought she was ready. Although people believed double penetration was something that was a given in a threesome, for them it wasn't usually the case. It had something to do with how well-endowed they were. It wasn't a simple, easy feat.

But it was doable and Kaden damn sure wasn't going to deny her request.

"We'll go slow," he promised.

When she nodded, he breathed a sigh of relief. Not because she agreed but because she trusted them enough to do so.

Bristol tried to roll on top of him, but Kaden stopped her, kissing her as he shifted, his hand sliding down to her thigh then slowly moving upward.

"I get to take that sweet virgin ass, baby."

"Come here," Keegan urged, now positioned correctly on the bed. "You're gonna ride me."

Bristol inhaled sharply, a sound Kaden enjoyed.

Then she was moving over Keegan, straddling his hips and leaning down.

Kaden could hear the wet sound of their mouths and tongues exploring, their soft grunts and groans as skin rubbed skin, but his focus was on getting her ass ready to take his cock. He knew he couldn't rush this, but not doing so was a testament to his will-power.

After riffling through her nightstand drawer, Kaden found a bottle of lubricant. He would've given Bristol shit about it simply to watch her blush, but again, his mind was on other things.

The instant he was kneeling on the bed, Bristol's entire body went rigid.

Kaden leaned over and pressed a kiss to her spine. "Relax, baby. We've got a ways to go before my cock gets anywhere near this beautiful ass."

Clearly knowing she needed a distraction, Keegan pulled Bristol back down to him, those kissing noises erupting again.

Kaden went to work, generously lubing his fingers.

Ensuring she knew where his hands were at all times, Kaden put one on her hip after pressing in the center of her back to get her to lean down more, angling her ass toward him.

He teased her with his fingers for long minutes. Slowly at first, rimming her, awakening those sensitive nerve endings. The more Bristol moaned and rocked, the more he gave her, starting with one finger, then two, until finally he had three fingers buried in her ass, fucking her slow and easy, pushing in deep. Every time she would relax, he would scissor his fingers, loosening those muscles as much as he could.

"Are you ready, baby?" Keegan asked her.

"Yes," she said on a raspy breath, her body rocking against the fingers impaling her. "God yes."

Kaden continued to finger her ass while Keegan shifted her so she was sitting astride his cock. Kaden watched as Keegan's cock parted her pussy lips and slid deep inside. And then she was filled completely.

Bristol grunted.

"Too much?" Keegan whispered.

"No. Just … go slow."

Kaden was already going slow, so he continued, pushing his fingers inside her when Keegan pulled out. They continued like that while Kaden lubed his cock then added a generous amount to her ass, still penetrating her with his fingers.

"I'm gonna fuck you now, baby. You ready for my cock?"

She sucked in air and breathed out something that sounded a lot like yes but was muffled by Keegan's lips.

He wasted no time. Kaden took the reins then, prodding her asshole with the head of his cock, pushing against her body's natural resistance while Keegan remained perfectly still beneath her. Inch by excruciating inch, he went in deeper. His head spun as the heat of her ass enveloped him, the tight ring of muscles parting as he pressed his hips forward. It took a while, but her body eventually relaxed, allowing them to fill her at the same time.

And then he was moving.

Kaden got lost in the sensations of her body moving on him as he gripped her hips, pulling her back and pushing her forward on his cock. He admired the long line of her spine, the smoothness of her skin. She was clearly distracted by the two cocks filling her impossibly full because she let them do all the work. They continued like that for long minutes, his cock sliding in and out of her ass as the pleasure robbed him of all thought.

When he paused, buried to the hilt, Keegan began to move. Slow and deep, he rolled his hips beneath her.

"Fuck yes, darlin'," Keegan crooned. "You're so damn tight like this."

His brother continued his crass monologue until he was groaning in earnest.

And with one quick look over her shoulder, Kaden nodded his head and they began to move together, alternating as they filled her. Bristol moaned when they did, her body coming to life as though she was chasing her own release.

"Oh, God!"

Her ass tightened on his cock.

"That feels … good. Surprisingly good." She moaned and sighed, rocking with their movements. "Don't stop. Please … oh, God, don't stop."

Taking her pleas as their cue, Kaden began to fuck her with shallow strokes. Faster, harder. Keegan matched his pace from beneath her until they were rocking her body between them.

"I'm … oh, God, yes!" Bristol cried out, her orgasm hitting without warning.

Her ass clamped down on his cock and Kaden came in a rush. His garbled groan was followed by Keegan's deep, bellowing grunt.

Kaden carefully dislodged, moving slowly so as not to hurt her. Then he padded to the bathroom, cleaned himself up, then grabbed another washcloth, got it wet, and returned to the bedroom. Bristol was lying with her head on Keegan's shoulder, her leg thrown over his thigh. To his surprise, she didn't balk as Kaden cleaned her thoroughly.

"That was ... amazing," she whispered with a contented sigh.

"Yes, it was," he agreed, pulling her into him so he was spooned up against her.

Keegan disappeared for a moment, then returned to join them on the bed, sandwiching Bristol between them as the three of them drifted off.

KEEGAN DIDN'T KNOW HOW LONG HE'D BEEN asleep, but he woke slowly, both Bristol and Kaden sleeping soundly beside him, the three of them crowded on her queen-sized bed.

A smile was immediately on his lips as he opened his eyes and peered up at the ceiling of the dark room. He didn't move, not wanting to wake Bristol. He had no idea what time it was, but since his stomach wasn't rumbling, he figured it wasn't quite morning.

His thoughts shifted to the ranch, to the morning chores that needed to be done before they headed to the shop. They had Cassius to handle them for now, but it wouldn't be long before he would be up with the sun, taking care of things. Him and Kaden.

Bristol would be there, too. And in the not-so-distant future, a son or daughter, as well.

It had been a long time in the making, but they were finally living their dreams. A ranch in Coyote Ridge and a sweet woman at their side. What more could they ask for?

"You awake?"

Keegan turned his head at the sound of his brother's voice. "Yep."

Neither of them said anything more and Keegan wondered if Kaden was thinking the same thing he was: they should be in a bigger bed.

As it was, his feet were hanging off the bottom, his shoulder hugging the edge. It would've been irritating if it weren't for the fact Bristol was naked between them. That was enough to forgive any discomfort he might've found with the bed.

But they would be getting a new one. One big enough for the three of them to sleep comfortably with Bristol between them every night.

Keegan would start looking online immediately.

But first he was going to wake up their sweet woman.

Using only his mouth.

Epilogue

Two years, eight months later
Saturday, August 12, 2023

"Okay, Princess P," Keegan called out when he stepped into the living room. "It's time for lunch."

He heard sweet girl-giggles and then Kate's head poked out of the blanket fort.

"Which one?" she asked. "There are *two* Princess Ps in this castle."

Keegan grinned. "Both of 'em."

More giggling.

"You think you can wrangle them, Kate?" Keegan asked when he perched on the arm of the couch, waiting patiently.

"Can anyone?" she countered then ducked back inside.

"All right, ladies," he said to the two-year-old twins who were still hiding in the elaborate blanket fort they'd convinced him to build.

Okay, fine. Maybe they hadn't really convinced him. He'd come up with the idea all on his own. It was something he did often when Bristol and Kaden left him alone with the girls. Since Bristol wasn't all that fond of him stealing the blankets and pillows, not to mention the barstools, for his works of art, he had to wait until they were alone, which was generally on Saturday mornings when Bristol and Kaden ventured out to the grocery store.

"Hey, Kate," he called out.

Once again, she poked her head out.

Keegan relied on Kate, just a few months shy of turning nine, to be the leader of the rambunctious duo who had learned early on that they could run roughshod over him. Well, he let them believe they could because, come on, they were just the cutest kids on the planet.

"Think you could do me a favor?"

One little head poked out beside Kate's, then another identical one on the other side.

"Sure."

"I'm gonna need to feed the chickens in—"

"Chickie!" Paisley squealed as she launched herself out of the fort, getting to her feet and darting over to him.

Payton wasn't far behind her, both girls banging a little fist on his knee while staring up at him with wide, hopeful eyes that were the same blue gray as Keegan's and Kaden's.

"What? You wanna feed the chickens?" he asked.

They both nodded enthusiastically.

Kate crawled out of the fort, got to her feet, and smiled. She knew how this worked because she'd been around the ranch plenty as of late. She often came over to help with the twins, and now that Bristol was nearing her fourth month of this pregnancy—only one healthy boy this time, according to the doctor—Kate continued to offer to lend a hand.

Keegan couldn't deny they needed as much help as they could get. Luckily, they had it. His parents were always offering to help out, as was Eve, who had taken to her nieces more so than anyone had expected. And the rest of the Walker clan was always around to pitch in, paying them back for all the times Keegan and Bristol had volunteered to babysit over the years.

"Okay, so here's the deal," he told the girls in a conspiratorial whisper. "We have to eat all our lunch before we can feed the chickens. You think you can do that?"

More head nodding.

"But you know what we gotta do *before* we eat?"

"Clean," Payton announced, pointing at the fort, which was quite possibly his most impressive to date.

Keegan kinda didn't want to take it down before Kaden and Bristol returned to see it for themselves.

"Let's get a picture first," he told the girls. "Then we'll clean it all up."

Kate strolled over, held out her hand for the phone.

After passing it over, Keegan joined the twins in front of the fort. He got down on his knees, grabbed them around the waist, and tucked them under his arms while they giggled uncontrollably. All three of them made funny faces for the camera.

Kate clicked away, then announced, "All good."

As they'd done plenty of times before, Payton and Paisley turned to the fort, and began dragging the pillows and blankets down, which was quite the feat for them. As was their routine, they shoved everything in his direction.

While Kate took the barstools back to the kitchen, Keegan grabbed the blankets, folded them neatly, and piled them on the end table. He left the pillows for the girls, waiting until they were ready to heft them up onto the couch.

"The chickens don't really need to be fed, do they?" Kate asked, her lips hardly moving as she spoke under her breath.

Keegan laughed. "What do you think?"

She rolled her eyes. "Those birds are gonna get fat."

Maybe. But seeing his girls giggle and smile made it all worth it.

Of course, they would wait until Bristol and Kaden got back from the store so they could handle the chore as a family.

After all, that was what they did.

All In

BRANTLEY WALKER:
Off the Books

Brantley Walker has dedicated his life to fighting for his country. Having given seventeen years to the US Navy, the last ten as a SEAL, the mission was the only thing he knew, the only thing that mattered. He never even considered what life would look like after the mission was over.

Until he's forced to.

After spending months recovering from career-ending injuries, Brantley finds himself back in his hometown of Coyote Ridge, Texas. Now a permanent resident once again, with the full support of his family and friends, he sets forth to start over, forced to figure out what to do with the rest of his life, which, as it turns out, is far easier said than done.

Then the unthinkable happens.

When his cousin Travis's daughter is kidnapped, Brantley puts himself right back in the action, partnering up with Reese Tavoularis to find the little girl and bring her back home where she belongs.

Along the way, Brantley and Reese end up immersed in another mission. Only this one results in a journey that takes them in a direction neither of them expected to go.

Prologue

June 2019, Location Classified

"ABORT! ABORT!"

The words were shouted through his earpiece, but Brantley Walker was having a difficult time hearing them. Probably had everything to do with this godforsaken ringing in his ears.

To top it off, he couldn't see a damn thing. What was left of the dilapidated concrete building was filled with dust, dirt, and debris, which not only affected his eyesight but was permeating his lungs, making it damn near impossible to breathe.

"Phantom One, get your ass outta there! Now!"

Coughing in an effort to expel the dust from his chest cavity, Brantley shook off the initial shock and pain, taking stock of his surroundings.

"Phantom One! Do you read?"

Did he? Brantley wasn't sure.

"Phantom One? Goddammit, Phantom One? Comm check."

Before he could force a few words to assure his team he was still in one piece, sounds came from above. Instinct and training caused him to go completely still, only his eyes moving to scan the space.

The main floor—now above him—of the single-story house had given way, sending him careening into what appeared to be some sort of concrete bunker beneath the structure that had supposedly housed the hostage they'd been sent in to retrieve. Intel had placed the thirty-year-old nuclear physicist here. Right fucking here, which was the only reason Brantley and his SEAL team had slipped silently into the building, intending to be in and out in under a minute.

Bad news: the fucking scientist wasn't here. Worse news: the tangos were moving in.

"Phantom Two, I don't have eyes on Phantom One. Repeat, I don't have eyes on."

"Roger that, Phantom Six. Fall back. We'll get eyes on him."

Would they? Brantley had an eerie feeling no one was going to see much of him once this was over.

How long had it been, anyway? A minute? Ten? Not that it mattered. The mission was a goat-fuck of epic proportions. The extraction team was likely gone, his own team scattered about. The most he could hope was Phantom Team was nearby, keeping a close eye on the exterior.

And here Brantley was, in the middle of it all, surrounded by broken slabs of concrete, rebar, and dirt, all piled high in the space, offering absolutely no protection should one of those damn tangos appear above his head.

The bad guys had been expecting them, the proof in the explosion that had triggered soon after Brantley had entered the premises. The explosion that had rocked the floor right out from under him, sending Brantley deep into the earth with the aforementioned concrete, rebar, and dirt. Not all of which had been beneath him after the descent into this fucking hole.

Speaking of bad guys…

The voice was growing louder from above, the language one he didn't recognize. Not surprising considering the hotbed they'd dropped into. God only knew which terrorist group was leading the charge in this shithole. Probably not the one they'd suspected considering everything they'd believed up to this point was proving to be bullshit.

"Phantom One. Sit tight. We're making our way to your location."

Unable to speak without revealing himself to the fucker stalking him, Brantley kept his trap shut, clamping his molars together as he attempted to heave the concrete slab off his fucking leg. Damn thing had trapped him in place, no doubt shattering his leg on impact. The pain threatened to blind him. He forced his heart rate to slow, honing the skills drilled into him by the US military. He would get out of this if he kept a level head.

All In

It took tremendous effort, but Brantley managed to shift the concrete slab enough to allow him to drag his leg free. Once he did, he slid backward into the darkened corner, the spike in his adrenaline making him light-headed. Aside from the debris, there was no protection or cover, but at least this way the fuckers would have to come into view to take him out.

The only thing he could do right now was sit and wait.

A grunt escaped before he could swallow it down. His leg was broken, no doubt about it. But unless he wanted to add more injuries—like a bullet to the skull—he had to swallow the pain. Not easy to do as he dragged himself deeper into the space, over the piles of rubble that had come down with him. As he shifted, one of the sharp ends of some rusted rebar stabbed into his thigh, dragging through his flesh before he could stop it.

Son of a fucking bitch.

A blaze of fire ripped through him as he manhandled his left leg, unhooking his flesh from the rusty metal. Gritting his teeth, he fought the darkness that threatened to take him under. No way could he pass out now. Not if he wanted to live through this clusterfuck.

The only sounds he heard were his ragged breaths and the voice growing louder as it came closer. Without looking, he knew someone was above him, staring down into the rubble. It wouldn't take much for the asshole to find him.

A flashlight clicked on.

Mother. Fucker.

That beam of yellow light swung through the room, passing over his injured leg more than once before his terrorist visitor hopped down onto the pile of concrete. There was no stealth to the guy's movements, telling Brantley he wasn't worried that he'd be found by the enemy. Then again, at this moment, Brantley was the enemy, the intruder, the guy who didn't belong.

Brantley gripped his Sig firmly in his hand, ignoring the blinding pain that was threatening to darken his vision.

The beam of light grew brighter, cutting through the dust lingering in the stifling air. Lifting his hand, supporting it with his left arm, Brantley leveled his sight on the tango. Best-case scenario had him taking the bastard out, which he could do in his sleep. The only problem with that, the shot would most definitely alert his terrorist buddies, and at that point, Brantley'd be a sitting duck.

"Fall back! Phantom Team, fall back!"

The words were in his ear, but they sounded as though they'd been blasted through a bullhorn. A semaphore flag would've been less of an announcement of his presence.

The tango started shouting something over his shoulder, the beam of light landing on Brantley's wounded leg again. He held his breath, not moving a muscle, praying like fuck the dickhead would suddenly go blind. Otherwise, there would be nothing more he could do.

More shouting. Despite his inability to translate, Brantley wasn't an idiot. Fucker was calling out to his buddies, inviting them over for the party.

The fact that no one came—bad guys or good—should've been a sign, but Brantley's brain was fuzzy, his body one big throbbing heartbeat. Blood coated his BDUs, oozing from the open wounds. No doubt, if he looked close enough, he'd probably see his femur poking out of his skin. The thought made him woozy, which was saying something considering he didn't have a weak stomach.

"Phantom One." This time the voice was soft, almost reverent, which was telling. Things weren't looking good from their vantage point, either. "We're comin' for you, buddy. We're comin'. Hang tight."

The terrorist in front of him started kicking rocks aside, moving closer. Brantley couldn't see the weapon in his hand, but he didn't need to. Asshole was no doubt armed with whatever assault weapon they'd managed to get their hands on. At this point, it wouldn't surprise him if it was a fucking rocket launcher.

More yelling, more urgency. Based on his frantic shouts, the guy wanted backup, but they still weren't coming. Seconds ticked by while Brantley maintained his position, pretending he was invisible but knowing this asshole had found him. Only reason the fucker didn't shoot him full of holes was because he was more valuable alive than dead. Which meant, any minute now, he would be dragged out of here, thrown in a fucking hole, where they'd ensure the shattered femur was the least of his worries. It was a risk he took whenever they went out on a mission, so he was at peace with it.

But Brantley wasn't ready to give up yet. The longer he could hold this bastard off, the better chance his team would get here.

The beam of light moved, lowered, which meant the guy had made it down to Brantley's level. It began a slow creep up his leg, his torso. The tango's face came into view, his dark eyes following the yellow glow. Right before it could blind him, Brantley pulled the trigger, nailing the bastard between the eyes. He took a deep breath, gritted his teeth as the reverberation sent agony rippling through his leg.

A deafening silence followed the gunshot, the ringing in his ears right on its heels. There were no pounding footsteps, no voices calling out his location. For a brief moment, Brantley thought the stars had aligned, that the bad guys had taken a dinner break, retreating.

"Phantom Team," Brantley rasped, his words scratching along his throat, sending his diaphragm into spasms. "Need help."

"Sit tight, B," came the response.

"Not goin' anywhere," he said softly.

"B, we're comin'."

No, they weren't. He could hear it in that tormented voice. Something was keeping his team from coming for him. Either they were pinned down or—

That was when he heard it. The familiar whistling sound alerted him to a big fucking problem. The only thing he had time to do was scramble in his brain for a prayer that might get to the big guy's ears before—

The blast shook what was left of the house overhead as well as the ground beneath him. Another was right behind it, closer, bringing the building down on top of him. The third was just icing on the fucking cake.

Sometime later—hours, days, who knew—his team would do as they promised. They would eventually find him, dig him out of the rubble, evac his battered and broken body, deliver him to the nearest medical facility, where he would cling to life for weeks. Numerous surgeries would be performed to repair the extensive damage to his leg, drain the fluid off his brain, and ultimately keep him alive. Months of agonizing therapy would follow, during which Brantley would finally learn how to use his leg again.

Nine months after that clusterfuck of a mission, his superiors would add insult to injury, releasing Brantley from his duty as a United States Navy SEAL.

Good news: he was alive.

Bad news: every-fucking-thing else.

ALL IN is available now!

ACKNOWLEDGMENTS

Of course, I have to thank my wonderfully patient husband who puts up with me every single day. If it wasn't for him and his belief that I could (and can) do this, I wouldn't be writing this today. He has been my backbone, my rock, the very reason I continue to believe in myself. I love you for that, babe.

Chancy Powley – You continue to come through for me in every way. You even tolerate my inability to answer my text messages in a timely manner. I will apologize for that now and for all future instances because we all know, I'm horrible at it. Just keep in mind, you are the absolute best friend I have and I am forever grateful for your friendship.

Jenna Underwood — Because you continue to be my friend despite the fact that I am the world's worst friend. Thank you for always being there for me and for the postcards. They make me smile.

I also have to thank my street team – Naughty (and nice) Girls – Your unwavering support is something I will never take for granted.

I can't forget my copyeditor, Amy at Blue Otter Editing. Thank goodness I've got you to catch all my punctuation, grammar, and tense errors. I also want to say thank you to Rebecca at Fairest Reviews Editing for giving me a different perspective and making some terrific suggestions.

Nicole Nation 2.0 for the constant support and love. You've been there for me from almost the beginning. This group of ladies has kept me going for so long, I'm not sure I'd know what to do without them.

And, of course, YOU, the reader. Your emails, messages, posts, comments, tweets… they mean more to me than you can imagine. I thrive on hearing from you, knowing that my characters and my stories have touched you in some way keeps me going. I've been known to shed a tear or two when reading an email because you simply bring so much joy to my life with your support. I thank you for that.

About Nicole Edwards

New York Times and *USA Today* bestselling author Nicole Edwards lives in the suburbs of Austin, Texas with her husband and their youngest of three children. The two older ones have flown the coup, while the youngest is in high school. When Nicole is not writing about sexy alpha males and sassy, independent women, she can often be found with a book in hand or attempting to keep the dogs happy. You can find her hanging out on social media and interacting with her readers - even when she's supposed to be writing.

Want to know what's coming next? Or how about see some fun stuff related to Nicole's books? You can find these, as well as tons of other stuff on Nicole's website. You can also find A Day in the Life blog posts, which are short stories about your favorite characters, as well as exclusive contests by joining Nicole Nation on Nicole's website. To join, simply click **Log In | Register** in the menu.

If you're interested in keeping up to date on any new releases and preorders, you can sign up for Nicole's notification newsletter. This only goes out when she's got important information to share.

Want a simple, fast way to get updates on new releases? Sign up for text messaging. If you are in the U.S. simply text NICOLE to 64600 or sign up on her website. She promises not to spam your phone. This is just her way of letting you know what's happening because Nicole knows you're busy, but if you're anything like her, you always have your phone on you.

Connect with Nicole

Website: NicoleEdwardsAuthor.com

Facebook: /Author.Nicole.Edwards

Instagram: NicoleEdwardsAuthor

DEAD HEAT RANCH
Boots Optional
Betting on Grace
Overnight Love

DEVIL'S BEND
Chasing Dreams
Vanishing Dreams

MISPLACED HALOS
Protected in Darkness
Salvation in Darkness
Bound in Darkness

OFFICE INTRIGUE
Office Intrigue
Intrigued Out of the Office
Their Rebellious Submissive
Their Famous Dominant
Their Ruthless Sadist
Their Naughty Student
Their Fairy Princess

PIER 70
Reckless
Fearless
Speechless
Harmless
Clueless

SNIPER 1 SECURITY
Wait for Morning
Never Say Never
Tomorrow's Too Late

SOUTHERN BOY MAFIA/DEVIL'S PLAYGROUND
Beautifully Brutal
Without Regret
Beautifully Loyal
Without Restraint

STANDALONE NOVELS
Unhinged Trilogy
A Million Tiny Pieces
Inked on Paper
Bad Reputation
Bad Business

NAUGHTY HOLIDAY EDITIONS
2015
2016